NOWHERE ON EARTH

Vincent J. Sachar

Divont Publishers

ISBN-13: 9780989813358

ISBN-10: 0989813355

Library of Congress Control Number: 2016901842

Vincent J. Sachar, Miramar, FL

DEDICATION

To my wife, Gwen. Mark Twain's wife, Olivia Langdon Clemens, provided the first read of Twain's manuscripts throughout their 34-year marriage up until the time of her death. While I certainly am not a "Mark Twain," I do have a "Livy" in Gwen who spends countless hours providing the first read of my manuscripts and provides immeasurable assistance in collaborating with me.

To readers everywhere who have discovered the magic world of books. "A reader lives a thousand lives before he {she} dies. The {person} who never reads lives only one."
—George R.R. Martin

SPECIAL THANKS

Original cover design photo provided by Jonathan M. Sachar

Chapter One

Wrong Place, Wrong Time

His heart was beating so fast that it seemed as if it might burst through his chest. At the same time, he was desperately trying to control his breathing. In the midst of all that was happening, at least he had the presence of mind to cup his hands over his mouth to avoid hyperventilating.

God, help me. Don't let 'em find me. Gotta get outta here. Help me. Oh God! I don't wanna die. I don't wanna die.

For Allan Wilpin, everything seemed to happen so quickly that he hardly had time to think. He had been a bit edgy to begin with, since, in violation of company policy, he had not clocked in on this night. However, that was the arrangement Allan had worked out with his supervisor, Jorge Rivera.

"Okay, so here what we do, *amigo*," Jorge said earlier. "You go to that appointment with your woman, yes? A good husband, he should be with his lady when the doctor, he gonna tell her about them lumps on her breasts.

You know, it probably is nothing, eh? But these things, they concern a woman. They concern her *mucho*. Yes?

Mira, Allan, I understand that. But you have to listen to me, *hombre*. Yes? Remember I got me a boss too—*no le gusta mucho*. An' he probably don't like me too much either.

He find out you takin' time off again, no tellin' what he gonna say. *Comprende?*

I tell you something. Jus' between you and me. Yes?

His old lady, she done left him for some dude she work with. So, he ain't all that big on the husband 'n wife thing. You know?"

Jorge agreed that Allan would leave early, but stay on the clock until 5:30 p.m. Jorge would clock Allan out. Wilpin would come back at night when

1

the late crew is on duty and finish some work that he was to have done by the next day. Under this arrangement, no one would know that Allan had left earlier in the day. In all fairness, Allan would work the hours that he clocked in for—just not exactly at the times that would appear on his timesheet.

Now, there was certainly nothing unusual about 18-wheelers pulling into the docking station at Bergam Industries. These big rigs seemed to just come and go. Like a pulse rate verifying life, their constant flow indicated that Bergam was alive and well.

It was, however, unusual for two of these tractor-trailers to arrive at Bergam at a few minutes after 1:00 a.m. It was also unusual that someone was directing a small skeleton crew of workers to unload the cargo from these two rigs and place everything in a separate room just off the warehouse docking station. That was odd. What was so special about the cargo brought in by these trucks?

Allan Wilpin intended to return to the warehouse at about 9:00 p.m., when the children were in bed for the night. Things did not work out that way. The doctor visit lasted much longer than anticipated. Despite the good news that Cecilia's biopsies revealed nothing more than benign cysts, Allan ended up not getting to Bergam until sometime much closer to midnight.

He normally would not even be out near the loading docks, but he heard the semis pulling in. His curiosity just got the best of him. As he peered out, he noted that there was no name, no identity on these two rigs. That was strange.

Never seen trucks that ain't Bergam's here. No markin's on 'em. This crew out there—I'd swear they ain't Bergam employees.

Allan had never known Bergam to use workers who were not staff and union members there at the company. All of the men in the dock area on this night were dark-skinned, with the exception of three men who were standing nearby. At first, Allan could not identify any of these men from where he was standing. Then a bolt of fear shot through him. One of the men was Paul Martin, Bergam's Chief Financial Officer.

The next thing to shock Allan was when he spotted security personnel patrolling that area. What's that all about? Bergam was a factory—not Fort Knox.

Allan made a quick turn to avoid being seen by a security guard and found himself facing a huge dark-skinned man headed straight towards him. The giant glared with an intensity that triggered a torrent of fear in Allan.

This enormous stranger had a two-way radio in his left hand. He was clutching a huge plumber's wrench in his right hand.

Call it instinctive. Label it foolish. Say it likely would not have mattered what he did in any event, Allan did not wait for anything additional to occur. He heeded some inner alarm that warned him not to spend time analyzing things.

Allan ran. He ran as fast as he possibly could. He ran down a wide aisle that was stacked to the ceiling on both sides with pallets filled with a vast assortment of electrical components and other supplies. The behemoth pursued. Allan could hear him shouting in a foreign language into his handheld.

There are by some counts several thousand languages spoken natively in Africa of which Allan was familiar with none. Yet something within him immediately sensed that what he was hearing was some African dialect. He could be wrong. It could be French or Portuguese or... no, it sounded African to him.

After a few twists and turns, Allan finally made his way into a small windowless room used by staff supervisors when the need arose to prepare a quick report. A metal desk was angled to the right rear corner of the room. It had a front plate that extended to the floor. Allan left the light off, quickly closed the door, and ducked down underneath the desk. He could hear the activity throughout the area. They were the sounds of people running in various directions, occasional comments, commands, and communications through handheld units likely synchronized to the one the giant had.

This can't be happening. Maybe I should just step out and reveal myself. I ain't done nothin' wrong. Okay, I am in the building without clockin' in. That ain't good. Man, I don't want to get Jorge in trouble for tryin' to help me. Mr. Martin ain't likely to be a happy camper if he learns I left early and made it look like I was still at work. I could get in big trouble here. They might fire me.

Allan Wilpin needed this job—needed it badly. He had to stay on a payroll. He and Cecilia were already behind on several monthly payments.

3

Now here he was hiding in trepidation in a darkened little room while people were searching all over for him.

His body shook. He was drenched from head to toe and the perspiration continued to flow. He was feeling weak and lightheaded.

Why were these men searching so urgently? What was the big deal about an employee on the premises at an odd hour and in an area of the warehouse that did not generally have a late-night crew working?

Ah! That *was* the point—the very point. And Allan knew it. The issue was not why *Allan Wilpin* was there nor what *he* was up to. The issue was why *these men* were here on this night, at this time, and whatever it was that *they* were engaged in.

Wilpin sensed that he had inadvertently stumbled upon something that he was not supposed to see or know about. There was no big mystery to what had just occurred. Allan Wilpin was in the wrong place at the wrong time. Now, only one question of any significance remained. What would these men do to Allan if they were to find him?

They gonna kill me for sure.

It was a strange thought—an extreme supposition. Yet, Allan could not shake it.

Too late. They seen me there. They know I seen them. They will kill me. I just know it.

Allan's thoughts were running unbridled now. His breathing was heavy. Perspiration poured from his brow. His hands were clammy. His throat was dry.

Oh my God! What have I gotten into? How do I get outta this? Don't let 'em find me! I don't want to die. Dear God, help me!

Suddenly, the door burst open. The lights were turned on. Someone—no, more than one person—several people were there in the room. Wilpin held his breath. The room was small. Perhaps a quick glance and whoever had come in would be on their way.

Hope abounded. For the first time since he encountered the giant and began to run, Allan Wilpin saw a glimmer of light. He just might get out of this situation alive. Hell, he would stay tucked under this desk all night, if need be. Cecilia was asleep by now anyway. She would likely not notice his absence until she awoke in the morning. Surely, whoever these people were, they would be gone before the sun rose. If they had to schedule whatever they were doing at this ungodly hour when it was dark and the number of people present at the factory was so much lower than during the day, it only made sense that these folks would not be hanging around.

Allan heard the blissful sounds of footsteps headed out from the room. The lights were turned off once again. Hallelujah! He breathed deeply. He was still shaking inside, but at least, for the moment, he felt as if he had been granted an unexpected pardon from a sure death sentence. He found it difficult to believe that he had so narrowly escaped from the clutches of whoever these people were. Looks like he had really lucked out.

Ah! Allan should have known better. Such an escape would be far too easy. Besides, Allan had already proven over time that he was not a lucky man. Lucky? He actually tried his luck at a casino when he and his wife were on a cruise once. Luck? He lost everything he had. Ended up getting his folks to wire some cash or he and Cecilia would have been in big trouble. Yes, Allan was unlucky. Now he was about to live up to that negative reputation once again.

When the desk was suddenly ripped away from its position as if it consisted of Styrofoam and when the dark Goliath stood there laughing aloud, Allan realized that he had not been spared at all.

"Come out, come out where you are. Oohoo! You come. Hahaha."

Once again, the big man growled a few quick words into his walkie-talkie and turned the light on. Wilpin had no idea what the man was saying, but he was sure that others would be arriving in a matter of minutes. He was right.

First on the scene, escorted by one of the giant's colleagues, was a tall lanky man. His name was Frank Melvin. Allan did not know him, but he had seen the man once or twice before walking the factory with Paul Martin. Howard Dandley, a small portly supervisor, who Wilpin also had seen at the plant a time or two, was next. Three additional men arrived, who at first Allan might have described as being dark-skinned African-Americans. Somehow, Allan seemed to intuitively realize that the word "Americans" might more accurately be omitted in this instance.

5

Then, Paul Martin himself walked into the room.

"Who are you and what are you doing here?" Martin asked.

Allan did have his Bergam identification key card hanging around his neck.

"Wilpin, s-sir. Allan Wilpin ... uh ... Section 8, Plant Maintenance, uh ... Mr. Martin. Had some late-night ... uh ... work... ain't been done...need to ...uh...finish before tomorrow. I ... uh ... I...uh...came back in to...to finish... it."

Wilpin hesitated for a moment, in an attempt to gather himself and make a quick determination as to what he should say next.

"Listen ... uh ... Mr. Martin," Allan continued, "truth is, sir, I...uh...I left work early today. My wife...she...she had like...uh...a really important doctor's appointment. I went with her. My supervisor...uh...he let me go, knowin' I'd come back tonight... I ...uh...well, I ain't exactly on the clock right now, sir, but I swear to you, I ain't cheatin' Bergam or nobody, Mr. Martin. I ain't cheatin' nobody of a single minute of my billable time. No sir, not a minute."

Paul Martin smiled and placed one hand on Wilpin's left shoulder.

"Okay, okay, let's all calm down here. No reason for alarm or any more... uh...games of tag or hide'n seek, eh?" Martin said with a chuckle."You just happened to stumble upon the makings of a new top secret corporate project here. Needless to say, it is comprised of some highly confidential trade secrets and is something we absolutely do not want our competitors to even get a whiff of at all."

Paul Martin then turned to Frank Melvin.

"We are okay here, Frank. Does not seem as if Mr. ...," Martin reached out and turned Allan's ID badge so that he could read it,"Mr. Wilpin here saw anything that would compromise our project. Why don't you take Howard here with you and escort this man from the premises now since this is such a sensitive night here."

Martin turned towards Wilpin."Sorry, Allan, but you'll just have to find another time to finish up whatever you were doing. Tonight is a bad night to have anyone not screened for this project anywhere in this area."

"Yes, sir. I understand, sir," Wilpin said while nodding his head and moving closer towards Melvin and Dandley.

Paul Martin turned away to leave, then turned back again.

"Oh, and your wife, Wilpin. You mentioned a doctor visit. Is she all right, if I may ask?"

Oh...uh...yes, thank you, Mr. Martin. The...uh...the tests were all negative, sir."

"Ah! Good. Very good. That's what we want to hear.

Okay, Frank," Martin said, while turning towards the tall lanky employee."That's enough excitement for one evening. You know how extremely sensitive this project is and the importance that absolutely nothing spreads any further. I am counting on you to make sure that does not happen."

"Understand, sir," Melvin responded.

Allan Wilpin watched as Paul Martin and the others walked away. Frank Melvin and Howard Dandley did not speak as they accompanied Wilpin. They headed towards an exit door that he did not even know existed. Allan did not really care. He just wanted to get away from this place as quickly as possible.

Wilpin spotted the"Under Construction" warning signs that prohibited entrance for unauthorized personnel. He saw the signs indicating that this was also an area mandating that hard hats be worn, but again he did not care. Surely, his two escorts knew what they were doing.

Wilpin never even noticed when Melvin nodded and Howard Dandley flipped a breaker switch on a nearby wall. Wilpin never saw the hanging wires that Melvin pushed him towards, nor did he have any advanced notice before the fatal electrical charges entered his body through the top of his head and killed him instantly.

Chapter Two

A Lasting Peace

A solitary figure jogged steadily in the crisp early morning air. Hints of orange and red colors painted the sky as the sun peeked out from its nightly slumber and winked at the new day. A light breeze gently massaged his face as if to welcome him to another day in paradise.

His every step was precise, expending only the energy needed to move him along the five-mile course he had mapped out three years ago. That was when Jonathan Nova acquired his home on the pristine island of St. John in the United States Virgin Islands. He used this identity then, despite the fact that he was also using the name, Ronald Lane Woodruff. Over the years, former Navy SEAL Lt. Commander Kent Taylor used a number of identities as additional layers under which to hide.

On this morning, Taylor felt particularly alive and invigorated. He was more at peace than he had been in years. He breathed in the fresh tropical island air and tasted a hint of the briny ocean that surrounded this Caribbean nirvana.

Nearly two-thirds of St. John is protected as Virgin Islands National Park and is, therefore, undeveloped. A limited portion of the coastal land, mostly in the north and east, is private property consisting of many secluded private villas and cottages. The beautiful villa with its oceanfront views where Kent Taylor and his wife, Katie, lived was located in a cloistered area where there were no rental units available to tourists.

Kent smiled at the thought that Katie would now be awake getting the coffee started and waiting for her husband to return. When they first met, Taylor's solitary lifestyle resulted from a self-imposed exile. Katie had been the primary catalyst to revive Taylor's soul and pull him out of the abysmal pit that engulfed his life.

Years before, his pregnant wife, Rose, his young son, Drew, and Ray and Eve Devlin, his in-laws, were all murdered. The people behind the murders were prominent government officials, law enforcement officers, and others who sought to cover up their crimes. When Taylor determined there was no one he could safely turn to for justice, he set out on a course to avenge the deaths of his loved ones. Then, circumstances forced him to surrender his daughter, Emily, his remaining family members, and his own identity. For a time, he wandered aimlessly without any purpose or direction.

Kent Taylor anticipated a lifetime of regret over the loss of his loved ones and the life he would never get to share with his surviving daughter. There would forever be a myriad of "what ifs" related to all that had been stolen from him.

Afterwards, Kent Taylor could not imagine ever loving another woman. Nor did he believe that he would or could ever have even a scintilla of normalcy in his life again.

For nearly fourteen years, Taylor remained hidden away in a life devoid of goals, aspirations, hopes, or dreams to fulfill—until the day when Kent Taylor met Katie Dunham.

How deeply he now loved Katie! The very thought of her evoked a sense of disbelief that he had somehow been given an opportunity to share a life with this woman. If he harbored any notions of guilt when it came to Katie, it would be that he had her all to himself while the world was unaware that this seraphic creature walked on its shores.

At slightly taller than 6' with sandy brown hair and hazel eyes seemingly more attractive than normal for a man, Taylor's lean body now bore a rich, deep tan. His face was handsome and, despite his inner toughness, friendly and inviting. From the moment Katie met Kent, she noted his keen sense of awareness, which was so strong that he almost seemed to be aware of things before they ever occurred. She felt deeply warm and protected by him in a manner that she had never before experienced.

Kent would describe his wife as "drop-dead-gorgeous" and his description would not simply be the high praise of a loving husband. Katie was exactly that with a curvaceous body at 5'5" tall, radiant brunette hair, almond shaped sparkling blue eyes, high cheekbones, and full lips.

Far beyond that, Katie was intelligent, witty, and possessed a warm and bubbly personality that Kent found to be irresistibly contagious.

In recent times, Kent had begun to write quite frequently in a personal journal. He had begun to do so after reading somewhere that this was often therapeutic for someone who had experienced great personal trauma.

Kent was reflecting upon Katie when he wrote:

Perhaps the most astonishing thing about Katie is the fact that she has absolutely no idea just how incredibly special she is. Everything about her just flows out from within, so naturally, so pure.

A series of events, combined with Taylor's need to remain hidden, led to his decision to relocate to the Virgin Islands.

Katie once asked her husband, "Will you ever find yourself bored, living such a peaceful life here on a remote tropical island?"

Kent smiled, pulled her close, and kissed her.

"First of all, Katie, if I am ever bored while having someone like you in my life, you might immediately take me to a hospital for a brain scan."

He remembered how she laughed at that remark and how much he loved her laugh.

He spoke to Katie about what his life was like before he met her.

"I am not sure that I can ever adequately describe the turmoil and the emptiness of my life before I met you. I guess I was tough enough to sustain the pretense that I was doing all right, when I honestly was not."

Taylor shook his head and stared off in the distance.

"I was dying a slow death. My life was so empty—so devoid of any meaning or purpose. You gave my life back to me, Katie."

Katie, a young beautiful woman, bearing the scars of a widow when she met Kent, believed the same in return. He brought new life and meaning to her. If there was ever such a thing as "love-at-first-sight," Katie believed that was exactly what she experienced when she first met Kent Taylor. He was living under the alias "Ron Woodruff" at the time and he concealed his past from Katie. Yet, somehow, she saw through the facade into the hidden true personality of the man she would eventually marry.

Katie often talked with Kent about his past as a decorated Navy SEAL.

"I will never regret that I worked so incredibly hard to become a Navy SEAL, nor that I served my country as I did. I will always hold the highest regard for my brother SEALs. Those feelings will never change.

What I do struggle with is the fact that I was away from home so much. Rose never openly said much about it, but I know it was starting to get to her. The kids were growing up. Drew had actually started kindergarten and I was never around. I missed birthdays and other special events. I never saw the first steps my children took and was rarely there to kiss them goodnight.

Beyond that, Rose had to live with the understanding that I might never return home. Before every deployment, I had to make sure my will was current and write letters to my wife and each child for them to read in the event of my death. You know there are wives of some SEALs who live with the fact that their husbands are, in a sense, already dead and not likely to return home from their latest mission. These wives begin to condition themselves that it is simply a matter of time before they end up as widows."

As he reflected upon the past, Kent recalled the years after his loved ones had died. What he feared above all else is that he would ever slip back into what he had become before he met Katie.

"Sometimes I feel as if there is a darkness lurking somewhere deep inside of me, Katie. I don't ever want to go there again."

Kent continued his steady jogging. As perspiration dripped from his brow, he felt the stinging saltiness of the liquid that slipped into his eyes. He smiled at the thought that his life was now so radically different.

I am now Jonathan Nova. I can never undo my past. I can never retrieve what I lost. If I focus only on my past, I will miss my now and my future.

The very thought of Katie broadened his smile and invigorated the hope that he had forged his way into a new existence never to return again to the solitary chasms that once dominated his day-to-day life. Back then, he initially attempted to push Katie away. His belief that he was cursed and that anyone close to him was at risk resurfaced even now at times. It generated, perhaps, the only genuine fear this man encountered. The thought that he would ever lose Katie or cause her to be in danger haunted him. He had to accept the fact that the wounds from his past losses had never fully healed. If so, they likely never would.

For a fleeting moment, Taylor was reminded that his life had always been one of great undulations. It seemed as if no matter what he was experiencing at any given time, there was always a destructive force lurking somewhere close by.

Maybe it would be different this time. Perhaps he had finally turned a corner and left misfortune in his wake.

If only he could believe that. Truth is, he sometimes considered that there was nowhere on earth where he would be completely free from the demons of his past.

As Taylor looked out over the scintillating blue waters, he spotted the billowing white sail of a small craft gliding in the distance. The tiny white dot stood alone in stark contrast to a seemingly endless blue sea. For years, his life had been like that. Moving under the direction of a wind, traveling but going nowhere in particular, living on the outskirts of a society to which he no longer belonged.

He tried desperately to let go of his yesterdays, but was never completely successful in doing so. He knew now that he never would be.

The image of his daughter, Emily, flashed through his mind. Kent Taylor did not merely think of her often. He thought of her every single day. How ironic that the greatest expression of his fatherly love was to completely avoid any contact whatsoever with his own child! He maintained his distance from her to protect her, his sister-in-law, brother-in-law, and their children from anyone seeking him.

Kent loved the fact that Katie, despite never having met or even physically seen Emily, spoke openly about her. She would often refer to Emily pursuing her college degree at Louisiana State University under the fictitious name of Rosemary Chambers. In fact, as a point of reference, Katie went online and perused the website of LSU, so she could talk about the university more intelligently.

At times, Katie would spot some article of clothing or a small piece of jewelry and say things like, "Ooh! I'll bet Emily would love this and surely it would look great on her."

It was just one more thing that Kent loved about Katie.

❖

Jonas Blair stood outside his home, sipping his hot morning cup of coffee before heading to his office. He brewed a cup of French Vanilla flavored coffee this morning. Tasted good.

Blair turned around for a moment and stared at the home that he shared with his wife, Sally, and their baby son, Taylor. A soft breeze tousled Jonas' curly blonde hair. No problem there. At 6'2" with blue eyes, Jonas looked good whether or not his hair was neatly groomed.

At the moment, he was deep in thought. It was ironic, even somewhat amusing, to think that Jonas and Sally Blair, former FBI field agents, were living in a house that a serial killer once owned. Compounding that irony was the fact that the killer was also the man who saved both of their lives.

Jonas knew the identity of the man. Sally did not. Kent Taylor was identified in the FBI crime pages as a notorious serial killer commonly referred to as the "Ghost Assassin."

Kent Taylor saved our lives. He was supposed to be the bad guy. Yet, the man Taylor saved us from—the man who was about to kill us—was a sworn federal agent. No, check that, the man who was poised to murder us was more than that. He was a colleague, a supposed friend. He was senior to us in rank within the FBI.

Kent Taylor is the reason Sally and I are alive, married, and even have a child. He defied everything we were ever taught about the criminal mind. Serial killers are not supposed to risk their own lives to save the lives of federal agents. They're supposed to be the ones with the sick minds that we were sworn to capture or even kill, if necessary. Hah! Go figure.

Some fifteen months had passed since Jonas and Sally resigned from their positions as federal agents and moved to this area in upstate New York. The nearest town, The Village of Halston, was about twelve miles from their home. The larger city and county seat, Comstock, was where Jonas' law office was situated. It was twenty-three miles west of Halston. Sally was now a teacher in the Halston elementary school system.

Married, living in the country, working secular jobs, a baby—their lives had certainly changed and become so calm and normal.

As Jonas prepared to turn around and go back into his home, he heard the susurrant morning breeze that caused the tree leaves to sway and signaled that a storm was headed their way.

Ah! There are some storms for which you can never be fully prepared.

Chapter Three

Bergam Industries, Inc.

Richard Kelser was seated at his desk when he spotted Paul Martin heading towards his office. He quickly glanced at his watch to check the time. Martin was a bit early since their scheduled time at the racquetball court was not until 6:30 p.m. Richard considered that Paul might want to make a stop at the sport shop. He waved Martin into his office and started to chide him a bit.

"You know, Paul, there's nothing you can get—new gloves, wristbands, whatever, that will help you finally beat me in a best-of-five match."

Paul Martin did not smile. He bent his 5'11" body over for a moment, took a deep breath, and pushed his dark brown hair away from his face. He raised his palm up towards Kelser and spoke with a strong sense of urgency dominating his speech.

"We've got to talk, Rich. We may have a major problem. A major problem."

Kelser was immediately arrested by the tone of Martin's voice and the look of deep concern that was apparent on his face. He started to bring his 6'4' body to his feet, then changed his mind and settled back into his chair.

Kelser with his square jaw, deep-set brown eyes, and buzz-cut light brown hair looked more like a guy in the military than a corporate executive. Nevertheless, his corporate credentials were unquestionably strong. Richard Wayne Kelser was in his sixth year as Chief Executive Officer of Bergam Industries, Inc., a privately owned company that had been in business in Chester for the past thirty-two years. Bergam originally manufactured electrical components for several small household appliances and tools. Over the course of time, the Company had undergone a number of changes at Kelser's direction. They adapted to the technological advances in products for which they provided integral electronic components. Kelser was also credited with acquiring an exclusive account with RedMark, a company headquartered in Chicago. RedMark manufactured small household appliances globally. They pretty well cornered the market on several of their products. By virtue of this and several other key clients, Bergam had performed well. In fact, they exceeded their annual revenue projections for each calendar year since Kelser's began his tenure as CEO.

Within the first month or so of Kelser's status as the company's executive leader, he released the man who had served as Bergam's Chief Financial Officer for nearly twenty years and promoted Paul Martin to that position. Since that time, the two men had forged a strong personal friendship that extended beyond their relationship as colleagues at Bergam.

Martin closed the door to Kelser's office and sat down in one of the two chairs facing the desk. Paul had returned to the plant that morning after spending two days visiting with a client in St. Louis. The two men had been together briefly earlier in the day. Upon his arrival, Martin assumed the role as the primary host to guests from a potentially new customer who arrived for a tour of the factory. He had taken a few minutes to introduce them to Kelser.

"Rich," Martin began, "I have reason to believe that someone was in my computer while I was out of the office and ..." Martin hesitated as he prepared to introduce the most crucial aspect of his concerns. "And it appears that whoever it was accessed the password-protected files."

Kelser froze. His gaze caught Martin's eyes. He leaned forward, as he now bore that same deep look of concern that Paul Martin had when he first entered the room. Kelser was aware that Martin had any number of password-protected files. However, he understood that Martin was clearly referring to a select number of high-level data files. They were files that only he and Paul Martin had awareness of and were able to access.

Kelser sucked in a breath of air, leaned back again in his chair, and spoke calmly.

"Okay, Paul, okay. Take a deep breath and start from the beginning."

Martin sighed, paused for a moment to collect his thoughts, and took a couple of deep breaths.

"As you would expect, Rich, I've pretty much been tied up all day with the folks from Luxaton. When I wasn't touring the factory or introducing them to you and our staff, I was with them in the executive conference room. I didn't really get back to my office until a short time ago after they all left the premises. That was the first time today that I actually booted up my desktop computer.

That's when I spotted a few things that raised my suspicions that someone had been in my computer while I was out of town. Look, man, I'd be the first to admit that my computer forensic skills are limited. But as I dug in a bit further, I became more convinced."

Kelser interrupted.

"Okay, Paul, let's assume for the moment that you are right. When would this most likely have occurred?"

"Yesterday. Most likely, some time yesterday, Rich. I was in St. Louis on Tuesday and yesterday. Both Linda and Jacob were in on Tuesday and both were out of the office yesterday. Linda was with me in St. Louis. Jake was at that conference in Atlanta."

Kelser assumed that Martin's assessment was likely correct. Linda Niles, Paul Martin's executive assistant, and Jacob Russert, the office comptroller, were the two people situated close enough to Martin's office to notice if someone entered it at any time.

"There's more, Rich. As you know, Linda is the only other person who has security card access to my office. And ... uh ... like I said, she was with me yesterday in St. Louis. Had her fly in Tuesday evening so she could assist me with a few client presentations I had planned for yesterday morning. Then she joined me for a client dinner. Hell, I didn't have time to fly back to Meg and the kids last night, so Linda and I took an early bird flight together this morning. We headed straight to the office in time for the arrival of the Luxaton team."

It was no big secret to Kelser that Paul Martin was having an affair with Linda Niles, nor was it of any great concern to him. Kelser was divorced. His ex-wife and two children lived in California. None of his current women "friends" worked at Bergam.

"I had Leo," Martin continued referring to Leo Pawlowski, Bergam's chief of security, "do some checking for me. Had him look to see whether anyone entered our fourth floor executive office area prior to normal office hours or at any time after the office closed on either of the past two days. No one did. His search came up negative. But my office access records for yesterday show an entry to my office at 3:58 p.m."

Kelser leaned forward in anticipation of Martin's report on who had entered his office while he was in St. Louis.

"That's just it, Rich," Martin began in response to the question that Kelser had not verbalized. "I just got this from Leo and headed straight over to you. Our security system report indicates that the person who entered my office yesterday while I was in St. Louis was... me."

Kelser neither spoke nor changed his facial expressions. It was no wonder that the man always fared well in the monthly poker games he engaged in.

"And you've never had a lost or replaced access card, I assume," Kelser interjected.

"Right, never have. And, of course, the only two people who can authorize that a security card be made for my office are you and me—and we've got to do it with a written, executed form. No one else has that authority.

Martin's head had been down and shaking when he suddenly lifted it upright.

"Hey Rich, before we go any further, let me mention that I never told Leo that I had any questions or concerns regarding the access to my office yesterday. He does not know I was out of the office. I never even hinted about the possibility that someone used a duplicate of my security access card to gain entrance to my office. I told him that we have a large potential client that is a real stickler on security. Said if our negotiations with them progress, they will likely be sending in some security analysts to our plant before signing on with us. Told Leo that I was simply asking a few questions myself to see how well our system reports are functioning. I told him the potential client's name is still confidential, but, if anything further develops, we'll make sure he gets advanced notice."

Kelser nodded. He paused for a moment, stared at Martin, and waited for his next response. He knew that Paul Martin was a man who would continue to ponder and explore. He knew, despite the relatively short time since he had become aware of all of this, Martin would stay on it until he had an answer.

Once again, Paul Martin answered a question that Richard Kelser had not yet asked. .

"Louie," Martin said, identifying his strongest suspicion as to who might have entered his office and accessed his computer files. "It's no big secret between you and me that I don't trust that guy. Merkel is someone who has concerned me for some time now. And the little twit has both the computer savvy to get past my password protection and the general knowledge of our shipping records to know what to look for once he gets in my files.

I've told you we should get rid of Merkel. Hell, I've told you this a number of times, Rich. I just don't trust the man. I haven't been comfortable just sitting on our hands while that little weasel is around. I mean, how many times do I have to..."

Kelser stood up and placed an open palm within inches of Paul Martin's face.

"Chill, Paul. Calm down. And I mean now. The last thing we need is to panic and lose our cool. You hear me?"

Paul Martin's face turned pale.

"Y-yeah, I hear you Rich," Martin said, dropping his head, slumping his shoulders, and sighing deeply. "Sorry, man. Guess this whole thing has got me spooked."

Kelser sat back down. He folded his hands on his desk and spoke softly.

"Listen to me, Paul. No matter what happens, we have to remain calm."

"You're right, Rich. I know you're right. Guess that's why you're the boss man here and not me," Martin said in the hope that his feigned humor would help him regain some of the composure he had lost.

Kelser smiled.

"Okay, Paul. Okay. Now, let's talk this thing through.

Why do you think Merkel would do this now? The one thing we have always agreed upon when it comes to Louie is that the man is a coward. He's a worm. It takes a certain amount of gumption for someone to hack into our security system, counterfeit an access card to your office, sneak in, whether during the day or night, and start screwing around with your computer.

Guess I wouldn't have pegged Louie Merkel as possessing the kind of pluck needed to carry through with something on this level. What would motivate him to take a chance doing something like this now?"

"Thought about that, Rich. My guess is he'd be motivated by the one thing that most defines the guy's personality. Fear.

Wilpin's death could be what pushed Louie over the edge. Probably convinced him that he needs some kind of insurance to be sure that something ... uh ... accidental doesn't happen to him."

Kelser's head snapped up and his jaw tightened at the mention of Allan Wilpin.

"We've already had a full-scale investigation into Wilpin's death. The official finding ruled that the man's death was an accidental electrocution resulting from Wilpin's failure to follow and adhere to standardized safety procedures. There hasn't been even the slightest hint that Wilpin's death was anything other than an unfortunate, but preventable, accident."

Martin's head was nodding, but his head movement was not an indication that he fully concurred that Kelser's analysis was the final word on this subject. His response to his corporate CEO and friend was delivered at a softer tone, despite the fact that no one else was within earshot of the discussion that he and Kelser were having.

"Rich, I don't know, but it is possible that no one has suspected any foul play in Wilpin's death because no one has any inkling that anything illicit might be taking place here at Bergam. Merkel might very well be someone who hasn't bought into the theory that Allan Wilpin got careless one night and ended up getting fried."

Kelser closed his eyes, as if he were attempting to block out all other distracting thoughts and focus solely on the next steps that needed to be taken.

"Okay, Paul, now we are beyond just sitting back and keeping an eye on Merkel. If Louie has some potentially damaging data in his possession, we need to get to him now. We need to find out what he knows and what he has before he passes it on to someone else. If we get to work on Louie, I have no doubt that he will spill his guts to us before he takes another step. Is Merkel still here now?"

"Don't know. I'll send an urgent text. Tell him to report to my office now, regardless of where he's at. Believe me, that will shake him up big time. We'll meet at my office first before I bring him to you. No sense giving the guy a heart attack by even mentioning you initially."

"He can have his heart attack afterwards. First, we resolve this with him. If he has anything he should not have, we end this tonight whatever that means, whatever it takes.

Put Melvin and Dandley on notice that we likely will be in need of their...uh...services tonight."

Chapter Four

In a Flash

His current year Honda Civic was parked inconspicuously in a strategic spot. It provided him with the ability to see the law office. Yet it was far enough away to avoid any indication of his intended destination. The man sat in his car continually rubbing the back of his neck. His eyes were rapidly blinking. His hands would not stop shaking. Every few minutes he battled against a desire to drive away. He thought about getting on a highway and driving to some distant place where no one knew him.

But they'd find me no matter where I went. They would never quit looking for me.

Someone nearby started a vehicle and he was so startled, he banged his knee against the bottom of the steering wheel. He was rapidly losing weight over these past months. The thought crossed his mind that he could die of a sudden heart attack.

This was not the first or last time that he considered that cardiac arrest might be a much more palatable solution to the web that entangled him.

Louis Merkel had been here before on several occasions. He had been planning things for some time now—ever since a man named Wilpin was electrocuted at the plant.

By now, Merkel was familiar with the office routine. He knew that this attorney was a single practitioner. He was aware that the only other person working in this law office was an elderly woman who sat at a desk in the office reception area. Merkel correctly surmised that this woman handled the routine office chores of answering the phone, making copies, preparing some documents, and handling the mail.

He noted that sometime around 4:00 p.m. each evening, a young man entered the office and provided some form of general cleanup. He usually finished his work at 4:45 p.m. or so by loading a garbage bag or two in the dumpster behind the building. The elderly woman left the office each night right around 5:00 p.m. The attorney, Jonas Blair, would normally remain in the office some thirty minutes to an hour afterwards.

Merkel had battled for weeks before he finally garnered enough courage to take the steps he was taking now. He knew what was at stake if his employer got even a hint of what he was doing. Then again, he also believed that if he did not get some kind of leverage, these people would have no problem making sure he ended up dead like Wilpin.

Last night, when Merkel arrived, the office was empty. Before he walked away, Merkel stuffed an envelope containing a USB flash drive in the mail slot at the office front door. As he did so, his hands shook and his heart thumped heavily and beat rapidly within his chest to a point where Merkel feared he might actually have that heart attack. Afterwards, he spent the night questioning what he had done.

What if the attorney calls the factory and asks about the flash drive? What if he gives it to the sheriff and they find my fingerprints on the envelope? What if Goodall's people followed me and saw what I did? How do I know this attorney isn't corrupt?

By the time the sun arose, Louie had a night without sleep and a blood pressure level that was through the roof.

Tonight, his physical well-being and stamina will undergo an even greater test. Tonight, he intended to follow up on his delivery. This was one more step across the "bridge of no return."

❖

Jonas Blair sat at his desk, propped his feet up, and began reading several motions which he intended to file in court the following day. His piercing blue eyes, temporarily tucked behind a pair of reading glasses, focused upon the mysterious manila envelope.

He heard Claire Reeves, his office assistant, in the small copy room nearby.

"Hey Claire, this flash drive you left on my desk, there was nothing else with it?"

Claire stepped into his office with a pile of documents in her arms. When Jonas acquired this legal practice from the retiring previous owner, John Roberts, Claire agreed to come along with the deal. Jonas never pushed the issue of asking Claire just how old she was, but his guess of 64 years old would have fallen short of her age by four years. He knew she was a widow with a daughter that lived somewhere out-of-state, but not a great deal more about her personal life. She was a prim and proper woman, always dressed professionally, her grey hair regularly tended to by a local hairdresser. She was petite at 5'2". Her reading glasses hung neatly on a chain around her neck.

"No. No postage on the envelope, just your name printed on a label. Only thing in the envelope was that storage drive. That's it. Nothing more."

Jonas reached over and held it between his index finger and thumb.

"You know, I took a chance and viewed it in my computer and I'm not one step closer to the answer of why someone left this thing with us."

At her advanced age and after years of office work experience, Claire had learned the art of listening far more than offering her opinion. She stood there with a curious expression on her face, but said nothing. Jonas looked up at her and answered her unasked question.

"A bunch of shipping reports from that Bergam manufacturing plant over in Chester. Looks like they all relate to a particular source out of Africa, but I cannot even identify the product or products being delivered. I can see that there is also some additional material on that drive, but I cannot understand any of it. Bunch of encrypted files. I cannot make sense of it at all."

As he continued to focus upon the small object wedged within his fingers, Jonas spoke, evidencing a mind flooded with a barrage of thoughts.

"Why in the world should any of this data be of interest to me? Bergam is not one of my clients. I don't even know much about Bergam, except that they employ a large number of people and are responsible for a good many trucks coming in and out of the surrounding area."

As Jonas sat shaking his head, Claire responded.

"A mystery, indeed. I do not recall John Roberts ever having a Bergam client either. He once explored whether there were any opportunities to provide legal services to them, but told me they were a rather private company. Said their factory, isolated and fenced in, looked like a prison." Claire giggled at her own last comment.

"I do recall," Jonas said, "that about a month or so ago, an employee was killed at the plant when he came into contact with a hot wire. But, no one has approached us to handle a wrongful death claim. And, even if they did, a bunch of shipping reports likely has no relevance to employer or employee negligence."

"Well, I will keep my eyes and ears open for any follow up to our little office mystery," Claire said with a chuckle.

Claire's comments caused Jonas to laugh.

"Yes, you do that, Miss Marple," Jonas said referring to the Agatha Christie character who acted like an amateur consulting detective.

Claire was still laughing along with Jonas, as she turned and left the room.

❖

At 5:04 p.m., Merkel spotted the small, gray-haired woman exiting the office. He extended the time an additional ten minutes before getting out of his car.

Jonas Blair occasionally had someone enter the office after Claire left, so he was not all that surprised when he heard the front door open. He rose from his desk and entered the reception area.

Louis Merkel was a small man somewhere in the range of 5'4" in height and slightly built. Blair estimated his age to be around fifty years old. The man wore thick glasses that hung loosely from his long, hooked nose. He was wearing a brown tweed suit minus a tie. Upon entering the office, this man removed the gray fedora that covered his head. The remaining hair encircling his balding head was of a dull black color mixed with gray strands.

As Blair walked towards him, Merkel extended his slightly trembling hand and spoke quietly.

"Evenin', sir. I ... uh ... I assume you are attorney Jonas Blair?"

Jonas smiled and nodded.

"I...uh...I hope it is not too late for me to ... uh ... talk with you?"

The man continually looked towards the front door.

"May I ask who you are?"

"Merkel, sir, Louis Merkel, Mr. Blair. I ... uh ... I need to talk to an attorney. I realize that I ... uh ... I do not have an appointment, sir, but I was hoping ... uh ... hoping that you could ... uh ... spare a few minutes to discuss a certain matter with me."

The man was definitely quirky. His apparent nervousness did not overly surprise Blair. People seeking an attorney were often, at least initially, uncomfortable in doing so.

"Sure, Mr. Merkel ..."

"Please, feel free to ... uh ... to call me Louie. Most ... uh ... everyone, both my friends and enemies," he said, in what Blair took as a stilted attempt at humor, "they...uh...call me 'Louie'."

"Okay, Louie, it is.

Would you like to step into my office where we can discuss whatever it is that you have on your mind?"

"Uh ... yes, sure. Talking in your office would be ... would be best. Mr. Blair."

The little man turned his head back towards the front door of the office.

"Would it be okay if we ... lock your front door here ... uh ... just to be sure that no one interrupts us?"

Okay, so this strange little man did not want anyone to know that he was meeting with an attorney. No big deal. He was certainly not the first person to feel that way. Blair walked past Merkel to the front door, locked it, and ushered his visitor into his office.

❖

"How long you say he been in there?"

He could picture the boss' face getting increasingly as red as the man's hair. He was personally very glad that they were conversing by phone. He was also pleased that on a hunch he decided to follow Louis Merkel on this day. The boss had to be pleased with his work, even if the man would never say so.

"He ain't been in there all that long, Sonny. You want I should find a way to bust up their meetin' or somethin'?"

"No, no. That would not be a smart move in front of an attorney—especially this attorney. Tell you what. Just let it go. We'll let the guys at Bergam handle this for now. Hahaha. 'For now'—I like the sound of that. Hahaha. Just for now."

Chapter Five

A Very Strange Office Visit

"Please have a seat, Louie. How can I assist you?"

"If I may... uh ... sir, just a few preliminary matters before we proceed. The things that I want to discuss with you, am I ... uh ... am I assured that everything I say to you will remain between us only? I mean, whatever I tell my lawyer is between me and him, right?"

For the first time since he had arrived, Merkel was making direct eye contact with Jonas. This was clearly of the utmost importance to the little guy.

No big deal. This was not the first time that a potential client wanted assurance that conversations with an attorney were confidential.

"Louie, if you either retain me as your attorney or are attempting to, our discussions will fall under an evidentiary rule commonly referred to as the *attorney/client privilege*. Based upon that rule, I am prohibited from disclosing our communications to anyone without your permission. So yes, anything you tell me is, as you stated, between you and me.

You do need to know, however, that the rule will not apply if you are seeking my counsel for the purpose of committing a crime or wrongful act. Attorneys are duty-bound to report when someone tells us that they are about to commit a crime."

Merkel smiled nervously, shook his head several times, and hunched his shoulders before speaking again.

"Oh no, sir. I-I can certainly assure you that I am ... uh ... I am not about to commit a crime. Oh no, sir, nothing like that. Not at all."

Merkel was slowly spinning the rim of his fedora in his hands, occasionally stopping to push his glasses up on his nose.

"Nothing illegal at all, Mr. Blair. I... uh ... I even pay my taxes on time and stop at red traffic lights," he declared with another awkward attempt to be humorous and disguise his discomfort.

"So, there you go, Louie. Have I sufficiently answered any questions you may have?"

"Yes, sir. Thank you."

Louis Merkel sighed, relaxed his body a bit more. He gently dropped his hat onto the floor next to his chair and reached towards the back pocket of his trousers. He pulled out his wallet, opened it, and extracted ten one hundred dollar bills.

"Okay, then I'm ready, sir.

I want to hire you ... uh ... retain you, I guess the ... uh ... correct terminology would be ... as my lawyer...uh...that is. I am...uh...concerned... very concerned about something at my place of employment. Might be some wrongdoing there."

Merkel gulped, breathed deeply, and shook his head. Then he extended his hand towards Blair.

"Here's some advanced cash to get things started."

Blair held up the palm of his hand towards Merkel.

"Whoa, hold on a sec. I think you should know that I am not a criminal attorney. If you need a good criminal lawyer, Louie, I am sure I can recommend someone to you who is far more qualified..."

Merkel interjected, speaking loudly at first, before Blair even finished his statement.

"No ... no, Mr. Blair. No ... uh ... you are the lawyer that I want helping me. I want a lawyer who once worked for the FBI. I need someone who I believe would be...uh... best-suited.

I took the time to check out your background, sir, before I even came here."

"You are correct, Louie, that I was an FBI field agent, but I left the Bureau more than a year ago."

"I am aware of that, sir, but I believe that you will be in the best position to advise me, as well as handle the ... uh ... the things that I want to tell you about."

Louie was perspiring quite heavily now. He removed his glasses from his face and used his handkerchief to wipe the perspiration. He began twisting his neck as if it were sore and blowing out a series of short breaths.

"I ... I *need* you to help me, sir. *You've got to help me.* I don't know who else to turn to, Mr. Blair. *I need you.*"

This was the first time since the moment that Merkel first entered the office that he spoke with a deep sense of urgency. Blair wondered what could possibly be generating this much fear. At the same time, he felt a sense of empathy towards the man. He disliked seeing anyone in such a state.

Jonas was silent for a moment or two as he continued to gaze at Louie Merkel.

"Okay, okay. Let me ask you a few preliminary questions, Louie, and let's see just what we can do here to help you.

This matter that you want to discuss with me, I believe that you indicated that it is in some way related to business or, more precisely, your place of employment?"

"It ... uh ... it has to do with where I work ... uh ... my employer. So, y-yes, it is business-related, I guess you could say."

"All right. Let's start there, Louie. Who is your employer and what is your position?"

Louie fidgeted again, cleared his throat, and struggled to speak. Jonas reached behind his desk to the credenza for a glass. He filled it with water from a pitcher. Merkel took two large gulps of water, then wiped his mouth with his handkerchief.

"I'm an accountant. I mean, not exactly. I sort of work in the shipping department. I keep records. I validate the accounts of shipments received and sent.

I am not a CPA or anything like that. Not at all. I just deal with shipments. I ... uh ... I work for Bergam Industries at our manufacturing plant over in Chester. I report directly to Mr. Paul Martin. He's...uh... well, Mr. Martin is our company CFO."

Merkel froze, pushed his glasses back, and began swaying a bit in his seat.

"Y-you… uh… you would…you know…tell me if you have some kind of conflict of interest, right? I mean…if…you know…uh…if Bergam is one of your…clients?"

Jonas lifted a palm up towards Merkel.

"Relax, Louie. Yes, of course, I would disclose that and…no…Bergam is not a client of mine."

Blair leaned forward in his chair reached for the flash drive and lifted it up for Merkel to see.

"I take it, Louie, that you are the one who delivered this to our office last night?"

"Y-yes … uh … well I came by … and … uh … I had it with me. It was only about twenty minutes after five, but no one was in the office. I … uh … well … I had to leave it somewhere safe. Couldn't take it back with me … if anyone … found me with it …"

Merkel froze as his cell phone began to vibrate in his coat pocket. He took one quick look at a text message that popped up, turned pale, and rose from his chair.

"I-I've got to leave. Got to go now, Mr. Blair. I can't stay here."

Blair rose from his chair. "Hold on, Louie, if you're in some kind of trouble, tell me what's going on. Let's see if I can help you in any way."

"N-no … uh … no time for that now, sir. No time.

You're my lawyer, right, Mr. Blair? For now, at least? I … uh … I gave you a retainer and I'm saying that I want to hire you.

I'll be back. I'll be back tomorrow."

Merkel walked swiftly out of the office into the reception area.

"The flash drive, Louie. What about the flash drive?"

Merkel turned around quickly.

"Oh my God! Oh my God! I'm not thinking clearly at all. Y-you need to place it in a safe. Surely, you have an office safe. Surely you do.

Place it where no one can get to it. The data contained on it is a sampling of reports that … uh …that help tell the story. I-I'll explain everything when I come back tomorrow."

And just that quickly, Merkel unbolted the office door and was out onto the sidewalk. Blair watched him as he dashed down the street, which Blair understood to mean that this man had not parked his vehicle too close to the law office.

Jonas Blair walked back towards his office greatly perplexed by all that had just occurred. He looked back at the USB flash drive and decided to do just what Louie had stated. He opened his safe and placed it inside.

"Oh well. At least part of the mystery is solved. We will have to wait until tomorrow when Merkel comes back, to get the rest of the story," Blair muttered.

But Louie Merkel did not come back the next day or any day. This evening would be the last time Jonas Blair would ever see this man.

Somewhere that breeze was building in force, preparing to unleash a storm that Jonas could never have anticipated.

Chapter Six

Daddy's Little Girl

Sitting alone at night in the Hill Memorial Library on the Louisiana State University campus provided Rosemary Chambers with some quiet time to reflect upon things other than her studies. It was shortly after her high school graduation when Rosemary first learned the truth.

It occurred on a day when she was alone with her aunt and uncle. Her cousins Arthur, Jr. and Stacey were not at home. Following dinner together at Rosemary's favorite seafood restaurant, she returned home with her Auntie Marcia and Uncle Glen.

"There was never any intent to deceive you," Auntie Marcia told her, as she looked upon her niece through tearful eyes.

"No, never," Uncle Glen interjected. He squinted his eyes and clenched his hands tightly into a fist. "We sought only to protect you," he uttered through a tightly held jaw. "We would do anything to keep you and our entire family safe."

It was at that time that her aunt and uncle, two people who had assumed the role of her surrogate parents over the past fourteen years, unlocked the long hidden truth.

"It is true that we-we *are* your aunt and uncle by blood," Marcia began.

She rose from the couch where she had been seated next to her niece. Her face was tight. Globules of crystal tears dripped slowly from her eyes.

"That part is true. Your mother was my older sister and I loved her so incredibly much. She was my best friend."

An eerie presence seemed to permeate the room. Rosemary felt a tightening in her chest and a fluttering in her stomach. She stared up at her aunt and glanced over at her uncle. She had never before witnessed or sensed such strange behavior from either of these two. If anything, her Uncle Glen

33

was usually quite reserved and laid back. Auntie Marcia had more spunk, for sure, but Rosemary had never seen her so deeply distraught. These two adults had always been rock solid, stable, and predictable in their love and support. What was so different about this night?

Marcia was pacing now and wringing her hands. As a result, Rosemary's uneasiness was steadily increasing. Her mind began to race with an abundance of thoughts, many of which she had never before even entertained.

What is going on here? Surely, they are not preparing to tell me they are divorcing. No. Preposterous. Sickness? Money problems? Releasing me totally on my own?

Could it be that now, since I just graduated from high school and will enter college in the fall, they want me out of their house? Surely, that is not the case.

Rosemary held her hands together on her lap in an effort to hide the fact that she could not stop them from shaking. Her lips were trembling. Her heartbeat was racing.

Marcia broke the chain of thoughts that had been racing through Rosemary's mind with her next comments.

"Like I said, it is true that your mother was my older sister. But...but...our names...that is our true names are not as you know them to be today, darling.

My-my name is Lisa," she said, stating something she had not said to anyone for a long time.

Rosemary watched as her aunt continued to move about the room, speaking very rapidly, while occasionally closing her eyes and taking a calming breath.

"And your uncle...his real name is Arthur. Our last name was Grazier—Arthur and Lisa Grazier. And my maiden name...uh...your mom's maiden name also was Devlin. Our parents were Ray and Eve Devlin. Your cousins are Arthur, Jr. and Stacey, not Harry and Helen."

Rosemary quickly turned to face her uncle. He nodded his head in agreement and smiled—a very forced smile.

"Y-you were not born with the name Rosemary Chambers. You...you are Emily...Emily Rose Taylor."

Lisa stated that as if that name should have some particular meaning to her niece. It did not. Emily was a three-year-old child when the story of Kent and Rose Taylor dominated the airwaves. She sat stone-faced, knowing that more was yet to come.

"Your father was Kent Taylor. Your mom, my sister, was Rosemarie Taylor."

Through a proverbial boatload of tears, sighs, hesitations, quivering voices, and deep fears and concerns about how their young niece would react, Arthur and Lisa told Emily everything that had been held back from her for years. It was the very first time Emily had ever seen her uncle shed a tear.

Learning that she and her family were under a form of witness protection, hearing for the first time that she once had an older brother named Drew, and that her mother was expecting another child when she died were the first things to shock Emily. Being told that her mother, brother, and grandparents were murdered was an incredible burden for a seventeen-year-old girl to bear. The revelation that her father was a storied serial killer, who also did not die in the manner that she had previously been told, could easily have pushed Emily over the edge. Fortunately, it did not.

Emily sat with her mouth wide open. Without uttering a sound, tears poured from her eyes. Her body shook and trembled violently. Her Uncle Arthur moved next to her and took her into his arms.

Lisa knelt on the floor sobbing, with her arms wrapped around Emily's legs. She told Emily how it came to be that she did not die with her mom, brother, and grandparents. She revealed how Emily's father died.

At one point, Lisa recalled the last time she ever saw Emily's dad. To her knowledge, that was also the last time Kent ever saw his daughter.

Lisa could see the scene reoccurring within her mind. She related the incident to Emily.

"You were three-years-old asleep in bed. Your daddy just stood there staring at you. It was as if he were paralyzed... frozen in time... breathing in every last moment, trying to force a lifetime into a few short minutes.

I will never forget the words he whispered to you.

'Always, my darling,' he said as he placed his lips against your cheek, 'always, with my every last breath and beyond, I will love you.'

That was the very last time any of us ever saw your Daddy. He arranged everything to save and protect our lives, but he could not save his own."

Later that evening when Emily retired to her bedroom, she stood in front of a mirror and stared. Tears flowed from her eyes, as she found herself questioning just about everything in her life. A myriad of thoughts and images raced uncontrollably through her mind. Nothing was as it had been before. The very foundation of her life had been stripped away and she was left staring into a deep, bottomless pit.

Throughout that night, Emily buried her head in her pillow in an effort to muffle the sounds of her sobbing. She cried so deeply and so long, that her ribs ached and she had to fight against vomiting a number of times.

These were extremely difficult disclosures for a young lady to handle, but Emily was the offspring of the combined genes of Kent and Rose Taylor. Initially, Emily, rightly so, felt devoid of everything she had known about herself since her childhood. It remained true that her life had risen from the ashes of a tragedy, but now the details of the calamity that had thrust her into the loving care of an uncle and aunt had significantly changed.

Over the next six weeks prior to the beginning of her first semester of college, Emily fought hard to control her emotions. This was not an easy task. However, despite a heart that ached and tears that flowed with little or no advance warning, Emily knew that she would prevail. She was also mindful of the fact that she still shared her life with a family knitted to her by blood and by a common tragedy that had also upended their lives.

Still, Emily's eyes would fill with tears when any little thing opened these new floodgates. Spotting a family consisting of a father, mother, little boy, and his younger sister was a trigger. Seeing a pregnant woman pushing a shopping cart in a local grocery store was enough to fill her eyes with tears. The sight of a family together or a mother with a newborn baby pierced her heart. Just the very thought that she not only lost her parents, but in essence, lost all her siblings and her grandparents could plummet her spirit to depths she had not previously known.

Emily held no resentments with regard to all that had been kept from her for so many years. She understood that everything that had been done was based upon the need to keep the surviving family members safe. She was told, and believed, that the plan to falsify stories and hide their true identities was originally hatched by her father. She remained sure of the love of her aunt and uncle.

Okay, so the identities of her parents just completely changed. And she now was aware that they both died in a manner shockingly different than she had originally been told. Yet, despite all of that, the genuineness of a few key things had not changed at all.

The deep love that her aunt had always expressed for Emily's mom was not fabricated. Added to all that, Emily was now aware that her aunt lost her own parents on that very same day. In fact, Arthur and Lisa lost loved ones and had their own lives turned upside down at a time when Emily was too young to comprehend all that had occurred. In those earlier years and so many since, Arthur and Lisa had carried the burden of these deep hurts alone.

Following her initial shock and even during her times of grieving, Emily began to explore. Quietly, on her own, she dug into the archives of newspapers, magazines, and media videos. Her eyes flooded with tears and she sobbed when she first saw photos of her mother, her brother, and grandparents in the initial reports about a fatal home fire. She cried tears of joy when she spotted her resemblance to her own mom.

Emily saw those and other photos again when the media latched onto the reports about her father. She questioned whether she was the only young girl to ever first see pictures of her own family by scouring through news related to old death notices and crime reports.

As she stared at photos of her dad and mom, Emily immediately felt as if she already knew them. Had she ever seen them before? Perhaps she had. In her dreams?

Her mom was beautiful. Her dad was handsome. Her older brother was adorable and looked like her dad. Her grandparents appeared to be so warm and friendly.

Based upon what her Aunt Lisa told her, Emily constantly recalled the last words her father ever said to her. She embraced them and held tightly to them. Although it did not change a thing today, just knowing that her parents truly loved her meant the world to Emily.

The mixture of joy and sadness that she felt during these moments generated a pain within her heart that was almost too much for her to bear. Yet, at the same time, Emily felt a sense of rebirth and renewal. At last, she was reconciled to her parents, her brother, and her grandparents. And she still had a living, loving family with her Uncle Arthur, Aunt Lisa, and her cousins, Arthur, Jr. and Stacey.

Emily learned more about her mother—a prosecuting attorney with a strong reputation for fairness. She gleaned and garnered a deeper exposure to the story concerning Commander Kent Taylor, the notorious *Ghost Assassin*, whose cunning and skills baffled America's best law enforcement experts and captivated the attention of a nation.

"Your dad was a Navy SEAL. In fact, he was one of the very best of them," Lisa informed her. "And let me tell you, darling, he adored your mom, you, and Drew. The three of you were his entire life. My sister, Rose, adored your daddy in return.

My parents had a great relationship with your dad. Rose used to kid Kent and question whether he married her so that he could be around her dad and mom."

Whenever Lisa spoke about anything related to the past, she would laugh and she would break down and cry. Even so, she would press on, desirous to now share family remembrances that had been so deeply locked within her for so long.

Lisa and Arthur had not yet told Arthur, Jr. and Stacey these things. The day was nearing when they would do so, but they believed there was a priority that existed for Emily. Kent and Rosemarie Taylor were her parents. Drew was her brother. The truth had to begin here.

Lisa and Arthur were deeply concerned, even afraid, of the effects of telling these things to Emily. At the same time, they could not justify never doing so. It was something the two of them struggled with over the years.

The fabricated story that Emily had been told was that Mark and Sylvia Chambers were killed when a single engine plane piloted by Mark went down. The Chambers' 3-year old daughter, Rosemary, was then taken in by her uncle and aunt, Glen and Marcia Bennett. Her aunt and uncle accepted and treated their niece as if she were their own child, but they opted to keep young Rosemary's birth name intact as a remembrance to her parents.

The fabricated story was elaborate and extensive. There were documents—all kinds of documents. There was a false copy of Rosemary's birth certificate. She now learned that the year of her birth was correct, but the date was not. There was a false copy of her parent's marriage license. And there were photos—a whole album or two of a man and woman purported to be Rosemary's parents, even though they were not. She marveled at the depth of the lies, but knew they were contrived to insulate and protect.

It was comforting to Emily that, over the years, Lisa had provided a true, though incomplete, picture of the personality characteristics of her parents.

Over time, Emily began to wonder what her dad was actually feeling in those last months when, with no one he believed he could in any way turn to, he struck out on his own to avenge the deaths of his loved ones. She considered just how great his despair must have been. She could easily see that he had been betrayed and stripped of everything he valued in life. She could not fathom how he must have felt when he returned home after being injured and incarcerated in a foreign prison camp only to learn that his primary reasons for living no longer existed. How deeply his heart must have ached when he learned that the very love of his life had been murdered and any future hopes and plans he once shared with her were now buried beneath the earth.

They killed you, Mom, because you were a woman of integrity. Oh, how I love and miss you! I will always love you and be proud of you.

My dad was a hero even before my mom, brother, and grandparents were killed. And he remained a hero even up to the time of his death.

I will never stop loving you, Daddy, and I will always be proud of you.

Oh God! How I wish you were here today! How I would want you to be proud of me.

Emily wished above all else that she could have even just a moment to hug and kiss her mom and dad and her brother. She considered that she would trade the rest of her life, everything, and anything, for just a few minutes to be with those whom she had lost. Prior to this time in her life, Emily would fantasize that she was with her parents, talking, sitting together, and laughing. Now her fantasies bore an even deeper sense of reality and included a brother and grandparents.

It did not bother Emily that her father had struck back as he did. Perhaps, it should have, but it did not. She was not a vindictive person. She abhorred violence. Even so, she would never view her daddy and what he had done in a negative light.

Oh, how deeply she wished that she had one opportunity to sit with him, look into his eyes, and talk with him about all that had occurred. She would not judge him in any way. She believed that she understood why he reacted as he did. She just wondered what he would say.

All of these things generated a new and penetrating question that was now rooted deeply in Emily's heart and soul. She wondered about something additional that pertained only to her. Reflecting upon her parents, their shared love, and her dad's reactions to the murders of his wife and family members, Emily wondered—she wondered above all else if she would or could ever in her life find a man who would love her *that* much.

Chapter Seven

Her Father's Daughter

Jonas finished gathering up things and was ready to head out for the day when he heard the front door to his office open. For a moment, his mind flashed back to the evening when Louis Merkel had come to his office. More than two weeks had passed and the man had never returned. Jonas resolved that he would simply wait for Merkel to contact him. He considered that the man would be back when he was ready to do so.

Jonas stepped out into the front room just as the woman was closing the door. Her braided auburn hair bore tight curls. She stood about 5'5" in height. Her skin was lightly freckled denoting its fairness. Nice figure. Girl-next-door pretty. Jonas' initial assessment was that she was likely in her mid-twenties. He did not recall ever having seen her before.

Jonas reached her as she turned from the door. She extended her hand and spoke rapidly in a tone that was polite, yet very assertive.

"You are attorney Jonas Blair, I assume."

A quick nod from Jonas provided her with the impetus to continue speaking.

"Mr. Blair, my name is Julie Hancock. I apologize for coming to your office without an appointment, but I have a very limited remaining time here in the area and was hopeful that I could have a moment to speak with you before I head back downstate."

"What can I do for you, Ms. Hancock?"

"Sir, I came into the area yesterday evening because I have been unable to locate my father for days. His cell phone is apparently turned off. I have done everything I could think of to determine where he might be. I checked at his place of employment, but they told me that he had resigned some two weeks earlier and did not disclose his plans. I went to his home. It looked as if the mail had not been picked up for several weeks. Nothing else appeared to be out of order.

I spoke with his neighbors and local merchants in the area where he lives. I have been unable to determine where in the world he might have gone. It's as if he disappeared, which is totally out of character for him."

"Okay, let's take this one step at a time," Blair responded. "Who is your father and why have you come here to me?"

"My apologies, sir. His name is Louis Merkel. My parents divorced sixteen years ago, when I was eleven years old. A few years later, my mom remarried. At the time, I took the name of my stepfather, Aaron Hancock.

About two and a half years ago, I got back in touch with my natural father. I found him to be a bit of a recluse, a bookworm, somewhat quiet and shy. I could readily see why he and my mother eventually drifted away from each other, but I have come to enjoy knowing him."

"And what brings you here to me today?"

"My dad lives in a duplex over at Fairway Meadows. He told me where he hid a spare key to his place. I went in and, as I stated, found everything to be in order. I mean my father is very neat. He's actually quite anal, Mr. Blair. He has everything neatly placed and arranged in his home. His clothes hanging in his closet are arranged by color to a point where even the hangers he uses match the color of the shirt or pants hanging on them.

Anyway, on a small desk located in the corner of his bedroom, I found an address book. There was a loose piece of paper tucked inside it that had your name, phone number, and identified you as an attorney. In fact, my father had written the words, *Attorney, former FBI agent.* That caught my attention, so I wanted to check with you and see if you might have any idea where my father might be."

Blair was listening attentively. He was hesitant to mention anything about having a brief encounter with Louis Merkel. Added to that, Blair had no way of knowing whether this young lady was truly Louis Merkel's daughter.

"Have you contacted the police? Maybe file a Missing Person's Report with them?"

"I did call the County Sheriff's office. They stated that I could, of course, report my father as missing. After talking with them, I realized that I don't have much of a basis for that. For all I know, he might have taken a few days off before starting a new job. His car was not in the driveway at his home, so he could have simply gone somewhere without telling me. We would speak often, but not every week."

"Based upon what you have told me, Ms. Hancock, you do not have enough to warrant a response from the Sheriff's Department. I mean, at this point in time, even you cannot say for sure that your father can be classified as a missing person."

Julie Hancock did not respond immediately and when she did not, Jonas noticed that it was not a loss of words or what to say next that generated her hesitation. She was making a concerted effort to control her emotions.

"It … it took me years, Mr. Blair, to finally link back up with my own father. Some of the reasons for that can be blamed on him, but there's no doubt that I am culpable also. There were times when he tried to reach out to me and I ignored him.

Now, I am finally back in touch with my father and …and I just don't want to lose him again. I mean … am I making any sense at all, sir?"

Blair nodded and spoke a bit more gently. "Yes, of course you are. Look, I don't know if I can be of any help to you. I had some very limited initial contact with your father a few weeks back, but have not had any follow-up with him.

I will do some checking and see if I can help you locate him. I just don't want you to get your hopes up too high on that. Like I said, I am not sure that I can do any better than you have. In the end, we all just might have to wait until we hear back from him."

Even as Blair spoke, he knew that if Louie Merkel did not want to be found, they would likely never know where he was. And, if something had happened to the man …

"Thank you, Mr. Blair. Thank you so very much. Just knowing that someone else is checking on this is itself a comfort to me." She handed Blair her business card, which listed her cell phone number.

Jonas stood still for a moment as he watched her exit the front door. He honestly did not know what to think. There was no doubt that Louis Merkel was deeply troubled, even frightened, on the day that he came to

Blair's office. The man did leave some data that he deemed to be extremely important. But Jonas had no idea what Merkel was concerned about and what the data he left revealed.

I am not involved in criminal investigations any more. I left all that behind when I resigned from the Bureau. If Julie Hancock is concerned about her father, she needs to work this out with the proper law enforcement agency. She needs to establish some grounds to warrant the possibility that her father is a missing person.

If Julie Hancock had appeared at his office and Jonas never had an encounter with her father, he would have simply insisted that she deal directly with the county sheriff's department. However, he was sure that Louie Merkel was frightened about something related to his workplace. Now, suddenly, Louie Merkel quit his job without informing his daughter and seemingly vanished from the area.

Jonas Blair was striving to push everything aside and accept the fact that there was nothing troubling about this scenario. Yet, Blair's instincts were telling him that Julie Hancock clearly had reasons to be concerned for her father.

They watched silently, hidden away, as Julie Hancock exited Jonas Blair's office.

"That'd be right at twenty-eight minutes she was in there, Sonny."

The speaker was Mugsy, the driver of the car. He turned towards his front seat passenger. "What do you want me to do now?"

Sonny Goodall was a tall man at 6'5" with a shock of red curly hair that he jokingly said made him look a bit like the clown, Ronald McDonald. When Sonny made a statement like that, he roared with laughter. No one else would ever dare to make a similar comment.

Mugsy was a short, stout, pug-faced former amateur boxer, named Michael Portello. He gave the appearance that he lost far more fights than he ever won. Sonny was the one who came up with the name "Mugsy." It was not a name that Portello particularly liked, but no one ever argued with Sonny Goodall about anything.

Goodall lifted his head from the crossword puzzle he had been working on. He kept the cigarillo in his mouth as he prepared to respond. The smoke emitting from Goodall's little cigar floated softly above his head. Mugsy accepted that as a positive sign, since whenever Sonny was agitated he puffed more mightily on his ever-present cigarillo.

The two men had been following Julie Hancock from the time she left Bergam Industries, returned to her father's home, and drove to Blair's law office. As the head honcho of Sonny Goodall's Private Investigators Agency, Sonny often passed surveillance and tailing a suspect on to one of his staff, but this matter was top priority and too lucrative an assignment to mess up.

"Hold back for a sec, Mugsy, then follow her one last time. We'll learn more about this lawyer visit later, but first we make sure Ms. Hancock is headed back to the Big Apple."

Two deep puffs on the burning ember in his mouth sent a cloud of smoke hovering above Sonny's head and wandering like a wayward cloud towards Mugsy. Goodall turned his head before glaring deeply into Mugsy's eyes. The little guy always made a concerted effort not to be intimidated by Sonny's tactics, but he never succeeded in doing so.

"Bottom line is this, Mugsy. If this attorney sticks his nose in this stuff, he'll only end up putting himself in a very bad spot."

Sonny took the cigarillo from his mouth, held it between his thumb and index finger, and jabbed it, for emphasis, towards Mugsy's face.

"Yesiree, Mugsy my boy, anybody messes with anything where Sonny don't want ya ta be and they end up in a very bad spot. But it ain't bad for us, ya know? 'Course that'll give us opportunity to add to our billing hours. Hahaha."

Sonny roared with laughter at his own attempt at humor because he believed he was that witty. His driver laughed also because Sonny was someone you would never want to upset.

Chapter Eight

The Things We See

Andy Maynard had just celebrated his one-year anniversary with the county sheriff's department. Standing at 6'3" with a chiseled body not carrying any excess weight and his short black hair shaved on the sides, Andy looked more like a U.S. Marine than a county sheriff deputy. His easy-going country boy personality was a stark reminder that Andy was a local. He starred as a tight end at Freeport High in Comstock and likely had a very real shot at a major college football scholarship had he not torn an Achilles tendon late in his senior year.

Even so, things were now going in the right direction for Andy. He and Donna, his wife of four months, had just learned that their first child would be coming along sometime within the next seven months or so. Once he was switched from night duty, Andy was ready to resume some evening classes in his pursuit of an associate degree at the local junior college.

Yet, despite the positive things occurring in his life, a few recent incidents had Andy both confused and very much concerned. If some of the things he had seen lately were as he suspected, he had inadvertently identified something that would be a major problem. But Maynard was a young, inexperienced deputy who struggled with the fact that he could be completely wrong in his judgment. If he dared to talk to anyone about this, if he spoke to Sheriff Devlin Miles and proved to be wrong, he likely would never recover from the department backlash he would receive. The only thing potentially worse than a dirty cop is someone who accuses others on the force of wrongdoing and proves to be incorrect. Andy placed a wad of gum in his mouth and chewed more vigorously than normal. He tried to push all of these thoughts out of his mind before he got himself into a heap of trouble.

Andy Maynard had not said a word to anyone about the things troubling him. The closest he had come was one night when he was on duty along with Walter Albert, who had been a deputy sheriff for twelve years. The two men were sitting together at the sheriff's office before heading back out on patrol in their vehicles.

"So, let me ask you something, Walt," Andy began. "Ever have times when you think you might be seeing things that could be criminal behavior, but you just aren't sure?"

Albert finished his latest gulp of coffee, before responding. "Not once, but many times, Andy. What we do for a living is not and won't ever be an exact science. There are no foolproof 'red flags' that pop up or buzzers that go off guaranteeing us that something we may be seeing or sensing is, in fact, the real thing.

Along with the facts and forensic evidence, we've got intuitions, suspicions, and questions that bombard our minds. And the crazy thing is that they all can have a place when it comes to criminal investigative work. Sometimes we follow a trail for a while and find ourselves at a dead end. Sometimes your number one suspect to a crime falls so far off the radar that you wonder what caused you to ever consider this person in the first place.

It's all part of what we do as we try, as best as humanly possible, to respond properly to a situation, unravel a mystery, or, in some cases, begin tracking something that just doesn't seem right—at least at first."

Maynard never told Walt Albert that he actually did have something in mind when he asked the initial question, but he heeded Albert's insights and determined to quietly pursue things he had noticed.

It all started about three weeks earlier when Andy was cruising on his late-shift patrol and, right at 2:00 a.m., he spotted two sheriff's deputies. They were coming out of one of the storage buildings behind Phelp's Transmissions Repair Shop on Baltic Avenue, just off Atlantic Boulevard. Seeing two off-duty deputies out at this hour caught Maynard's attention. The fact that these storage areas were located in a seedy section of Comstock, added to his curiosity.

The two deputies had not spotted Maynard, since their backs were to the road as they were locking up the building. He started to head over towards them when another vehicle pulled up and the driver spoke to them from the window of his car. Within a few minutes, the driver pulled away, the two deputies quickly hopped into their car and left the area.

At the time, Andy Maynard treated the incident as somewhat curious, a bit odd, seemingly out-of-the-norm, but not necessarily anything much beyond that.

On the following night when Maynard reported for duty, he was given a quick report by Deputy Margaret Schiller, who had just completed her shift and was headed home.

"Not sure if you caught the news that old man Townsend's home had been burglarized last night," Schiller began. "That's the fourth burglary in the past three months in our county. Don't need to tell you that for us, that's a major crime wave."

"Hmm," Maynard responded. "So, they get away with much?"

"Well, you know Ned Townsend made a ton of money over the years in real estate dealings. Remember, he sold the property where Walmart put up their supercenter and a Sam's Club and that was just one of the deals where he made a hefty profit. So we already have a list of several valuable antiques, jewelry, and a number of other pricey items that are missing."

"Whew!" Andy exclaimed. "So...uh...who called it in?"

"Townsend's granddaughter. Name is Penny Wright. She's been checking on the place while Ned and his wife, Martha, are overseas. Sheriff's here tonight. He's gonna talk to you all before you head out patrolling. Believe he's adding a few additional deputies to patrol tonight."

"So, we get a talk from the man tonight, eh? Thanks for the update, Mags," Maynard responded, referring to Deputy Schiller by a nickname commonly used for her within the department.

❖

Three nights later, Andy Maynard caught the report from dispatch on his car radio that a neighbor next door to the home of Jennifer Foster called 911 to report a potential burglary of Ms. Foster's home. Two deputies much closer to that location responded, so Maynard stayed within his designated patrol area.

Over the next few days, Maynard carefully backtracked, checking the records on the recent five county burglaries. In each instance, the occupants of the homes burglarized were out-of-town. In each instance, the residents owning the homes had informed the Sheriff's Department that they would be away. Yet, in each instance, Andy Maynard never received word that these people would be away so as to prompt him and other officers on duty to do a couple of drive-by trips to check on the house during that time—a standard departmental procedure. The calls informing the Sheriff's Office that these residents would be away were received by dispatch and passed on to several officers on duty. Two messages were forwarded to Jimmy Welcher, two were forwarded to Caleb Grant, and one was actually passed on to Sheriff Miles himself.

Andy Maynard's concerns reached a much higher level once he learned these things. The two deputies who were at the storage building the night he spotted them were Welcher and Grant. The driver of the car that pulled up to speak with them was Sheriff Devlin Miles.

❖

When Bubba Falkirk purchased his pre-owned boat, replete with a front casting deck with dry storage, vertical rod holders for three fishing rods, and a Yamaha 15 hp. 2-stroke engine, he thought he was elated.

"I'm tellin' ya," Bubba told his wife, Carly, "I feel like I just died-and-gone-ta-heaven."

Carly did not feel that getting up before the sun and hopping in a boat trying to catch a bunch of fish she would not eat anyway was hardly something heavenly. But if it made Bubba happy, Carly was fine with that.

When he was out on the water watching the sunrise, Bubba was truly in his element. He marveled as the early morning mist slowly rose up from the water's surface like a curtain opening up over a stage. He loved the sounds of occasional ripples on the water and the wakeup calls of local birds.

However, when he made this morning's trek to Fischer's Pond, he anticipated catching some bass or perhaps a catfish now awakened from its winter hibernation at the pond's bottom. He never anticipated spotting an automobile submerged in the water.

Andy Maynard was headed home following his night shift duty when he heard the report that a local fisherman had spotted a vehicle in Fischer's pond. He arrived just in time to see the current year silver Honda Civic being pulled from its watery grave.

"Hey, so watcha got there?" Andy called out to Deputy Denny Grimes.

"Hey there, Andy. Got us a vehicle doing some underwater swimming or5 scuba diving, man. Unless they got somebody locked away in the trunk, there ain't no occupants. Had two divers help with getting the vehicle out. Now we got an additional team of divers coming in to do some searching in case we got us a body or two somewhere in there."

Andy chatted a bit longer with Grimes before leaving and continuing his trip back home. He would be off-duty tomorrow and then start working the day shift on the following day. There was not a whole lot more he could contribute to the activity there.

The vehicle was registered to a Mr. Louis Anthony Merkel, 117 Greenway Drive in the Fairway Meadows subdivision.

Neither the body of Mr. Merkel nor anyone else was found in Fischer's Pond.

Chapter Nine

Yesterday's Memories

Katie giggled aloud as Kent entered the bedroom carrying a tray with two cups of coffee, some orange juice, French toast, and a couple of boiled eggs.

"How is it that I merit room service this morning? What's the occasion? It's not my birthday. Not our anniversary."

"And why, my dear, must it be some type of special occasion for me to gather up a few things for you as you rest in bed this morning? Besides, this could be a ploy on my part to keep you in bed as I climb back in."

Katie laughed aloud, as Kent helped to prop up her pillows and get to a seated position. "You'll never have to resort to trickery with me, mister. Hah! If anything, it might be the other way around."

Taylor laughed with her as she propped up his pillows and opened the covers for his reentry. God, how he loved this woman!

"So what's on the agenda today?" Katie said with a slight smirk.

"Well, I'm thinking about herding up the cattle to give them their shots, then baling some hay for the winter storage, and, if time permits, mending the fences out on the north forty."

Katie was laughing hard now.

"Hmm, we don't have cattle, we don't bale hay, we do not have fenced pasture land, and, heck, we don't even have winters here in the tropics."

"Well then, I guess I can cross all of those chores off of my list, eh? My work is done for the day."

Kent loved Katie's laugh.

"Hey," Kent said, "You've been wanting to go to the market. We can do that this afternoon."

They ate their breakfast together, laughing and chatting lightly as they did.

Soon, Kent and Katie were lying back with Katie's head resting against Kent's body.

"I've had some dreams lately, Katie. Surprised me a bit, but I think maybe they are kind of therapeutic for me. It's as if I have things tucked away deep inside of me and they finally surface in an effort to free me of the past."

From the very beginning of their relationship, Katie purposed never to push Kent into having to discuss his past. In fact, in the initial phase of their time together, Katie knew Kent as Ron Woodruff and had no awareness of anything much beyond that.

"Would you be willing to share your dreams with me, Darling?"

In addition to providing Taylor with an outlet for anything bottled up within, the very act of sharing openly with Katie was restorative for him. He had lived a solitary existence for so many years. This, combined with the secretive, confidential nature of his former position as a Navy SEAL, made it difficult for him to open up to anyone.

"I dreamt I was sitting and talking with Carlos Martinez and Wilson Brown."

Katie knew precisely who these men were. They were two fellow SEALs that Kent attempted to save while on his last covert mission overseas.

"They were so alive, Katie. The dream was so real. Then suddenly I remembered that they were dead and I asked them about that. They never did answer me. For a moment, I wondered if I was dead also.

Weird stuff, but that's how dreams are most of the time."

Katie smiled and hugged her husband even tighter. He continued to talk.

"I never told you about all that happened that day. We were in Yemen. The suspected terrorist that we were sent out to capture was now in our custody. We set up a camp for what would be our last night in that country. We were all feeling good. Our mission was just about over.

The missiles that struck our camp came without any warning whatsoever. One minute, things are quiet and calm. Next minute, you feel as if you are in the very center of hell itself."

There was a strong element of stress in Taylor's voice now. He was grinding his teeth. He clenched his jaw. He began to rub the back of his neck. His eyes seemed to be focused upon something that occurred years ago. He appeared to be somewhere back in time.

"In the midst of fire and the putrid smell of death, there's this high piercing sound, like a scream or a shriek. My ears were ringing. You want it to stop. My God, you wish you could just silence it.

At first, an adrenaline rush disguised my pain. I did not even realize how badly wounded I was. Let me tell you, that ended quickly. I was in intense pain and disoriented from having been thrown through the air and slammed against the ground by the blast that hit our camp. I was light-headed and my mind was in a fog. When something like that happens, Katie, you kind of feel as if you are deep inside some kind of a dream.

I remember running—racing away from the fire. Then I turned back. I had to know what happened to Carlos and Willie. I had just been talking with them on my handheld before the blast occurred.

Then I spotted them lying on the ground close to each other. They were unconscious."

Kent focused back for a moment on Katie. As their eyes met, she could see that her husband was genuinely reliving a nightmare. Katie reached up and placed the palm of her hand on Kent's cheek.

"One part of your mind tries to convince you to run away, that it is too late, that they are likely dead anyway. But, within your heart, you know that you must try to save them. You cannot leave them behind.

Your mind is in conflict. You have been trained to survive. You have been trained to save others. You have lived under the SEAL code to 'Leave no man behind.' When I was a SEAL, it was unwritten, but we were all committed to it. It was inscribed somewhere within us.

I was never so frightened in my life."

Katie gazed deeply into her husband's eyes.

"I cannot imagine you ever being afraid of anything. I see so much courage in you, Kent."

Taylor stared more intently into Katie's eyes.

"There is no need for courage without the presence of fear, Katie. I have been fearful many, many times."

Kent sighed. His eyes once again took on a far-off look. Katie was very aware that even after the passage of years, there were things etched so deeply in her husband's mind that the images remained very clear to him.

"I just don't think I could ever forgive myself if I had just run away. I am so thankful to this day, Katie, that I did rescue those two men. The three of us ended up in a small cave. I have no idea how we ever got there. I cannot honestly even tell you where it was. Yet, I can still see it. I can smell it even to this day."

Katie softly began to rub the back of Kent's left hand. Her voice was slow, soft—almost melodic.

"If Carlos and Wilson were able to sit with you today, Kent, I believe they would thank you for all that you did and risked in trying to save their lives. Darling, you do realize that you honestly did everything you possibly could to save them, don't you?"

Taylor paused for a moment, then sighed deeply.

"Yes. Yes, I know I did. I-I think the thing that bothers me most, Katie, is that I hardly had time to grieve for them.

First, I woke up in some local village where an old retired Yemeni doctor saved my life. Then I ended up in a Yemeni prison camp. Then, by the time I got back home, well… my whole world had been turned upside down."

Kent sighed deeply. He stared down at his empty hands and spoke in a more flat, monotone voice.

"Carlos and Wilson were good men, Katie. They were good soldiers. They both had family. Carlos was divorced, but had two young daughters that he loved. He was very proud of them.

Wilson was a great guy. He was very gregarious, warm, kind of like a big, strong teddy bear—although no one ever called him that."

Taylor laughed at his own remark. Once again, he seemed to be focused upon another time and place, but now these memories were not as dark and foreboding.

"Wilson had a son with a woman he had known and been with for years. They named the boy Wilson Brown, Jr. Wilson kiddingly called him "Hashbrown." He was so incredibly proud of that boy of his.

Anyway, Wilson told me that he was ready to marry the boy's mother, Gloria, soon after we got back to the States. I met her a few times. Great gal. Knew how to handle Wilson like no one else on earth," Taylor chuckled. "You know Wilson asked me if I would be the best man at his wedding and bring Rose and the kids to the ceremony.

They were both good men—Carlos and Wilson. Tough, good soldiers, patriotic, so reliable you could put your life in their hands."

Taylor was clearly in much more positive spirits now.

"Well you know, Mr. Taylor-Woodruff-Nova, they both sound a lot like you."

"Ah," Kent said with a big smile, "flattery will get you…uh…everywhere."

Then he drew Katie closer and kissed her deeply.

Chapter Ten

Searching for the Owner

"Welcome to 'on-the-clock when the sun is out,'" Sheriff Devlin Miles said with a big grin, as Andy Maynard entered his boss' office. "Have a seat there, son. Sit down and take a load off."

Miles, at forty-four years old, had recently been elected to his fourth two-year term as county sheriff. At 5'10" tall with slight traces of his red hair, mixed with gray, atop his otherwise baldhead, Dev had put on a few pounds since the day he joined the department twenty-two years earlier. Nevertheless, his burly frame generated an appearance of strength.

This was Andy's first day working the dayshift. Dispatch informed him on his drive to the station that the sheriff wanted to see him right away.

"Uh, thank you, sir," Andy replied."So, I'm excited about the opportunity to work days. I'm lookin' to get a better sense of all that takes place on the other side of what I've been doing so far."

"Well, that's good thinkin' right there, Andy, mah boy. You got that right. Different crowd these daytime folks. Makes us have to police a bit differently than at night. Darkness gives us an added excuse if we come across a bit too harsh in dealing with someone.

Now, I ain't talkin' 'bout being too physical now, boy. No excuse for officers of the law getting contrary when it ain't really called for.

I'm talkin' 'bout things like how ya approach a stopped vehicle at night usin' a loudspeaker rather 'n jus' a getting outta your vehicle 'n all.

Anyways, we don't have that same cover when it's daylight outside."

Andy nodded. He made a concerted effort to appear comfortable with the county's highest elected law enforcement official. However, the image of

Sheriff Miles talking with two of his deputies late one night at the storage building continued to press its way into Andy's mind.

"So, I'm just more than glad to add to all that I'm learning as a member of your team Dev," Andy said, still feeling no less awkward.

"Andy, mah boy, I asked you to come by here this morning 'cause ah'm needing something in particular from you, son. Looks like ol' Denny Grimes' grandma up and died. Family's from up near Plattsburgh, Clinton County. Denny and his family are headed up that ways right about now."

Miles reached for his coffee mug, took a gulp, wiped his mouth with his sleeve, and continued.

'Lissen here, Andy. I had Grimes checkin' on a missin' person case. Ah'm talkin' about the guy whose car showed up in the mud at the bottom of Fischer's Pond.

Let me tell ya, Andy, even a one-eyed possum would spot that our detectives are all tied up investigatin' this here string of burglaries we been havin' lately. So we need a little help from guys like yourself."

"So, I'm more'n glad to help in any way that I can," Andy responded, as he reached for a file that the sheriff was handing to him.

"This here's the case file that Denny's been workin' on. You gonna see what he learnt so far. There's a list of people Grimes either already spoke with or was fixin' to.

Would 'preciate it, Andy, if you'd step in where Grimes left off and take over 'til he gets back. We need ta stay on this before things get any colder on why this here car was scuba divin' in a pond and its owner ain't nowhere ta be seen."

❖

On the virginal island of St. John, Kent and Katie sat together on the veranda of their home overlooking the crystal blue Caribbean waters. Their marriage had already glided past the one and a half year mark and was moving well on its way towards forever.

"Hey, Katie, I just had an alarming thought. You and I were married here under the names Jonathan and Katie Nova. You suppose that means our marriage is not legal?"

Katie laughed.

"Well let me tell you, Mr. Taylor-Woodruff-Nova or whomever you are."

Kent was laughing along with Katie.

"I am convinced that marriage is not simply a piece of paper or a ring on a finger. What do you think, sir?"

Kent stood up. Pulled Katie close to him and spoke softly to her.

"I think that marriage consists of two people surrendering their hearts to each other, vowing to remain committed to one another forever. I have done that with you."

Then he kissed Katie deeply.

"In that case, I would have to say that I marry you every single day, Kent, and nothing will ever change that."

Kent and Katie sat back down. Armed with freshly made glasses of ice tea and positioned where the ocean breeze gently massaged their faces, they were once again simply spending time together.

For a moment, the gentle undulating ocean waves and the clinking of ice cubes as they sipped their tea generated the only sounds.

Kent spoke again.

"You know, Katie, sometimes I wonder how we will ever catch up on the years we missed, even when it simply comes to talking with each other."

"Hmm, maybe, because you spent so many years speaking to no one, just having someone, anyone or anybody around just gets you going," Katie said with a big smile.

"No, you are wrong, my dear. You could never be just anybody—never. But you do have a point there when you talk about what I was like for so many years. Day after day could pass and I never said a single word to another human being. And whenever I did speak, they were, I don't know, some shallow, innocuous words that I had to express to some stranger."

Katie rose from her chair, walked over to her husband, and sat on his lap.

"There's just no doubt about it, Aykuh, you most certainly have come a long way out from your cocoon."

Katie rubbed her face against Kent's face as they both laughed heartily.

Whenever Katie referred to her husband as "Aykuh," they both understood that she was referring to the fact that Jonathan Nova was simply the latest of a number of aliases her husband had. When she first met him, he bore the name Ronald Lane Woodruff. He had several additional false identities prior to that.

The"Aykuh" Katie teasingly used stood for"aka" or"also known as."

Now, here on St. John, Kent Taylor bore the name Jonathan Nova. The name really did not matter all that much to Katie, as long as she was the "Mrs." in front of it.

❖

Claire Reeves was seated at her desk in the reception area of Jonas Blair's law office when Andy Maynard stepped through the door.

"So, good morning to ya, Miss Claire," Andy beckoned, as he spotted the woman he had known since he was a young boy.

"Deputy Maynard," Claire responded, although she could just as well as referred to him as Andy and been well within the bounds of protocol. "Good morning to you. And to what do we owe the honor of your presence here today?"

"So, I've got a little something I'm workin' on and was hopin' I could have a little time with the man," Andy said referring to Jonas. "So, you think there's a chance I could have just a few minutes with Jonas?"

"Well, you're in luck, Deputy. He is here and does not have anyone with him at the moment. Give me a sec, please, and I'll check in with him."

Andy nodded and sat down in one of the guest chairs situated in the foyer.

Andy and his wife, Donna, knew Jonas and Sally Blair quite well. Donna was a teacher's aide who worked with Sally at Halston's Somerset Elementary School. Somewhere along the line the two husbands met, ended up going fishing together, and sat near each other at a few Freeport High football games. Blair was out of town for Andy's bachelor party, but Sally attended Donna's bridal shower. The Blairs were in attendance at the Maynard's wedding some four months earlier.

"Hey, Andy! How's it going?" Jonas had entered the foyer upon learning that Maynard was in the office. The two men shook hands and Jonas quickly steered Andy Maynard into his office.

"Hey, man, I'm sorry to just pop in here without advanced notice. So, I was nearby and you were on my list of people that I need to follow up with. I'm workin' on a case Sheriff Dev handed over to me a day or so ago."

"No prob at all, Andy. How can I help you?"

"So, the case I'm workin' on involves the car they pulled up from Fischer Pond recently."

"Oh yeah, saw something about that in the local paper, but they never gave any details on the vehicle owner. Only thing they did report was that they did not find the driver or anyone else in the pond,"

"Right," Andy continued, "So, Dev decided to keep the owner's name quiet at first, until we get a better opportunity to see if we can find the guy. So, the car belongs to a man named Merkel, Louis Merkel. Works or worked, I should say, over at Bergam in Chester."

Andy immediately spotted the reaction from Blair.

"So, I understand that you have had some contact with this man?"

Before Blair even responded, Andy provided some additional background.

"I contacted Merkel's daughter. Name's Julie Hancock. So, she came in from downstate yesterday late afternoon. She's stayin' at her father's place even now, after she provided us with some opportunity to look around."

"Yes," Blair responded. "I did have limited contact with Mr. Merkel and also had a visit from his daughter, Julie. She was trying to locate her dad and came across my name on a loose piece of paper in an address book that Merkel had.

Needless to say, Andy, I had no idea whatsoever where her father might be. Julie was quite concerned. Seems the man just up and quit his job at Bergam and, at least from his daughter's perspective, disappeared."

"Yes, that's pretty much exactly the story I got from Ms. Hancock. So, anything you can shed further about what you and Merkel might have talked about? I'm assumin' the man came to you for some legal advice?"

"Yes, in fact, Merkel left a retainer with me, rushed out after receiving a text message while we were together and said he'd be back. Never heard from him again.

I am bound by my attorney/client privilege with Louis Merkel, but I can tell you that I had the very strong impression that the man was troubled—no, make that frightened—about something related to his job. Claire did try to reach the man at his home at one point. I decided not to make any contacts at Bergam. Without knowing any more details at all, I did not want to let the folks at Bergam know that one of their employees was seeking out legal counsel."

Andy nodded. "Well, I've made contact with a man named Paul Martin. So, he's Bergam's top financial guy and, apparently, the man Merkel reported to. I'm hopin' he might be able to shine a little more light on this whole thing."

A few additional pleasantries, an inquiry as to how Donna was doing with her pregnancy, and a promise that they would both find some free time to go fishing again, superseded Andy's departure.

Blair did not mention the flash drive of data that Merkel left with him. A vehicle found on the bottom of a body of water does not send positive vibes about the welfare of its owner. Nevertheless, at this point in time, Jonas did not have a whole lot to go on when it came to where Merkel, might be. Did he ditch his own vehicle so that no one could possibly trace his whereabouts? Was Louie Merkel even alive?

For the moment, Andy Maynard was going to have to be the one to solve this puzzle. Jonas Blair would have to step aside, along with everyone else, and wait to see what unfolds.

Chapter Eleven

Nowhere to Hide

Akimba was returning to the family hut when he saw the smoke billowing high into the sky and heard gunfire. His heart began beating furiously. He became lightheaded. His legs felt like jelly as he dropped to his knees. He knew that his family was in dire trouble.

Akimba heard of incidents such as this throughout his and neighboring villages. The young boy had already been exposed to violence and death as his country, the Democratic Republic of Congo, continued to be at the center of what some referred to as "Africa's world war." Despite attempts to construct a meaningful transition of peace, government forces backed by Namibia, Zimbabwe, and Angola were even now in conflict with Ugandan and Rwandan rebel forces. According to some estimates, more than six million people had already died, either as a direct result from the fighting or from disease and starvation arising out of this embattled nation.

Akimba dropped the buckets of water that he had been carrying from a nearby stream—water that he was supposed to bring home several hours ago. He would have done just that had he not, as a typical eleven-year-old, gotten distracted skipping rocks across the water and staring at the tiny fish he spotted near the water's edge.

Despite his weakness and fear, he rose to his feet. He ran towards the small, thatched roof hut that his family called home. Akimba stopped, found some cover in a clump of bushes, and stared out at what was occurring. A band of men had already torched his home. He looked for his father, Mobula, and his mother, Shashan. He had three younger siblings—two sisters and a brother.

Akimba's heart was beating even more rapidly now. Fear had replaced all other emotions. He spotted the men holding his father captive as they forced his mother, his sisters, and brother to kneel on the ground. Rifle shots in quick succession felled each of them. Akimba's father was forced to watch the execution of his wife and children before he was also killed.

Jean-Pierre Muamba was among the men who were murdering young Akimba's family. His heart was beating so rapidly that he was having difficulty even breathing. As he witnessed the slaughter of this family, he felt sick to his stomach. He did nothing to aid in the killings of these innocent people. Yet, despite the fact that he was powerless to stop any of this, his body was riddled with guilt.

Muamba, along with Fabrice Zakuani, and Muteba Kyenge were all working undercover with America's CIA. It was an extremely hazardous position to be in, but in doing so, they believed that they could help prevent the slaughter of many more Africans and Americans. Now, as Jean-Pierre stared at the bodies of a father, mother, and three young children, he did not feel good about anything.

In such a short moment of time, Akimba was left an orphan, forced to survive by himself, assuming he was not found and also executed.

Tears poured from his eyes as Akimba turned away and ran, which spared him from witnessing his dead family members added as fuel to the fire consuming what had once been a place of safe haven for Akimba and his family. Earlier that day, his biggest issue in life was getting his chores done and not fussing with his sisters. Suddenly, life had taken on a whole new level of burdens and responsibilities.

Akimba was old enough to understand the ravages and consequences of death. What he did not understand was how such acts could be fueled by his country's vast mineral wealth or why to some it was important enough to kill others.

❖

"So, thanks for meeting with me, Mr. Martin," Andy Maynard said, as he was ushered into the office of Bergam's CFO. "No need to take up a whole lot of your time."

"Please have a seat, Deputy," Martin responded, as he accepted Andy Maynard's card. "Always glad to assist our law enforcement officers in any manner that we can. Appreciate the work you all do to keep our communities safe."

"So, I'm here, Mr. Martin, to inquire about one of your former employees, a Mr. Louis Merkel. I understand he terminated employment with you all recently. Seems we found Mr. Merkel's current year Honda at the bottom of Fischer's Pond, but we have not been able to find any sign of Merkel himself."

"Whoa!" Paul Martin exclaimed. "Heard something about a car being pulled out of Fischer's, but had no idea it was Louie's car. What in the world happened there?"

"Well, sir," Andy continued, "you might say that's what we're tryin' to find out. We don't have much to go on at all. So, I was hopin' you might be able to shed a little light on what might have been going on with Merkel. You know, his state of mind, whether he was troubled about anything...things like that.

So, let me begin by asking you, Mr. Martin, why Louis Merkel is no longer employed with your company. I understand from his daughter that he was with Bergam for something like sixteen years or so. So, are you free to tell me whether you terminated him or he left on his own volition?"

Martin nodded before speaking.

"Yes, well, in most instances, we leave discussions such as that in the hands of our very capable Human Resources people, but I do not mind telling you at all that Louie Merkel resigned from his position with us. In fact, I actually tried to convince him to stay on board. Merkel handled accounting matters and records related to Bergam shipments, both our imports and exports. He was a bit of a quirky guy, at times, real perfectionist, but that fit well with the demands of his job. He was thorough. Did good work."

"So, do you know why, in particular, he decided to quit his job? Did he have something else lined up? Another job slated somewhere?"

"I asked him that myself," Paul Martin responded, "as did our HR folks during his exit interview. But, if he did have another job, for some reason, he would not disclose it. He just said he was tired. Wanted some time to slow down a bit. Maybe do some traveling.

As I stated earlier, Louie was a good worker, but ... a bit of an odd fellow you might say. He was a very private individual—a real loner, who pretty much kept to himself."

Martin paused for a moment, rubbing his hand over his eyes, and spoke a bit more softly.

"My God! I hope nothing serious has happened to Louie."

"Well, as I say, Mr. Martin, that's what we're tryin' to find out. So, I am sure that you realize that findin' a man's new vehicle at the bottom of a pond is certainly not a strong indicator that all is well.

But, you know, I'm having a bit of a hard time tryin' to wrap myself around the fact that he suddenly up and quits his job with little or no explanation why. Next thing we learn is that the man is unaccounted for and his vehicle is at the bottom of a pond."

Paul Martin remained quiet.

"So, can you provide me, sir, with a contact at your Human Resources Department with whom I can speak? I'd also appreciate an opportunity to talk with any of Mr. Merkel's co-workers who might have some helpful insights."

"I'll follow up with HR and see who would be your best contact there and what we can find that would assist you, Deputy Maynard. I've got your number here, so let me check with Mary Sterling. Mary heads up our Human Resources Department. I will have someone from HR give you a call.

As to co-workers, Merkel was, as I said, pretty much a loner and his job was unique. That's why he reported directly to me. I am not sure that there is anyone who really worked closely with the man."

Andy felt a significant switch in the course of his discussions with Paul Martin. Suddenly, Human Resources contacts were unknown? Would Paul Martin not have had follow up with his HR folks following their exit interview with a man who was one of Martin's direct reports? And now Martin could not think of a single co-worker who might be able to provide some insight on Louis Merkel's demeanor prior to his departure and disappearance?

Blair stated that Merkel seemed very anxious, even frightened, about something that related to his job. Surely, others would have noticed something in one of their co-workers.

"All right, Mr. Martin, believe I have taken up enough of your time today. So, I'll just wait for that follow up with someone from your Human Resources Department and give you some time to determine whether there might be any others here at Bergam who might be good candidates for me to talk with about Louis Merkel."

Andy stood to leave, extended his hand to Paul Martin, and walked away. Once Andy was out of sight, Martin immediately reached for the phone to call Richard Kelser.

❖

When Andy called Jonas asking if he could spare some time to talk again, it was Blair who suggested they meet after work where they could also have a few beers and something to eat. Gino's Pizzeria and Italian Ristorante fit the bill perfectly.

"So what you're really saying, Andy, is that you are not entirely comfortable that Bergam's CFO was being straight up with you."

"So, I don't know exactly what it is, Jonas, but there was just something about this guy that made me feel as if he was stringing me along.

I really appreciate you taking the time with me, Jonas. Don't mean to bother you with my work, but it sure helps to have a good sounding board and, believe me, your training at Langley is well beyond anything I've ever received. Hell, I'm not even a detective and have no idea why Sheriff Dev chose me to handle this thing. First, he indicated I would step in temporarily until Denny Grimes returned. Then he said he needed Grimes on something else and I was to stay with this case.

So, like I say, I appreciate you spending time with me."

"Anytime, Andy. Glad to help in any way that I can. But, I kind of feel as if my FBI background is not the only reason you wanted to bounce things off of me. Am I wrong in sensing that something has got you a bit uncomfortable as to just who you can go to or trust over at the station?"

Maynard did a bit of a double take, then shrugged, grinned, and sighed.

"So, I guess I should have known that I can't slip anything past you. Here I was talking about Paul Martin not being straightforward and I'm doin' the same with you."

Andy told Jonas Blair about the deputies, Sheriff Miles, and the recent rash of burglaries.

"Okay, Andy, I think you very well may be on to something there. Problem is, as you know, you are dealing with a hotbed of coals. Before you make any move at all, you are going to need something a whole lot more solid than you have now. You best not even hint at anything implicating fellow officers in a string of burglaries.

I'm sure that I don't have to tell you how dangerous it is to even go so far as to include Sheriff Miles himself. Trust no one, Andy. If another officer comes up to you privately and expresses concerns similar to yours, do not reveal your own concerns. That is a pretty common ploy used when dirty cops suspect that someone on the force may be aware of wrongdoings.

Let me think about this a bit more, Andy. My immediate thoughts are that you are going to have to do some behind the scenes work. Find a way to become aware of any call-ins from people saying they are going to be away and would hope to get some extra patrol from the department. Be in a position to have eyes on that home and hope you can be there when the burglars show up. I have a really good camera for night pics without a flash that I can let you use. You know this will entail extra time and commitment from you. And hear me clearly, Andy, you cannot let anyone know what you are up to or even know about the suspicions that you have. You've got to be extremely careful. When dirty cops start to feel cornered, they generally will stop at nothing to avoid being discovered.

Andy, when I say stop at nothing, I mean you will seriously have to watch your back. You may find that you are playing with fire."

Chapter Twelve

The Seeds of Lies

It troubled Jonas that he was unable to reveal more to Andy Maynard with regard to Louie Merkel's strange visit and the flash drive he left at Blair's office. Finding Merkel's car submerged in a local pond raised the likelihood of foul play. Yet, it was not yet established that Louie Merkel was dead.

"I do believe that Andy is on to something with this case he is currently working on," Jonas was saying to his wife, Sally, as they sat together eating dinner at home. Little Taylor was already asleep for the night. "Andy is already a really good police officer and has the makings to go far in whichever direction he takes with his career."

Jonas first met Sally when she transferred into the New York FBI office from Chicago and joined Bill Gladding's task force. Sally's law enforcement pedigree as a former FBI field agent was on a par with her husband. Her computer forensic skills surpassed a good number of the FBI lab geeks.

When Donna Maynard, Andy's wife, was assigned as a teacher's aide to work directly with Sally, the two women formed a friendship that was not limited to a classroom.

"You know, Donna says Andy has surprised her with his smarts and the thirst for knowledge he demonstrates. She knew he was a good student in high school, but she says he reads all the time and can discuss world events with the best of them."

Jonas smiled. "They're just 'good people'—Andy and Donna."

"Yes, I agree. They are going to be great parents once their little one comes along. I am really excited for them."

The phone call from Mary Sterling, Vice President Human Relations at Bergam, opened the door for Andy Maynard's return to the prominent local company's headquarters.

"You will be speaking with Rosanna Castro," Sterling mentioned, as she sat with Andy in her office. "Rosanna conducted the exit interview with Mr. Louis Merkel. She will gladly assist in any manner that she can. Deputy Maynard, there are, as you would expect, certain areas of confidentiality that exist with respect to an employee's portfolio, but Rosanna will most assuredly provide whatever she can to help you. We are all very concerned about the welfare of one of our former colleagues."

"How well did you know Louis Merkel, Ms. Sterling?"

"I knew Louie Merkel well enough to say hello whenever I spotted him. From time to time, I ran into him, especially when he was meeting with Mr. Martin.

Bergam is a large Company, Deputy Maynard. I wish that I was able to know every employee well, but, unfortunately, I am just not able to do so."

"So you would not be in a position to have noticed any erratic or change of behavior in Louis Merkel in recent times?"

"Oh no. Not at all. I simply did not have that level of contact with that employee."

Following the time with Sterling, Ms. Castro greeted Andy. He handed her his card. Castro was an attractive young woman. Andy estimated her height to be about 5'4". Her body was tight and bore just the right curves in all the right places. She had dark brown curly hair that extended just beyond her shoulders, brown eyes, and high cheekbones. Her surname and a hint of an accent supported the fact that she was of Hispanic descent. Maynard guesstimated her age to be somewhere in the range of twenty-five to twenty-eight years old. She had been employed with Bergam just short of two years. Castro reported directly to Mary Sterling.

Rosanna Castro was polite and pleasant throughout their time together in a small conference room. Even so, there was something underlying her demeanor that Andy was working hard to discern when it suddenly occurred to him. Scripted. Rosanna Castro could have been reading to Andy, responding to his questions by following a prepared script that anticipated and directed her responses to any questions the deputy might raise. Andy considered the fact that people working in HR would have a tendency to be deeply conscious of boundaries related to privacy whenever discussing anything about a current or former employee. Nevertheless, this woman was not attempting to assist Deputy Maynard in his quest to determine the whereabouts and welfare of one of Bergam's former longtime employees. If anything, her conversation was slanted towards revealing as little meaningful insight as possible and sending the deputy on his way.

As a result, Rosanna Castro pretty much added nothing of any real value with regard to Louis Merkel. No, Mr. Merkel did not seem overly nervous, agitated, confused, nor deeply concerned about anything. No, he never gave any indication concerning his immediate plans other than some time to relax and, perhaps, travel a bit. No, he did not provide any information about a new employer and, in fact, gave the impression that he was not leaving Bergam to take another position elsewhere. No, Ms. Castro did not have an opinion on whether Merkel's decisions were rather strange or indicative of something beyond the norm occurring in his life. In addition, no, Bergam's CFO, Paul Martin, did not provide the names of any of the company's employees who might be available to speak with Andy about their former co-worker.

"So, I'll need you to get back with me, Ms. Castro, with the names of a few Bergam employees who likely would have had the most contact with Mr. Merkel over the past month or so. You can call me directly on my cell listed there on my card or just call the station and leave a message. I'll get back to you."

As he drove away from Bergam, Andy reflected back on the conversations he had with Mary Sterling and Rosanna Castro. What he was experiencing might simply be what you get when you go from talking to individuals and small businesses to these larger corporations. He had always heard that Corporate America was commonly gifted at dehumanizing their employees. Even so, he found that, once again, he was leaving Bergam with a bad taste in his mouth. He could not shake the feeling that these people were playing him.

These folks are stringing me along, telling me as little as possible. Why would they do that? What are they hiding? And you mean to tell me that no one in the entire company has had any contact with this Merkel in the past month or so?

Andy's thoughts likely would have continued on that track had he not been interrupted by a call from dispatch.

"Big One wants to see you in his office," the dispatcher stated with reference to Sheriff Devlin Miles.

Within the next thirty minutes or so, Deputy Andy Maynard was sitting in the sheriff's office feeling somewhat like a young boy called to the principal's office at school.

"Andy. Mind tellin' me why you was in the station before duty checkin' on whether we got any people callin' in for added patrol while they's away on vacation? You ain't on night duty no more. Fact, at the moment, you ain't even on patrol duty. I pulled you off, in particular, so's you could work on that missing person case."

The Sheriff was clearly agitated.

"Sorry, Dev. Just habit, I guess. You know, still on that mindset that there's certain things I need to stay on top of, even when I might not be workin' on patrol at the moment."

Miles said nothing as he stared at his deputy, locked into eye contact. Maynard knew the tactic was commonly used to intimidate a person.

"I didn't put you on a particular case so's you could be distracted by habits or nothin' else, Deputy. I want you focused on what I gave you. Is that understood?"

"Yes, sir," Maynard responded. "Understood."

Andy Maynard left following a hand wave by the Sheriff indicating that their time together was over. As he walked away, Maynard believed that Sheriff Miles did not simply call him in because he was concerned about his deputy's focus on an assigned case.

"Not good." Maynard murmured as he climbed back into his police car. "They know or at least strongly suspect. Believe it is time for me to really heed Jonas' words even more and watch my back."

Once Andy was out of sight, Miles picked up his cell phone and punched in a number.

"Yeah, Welcher here."

"Jimmy, we gonna have need to round up Grant later and have us a little meetin'. Seems like Deputy Maynard may be on to more'n we knew.

71

My shiftin' him over to days and puttin' him on an assignment that don't involve patrollin' didn't seem to help none either. Get ahold of Caleb and get back to me."

❖

She was packing her things at furious pace now, just throwing things together in a haphazard manner. No time to be picky. She would take whatever she could, abandon the rest. As a single woman living in a small furnished apartment, she would not be transporting anything that would not easily fit into her car. The primary goal she had was to get herself out of the area and get as far away as possible.

She felt uncomfortable from the moment Mary Sterling asked her to meet with Deputy Maynard. "We didn't follow protocol on this one," Sterling stated. "Company policy says we are to conduct an exit interview with every employee who terminates. Somehow Louis Merkel slipped through the cracks."

She was initially reluctant to tell a law enforcement officer that she met with an employee she had actually never even seen before. Then Rosanna Castro thought a bit deeper about this. She saw it as an added opportunity to put her in good stead with her boss.

Who knows what this Merkel guy was up to or why he quit. Mary Sterling reminded her staff many times that Bergam was an employer, not a babysitter. What people do away from the plant is their own business. Whatever happened to Merkel or wherever he might be had nothing to do with his employer.

It was after Maynard left the plant that Castro became increasingly concerned. Bergam still had hard copy personnel files, although HR was now budgeted for the costs of converting everything to paperless records. Mary Sterling was away from her office when Rosanna went to the file cabinets stored in an alcove near Sterling's office. She quickly pulled up Louis Merkel's folder. There was nothing out of the ordinary there. In fact, Castro was about to shut the cabinet drawer when she noticed a file a few folders back from Merkel's that was missing an identifying label. It was what she found in that file that caused her blood to run cold.

The file contained a record of an exit interview with Mr. Louis Merkel. According to the document, duly dated and initialed, that interview was conducted by Rosanna Castro. Someone had even forged her signature on the documentation.

Why had someone gone so far as to have me lie about meeting with Merkel and then create false documentation? Why not simply say that the man just disappeared one day and no one at Bergam knew why he had done so? What are they covering up? Are they trying to draw any and all suspicion away from Bergam? Why? Does someone know more about Merkel's disappearance than are admitting?

Fortunately, the workday was nearing an end. Rosanna, despite the fact that initially she could hardly breathe and her body was shaking, was able to contain herself well enough to not raise any suspicion before exiting the building for the day.

Now, as Castro continued to move quickly, her breathing, her every movement supported the fact that she was frightened. They had set her up and she knew it. Surely a company as large and successful as Bergam would be more than willing to sacrifice a young woman, rather than run the risk of exposing themselves to any wrongdoings.

Her thoughts were running rampant as she shut the door to her apartment and moved quickly to her car.

I've never done anything criminal. I should have known when they started playing up to me, telling me about my great potential and all. I'm their patsy. I'm the one who takes the fall if anything really bad ever happened to that Merkel guy. I'm the one who looks guilty. I talked to the deputy about conducting the man's exit interview from Bergam when truth is I never even met the guy at all. No one will ever admit that they told me to lie. In fact, they'll hand over the file that was supposedly created by me.

Rosanna was in tears as she drove away. Her hands were shaking and she felt sick to her stomach.

I'm the patsy. I'm set up to take the fall. I should have known. Stupid. Blind. Agreeing to lie to that deputy. I should have known.

❖

Andy Maynard passed the security gate at Bergam and pulled his police vehicle into one of the designated guest parking spaces. He had called Rosanna Castro's office phone at least a half dozen times, reached her voicemail, left a few messages, and never received a return call. Today he was looking for a face-to-face meeting.

During his drive to this plant in Chester, Andy had something different on his mind. Last night he was out driving alone. He had done so in the two-year old Chevy Caprice that he and his wife, Donna, owned, but, at one point, he still had this eerie feeling that he was being followed. Yet each time he made a tactical move, he saw nothing to confirm that he had a tail.

Guess I'm just spooked. There's no doubt I stirred up some serious suspicions with Sheriff Dev. No telling just what Dev and any of the others know or don't know. I just need to lay low for a while. Gotta let this thing blow over.

Chapter Thirteen

What in the World

"We are sorry Deputy Maynard that you did not receive a response from Rosanna." The speaker was Mary Sterling. "Truth is Ms. Castro is no longer with us," she continued. "We strive to retain our employees, but things just were not working out when it came to Rosanna. It is very important to us, with the number of employees we have here at Bergam, that we maintain a strong Human Resources Department to best serve the needs of our people."

"Are you able to provide me with an address for Ms. Castro," Andy inquired. This was not that big a deal to him. He pretty much figured he could track her down on his own. He asked the question to see what kind of cooperative response he would receive from Bergam's chief HR person.

When Sterling accessed her cell phone and quickly jotted down the address of her former employee, Maynard wondered if he was being a bit too negative towards these Bergam people. Of course, a sudden departure of an employee so shortly after Andy had spoken with her did generate suspicions.

His suspicions were fueled when he arrived at Castro's apartment, received no response from within, and then encountered a man named Ernesto Juarez.

"She no here, no more," Juarez volunteered. "She gone. No here."

Maynard quickly learned that Ernesto Juarez was a tenant who paid no rent. He also earned a small monthly stipend from the apartment building owners by keeping an eye on things and assisting other renants with small repairs or other needs.

"She no say nothing to nobody. Just all of a sudden, I see her putting the suitcase in her car. I ask what going on, you know? She say she have to leave and no come back. Her rent paid up. She, how you say, pay by the month…"

"A month-to-month tenant?"

"Si, yes officer, you right. *Mes a mes.* No lease. She just pay rent every month is all. I ask about her deposit she pay when she first take her place, but she say just keep it, you know? And do whatever I want with anything she leave inside."

Ernesto stood silently for a moment. The man appeared to be comfortable talking with a police officer, but likely was not as comfortable talking about other people behind their back.

"I am here because I am concerned for Ms. Castro, sir. I need to be sure that she is okay. I would appreciate any assistance you can provide. Anything more you can tell me will help me put the pieces together and may be the reason I find her before anything really bad happens to her."

Juarez nodded, started to speak, stopped for a moment, and then responded.

"She look scared to me, sir. She very frightened. Her body shaking, yes? Normally, she always smile. She friendly person, you know? But this time, no. This time, she very scared like I never see her before.

Where she go, she no say. I do not know, sir. *No lo sé.*

I hope you find her and help her. Ms. Castro, she is very nice young lady. She is good person."

❖

The Democratic Republic of Congo is the second largest country by area in Africa. It has an estimated population exceeding 75 million, which makes it the fourth most populous nation in that continent. This Central African country lies on the Equator, with one-third north and two-thirds to the south. South of the Equator, the rainy season lasts from October to May. North of the Equator, the rainy season extends from April to November. As a result, the Congo receives very high levels of annual precipitation—eighty inches in some Congo locations. The Congo Rainforest is second in world size, only exceeded by the Amazon.

However, rainfall and thunderstorms have not been the primary identity of tempestuous activity in this nation. The ravages of war earn that dubious distinction. Millions of deaths have been left in its wake. Even now, the death toll continues to rise at an alarming rate of regularity.

The economy of the Congo is heavily reliant upon mining. The DRC is the largest producer of cobalt ore in the world, with some 80% of the world's cobalt reserves within its borders. It is also a major producer of diamonds and copper.

By some estimates, at least one-third of all the diamonds mined in the Congo are smuggled and sold to perpetuate the ongoing fighting throughout that region.

Efforts have been made to inhibit trade in conflict resources in the hope that this would reduce the incentive to extract and kill over them. In 2010, the US Congress enacted the "Dodd-Frank Wall Street Reform and Consumer Protection Act" which requires manufacturers to audit their supply chains and report conflict minerals usage. But just as with any law stretching across continents, legislation itself cannot control what it cannot see.

In the city of Lubumbashi, within the eastern portion of the Congo's Katanga Province, the blackness of the night served as an additional cover as he slipped through back alleys. He emerged from his hiding place for the sole purpose of scrounging up some food and adding to his limited supplies. He had already sent out a distress signal to his contacts back in the United States. His only hope now was to stay hidden long enough for them to reach him and bring him to safety.

Katanga Province has a land area larger than California. The Katanga Plateau is known for its farming and ranching. The eastern portion, with its capital city of Lubumbashi, the second largest city in the Congo, is the rich mining area. Cobalt, tin, copper, uranium, radium, and diamonds are mined there. It is also in that region where Jean-Pierre Muamba, Fabrice Zakuani, and Muteba Kyenge infiltrated the armed group that was of great interest to the United States Central Intelligence Agency. Like other armed groups in eastern Congo, they used mass rape as a strategy to intimidate and take control of mines and trading routes. Like other armed groups, they earned vast sums of money from the ores that produce tin, tantalum, tungsten, and gold—the majority of which end up in electronic devices such as cell phones, computers, and portable music players. Unlike other armed groups, the CIA had learned that there was a direct link between this armed group and terrorists with aims towards the United States. Moreover, someone, some person of significance living in the US and unknown to the CIA, was a key player in this activity.

Muamba and the two other Congolese men were strategically associated with America's powerful intelligence-gathering agency. Over the course of time, they had successfully penetrated the armed group that they informally referred to as BK1. This was a code name with no real meaning except to aid in the communications between these three men and their CIA contacts. Until recently, the three men had remained undetected, but that suddenly changed with fatal consequences.

Had Jean-Pierre been with his two compatriots when they were taken away, he also would have been tortured, before being bludgeoned with hatchets and killed. His corpse would also have been temporarily displayed as a message to the other group members. A savage merciless death is the only sure consequence for any who choose to betray the group to which some had been forcibly conscripted.

Muamba had been only minutes away. Since that time, he remained hidden, moving periodically from one place to another, trusting no one, avoiding the light of day, and making no further attempt to reach his CIA contacts. Once he received a communication that his rescue team was coming, he would coordinate a time and place for them to meet. Until then, he lived as the rat in the sewer, the mouse within the building walls.

As Jean-Pierre moved about quickly as a shadow in the night, he pondered once again how it was that he and his fellow agents had been discovered. His strongest inclination was that someone in America had leaked this information to the kingpin in the US. And that was yet another key piece to this puzzle. Muamba and his two partners had very recently learned the identity of this man in the States. Unless Jean-Pierre remained alive, the name of the man who was set to play a major role in a massive terrorist strike within the borders of the United States would go with Muamba and his cohorts to their graves.

Chapter Fourteen

On the Move

"Yeah, that's right. Mary says the deputy just showed up unannounced looking for Rosanna. From what we can gather, he had been anticipating a follow up call from Castro. When she never called, he started calling her and got nothing but her voicemail. So he decided to come here looking for her."

The speaker was Paul Martin. He was sitting with Richard Kelser in the CEO's office.

"Well, for what it's worth, it sounds like Castro's not doing any talking. How we doing with tracking her down?"

"We've got Sonny Goodall and his PI team on it. You know they're the best out there, Rich. Just a matter of time before they catch up with her. Sonny and his boys can track down the slickest of them and Rosanna Castro is hardly slick."

Martin was rubbing his hands on his pants legs and no longer making eye contact with Kelser.

"But...uh...you need to know that something major has popped up."

Kelser nodded, but said nothing, waiting for Martin to reveal this next piece of crucial info.

"Seems Louie Merkel may have had some contact with an attorney over in Comstock."

Kelser's attention shot up to an even higher level. He sat rigidly in his chair, while placing his folded hands on his desk.

"No telling right now what that was all about, but Merkel's daughter is back in the area. She called in and spoke with Sterling. As you would expect, Mary's done a great job in winning her over from when the daughter first contacted us after she could not locate her father. Mary gave her the sympathetic ear. Says this time she played up with the daughter on just how deeply concerned we all are over Louie being missing and his car showing up like it did. Told her we are all clinging to the hope that Louie is okay and hoping we might even hear from him again.

Anyway, during the course of the conversation, the daughter mentioned that after she left here last time she visited an attorney that her father had apparently gone to see. Man's name is Jonas Blair and, like I said, he's got an office over in Comstock."

Paul Martin hesitated before providing one more key piece of information."I've got Sonny personally following up on this, Rich. There are a lot of different reasons why someone goes to see an attorney. May even have something to do with Merkel setting up something for his daughter. We simply do not know enough yet. But this Blair ... he is a former FBI field agent."

❖

Sonny Goodall had never revealed the fact that Louie Merkel and his daughter had both visited attorney Jonas Blair.

"I decided they don't need to know until I want 'em to know," Goodall told a few of his key men. "Just remember. Bergam ain't the 'end-all-be-all,' even if they think they are. Hahaha. Even if they think."

Once Mary Sterling learned about the visits with Blair from Merkel's daughter, Mary relayed her knowledge to Paul Martin. Soon afterwards, Goodall conferred with Kelser and Paul Martin.

"We gonna take care of all that," Sonny casually stated in a conversation with the two corporate officials. "You just concentrate on what you're workin' on and we'll handle this stuff with Jonas Blair or anybody else. No problem. Ain't no problem at all," Sonny said, as he chuckled and twirled the unlit cigarillo in his hand.

"I already got operatives workin on dredgin' up Ms. Rosanna Castro," Sonny said. "Hahaha, those are two real good words right there—'operatives' and 'dredgin'. Hahaha."

Then just as suddenly, Sonny's cackling stopped. A stern face and a much lower tone of voice replaced it.

"When Sonny Goodall sets out to take care of somethin'," he said while jabbing his unlit cigarillo at the two men, "that somethin' gets done. So like I said, we gonna take care of everythin' that needs takin' care of."

It did not take very long for Sonny Goodall and his team of investigators to determine that Rosanna Castro had not gone to her parents in Baldwin, a small village located within the town of Hempstead in Nassau County, New York. Her mother was a housekeeper for an elderly wealthy couple there and her father was the groundskeeper.

Goodall also crossed Rosanna's sister, Marianna, off the list and an aunt who lived in Jersey City. But as Paul Martin had stated, Sonny and his guys were good—very good. They traced back to Castro's college days at Pace University in New York City. They discovered that Rosanna roomed with three other females in an off-campus apartment. She developed a particularly close relationship with one of her roomies, named Melissa Alvarez.

Rosanna and Melissa still had some contact with each other despite the fact that Alvarez now lived in Nashville, Tennessee. Between Melissa's Human Resources degree and her desire to make a mark in the music industry, the arts had won out. Alvarez lived alone in a small apartment. She worked by day as a waitress and had several local gigs she conducted in the evenings.

The Goodall team member who showed up unannounced at the Nashville apartment found Melissa there, but not Rosanna. Melissa did not fall for the guise that this man was working for an attorney seeking to utilize Rosanna as a potential witness to a severe multi-passenger car accident. This led to her undoing. It was also unfortunate that Melissa's passionate concern for a friend whom she considered to be vulnerable and in need of support and protection, spilled over into her contact with this man.

"You don't fool me one bit, mister," Melissa stated while pointing her finger at the man's face. "I know what you've done and as soon as my friend is strong enough, I'm going to march her right over to the police and have her report everything she knows."

Goodall's man determined then and there that Melissa would have to be eliminated along with Rosanna, but he intended to execute them at the same time. His plans went awry when the gag he placed on Melissa's mouth did not hold up and she, though bound tightly to a chair began to scream for help. The neighbor from the apartment next door, an elderly man who came to the door, was dragged inside only to quickly have his throat cut.

Melissa was also killed when another neighbor, a heavy-set woman, opened her apartment door and began shouting out, asking what was going on, and assuring that she had already called 911 for help.

"They're on their way," the woman bellowed. "The police are coming now."

Goodall's man was long gone by the time the police arrived, leaving the heavy-set woman to tell her story of a narrow escape from murder countless times. She did not know Rosanna Castro despite seeing her a few times. She never saw the assailant who left two dead bodies in his wake. Her story remained focused upon her own narrow escape with death.

Nashville police cars with their lights flashing, joined by two medical emergency vehicles, were all on the scene when Rosanna was within sight of the apartment building. By now, a small crowd had gathered at the scene and mobile media vehicles were well on their way. Rosanna carefully inquired as to what was going on and received sketchy reports that the young lady in apartment 211 and another tenant were murdered.

Rosanna was struggling to breathe.

Melissa dead? How? Why? Because of me? Are these the ones chasing me? Is it my fault that Melissa is dead? Yes, must be. But...how? How did they find me here?

Rosanna was not ready to entrust herself to the police. She feared that she would be criminally charged for her involvement back in Chester.

If they took her into police custody, the people searching for her would know exactly where she is. Then again, she might be set free and become an easy target. But if they found me here in Nashville, they will likely find me wherever I go.

Let them try. I will not make it easy for them. I cannot just stop and let them get me.

Oh Melissa, oh sweet Melissa! I am so sorry. Please forgive me. What have I done to you? Oh dear God, why is this happening to me? What have I done to deserve this?

So now, leaving everything behind and driving away with even less than she had when she ran from her apartment in New York, Rosanna Castro made her way back to her parked car and drove away. As she did, she realized that someone could have been watching from a distance for her return and prepared to follow her even now.

And if they get to her, she would once again be reunited with Melissa.

❖

"Listen dear. Your father will gladly take you back home tonight. He doesn't mind driving you home at all."

Donna Maynard laughed at her mother's remark. "I appreciate that, Mom," Donna replied as a big smile crossed her face, "but Andy already texted me. He has left home already and is on his way. I am perfectly capable of driving myself and I told him that a number of times. Andy is being so protective now that I'm pregnant. I laugh just thinking about it, but, in all honesty, it is kind of sweet. Andy is going to be a great daddy, Mom."

Andy was, indeed, on his way. Donna's mother picked her up at school and the two of them had a time of shopping together and dinner. Donna had driven to work in the morning with Sally Blair.

Soon Donna and Andy would be coming to Donna's parents' home with their little one in tow. That was a precious thought.

As Andy drove the car, his mind was focused upon the fact that he and Donna were expecting their first child and they could not possibly be any happier about it.

Andy turned off the main road onto a quiet back street that would eventually lead him to the home of his in-laws. There were no other cars around. He hit his brakes and brought his car to a sudden stop when he spotted someone lying in the road in front of him. Andy chose not to make a call with his cell phone until he had at least some better indication of just what he had stumbled upon.

The deputy exited his car, leaving it running with the hazard lights on and the headlights still focused upon the man lying there. He walked over and called out to the man, but did not receive a response. He reached down to determine whether the man had a pulse. As he did, the man whirled onto his back and two quick snaps, sounding similar to a staple gun, added to the sound of the engine of Andy's car. As Deputy Andy Maynard's lifeless body dropped onto the asphalt, the man who just moments earlier had been lying still on the road, sprang to his feet, skipped for a moment, then ran away.

Afterwards, when the police and other emergency vehicles were on the scene, no one knew for sure just how long Andy had been lying there before a young man headed home after working at his fast-food job happened upon the scene and called 911. It did not matter anyway. The medical examiner determined that Andy died instantly when the first bullet exploded in his brain.

Chapter Fifteen

The Pace Quickens

Tears flowed from Sally Blair's eyes as she spoke with her husband. "I-I just can't believe it, Jonas. I just can't believe that Andy is dead. Donna is beyond devastated. I'm deeply concerned that she will lose the baby in the midst of her anguish. Why? Why would anyone do this?"

Jonas shook his head. He made a concerted effort to be strong for Sally, while at the same time, his own heart was grieving. Like Sally, his time as a federal agent aided in developing a toughness when it came to dealing with tragedy. Even so, it did not exempt him from the emotional turmoil associated with something like this. He liked Andy Maynard—liked him a lot. He also was deeply saddened by the fact that Andy's wife, Donna, would now bear a child without Andy around. This sucked big time. Beyond the sadness that he felt, Jonas was angry and could not find anyone at whom to direct his festering anger. As best he could tell, the law enforcement officers, despite an influx of others donating their time from nearby communities, were clueless as to who was behind this seemingly purposeless murder.

The initial reports were sketchy. The media described this as a bizarre incident. Sheriff Devlin Miles went on public record that he and his men would never rest until they identified the murderer of this fine young deputy and brought the killer to justice.

Jonas Blair began to consider the possibility that Andy's killer might never be found. For the first time since he walked away from his position as an FBI agent, Jonas was preparing to do some personal investigation.

"I'm not sitting back on this one," he informed Sally. "I won't interfere in the investigative work being done, but I just can't sit back and do nothing."

Sally smiled despite her tears. "You know I will help you, Jonas, in any way that I can."

❖

The size of the team investigating the murder of Deputy Sheriff Andy Maynard continued to swell as law enforcement officers from other police departments volunteered their time.

Sheriff Miles was sitting in his office with deputies Caleb Grant and Jimmy Welcher. They had agreed to meet early before the building filled up with officers working their regular shifts and others on a task force investigating Maynard's shooting.

"There ain't no reason why Andy's death should lead to anything involvin' us," the sheriff began,

"but, just to be sure, I want you guys workin' on separate teams. Remember you gotta be keepin' your eyes and ears open. Y'all need to just stay calm and focused. Ya unnerstand?"

The two men nodded, but did not have much to say. It concerned Devlin Miles that the men he shared dark secrets with were clearly nervous.

"Now you guys listen to me and listen real good. If you don't like havin' a whole bunch of lawmen sniffing around, turning up every rock they come across, just give some thought to what it would be like bein' surrounded by a whole bunch of inmates in the pen, some likely located there 'cause we got 'em arrested in the first place. You guys keep that in the back of your minds and I believe you'll get the picture of what we need to do to keep the focus away from us. Are you guys reading me.?"

"Loud and clear, Dev," Caleb Grant answered.

"Yeah. I gotcha," Jimmy Welcher said, while nodding his head.

"Good," Miles responded just before reaching for his coffee cup. He took a sip, wiped his mouth with the back of his hand, and spoke again."Glad to hear we on the same page, boys, 'cause we in this thing together. Sink or swim, it's the three of us. And I ain't plannin' on none of us sinkin'."

❖

"Do you know what in particular she wants to talk about? Did she say anything more to you?" Jonas was driving with Sally headed to the home of Donna Maynard.

"No," Sally responded. "She asked if there was any possibility that you and I could come and talk with her. Then she started to cry and I did not want to push things any further. I simply told her that I would get in touch with you and we would come to her home.

She is so distraught, Jonas. It makes me think how I would be if I ever lost you."

Jonas reached over, took Sally's hand in his, and spoke softly. "Well, first of all, you are not going to lose me, Sal. We both already had our 'should-have-died' moment, so I believe we have a full lease on life now. And, yes, I know how much Donna loved Andy and with a baby coming ... Whew! This is just heartbreaking."

Before long, Jonas and Sally were seated with Donna in her living room. "I apologize for interrupting your day. I realize that you both are busy..."

"No, Donna," Jonas interrupted, "you are not bothering us at all. We are honored that you would reach out to us. You know how we felt about Andy..."

"And how we feel about you, Donna, and that little one inside you," Sally joined in. "We are here for you."

Donna Maynard fought against the tears forming in her eyes and spoke again. "I asked you here because there are some things troubling me, things I am not sure how to handle. There are no two other people on earth that I believe I can trust more than the two of you.

In recent months, Andy was troubled. Oh, he tried to hide things from me, not wanting to burden me. That was especially true once he knew I was pregnant. He was ... he was so..." Donna was struggling to fight back against her tears. "I-I c-can hardly tell you ... [sigh] just how excited Andy was about this baby."

Donna paused to compose herself. Sally reached over and held Donna's hand. "A few days before he ... before I ... uh... lost Andy. I got him to sit with me. I told him that I could sense how troubled he was and all. He, of course, mentioned how he did not want to burden me with things, but I told him, 'No, we are a couple and need to share things with each other whether they are good or bad.'"

Jonas calmly interrupted. "Andy did talk with me about some of the concerns he had about Sheriff Miles and a few of the deputies."

"Yes, Andy told me that he had confided in you and I was so very happy to hear that. He respected you so very much, Jonas."

Donna's words penetrated Jonas. He had already gone from simply grieving over Andy's death to the secondary emotion of anger towards whoever was responsible for this tragedy.

"But it wasn't only the sheriff's department that was troubling Andy," Donna continued. "You know he was investigating the disappearance of that man whose car was found at the bottom of Fischer's Pond."

"Yes," Jonas interjected. "A man named Louie Merkel."

"Andy felt as if he was getting the runaround from the people over at Bergam Industries where that man worked. He believed they were definitely hiding something. He knew that messing with Bergam could stir up a whole lot of trouble in the community, but he was convinced, as he put it, that they were 'dirty.'

I think …," Donna paused once again, as she struggled to keep herself composed. "I-I think that Andy was scared. I had never seen him like that, but I think with me, the baby coming, he did not want to upset me too much. Andy was scared of something just before he died."

❖

"Okay, so what are you saying?"

"Well, I don't know exactly. Could simply be neighbors paying their respects once again to the widow, ya know? All I know is what I told you."

"Okay, so tell me again. And don't leave nothing out."

"Well, like I say, it was late morning, you know? And the deputy's widow got a visit from the lawyer fellow out of Comstock and his wife. In and of itself, that ain't such a big deal, but the wife, she's a teacher, you know? So it means she had to break away from class and her husband had to interrupt his lawyerin' so's they could visit Maynard's wife, if ya catch my drift.

I mean, why not visit later when school's out or when the lawyer might simply leave early for the day? That and the fact that both them folks used ta be FBI just raised my suspicions a bit.

I may be overreactin' or something, but I felt it were enough for me ta quickly let ya know."

"Well, you were right to do so. Good job. We will take it from here."

Chapter Sixteen

Trapped

Sonny Goodall and two of his men entered the office of Jonas Blair. Sonny showed his PI credentials to Claire Reeves. Despite Sonny's wide grin and attempts to be polite and civil with Claire, she did not feel comfortable with any of these three men. If she were in a position to describe them to Jonas, she likely would have referred to them as thugs.

Soon, the three men were seated with Blair in his office.

"Attorney Blair," Sonny began after he handed his credentials to Jonas,"we have been retained by the folks over at Bergam Industries to assist in recovering some highly confidential stolen property."

Blair was relaxed, maintaining a very calm and collected demeanor. "So what brings you gentlemen here to me?"

"Well, sir," Goodall began, "we have information that a former Bergam employee, a Mr. Louis Merkel, visited you here in your office shortly before he terminated his employment and seemingly vanished."

"Ah yes," Jonas interrupted. "Merkel is the owner of the vehicle they found at the bottom of Fischer's Pond, as I recall."

"Yesiree, counselor. One and the same," Goodall quickly answered. "We have reason to believe that Merkel is the one who sunk his own car there then came up with some other means and left this area."

"That is an interesting theory," Blair said. "And just why would a man do that?"

"Mr. Blair, we believe that Louis Merkel stole data from Bergam that relates to some highly-confidential plans and schematics. They relate to a new and state-of-the-art design that could be worth several billion dollars, that is billions, sir, not merely millions, in future revenues to the company. This material is so secretive that Bergam has not gone to the police with this matter, but chose to turn the matter over to me and my private investigation team. They do not want to even inadvertently tip their hands to any of their competitors nor tell anyone the details of their future plans."

Sonny paused and stared. Jonas immediately recognized this as an intimidation technique. It would be ineffective against a former trained federal agent.

"We are here today to solicit your assistance, Mr. Blair. I am authorized to inform you that even though the property that we believe Merkel took rightfully belongs to Bergam, the Company is most willing to pay a very handsome five-figure recovery fee to anyone who aids in getting this back to Bergam."

Jonas hesitated for a moment, smiled, made eye contact with each of the men in his office, then spoke again. "I am free to confirm that I did meet with Mr. Merkel here in my office. I am not at liberty, based upon attorney/client privilege, to disclose my discussions with the man.

However, I can assure you gentlemen that Louis Merkel did not provide me with anything even similar to the property that you allege he stole from his former employer."

Sonny Goodall smiled, nodded, rubbed his chin, and then breathed deeply. As he did, his demeanor changed. His eyes narrowed as he glared at Jonas. His voice was tighter.

"Well, let's just say I want to be sure that we are communicating very clearly to you, Mr. Blair. Bergam's recovery of what Merkel stole is of the utmost priority. We, on behalf of the Company, intend to get that property back regardless of what it takes to do so. I advise you, sir, to take this matter very, very seriously."

Jonas sat silently and stared back at Goodall. He caught the man's subtle threat.

"Here's my card should you suddenly think of something helpful to our cause or come across some additional information. Do remember the recovery fee that Bergam is willing to extend to someone like yourself. I assure you, sir, it would go a long way in aiding a young married couple with a baby."

Jonas felt a chill racing through his body, as Goodall stood and turned to leave the room along with his two aides. They were through the reception area and out the door before Jonas even rose from his chair.

❖

With a stop in Jackson, about an hour short of Memphis for gas, a restroom break, a couple of diet Dr. Peppers, and a few bags of chips, Rosanna Castro was in Memphis in just a bit over three and a half hours from Nashville.

Her trepidation after learning that her friend Melissa was dead was now replaced by an adrenaline rush that spurred her on to find some way to protect herself. She was overwrought with guilt that she had caused her friend to be killed. But, there was nothing she could do to save Melissa now. Her focus had to be upon her own safety. She needed to come up with some kind of a plan to hide somewhere beyond the reach of Melissa's killers.

Rosanna shuddered at the thought that whoever would be looking for her was far more astute in what to look for when tracking someone. After Melissa had been killed, after Rosanna's presence in Nashville had been discovered, Rosanna quickly stopped at an ATM and withdrew the maximum $500 from her checking account. From that point on, she would revert to only using cash and leaving nothing that would be traceable to her credit card. Now, that money would serve her purposes, but it could only stretch so far for so long. She had another $800 remaining in her checking account, which represented all she had left. But she simply did not know whether there was any way to reach that money without revealing her location to someone anxious to find her.

Every time Rosanna saw a police car, she had conflicting feelings. She feared turning herself into the authorities. However, she wondered if she should simply turn herself in and take her chances.

She journeyed onto Interstate 55 and onto the Memphis-Arkansas Bridge, across the Mississippi River and into West Memphis, Arkansas. Rosanna had no assurance that anything she was now doing would provide greater protection from anyone pursuing her. It simply felt better to be entering into new states even more distant from her starting point in New York. If they were going to catch up to her, they would have to fight to do so.

❖

Following the visit and veiled threat from Sonny Goodall, Jonas contacted the FBI regional office in Buffalo, New York. He was informed that Agent Marshall Price was doing some unrelated investigative work within striking distance of Comstock and would be notified. Within a few hours, Jonas received a call from Agent Price. On the very next afternoon, the FBI field agent was sitting in Jonas' office.

Price exchanged all the expected congeniality to a former agent, listened to all that Jonas had to say, and shared some limited insights of his own.

"Yeah, you know what it's like, Jonas. You find yourself working in an area, you pick up scuttlebutt here and there even on cases that you're not working on. Bergam Industries is a big reason why a whole lot of people in this area even have jobs, whether directly with them or ancillary jobs spawned by Bergam's presence. Means you have a lot of people who are going to feel protective towards that company. When you think about it, Jonas, keeping that company both prosperous and competitive impacts upon entire communities. The fact that somebody pilfers insider info worth a great deal of money to Bergam and future job opportunities to locals is not going to sit well with a whole lot of people. Folks around here are real sensitive about safeguarding their own future.

I will be within a 20-25 mile radius of you for the next several months or so. Don't hesitate, man, if you need anything. I'll also be more than glad to check on your wife and little one from time-to-time, even if it's just a drive-by for you and your sister's family next door. I'm here for you, man. You just say the word."

The two men continued to chat. They traded names of FBI agents they both knew and Price updated Jonas on some newsy items that occurred after Blair had resigned from the Bureau. But by then, inner alarms and warnings had already sounded for Jonas. He was very careful not to reveal any hint of his suspicions to Agent Price and did a great job in concealing all that was now the dominant stream of his thoughts.

Sonny Goodall said that Bergam had not revealed anything about Merkel's alleged theft to anyone other than their hired private investigators. Yet, FBI Agent Marshall Price knew. He referred to someone taking valuable insider info from Bergam.

Beyond that, Jonas mentioned the veiled threat against his wife and child when he spoke to Price. But he never mentioned anything about his sister and her family living next door.

Yes, it was possible that Price picked up on some background info before he came to Blair the very next day. However, Jonas did not think that was likely the case. Rather, his strongest suspicion was that FBI Field Agent Marshall Price was dirty. He was likely in bed with Bergam and their fees and bonuses.

Jonas waited until Price was gone before grabbing his cell phone and making the call to the one person that he was sure he could trust. His hand shook as he dialed the West Coast phone number.

❖

Four days after his time with Agent Price, Jonas received a phone call on his cell. The caller's ID was hidden.

"Mr. Blair, how are you, sir? Sonny Goodall here. Listen, I'm calling to see if maybe you've had any additional thoughts or insights regarding our discussion last week. Perhaps you've had a chance to reflect back a bit. Maybe you recall something about Mr. Merkel that might help us to find what he stole from my client?

I don't have to tell you, Mr. Blair. You've been around the block a time or two, but people get desperate and bad things happen that could otherwise have been avoided. I just want to do all I can to make sure things like that don't happen. Ya know?"

Yet another veiled threat. Goodall will now attempt to provoke me. Men like Goodall are bullies. They use those tactics to get someone to slip up, maybe reveal something they should not.

"Well, like I told you before, Goodall, I have no idea what you're talking about when it comes to Mr. Merkel stealing anything from his employer. Nor do I have any idea where whatever it is might be if the man did take anything he should not have."

"I'd likely be thinking about a flash drive, sir. Merkel most likely stored everything on a drive. Maybe kept a copy himself and gave something to his attorney."

"Sorry I cannot help you there, Goodall. My meeting with Merkel was short, interrupted, and a one-time encounter."

"Can't help me or won't help, Blair?"

Blair knew that he had to tread lightly when dealing with Sonny Goodall and his "thugs" as Claire would refer to them. He heard what Goodall initially said. He referred to "something about Mr. Merkel that might help us find what he stole." Goodall was looking for the flash drive, but did not seem to be looking for Merkel. Blair could not help but wonder whether the PI and his boys already knew where Louie Merkel was. Could it be that they had found Merkel, but never found what he had taken?

"I'd suggest that you and your team make a serious effort to locate Mr. Merkel and stop wasting your time talking with me," Jonas said.

"Well now, I sure don't mind chattin' with you, Counselor. You seem like a nice enough fella. And sooner or later, you just might have a major recollection about some things. Hahaha. Yesiree, a major recollection."

❖

Claire had asked for the day off as her daughter was flying in from San Antonio. As Jonas entered the office that morning, he was glad that Claire would not be in. Someone had entered during the night and had been searching for something.

File drawers were left open and some files were piled on top of a cabinet or on the floor. Desk drawers had been searched. Perhaps the most astonishing fact was that the office safe had been accessed and the door was left open. Blair was sure that the open safe door was intended as a message that his intruders should not be underestimated. He also knew that they were searching for the flash drive left with him by Louie Merkel. Blair was very thankful that he had removed it from the safe following Goodall's visit to his office.

Jonas Blair began to tidy things up knowing that he would not report this to the police nor contact Marshall Price. He would have to come up with his own plan of action.

Blair had pretty much restored order to his office when his cell phone rang. Once again, the words "unidentified caller" appeared on the screen.

"Jonas, top of the morning to you, sir. This is Sonny."

Hmm...we're on a first-name basis now.

"Just checking in. I'm concerned that I may be owing you an apology. I got me a really outstanding team here, working under my PI license. But, you know, my boys tend to get a bit too exuberant, I guess you might say—especially when we're working a case with such a high-profile client like Bergam. My guys are well aware who butters our bread. No Bergam, no guarantee that all my men stay on my payroll. Plus, in addition to our normal fees, Bergam has offered a very nice reward to us for the return of their misappropriated property."

"Why don't you just get to the point, Goodall. It was your folks that broke into my place last night—a felony I might add."

"Aw, c'mon now, Blair, a guy like you, of all people, should understand. You know what it's like when people, even federal agents, get a bit too excited. Before you know it, they begin kicking in doors and pushing their way into situations that could be labeled as outside the acceptable parameters of their lawful authority.

Now I ain't saying that makes it right. I'm just saying these things happen sometimes."

"I am telling you to back off, Goodall. I already told you that I do not know anything about what you are looking for. So back off."

"Ah! Sounds like we've upset you, Counselor, and for that I profusely apologize. You know, I deeply respect another man's privacy and his concern for the welfare of his loved ones."

"Now, you listen to me, Goodall," Blair was screaming now, "if you or any of your goons come anywhere near my family, I swear I'll..."

Blair heard the phone disconnect. Sonny Goodall was gone. He had delivered his message.

Chapter Seventeen

Take the Offensive

At this time of the year, it was dark by sometime around 6:00 p.m. In Jonas Blair's neighborhood, if one could even refer to an isolated location where only two homes exist within the radius of a few miles as a neighborhood, that darkness arrives even earlier. It is also much more pronounced.

Sally Blair had little Taylor warmly dressed and all wrapped up in blankets, as she prepared to leave.

"Okay, so I'll be right next door with Jen. We'll have all the kids settled and watch a movie together while Danny is out of town."

Jonas smiled. He enjoyed the fact that his wife and his sister got along so well.

The conversations with Sonny Goodall continued to trouble him.

He stepped outside with Sally, as she headed for the car. Despite the short distance between these two isolated homes, Sally and the baby would drive over to the Roberts' home.

As he watched his wife drive away from the property, Jonas reflected back on the fact that he and Sally Forrester had worked together as federal agents with the FBI when they fell in love. They were careful not to show affection to each other while on duty and to not permit their relationship to interfere with their duties as sworn federal agents.

Then came the day when their lives were in jeopardy. In fact, they were in a precarious situation that brought them at the very point of being murdered by a fellow federal agent. At the very moment when Agent Michael Burns was beginning to press the trigger of a weapon held against Sally's head, a man appeared seemingly out of nowhere. He fired a perfectly placed shot that immediately dropped Burns and spared Sally and Jonas from an otherwise certain death. That man, unknown at the time to Sally and Jonas, was Kent Taylor. Afterwards, Jonas Blair learned the identity of the man who had saved his and Sally's life. To this day, Sally did not know this man's name.

Now, Jonas Blair and Sally were no longer together as federal agents working for the Bureau. They were husband and wife. They were father and mother to their newborn child. Unfortunately, they were also persons under a threat from a man named Sonny Goodall, his team, and possibly certain key employees of Bergam industries. Jonas reflected upon all that was happening.

We weren't spared from death only to become victims to these people. If I have to, I will kill Sonny Goodall and his gangster friends. The same goes for anyone at Bergam who even considers threatening Sally, Taylor, or my sister and her family. I will kill them without hesitation, regardless of whether I die along with them or end up in a cell for the rest of my life.

And just that suddenly, Jonas was reminded of Kent Taylor, the decorated Navy SEAL, who killed those who were directly or indirectly responsible for the murders of his loved ones.

"Fine. I'll join you in hell, Kent, if that's what it takes," Jonas muttered to himself, "but no one is going to touch my family. No one."

Normally, Jonas would hear any vehicle that approaches his property, but he had the television sound up as he watched an exciting NBA game. However, he muted the television when he heard the chime signaling him that he had just received a text on his cellphone.

"Hey there, Jonas. Just thought you should know we are here. Yesiree. We are right next door at the Roberts' home. I see that your wife and little boy are here also. Now ain't that nice. Man, is there anything in life more important than our loved ones?"

The text stopped there and was immediately followed by another.

"Don't worry, Blair, they are safe *this* time. But the clock is running and only you can stop it."

The immediate shock that flashed through Blair's body was quickly followed by an inner call-to-action. He ran to his upstairs bedroom. He loaded a clip into his automatic weapon and placed two more clips in his pockets. Then he holstered the gun, ran down the stairs, and out the door into the night air.

Jonas ran into the woods that separated his property from the Roberts' home. Sally, Taylor, Jen and the children. Blair's heart was pounding within his chest. His body was drenched in perspiration. He ran without regard to any noise he might be generating. He ran dodging trees, seeking any non-resistant path to the house where his loved ones were located. He ran through briars and brambles that scratched his body. He ran with abandon. His training at Langley, his experience as an FBI field agent were all forgotten.

Suddenly, something reached out from behind a tree and clotheslined him. The combination of his movement, the obstructing object striking against his throat, and the shock arising from this unexpected occurrence would most assuredly have knocked Jonas to the ground, but the arm that struck him was now wrapped around his neck. Within seconds, a blackness draped over his mind and consciousness.

❖

Once Rosanna Castro entered Arkansas, she was determined to keep traveling. Her goal was to tuck herself away somewhere further within the borders of this state, though she had no idea where that might be. She drove across US-64W initially passing flat, flooded lands where rice was grown. She carefully watched her speed as she passed through one small Arkansas town after another. When she saw a sign pointing towards Searcy/Little Rock, she merged onto that ramp and continued until she found herself in the city of Searcy. She was pleased to find a choice of motels, as well as places to eat.

She made a quick jaunt around the County Courthouse, admiring the building that was originally completed in 1871. She stared up at the large clock tower that housed an 1855 bell that resembled the Liberty bell.

"Thank you, thank you, Holy Mother of God," she whispered quietly as she blessed herself. "Nice place, this Searcy, yes? You know, a little something to eat, then a nice relaxing shower, and a good night's sleep is what I need. I'll be able to think more clearly in the morning."

Rosanna smiled as she pulled up to the doors of her motel of choice. "Hello Searcy, Arkansas," she whispered again. "Just give me a night to catch my breath. That's all I'm asking from you."

❖

The voice emanated from the earbud in his left ear. "How we doing there, Ghostie?" The man smiled, then responded feigning annoyance. The "Ghostie" reference traced back to the nickname, *The Ghost Assassin,* he first bore when his vengeance killings shocked the nation. "Cut out the ghost stuff, old man," he said before responding directly to the question that was raised. "Got him back where he belongs. He's beginning to come around. How are things on your end?"

"They're gone now. Passed me a few minutes back. Give me a few and I'll be there."

"Copy that," the man responded. "Try not to get lost on the way," he said with a chuckle, knowing that there was only one road in to where he was located.

Jonas Blair was stretched out on his living room couch. It took a few moments after he opened his eyes for him to realize where he was. His night had certainly changed rapidly with a series of major shocks!

First, he received a text informing him that Sonny Goodall was outside the house where his wife, his sister, and the children were. Then, someone rendered him unconscious in the dark woods. Now that "someone" was sitting on the end on the couch checking the wet cloth he had placed against Jonas' throat.

"You...Kent...Jonathan Nova. What? How?"

"Hold your breath. Give yourself some time to regain your senses, Jonas." The man speaking was, indeed, Kent Taylor. "Got a call from your old boss. Seems Mr. Gladding was very concerned about his former protégé.

Bill and I linked up at the airport in Albany—a bit of a hike from here, but it offered the best options and least gap for travelers coming in from our unique locations. Bill had a nice black SUV lined up and we drove the rest of the way here."

Jonas was much more alert, as he sat up and took a drink from a glass of water that Taylor handed to him. "But what were you doing out there in the woods?"

"We were headed your way when we noticed a vehicle ahead of us. Saw it turn onto your frontage road. We acted as if we were going straight. Bill dropped me off where I could proceed on foot rather than have us draw attention by driving in. When I saw that the vehicle did not stop at your place, I headed over to your neighbors' through the woods to check things out.

You know, I am kind of familiar with the neighborhood," Taylor joked, referring to the fact that he had previously owned and lived in the Blair home for five years.

"I could see that whoever was in that vehicle was scoping things out. I assumed they would find a way to let you know they were or had been in the neighborhood. For all I knew, you were in that house also. Then I heard someone racing through the woods, making enough noise to raise the dead. Once I determined that it was you, I made my move to slow you down before you triggered a real problem on that end."

Jonas stared for a moment at the man he first encountered when he and Sally were in dire straits. The second time that he saw Kent Taylor, the former Navy SEAL was saving the life of the legendary field agent, Bill Gladding. The last time he was with Kent Taylor, Blair and Gladding journeyed with him to southern Louisiana where Taylor saw his daughter and surviving family members for the first time in fourteen years. Taylor's daughter, brother-in-law, and sister-in-law all believed that he had died years earlier. He did nothing to dispel that belief as he gazed upon his loved ones from a distance.

Now this man, this unique man, who was in the crime annals of the FBI as one of the most skilled assassins they had ever encountered, was back in the life of Jonas Blair. The *Ghost Assassin*! Once again, he appeared like a ghost and, once again, he likely spared Jonas from a dangerous situation.

"What in the world were you thinking, Blair? If you encountered someone other than me in the woods, you might very possibly already be a dead man. In a situation like this, you've got to come up with a better strategy than running straight into something like a crazy bull or the proverbial chicken without a head."

"I know. I know you're right, but you've got to understand, man. We're talking about my family..." Jonas hesitated when he realized that he was speaking to a man who completely understood what it was like to feel intense emotions when someone is doing or has done something to your family members.

Taylor quickly discerned Jonas' reactions and responded. "Listen to me, Jonas. I understand what it is like when someone reaches out against your family members. And I am convinced, based upon what you have told Gladding, that you have a situation here that has to be dealt with now. Let me tell you, man, up-front and nothing held back. If you cannot control your emotions and focus, you will be of no use to anyone—and that includes your family members."

Jonas nodded slightly, very slightly due to a neck that was still sore. "I hear you, Kent. I hear you loud and clear. When I realized that Sally, Taylor, my sister, and her kids could be in danger, I reacted, rather than acted. I know you're right."

"Listen to me, Jonas. Bill is on his way here now. We will sit together. The three of us will come up with a plan. Maybe I should say the four of us, Mr. Blair. I do not know how much you have told your wife, but, if she is not privy to what is going on, it seems to me that it is time to enlighten her. Besides, as I recall, your wife was also a federal agent and likely has got some pretty strong credentials of her own."

Taylor smiled at his own last comment and Blair smiled along with him. "Yeah. Guess I have been trying to protect Sal and the baby without respecting the fact that Sally is smart, tough, and has as much right as me to know what is going on."

Taylor nodded. "Like I said, Jonas, we can develop our strategy together. Bill and I will need you to fill us in on everything that has transpired to this point. But I do have some initial thoughts even now,

Jonas. I believe, based upon what happened here tonight, it is time for us to reverse things."

"Reverse? What does that mean, Kent?"

"It means that we do not sit back any longer and wait for their next move. It means that we take action and go on the offensive. They're picking a fight—so let's give it to them."

Chapter Eighteen

A Path of Destruction

No plan was perfect and Rosanna knew it. The people tracking her were like human bloodhounds. They had already proven that when they located her in Nashville. The "Music City" is a long way from her starting point in upstate New York.

Earlier that evening, Rosanna made a quick trip to the local Walmart Supercenter to purchase a few needed items. Now she returned to Walmart with a different purpose in mind. She parked her car, made sure that nothing that would further identify her was anywhere within it, and locked it. She reached into her purse and found the slip of paper where she had written down the phone number for a taxi before she left her room. Her cab ride will end at a destination short of the motel.

By the time Sally entered the house, Kent Taylor left the kitchen area and was waiting in the living room. Sally immediately spotted Bill Gladding. The moment that Jonas took the baby from Sally, Gladding was on his feet hugging Sally with a big smile on his face. Sally's smile matched Bill's.

"Wow! What a surprise this is," Sally said. "If Jonas had given me a thousand guesses as to who was here, I just don't think I would ever have gotten it right. I am so happy to see you again, Bill."

"Likewise Sally, you look great. Now let me see this little guy you've got there."

Jonas had managed to unwrap Taylor from his blankets and remove his hat and coat without waking the baby. He handed him to Gladding who immediately evidenced the additional comfort he had with children resulting from his increased role as a grandfather.

Jonas turned towards Sally.

"Listen Sal, I am sorry. I have not told you about some things going on. Didn't want you to be concerned. I apologize for that.

You also need to know that we have another guest here tonight. He has been waiting in the living room to provide you with an initial opportunity to see Bill. Also, you kind of know this man, even if you do not know his name."

Taylor took that as a signal from Jonas and entered into the kitchen. Sally gasped. The expression on her face pretty much said it all. She was shocked to see the man who had saved her life and the life of her husband. Her eyes were flooded with tears.

Sally relived that fateful day time and again. She and Jonas were chained to the walls of an old seafood processing plant. FBI Agent Michael" Bernie" Burns shockingly turned out to be the mole for whom Bill Gladding and his team were desperately searching.

"Oh my God! Oh my God. You? Are you kidding me? I-I never thought I would ever see you again. Y-you don't know. You could not possibly know how many times I've pictured your face in my mind. Dear God! So many times I wanted so much to somehow be able to thank you for what you did for Jonas and for me."

As she spoke those words, tears flowed from Sally's eyes and continued even as she walked up to Kent Taylor and hugged him. Her body shook as Taylor held her in his arms.

"Sal, I want to introduce you to Jonathan Nova. Yes, he is the man who saved our lives."

Taylor spoke quietly. "Sally Blair, it is an honor to officially meet you. And listen, before you go too far with these accolades about me saving your lives, you might want to tone that down a bit. In a way that I am not sure I can explain even now, I think the very day you are alluding to had a part in helping to save my own life."

Then Kent smiled and moved towards the baby that was still in Bill Gladding's arms. Gladding handed the child to Kent Taylor. This is our son,

Taylor," Blair began, but he paused when Kent Taylor's reaction to the baby's name was so strong.

"Yes," Blair said. "His name is Taylor. I suggested that name to Sally one night before the baby was born and she loved it. Guess now is as good a time as any to tell her why I ever thought of that name."

Taylor turned towards Sally and spoke again. "Yes, it is time to do a better job introducing myself to you, Sally. My name is Kent Taylor."

Sally paused before speaking again. "Makes our son's name even more special," she said.

"That name, 'Kent Taylor'...there was a Navy SEAL who...uh..."

"Yes, I am that man, Sally. Reports you may have heard or read stated that I died some fifteen or so years ago. Obviously, I did not."

"Thankfully, you did not," Jonas stated.

"We will fill you in on everything, Sally. Let me first state that there's a really unique perspective here in this room tonight," Bill Gladding stated. "Kent Taylor also is the man who saved my life, Sally. He killed the assassin we called the *Night Shadow Killer*. Every act of bravery attributed to your husband was true, but we covered up the fact that the bullet that killed that assassin was fired by Taylor."

Taylor was visibly uncomfortable with all the talk praising him. He quickly moved to change the subject.

"And I am going to go out on a limb, Sally, and say that you likely do not believe that Bill and I stopped by tonight for a social visit."

Gladding laughed. "Well, you know, we just happened to be in the neighborhood."

Jonas responded. "I called Bill because I sensed that trouble was brewing. I knew that you and I were going to need some help."

"Well, from the look of things," Sally responded, "I cannot imagine two better people to have on our side."

❖

Rosanna made sure that she was standing at the front of the store and nowhere near her parked car when the cab arrived. She hopped in and gave the driver the address where she was headed. She felt good to be in a taxi. Soon she would be safely tucked away in her room and able to get a good night's sleep.

The driver never said a word from the moment she entered the cab. Now, as they approached the area where she wanted to be dropped off, she saw that he was not slowing down.

"You missed the turn there. My street is in that little section of houses. You'll need to turn around and go back."

But the driver did not turn around. He abruptly stopped the taxi and suddenly without warning another man entered the back seat where Rosanna was seated. She felt the blood drain from her face. This could not possibly be happening! After a momentary pause which allowed her to further analyze the situation she was now in, Rosanna reached for the door handle with the intent of jumping out of the taxi."

The man seated next to her reached over and grabbed her wrists tightly. "Now, now, Ms. Castro, you could get hurt jumping out of a moving vehicle. You should know better than to even think of doing such a foolish thing. Good thing I am here to protect you, eh?"

"Please! Let me go. I won't tell anyone anything. I swear. I won't say a word to anyone. I-I don't even know what's going on anyway. Please. Just let me go. Please. I'm begging you. Please just let me go."

Soon with her mouth taped shut and her arms tightly fastened behind her back, Rosanna Castro was in too great a state of shock to appreciate the scenery on the ride out of town. They drove on Highway 36, climbed Joy Mountain, out of White County, and into Cleburne County. Rosanna never saw the sign announcing that they had now entered the city of Heber Springs.

It would be close to two weeks before Rosanna's body was found in a wooded area near the Little Red River and the Greers Ferry Dam. It took even longer for the Cleburne County Sheriff's Department to positively identify the body and that only occurred following an exhaustive search of nationwide missing persons reports.

It would have been beneficial to law enforcement officers investigating her death if Rosanna's car had been identified as an abandoned vehicle in the Walmart Supercenter parking lot. But there was no chance of that occurring.

A tow truck removed Rosanna's car before her taxicab even reached Heber Springs on the night of her death. The reason for her murder was also quite a mystery. There was no evidence of a sexual assault. With no car nor purse, robbery could have been a motive, but the criminal investigators could not be sure.

From a town named Chester in upstate New York to Greers Ferry, Arkansas with several bodies strewn along the way, the mystery hidden within the walls of a manufacturing company by the name of Bergam Industries was not something that could easily be solved.

How many more lives would it take to even begin to get some answers?

Chapter Nineteen

Reunited for Battle

The plan was set. Taylor, Gladding, Jonas, and Sally had gone over everything for nearly three hours. Jonas revealed all that he had encountered with Louis Merkel and his conversations with Andy Maynard concerning the Sheriff's Department.

"We have two primary issues here," Bill Gladding stated. "There is every reason to believe that Deputy Maynard's murder was premeditated. What we do not know is who was behind it. The Sheriff's Department? Bergam Industries? Could easily have been either one."

"Right," Taylor spoke next. "But the people threatening Jonas are clearly linked to Bergam. They already tipped their hand that they were aware that Merkel visited Jonas."

"They may have killed Merkel," Sally added. She looked over towards her husband.

"Yes," Jonas added. He spoke openly to everyone, but it was clear that he was also responding to Sally's deepening concern. "They likely believe that I have evidence that would incriminate them."

Sally joined in next. "So I believe that I should go through that flash drive that Merkel left with Jonas." Everyone nodded in agreement, as Sally's computer skills were extremely good. "We know so far that there are shipping records primarily coming out of Africa that do not yet mean a great deal to us. Then there are encrypted files. As I told Jonas, there are primarily two ways to unlock encrypted files. The easiest and most obvious way is to contact whoever created them and get the password. Needless to say, with Louie Merkel missing and the fact that we cannot go to Bergam with this, that option is out. Another method is to run it through a password hacking program and wait. Problem with that is depending on the encryption used, we might be waiting like hundreds of years."

"I may be wrong," Taylor said, "but I don't think the waiting hundreds of years is a particularly good option for us."

Everyone laughed.

"I don't know, Kent," Gladding said, "you've already come back from the dead once. I am already thinking of calling you Mr. Revenant, as it is. You might be able to make it through the hundreds of years, but I am quite sure none of the remainder of us will."

Everyone laughed again.

"Seriously," Gladding said, "after 9/11 and the establishment of the Department of Homeland Security, the government tightened up the reporting requirements for any and all international imports. It's very possible Bergam is involved in bringing something in that is not being properly reported to the feds."

"And if they are," Taylor added, "then whatever they are involved in may be a whole lot bigger than an upstate NY company failing to properly report some imports."

"At this point in time," Gladding continued, "we are only guessing. We have no idea what is going on."

"Yeah," Jonas interjected, "except that it may be the reason why we already have a few dead people."

"Well, I'll do whatever research I can and see if I can make any sense of why a list of shipments and encrypted files seem to be so incredibly important to some people around here," Sally said. "With a little luck, I might find some way to shorten that hundreds of years gap in time."

"Great, Sally," Gladding said, "that's a good start. We have to assume that something funny is going on inside Bergam. It is very possible that the employee who was electrocuted may also have been murdered."

Gladding hesitated before uttering his next comment. "Guess it is rather clear that there is only one way to find out what it is."

Kent Taylor chuckled. "Sounds like a guy like me needs to get inside there and check things out."

"I want to go in with you," Jonas interrupted.

"Okay, here's my opinion, for what it's worth," Gladding said. Everyone turned towards him awaiting his next words. "Kent and Jonas go in... "

"Whoa! Hold on." Taylor interrupted. "You've got yourself a newborn, Jonas. No sense you putting yourself at risk any more than necessary. I can go it alone."

"No, Kent. My life is not any more important than yours. Hell, if anything, this is more my fight than yours or Bill's.

Besides, there's no reason for you to ever be alone again."

The words penetrated Taylor. The last time he had ever worked together in concert with others was on his last fatal mission as a SEAL. Taylor said nothing as he stared into the eyes of Jonas, then Bill Gladding, and ultimately Sally Blair.

"And you, Sally?"

"Jonas is right, Kent. We are all in this thing together. Of course, it concerns me that Jonas would attempt to enter Bergam—just as it concerns me that you will be at risk.

Listen, I am expecting that whoever goes in comes back out safely. If we don't feel that way, then no one should be attempting to do this."

The silence that ensued evidenced the general agreement that Taylor and Blair would be the ones to enter the Bergam factory.

"Okay, so now that we've settled that," Gladding continued with a smile, "here are some preliminary thoughts I have. We pick up some audio equipment we need and I station myself outside the grounds in the SUV."

Taylor had not spoken again when everyone turned towards him somehow anticipating that he would be the next one to say something. It was a correct assumption. The look on Taylor's face clearly indicated that he was already putting together some of their next strategic moves.

"Okay, so the first thing we will need to do is scope out the place. Get a sense of where their security people are situated and what their general patterns are. We also need to know what kind of security system Bergam has in place. I think that I should be able to determine that by hacking into their systems."

Bill Gladding laughed. "Hey, Jonas, Sally, we sure have come a long way from our days with the Bureau. Now we're hatching out a few crimes that we are about to commit."

Sally Blair laughed aloud. "It has always been said that it is a fine line between a law enforcement officer and a criminal. Looks like we are proving that to be true."

Sally turned towards Taylor. "Kent, if you are willing to share some insights with me, I can do the … uh …investigatory search into Bergam's systems. This way you, Jonas, and Bill can concentrate on the strategy of how you are going to enter that factory…"

Sally made eye contact with each of her three cohorts.

"And…how you are going to get back out safely."

"Not sure how aware you are of my wife's computer forensics expertise, Kent. She is rather incredible."

"Hah! This is awesome," Sally said. "I have often wondered what it would be like to use my forensic skills for the dark side."

Jonas was laughing now. "My wife, the computer hacker. I like it. It's got a nice ring to it."

Everyone laughed. Sally reflected upon the fact that even though they were about to embark on some serious actions, everyone appeared to be loose and relaxed.

"Bergam will have internal security cameras. We need to take a look around before we actually enter the building," Taylor opined.

"Sally, once Kent helps you with whatever you need, we need to consider where in particular we should start looking once our guys are inside," Gladding said.

As he spoke, Sally could not help but be reminded of recent past times when Special Agent William Gladding was her commanding officer within the FBI. She trusted the man then and found it easy to respect and trust him now.

Sally was already greatly intrigued by Kent Taylor. Without question, she and Jonas owed their lives to him. Even so, there was more to this man than even that one incredible encounter displayed. He emitted a strength and generated a confidence that Sally immediately sensed. She liked him. She trusted him. She was glad that she, Jonas, and Bill were on the same side as him.

Bill Gladding, her husband, Jonas, and Kent Taylor. Seeing these three men together in her kitchen generated a confidence that everything was going to be all right.

"In addition to getting a general feel for Bergam's security, I will check out areas within range of the loading docks. My goal there will be to try and find out whether something questionable is coming into Bergam," Sally said. "I will be looking for areas where they would, at least initially, store things."

"Right, Sal," Jonas agreed. "See if you can identify areas where Kent and I need to get a better look."

"They will be very secure locations," Gladding added. "I would expect them to be close to the loading docks."

"Before we do anything," Taylor said, "we will have garnered a great deal more insight on both the exterior and interior of that factory."

Jonas smiled. A short time earlier he was racing through the woods concerned about the safety and welfare of his family. Now reinforcements were on the scene.

❖

Jean-Pierre Muamba was hungry, thirsty, dirty, tired, and scared. He and his partners, Fabrice Zakuani and Muteba Kyenge, had worked undercover for the CIA with much success—until recently.

None of the three were trained agents. The key to their success was primarily due to the fact that they were all countrymen of the Congo. Moreover, they had been conscripted into one of the illicit gangs from their youth, so they did not need to find a way to gain the confidence of the gang leaders. From a personal viewpoint, another key to their success existed in the fact that they had each other.

Now, with Zakuani and Kyenge dead, Muamba was on his own. He no longer had anyone around him on a daily basis to help him in any manner. Zakuani and Kyenge had been identified as traitors. Muamba's close association with them implicated him. If found by the gang, he would be tortured, interrogated, and slain. He had no choice. He had to remain hidden and hope that he would be rescued before he was found and slaughtered.

But, Jeanne-Pierre, despite his lack of formal training, was well aware of something else that he and his two partners had discussed a number of times.

"We must remember always," Fabrice Zakuani stated, "that, in this America, we are dealing with those who use people. As they say, these Americans, they chew them up and then spit them out."

When Muamba questioned the meaning of Zakuani's statement, Kyenge interjected.

"What Fabrice say, is if we are ever exposed, the US of A, they will deny any association with us. They play with human lives as one plays in a game of chess. To them, we are, one might say, merely pawns. Our loss would not be monumental to them."

But, that was before word had been sent back to America's chief spy agency that these three men in the Congo had uncovered the identity of the key player hidden away in the United States. Muamba was too frightened to think very clearly. Had he done so, he would have realized that he was no longer a pawn. The information he had concerning the identity of someone located in America changed the nature of the chess piece with whom he could now be likened. Muamba was now clearly on the level of the queen or, perhaps, the king.

The local media continued to pressure Sheriff Miles for answers with regard to the murder of Deputy Andy Maynard. It had been a number of years since Maynard graduated from high school, but his reputation as perhaps the greatest athlete to come out of Comstock's Freeport High School was revitalized. The news of his tragic death went viral throughout the area. Moreover, the sympathy for his widowed pregnant wife, Donna, was met with outpourings of kind and generous acts and an even greater anger at whoever was responsible for Maynard's death.

"We ain't got nothin' more to announce at this time," Miles stated at a press conference. "We dealin' here with an ongoin' investigation, so y'all gonna just have to be patient and let us do our job here. Ain't nobody more anxious to find out who done this atrocious thing and get justice for the untimely death of our colleague than us. But we all got to show some forbearance here. Believe you me, we ain't never gonna quit until we identify who was behind the murder of Deputy Maynard and we make 'em pay for what they done."

Chapter Twenty

Strategy Set

Blair marveled at how thorough Kent Taylor was as he, Taylor, and Bill Gladding scoped out the Bergam facility the very next night. He likened Taylor to a great cat, studying its potential prey before poising itself for the attack.

"We were superbly trained by the FBI," Jonas said one night while lying in bed with Sally. "I am convinced that we were with the greatest law enforcement agency in the world. Bill Gladding is outstanding. No doubt about that, Sal. But, I'm not sure just what it is about Kent Taylor. The man astounds me. No wonder he was so skilled that even those in law enforcement marveled at his stealth and cunning. The guy is actually scary."

The Bergam property was set off by itself at the end of a private road. A booth with security personnel was situated at the entrance to that road. An elaborate sign introduced the property as that of Bergam Industries, Inc. A smaller, less elaborate sign marked the property as "Private Property-No Trespassing." About two hundred feet down the road, the extensive factory building stood alone. An eight foot high fence topped off with razor concertina wire projected the appearance of a prison, rather than a manufacturing plant. It certainly sent out a message that breaching the secured perimeter of this property would not be an easy task.

The fence itself joined together at a front gate entrance. On one side of the manned security booth, single vehicles could enter. On the other side, double gates could be opened to permit large trucks to enter, take a different path than smaller vehicles, and reach the loading docks at the rear of the building. There was no other entrance to the property.

"Okay, so we see that there are generally two guards stationed at the front gate who pretty much remain within the booth located there," Taylor began, while never turning his head towards Gladding or Blair.

The three men were tucked away in a wooded area scoping out the factory with binoculars.

"Then we have two additional guards who are in that security vehicle. They drive around the building. But they do not have an established pattern. That indicates to me that they are not all that serious in patrolling and protecting the premises and the outer region of the building."

"Right," Gladding added. "They are doing what they have been instructed to do, but they do not expect anything of any real consequence to occur. Someone has to get past that gate for the security vehicle guys to even get involved."

"Which means," Blair opined, "that if the primary security on the exterior of this building is the front gate, then even illicit deliveries come in this way."

Gladding's eyes remained focused on the front gate as he spoke. As Blair observed his former boss, he reflected upon the fact that Bill Gladding was widely regarded as one of the greatest field agents in the history of the FBI.

"Exactly, Jonas. The front gate appears to be the only exterior area where these guys believe the perimeter can be breached. The two guards in the vehicle are a secondary backup in the highly unlikely event that someone gets past that front gate."

"What it also means," Taylor said as he turned his attention to directly meet Blair's eyes, "is that it is even more crucial that we acquire a solid reading of the level of security that Bergam has within their facility. Getting past the gate and into the building, difficult as that might be, is not the only challenge we are going to encounter. Everything we are seeing here tonight points to the likelihood of strong security within the building itself."

❖

Blair returned to his office in Comstock the next morning. The consensus among Blair, Taylor, and Gladding the previous night was that Jonas and Sally would return to work.

Jonas and Sally suggested that Gladding and Taylor stay with them at the house. "We have no idea if Goodall and his thugs will be around again. No sense risking that they spot you guys coming and going."

The goal was to keep things looking as normal as possible.

Suddenly, Kent Taylor was back at the home he had lived in for five years. His mind was flooded with a barrage of thoughts. He had responded to a call for help from Bill Gladding. Kent and Bill had taken turns saving each other's life. Yet, by coming here, Taylor risked exposure to a world that believed he was a dead serial killer. This, in turn, increased the risk of danger for his loved ones. At the same time, a failure to respond could usher Kent back into the dark chasms of a world defined by isolation and seclusion—a world he had once been trapped in for far too many years.

When Kent Taylor was active as a Navy SEAL, he lived with a deep commitment to his colleagues that they would always be there to support one another. This commitment was so strong, that it conflicted at times with the fervent love and commitment he bore towards his wife and children. He could be at home enjoying Rose and the children. Yet at the same time, fellow SEALs were often engaged in a potentially life-threatening mission and Taylor felt strongly that he should be there with them.

In a very real sense, that same level of commitment was now rooting itself in the relationships he had with Bill Gladding and Jonas Blair. It was a reason why he responded to Gladding when he learned that Jonas and Sally could be in trouble.

With a past filled with dark alleys and painful memories, Taylor did not have many places he could go to without encountering some painful remembrance. Now he was on the very property that once served as a habitat of escape—a place where some pleasant memories were adulterated by the fact that he was living as a recluse shut off from all else.

His inner struggles quickly dissipated when he dialed the number and heard Katie's voice.

❖

When Blair arrived at his office, he found FBI Agent Marshall Price seated in the reception area sipping some hot coffee that Claire Reeves had obviously provided. Jonas found it interesting that despite the outward appearance of friendliness and graciousness that Claire displayed, he could sense that she did not particularly like the man. Jonas found Miss Claire, as she was commonly known, to be one of the most astute judges of character of anyone he had ever known. The woman had all the grace and protocol of the first lady on an antebellum southern plantation, but she also possessed the cunning of a Fortune 500 CEO.

"Good morning to you, Jonas," Price called out just as Blair entered the building.

"Morning, Marshall. Good morning, Miss Claire. So...what brings you our way this morning, Agent Price?"

"I've got some things to attend to in the area today," Marshall responded, as he stood, transferred his coffee cup to his left hand, and extended the right in greeting to Blair. "Thought I'd drop by before the day got away from me."

Blair ushered Price into his office. Before he and Price even began speaking, Claire showed up with a cup of black coffee for Jonas. He often tried to convince her that he did not consider it her job to have to serve him coffee, but Claire disagreed.

"It's not a matter of subservience nor a gender issue," she would say. "It is simply a matter of respect and protocol for one's employer. I'm not sure just who changed the rules over the course of time and made everything an issue based upon race, age, gender, faith, or any number of other bases that often have nothing to do with a particular thing at all. Why do you often address me as Miss Claire, rather than simply by my first name?" she once asked.

"Well, that's simply the way everyone around here addresses you. It's ... I don't know... it's just a matter of protocol... a matter of resp..." But before he even completed the word "respect" he laughed aloud and jokingly questioned when she had acquired her law degree.

Claire closed the office door when she exited.

"Tough thing, that young deputy losing his life like that," Price began. "Understand you were pretty close to him. My condolences, Blair."

Jonas nodded his head in a gesture of politeness. He wasn't exactly sure how Price knew that Jonas had a friendship with Andy Maynard. And, at the moment, Jonas did not particularly care. "Andy was a good police officer and a good man."

Jonas did not believe that Marshall Price had come here this morning out of concern for Jonas nor to extend his condolences for Andy Maynard's death.

"They any nearer to figuring out who was responsible and what their motive might have been? The Bureau has not been formally brought into the case yet, although, as you would expect, we have offered to help in any way that we can. Word I got is that it may have been a random killing by some crazy with a bad itch against cops. All the law enforcement agencies in the area, besides assisting in the investigation, are on high alert. Of course, some people are wondering if Deputy Maynard's murder was related in some way to any of the cases he was currently working on."

Jonas shrugged. "Really can't say that I know anything more than you do."

Blair was making a concerted effort now to control his anger.

He's fishing! Trying to gauge how much I know or what my thoughts are with regard to Andy's murder. He's waiting to see if I say anything about Bergam Industries and the case that Andy was working on before he was killed.

"Went fishing a time or two with Andy. Sat with him at a few high school football games, but he never discussed anything related to his work.

Our wives work together at the school where my wife teaches. Like I say, he was a good man."

"Well, you know as well as anyone, Jonas, whether the badge you wear is on a federal, state, or municipality level, it doesn't take much to make enemies with someone and find a big target on your back."

Believe me, Blair, you're much better off practicing law than when you were traipsing around working for the Bureau sticking your nose in places where the law is just not welcome.

Yeah, you're much better off just minding your own business and staying out of trouble.

119

Well, glad I had a moment to stop by and pay my respects to you," Price said just before leaving Blair's office.

Blair did not believe for a moment that "respects" was what Price came to offer. A word of warning to stay away from Bergam and anything related to the investigation of Maynard's murder was a much better description of Agent Marshall Price's mission.

Chapter Twenty-One

The Need to Know

Everyone knew her as Rosemary Chambers, but now, for the first time in her life, she knew the truth. She was Emily Taylor and, until very recently, just about everything she was told about her past was a complete lie.

Emily would always love and deeply appreciate her aunt, uncle, and cousins with whom she had shared her life for so many years. She was confident in the love that they all shared together. She was completely settled about that.

However, all that she was now learning about herself, about her deceased parents, brother, and her dead grandparents was like a new birth to her. It was a path down which she had never before walked. It was a life that she had not previously known. In many ways, it was like a puzzle with so many pieces still to be found and locked into place. Beyond all of that, in a strange, yet fascinating way, it was also shockingly liberating.

Now my life, my past, all makes much more sense to me. It wasn't just happenstance that left me an orphan. It was not simply a dark fateful moment. Crazy at it seems, at least now I know there was a reason, a purpose behind it all.

In times past, Emily tried to convince herself that she had a few vague and distant memories of her dad and mom. When she looked at pictures of them, she conjured up remembrances of times together. She now knew all of that was simply a hoax. She was not yet four years old when her parents died. Hah! Not likely a three-year-old has memories. Besides, the pictures she had been given were not her true parents. Until now, she never knew that she had an older brother. She had been unaware who her true grandparents were. Now she was learning some deeper lessons about reality versus fantasy.

Suddenly, it was as if someone opened a treasure chest containing the truth about Emily Taylor, her family, and her past. She had a taste of this truth and it stimulated an uncontrollable desire for more—a voracious appetite. Her thoughts were consumed by this. She continued to dig in deeper, to do everything and anything to more fully identify the family members she had lost. She also dug deeper into the story of all that had happened to her mother and to her father. She wanted to know everything about her family members, everything that led to their deaths, everything relating to her father, the notorious *Ghost Assassin*. She would not cease to explore until she exhausted every possible branch of knowledge.

She sobbed and her heart ached every time she dug deeper into the history of her family. Yet, at the same time, she was overwhelmed with feelings of love and a sense of belonging.

One major frustration was that there was no one, other than her aunt and uncle with whom she could talk about any of these things. She was making friends on campus. She had suitemates in her dorm. Yet, there was no one with whom she could or would dare say a single word or share a single thought. At times, she felt as if so much was locked within her that, without some form of release, she might explode.

That was when she began to look outside of her own life, outside of her own circle of friends and contacts. Perhaps, there was at least one person with whom she could talk. This person knew her father. This person knew the details of all that occurred when Kent Taylor struck out against those who murdered her family members.

Her pursuit of this kept her occupied and to some extent served to assuage the pain she felt every time she reflected upon all that she had lost. The hurt she did feel was deeper than any she had ever before known. Yet again, the pain also played another role. It connected her to those whom she had lost. It further assured that they genuinely belonged to her and their existence was no longer hidden behind deceitful cloaks.

Although she had never known them, she loved her dad, her mom, and her older brother. She loved her grandparents. She only wished that she had been given the opportunity to be with them in ways she could remember and cherish.

It took a great deal of research, time, and effort, but Emily found the phone number for which she had desperately been searching. Her mom and dad had both uncovered the mysteries of scandals. Perhaps finding someone over the passage of time and movement was evidentiary that she also was a mystery-solver. Hah! Perhaps it was in her genes. She liked thinking of anything that might be genetic—anything passed down to her through her dad and mom, anything she shared with her brother and grandparents. Those links were special to her. She saw resemblances she bore to both her mother and her father. And this time these observations were not based in fantasy.

Her hands shook as she held her cell phone and began to punch in the number. She was not sure just what she would say or how she would even begin the conversation. Three, perhaps it was four, times she started dialing and then hung up before the call went through. She was about to hang up again this time when she heard the first ring.

❖

Kent Taylor was awake, lying in bed. His body was drenched with perspiration. His mind was racing. He rested his head on the pillow as he continued to make a concerted effort to slow his thoughts down and get some much-needed sleep. He knew that he had taken a risk when he responded to a call for help from Bill Gladding.

Years ago, in retribution for the involvement of the Guarino Crime Syndicate in the deaths of his wife and family members, Kent struck back. He stole millions from their coffers. They did learn that he had not died as reported and would have killed him if it were not for Bill Gladding's intercession on his behalf.

Years had passed. The Guarino clan had been systematically dismembered by a series of arrests and criminal indictments. Anyone of significance in that crime syndicate was now either dead or tucked away behind the walls of a federal prison.

His mindset shifted from concerns over what might happen to him if he failed to respond to the crisis that Jonas and Sally were in to what might be the personal impact when he does. He had lived that way for years, refusing to get involved in any way with the needs or concerns of others. That was a prison that he had no desire to ever live in again.

He had no way of knowing just what they were all headed into, but he knew enough to believe that they were dealing with people who were reacting because they had much to lose. Damn! He already had seen first-hand just how far people will go when they have that much at stake. His loved ones were buried six-feet under as evidence of that.

Years ago, Taylor utilized his training and experience as a Navy SEAL to strike back at those who directly or indirectly murdered his family members. There was never a need for him to reevaluate what he had done in terms of right or wrong. He never believed it was right to kill in revenge. He simply believed it had been necessary.

Kent Taylor was not afraid of what he might face. He was only afraid of what he might once again become.

❖

It is a long way from a Caribbean island to the upstate regions of New York, but Katie's every thought was centered upon her husband. She was glad that Kent had responded to a call for help from Bill Gladding on behalf of Jonas and Sally Blair. Yet, at the same time, her concerns were deep and heightened.

Katie loved Kent with all her heart. He was the strongest, most courageous, kindest man she had ever known. Her husband was a rock—someone she could trust and lean on no matter what situation she might be facing. Her husband also had a fragility that frightened her. It was hidden away, deeply tucked within him, but it was there. She knew it was there.

This man had been tested in battle. He had faced death a number of times. When carrying out a mission, whether he was deployed by his government to go overseas or a self-determined mission to right the wrongs that took the lives of his innocent loved ones, he always succeeded. But Katie knew that Kent bore deep scars, even wounds that had not completely healed—might never fully heal.

Katie rested her head on a pillow as tears softly fell from her eyes. Kent would be all right. He *had* to be all right. He was the essence of her life.

Chapter Twenty-Two

In the Battle Zone

Faces painted, dressed entirely in black, wearing black knit caps, two men stood outside the surrounding chain link fence in the one area where the external cameras did not reach. It was a small, very limited flaw in Bergam's security, but Sally Blair had detected it. Kent Taylor then devised the plan to capitalize on it. The two men quickly scaled to the top of the fence, cut the barbed wire, and headed towards a single rear door. Sally had already remotely turned off a separate camera that covered that seldom-used rear entrance.

Taylor wondered how he would feel as he engaged in conduct more aligned with his special forces training or his actions as the notorious *Ghost Assassin*. His concerns were answered quickly. He felt nothing at all. He had a job to do and he immediately set out to accomplish it. Taylor glanced at his watch, checking the elapsed time since they had last seen the security vehicle pass by this very spot.

"Right at two minutes, Jonas. Let's get moving."

Blair held the small flashlight for Taylor, as Kent, with hands moving as dexterously as an onstage magician, sought to unbolt the door that would grant them entrance to the factory.

"Should have this baby opened in just another few seconds," Kent whispered.

"Kent, hold on. Here they come..."

They both heard the sound of the approaching vehicle. For whatever reason, the guards were headed back that way. Taylor and Blair quickly threw their bodies behind a large outside air conditioning unit that was near the back door entrance. Both men drew their weapons and held their breath. The vehicle stopped right in front of the very door that Taylor had been attempting to open just moments earlier. One man jumped out of the vehicle. He spoke aloud to the two men still seated in the security vehicle.

"Thanks for the lift, guys. This door brings me a whole lot closer to my station. Now I won't have to hear Embers dressing me down for being late tonight."

"Embers is a jerk," the driver said. "Perfect example of a man who lets a little bit of authority go to his head. Catch you later, Fred. Just make sure you get that key back to us before you leave tonight."

Fred had a key that he used to open the door. He also clearly had to know the security code for the alarm system.

Taylor tapped Blair on the shoulder.

"Let's hope that is the only close call we will have tonight."

As the two men prepared, once again, to enter the building, Blair kept his weapon in his hand. He covered Taylor, as Kent carefully stepped into the building.

Taylor disarmed the door alarm by entering the four-digit code that Sally had learned earlier. Once again, a quick head nod and slight hand gesture from Taylor informed Blair that Kent would take the lead as they headed towards an area near the loading docks.

Suddenly both men heard the voice of Bill Gladding in their earbuds.

"I've got eyes on you now. You're clear on this...hold on...coming around the corner to your right," he warned.

Taylor held back and the moment the security guard came into view, Kent struck quickly and efficiently. His soundless attack was successful, as the guard lay unconscious on the factory floor. Blair pulled duct tape from his backpack, quickly bound the hands and feet of the guard, and covered the man's mouth.

"Okay, now, you should be seeing two guards coming up in the next fifty feet or so. They're located at the point where you will be turning right. They're standing very close together. Probably chatting with each other."

Good. Taylor thought. *Likely means they are relaxed, not expecting any company tonight. The longer our presence remains undetected the greater assurance that these guards will not be expecting anything out of the norm tonight.*

And he was right. The two unsuspecting guards never knew what hit them as Taylor and Blair each quickly stepped behind their man, established a chokehold, and rendered each guard unconscious. Once again, Blair bound and gagged the victims.

"Lookin' good, Ghostie and Whale Boy," Gladding chimed. Once again, he used a reference to Taylor's past identity as the *Ghost Assassin.* Jonas had already informed Gladding that the biblical character associated with being swallowed by a whale was Jonah and not Jonas.

"Well, no big deal," Gladding remarked. "I kind of like the nickname I've chosen and am inclined to keep it."

"Better let him keep it, Jonas. No telling what other horrific name he will come up with if you don't," Taylor had advised back then.

They all had a good laugh at that. Kent knew that Gladding would use the nicknames in an effort to keep everyone calm and focused. If there was one major difference with regard to Gladding now than in times past, he was more relaxed, even more prone to use humor than when Taylor first encountered him.

"Okay, guys," Gladding stated with some urgency. "At 3:00, you've got a lone wolf ambling towards you now."

"Copy that," Taylor responded.

Taylor and Blair took cover. The guard was walking rather causally. Taylor was about to make his move, when he stopped abruptly and spun his face towards Jonas. Taylor mimicked someone talking on a phone to warn Blair that the guard was apparently on his cell phone. Kent considered that they could quickly take control of the man, but did not want to risk that the other person on the phone would be alerted that this man was in trouble.

Now Taylor was in a bit of a quandary. He already knew, based upon insight that Sally had gleaned, that there were two guards stationed ahead outside of a door leading to a secure room near the loading dock area. In order to silence those men before they could radio or otherwise warn others, Taylor and Blair had to move as quickly as possible to render them helpless. A third guard would greatly diminish the odds of their success in doing so.

As a result, Taylor waited, made no move at all, and gave the appropriate signals to keep Jonas Blair at bay.

Jonas' heart was pounding. He knew the score and the need to stop this guard before he passed from the area where they were all currently located. The man was now precariously close to that point and still was chatting on his phone. Jonas spotted a bolt lying on the ground near his feet. He bent down slowly, picked it up, and tossed it to an area behind where the guard was walking. The sound of the bolt hitting the floor was not all that loud, but it was loud enough to catch the attention of the guard. As a result, the man quickly ended his call, slid his phone into his pocket, and started walking back to where he had come from to investigate.

Advantage, Taylor and Blair. In less than a full minute, they had their man unconscious, gagged, and bound.

Taylor and Blair moved cautiously towards the secured room where, based upon Sally's findings, they would most likely find whatever it was that was being hidden away. Taylor quickly checked in with Gladding, who updated his report.

"You've got the two, as expected, guarding the door to the targeted location. All else is clear."

No time to wait. Taylor and Blair were quickly approaching their intended destination.

When Taylor, Gladding, Jonas, and Sally were setting their strategy a few days earlier, Taylor provided the ominous warning about the required last steps in entering the room where they all believed something was hidden away.

"The very last part of our little journey will be the toughest," Taylor had said while going over plans with Gladding, Jonas, and Sally. "From what we can see, there are always two men guarding the entrance to that room. And there is no way we can approach that area without being seen. This is where we are most vulnerable."

"Any chance we could change clothes with any of the guards we will already have taken out or bring a change with us?" Jonas asked.

Gladding responded first. "No. From what we have observed, every night, when they change guards, the two leaving know the two coming in. A good number of these guys are off-duty police."

"Right," Sally added. "Got a few from the County Sheriff's Department, a few from the Chester Municipal Police Department, and a few state troopers.

I am seeing a pattern that the guards at the secured room in question appear to always be off-duty sheriff's department deputies."

The team considered using smoke bombs, tear gas, or anything else that would provide Taylor and Blair with additional opportunity to get close to these men.

"No can do," Sally said. "I cannot turn off all the smoke and fire alarms in that building. The moment I touch anything, an alarm goes off in the building and a silent alarm is immediately transmitted to the local fire department."

"Can't hit them with tranquilizer darts," Jonas said. "They are unreliable against humans. Too hard to gauge how many are needed. Plus the side effects can be fatal."

"If I can get within a range of about fifteen feet from these guys," Taylor said, "I can taser them. We hit them with 50,000 volts that can penetrate two inches of clothing and they'll be shocked for about thirty seconds. That's more than enough time for us to put them out and bind them."

Now as the two men approached, Blair moved out first. He had removed his black knit cap and wiped as much of the black paint as possible from his face. He ambled forward, lolling about, giving the appearance of an intoxicated man with no particular place to go.

The two guards snapped to attention, moved towards Blair, drew their weapons, and called out for him to halt.

All of that provided just enough time and distraction for Taylor to run forward. He had a long-range Taser gun in each hand. He quickly fired his weapons. The two guards were stunned. Taylor and Blair quickly rendered each man unconscious and bound and gagged them.

Taylor opened the locked door to the storage room that had been so closely guarded. Blair entered the room first. As he did, Jonas entered the code that would turn off the alarm system within that room. It was not until Blair moved closer to the stored boxes that Taylor spotted the laser beam that triggered a silent alarm. It was not something that Sally was able to detect.

"Jonas, we've got to find out what's stored in here and get out of this area as quickly as possible. They'll be coming for us, likely in a matter of minutes."

At the same time, they heard the voice of Bill Gladding speaking much more urgently in their ears.

"Silent alarm triggered. Get out of there now. You've got guards stirred up throughout the place. I see four of them running towards your location now. Get out of there now."

Taylor and Blair took a quick inventory and some pics with their cell phones. Taylor whispered the message back to Gladding.

"It's Coltan, Bill, and plenty of it."

They took a few additional pics before quickly exiting the room. Too late! There were already four men in view running towards them with their weapons drawn.

"Drop your weapon and put your hands in the air," Taylor whispered to Blair. "First thing we need to do is surrender."

With hands raised and their weapons on the floor, Taylor and Blair stood motionless as the four men, with their guns pointed, moved in closer. Blair was initially surprised at the fact that Taylor had surrendered so quickly and, in Jonas' estimate, so meekly. When the blur of Taylor's body in motion had two of the four men on the floor and Taylor fired shots into the legs of the two other men, Jonas realized that Taylor's ploy was simply to get these men closer in where he could take action against them.

"Bind and gag them quickly, Jonas," Taylor said, as he kept his weapon pointed towards their victims. Meanwhile Taylor checked on the gunshot wounds of two of the men and determined that no arteries had been severed. The men, despite the pain they were currently in, would not bleed to death.

"Looking good," Blair said. "Seems to me it's time to get out of this building."

"Okay, Bill," Taylor whispered. "Eyes on. Lead us out of this place." Taylor was met with silence. He pointed to a direction and he and Blair began running. "I'm not reaching Bill. Not sure why."

As they rounded a corner in the warehouse, they heard the shouts. "Drop your weapons. Hands in the air. Do it now."

Taylor's quick estimate was that they were surrounded by eight or so men. There would be no way out of this one.

Just as quickly, each of the men surrounding them were dropping their weapons to the floor. One-by-one, others appearing on the scene took charge. Several of the eight men surrounding Taylor and Blair had guns pointed at their heads. A few others had already been taken captive and cuffed.

"What in the... ?" Blair uttered. But Taylor did not have an answer. Someone had moved in. They had taken charge of the eight men and were now, with guns pointed, ushering Taylor and Blair to come with them.

Taylor walked slowly with two men pointing weapons and walking behind him. As always, Taylor would look for his opportunity to make a move. But as they rounded a corner and were completely out of sight of the eight men and their new captors, one of the men following Blair placed his weapon against Blair's temple.

"We are going to ask you nicely, sir," one of the men behind Taylor stated, "to calmly place your hands behind your back. If you so much as make a move of any kind other than what we have asked you to do, your friend here will be dead before you even have time to flinch. Do you understand me, sir?"

Taylor said nothing. Yes, he understood. He would not, under any circumstances, risk Blair's life. As a result, Taylor and Blair were both cuffed and led out of the building. They were placed into a van which drove away quickly. There was no resistance at the gate.

Chapter Twenty-Three

A New Enemy

"Answer, Bill. Answer the damn phone." Sally Blair was deeply troubled that she could not reach Bill Gladding nor Jonas. She began by making up a slew of legitimate reasons why they were not answering their phones. In her heart, she believed none of her contrived explanations. She knew that something had gone wrong. She would not know for sure what had occurred until the next morning when a black SUV pulled up at her home.

The two men showed their credentials—specialized skills officers with the Central Intelligence Agency. It was then that she learned that Jonas, Bill Gladding, and someone they described as a "third man" were currently in CIA custody. Sally permitted the two federal agents to enter the home and sit with her at the kitchen table. She offered them a cup of coffee, which they both accepted. Sally intended to find out everything she could from these two men.

Jonas, Bill, and Kent were in the custody of the CIA, at a place somewhere in the area of the Bergam factory. Federal agents had been watching activity at Bergam. These agents did not reveal why.

In remarkably fast fashion, Blair and Gladding had already been identified. Taylor had not and clearly Jonas and Bill had said nothing.

Finally, the conversation turned to the actual intent of the morning visit.

"Mrs. Blair," the agent named Eagan began, "we are aware that you are a former FBI agent. Needless to say, you would be very aware that knowingly and willfully making any materially false, fictitious, or fraudulent statement to me or my partner, as federal agents, is a crime. We certainly do not have to tell you that it constitutes a felony, under Title 18, United States Code, Section 1001.

We are aware that you were trying to reach both your husband and William Gladding.

With that in mind, Mrs. Blair, do you know the identity of the third man who was with your husband and former agent Bill Gladding at the Bergam factory last night?"

Sally smiled. "Do you by any chance have an extra card that I can pass on to my attorney? Since I will not be answering any questions this morning, I do want to be sure to give your coordinates to my lawyer.

More coffee?" Sally asked.

"Why do you need an attorney, Mrs. Blair? I asked you a very simple question. What do you have to hide?"

"Gentlemen," Sally's voice was steady and lower-pitched. Her eye contact was strong. "As federal agents, I am sure that you are very aware of my right to consult counsel. I will do just that. You can expect that your next conversation with regard to this subject will be with my attorney."

Sally stood, smiled, reached over, and opened the kitchen door.

"Gentlemen, have a great rest of the day."

The two men left and Sally was, once again, alone. The baby was still sleeping, which provided Sally with ample opportunity to reflect on all that she had gleaned from her early morning visitors. It was alarming to learn that Jonas, Bill, and Kent were being held by the CIA. It was of comfort to know that they were alive and unharmed. These two men did not address the issue of bringing criminal charges against Sally. She assumed that was something they would use in applying pressure against Jonas, Kent, and Bill.

This visit from two CIA agents clearly answered the question of whether illegal activities were being conducted by Bergam. Sally wondered just what it was that merited such strong attention from the world's greatest intelligence agency?

❖

Kent Taylor only had time for a quick survey within the guarded room near Bergam's loading docks, but that was all the time he needed to unlock the mystery. Bergam was not only engaged in illegal activity, they were engaged in some high level international illegal activity.

Columbite-tantalite, better known as Coltan, is a black metallic ore that, because of its heat resistance and ability to hold a high electric charge, is a vital element in creating devices that store energy. Coltan is used in cell phones, laptops, GPS systems, auto airbags, video game consoles, and so much more. The Congo possesses 80% of the world's Coltan. Countries such as Rwanda, Uganda, and Burundi are among those who have exploited Coltan from the Congo to support the war efforts that have resulted in the deaths of millions in Africa. For this reason, the United Nations, the United States, and other countries have developed strict reporting requirements from companies involved in the extensive use of Coltan.

Unfortunately, for some, the illegal acquisition of Coltan was worth the risks involved. From the Congo, where it is mined by rebels and foreign forces, to the refineries where Coltan is processed and converted to capacitors, to the major international corporations who will use this in a wide assortment of everyday products, there is a great deal of money to be made. Surely, it is enough to sustain ongoing war efforts year-after-year. Certainly, it is enough that the loss of some lives to assure that this activity is ongoing is also an acceptable part of doing business.

The houses utilized by the CIA team were located at the end of a cul-de-sac, some three miles from the Bergam factory. Gladding was currently in the primary house that also served as a headquarters for the CIA team working this case. There were two adjoining houses. Masters ordered that Taylor and Blair were separately housed in them.

The Counterterrorism Center (CTC) of the CIA operates under the National Clandestine Service and its Deputy Director NCS. The current Deputy Director was simply referred to as "TJ," to further protect his identity.

Phillip Masters headed up the team that was working on the case related to Bergam. Masters had eleven years of experience and a strong reputation as an intelligence officer. His name was constantly mentioned among the limited list of potential personnel who could ultimately end up in a position of high administrative rank at Langley, the headquarters of the CIA.

At 6' tall, weighing in at 180 lbs., with short blonde hair, and deeply set green eyes, Masters looked like he could still play left field for Vanderbilt's nationally ranked baseball team. Upon graduation and an honest assessment that his professional baseball opportunities would be very limited, Masters opted to go to Camp Peary, the Armed Forces Experimental Training Activity. Camp Peary, known as "The Farm," is rumored to host a covert CIA training facility.

"Come in," Masters called out in response to the knock on the door of the bedroom that served as his temporary office. Agent Benjamin Marlowe, who Masters often referred to as "Benjie," entered the room. Marlowe stood at 6'4", weighed 225 lbs. He was a tough, well-disciplined young agent, whom Masters had chosen to closely mentor. Masters lifted his head from his computer screen and fastened his gaze upon the young agent. He liked Marlowe, even saw a bit of himself in this upstart agent.

The look on Ben's face appeared to be a mixture of concern and confusion.

"We got us a problem here, sir, a big problem, I'd say."

"And just what might that be, Benjie?"

"Well, in line with what you anticipated, we got us two guys with government credentials. Guy in the SUV is one William T. Gladding, retired FBI. Strong rep. Youngest guy is Jonas Blair, also has an FBI past, but now has a law practice over in Comstock. Got their profiles coming your way now."

Masters waited, saying nothing. Marlowe stated that there was a major problem of some kind. He would wait for his protégé agent to expound on that statement.

"It's the third guy," Marlowe began. "His prints have a match... "

Once again, Masters waited without saying a word.

"The identity of this man is locked tightly under a need for top secret clearance. None of us on the team have ever encountered anything on that level. This one is bigger'n all of us."

Masters grimaced. This he did not expect. What he would soon learn was beyond his wildest imagination.

❖

"I am not going to play games with you, Special Agent Gladding. I have had time to check out your profile. You have a sterling reputation, sir, and I am going to honor that. In light of that, you will note that we have already removed your cuffs."

Gladding did not say a word nor did he make any eye contact with Masters. He simply sat calmly with his hand folded atop the table that separated the two men.

"At present, I have no earthly idea why you and two others broke into the Bergam factory as you did. I am hopeful that you will shed some light on that for me. But I will go first.

We have had the Bergam place under observation for some time now. We actually started moving a team into the area in the past eight weeks or so.

The details of where our suspicions came from are things that I am not at liberty to share with you. Suffice it to say, we have reason to believe that the Bergam folks are part of a network dealing in the illegal importation of Coltan. I am sure that I do not need to enlighten you on the fact that Coltan is used in more electrical devices than I can possibly cite———cell phones, an enormous list of electronic devices, electric cars, medical, and optical equipment. And the list keeps growing as new technologies come into play.

I am also sure that you are aware that Coltan is being used to support the ongoing wars in Africa that have directly or indirectly caused the deaths of millions."

Gladding lifted his head for the first time and looked directly at Phillip Masters. As Masters was speaking, Gladding determined that if he chose to show some cooperation, he might be able to derive even more insight from Masters. "So, we have inadvertently screwed up your investigative work to help resolve international injustices, Masters. Is that it?"

Masters paused, gulped, and quickly considered how much more he could or should reveal to Gladding. "I'm afraid it is more than that, Agent Gladding. We are not simply dealing with some greedy folks making a ton of money via illegal trade that ultimately results in millions of dead foreign nationals. Without question that would be enough in itself to warrant our deepest concern and activity.

By the way, I am sure that you are also aware that Coltan is ideal for smart bomb guidance control due to its conductive ability in extreme temperatures and capacity to move and hold electrical signals."

Gladding's furrowed brow was a clear indicator that he did not know why Masters had shifted the conversation this way. Masters was ready to provide the answer to Bill's unasked question.

"My team is a counterterrorism unit. Our concerns are a whole lot more than what happens over on another continent, Special Agent Gladding. In fact, we are a lot more interested in where the trail leads beyond Bergam. In this instance, we are dealing with direct threats to our national security. Threats that will impact right here on American soil."

Gladding's head snapped up and jerked back. His body became rigid. He stiffened his arms, leaned his body back, then forward. He had not anticipated this response. It was also not the sort of thing that Bill Gladding, a man whose entire career had been dedicated to serving his country, could simply ignore.

"Okay, Masters, now you've got my full attention. What in the hell are you talking about?"

"I am referring to a major terrorist threat here in this country. We started tracking this over in Africa. I am talking about people somewhere here in the USA, including a major player who is commandeering this. Someone whose identity we do not know.

I am talking about the fact that the illegal Coltan trade is merely the tip of the iceberg. The money derived from Coltan is being laundered and used to finance an underground operation.

So when it comes to Coltan, we are not only dealing with the loss of millions of African lives. We may also well be dealing with the loss of millions of American lives."

Chapter Twenty-Four

Unraveling a Mystery

Taylor remained cuffed as he sat motionless across from Phillip Masters. It was as if Kent Taylor hit some type of inner switch that ushered him into a catatonic-like state. His body was tucked behind an invisible shield. His head was down, his eyes seemingly focused on something that he alone could see.

"Who are you, mister? Who in the hell are you? What were you doing in that factory? How is it you are linked to two former federal agents?

We are going to need some cooperation here if you have any hope of escaping some very serious criminal charges, my friend. Breaking and entering, armed burglary, multiple counts of aggravated assault... Do you need me to keep going or are you getting the message here? You've got some big problems and, at the moment, I am the only person who it would benefit you to be nice to."

It was somewhat amazing to think that the room they were presently in once served as a bedroom for some family member before the CIA acquired the house. Now, all furnishings were gone and the room had been set up with a single bare table and two chairs. A tiny camera that transmitted both video and audio to a flat screen monitor in the adjoining room was hidden away discretely in an air conditioning/heating vent. It was barely discernible. Most people would never notice it. Kent Taylor, however, was not "most people."

Taylor remained completely unresponsive. Masters slammed his fist on the table and stood up. He kicked over the chair he had been seated in and walked towards the door. Masters had no idea just how impervious to all those tactics Taylor was.

Benjamin Marlowe had been watching on the flat screen. Now he was waiting outside the door as Masters stepped out.

"Watcha think?" Marlowe asked his superior.

"The guy is definitely trained. In fact, I am beginning to think he is highly-trained.

Whether he was also a Bureau agent along with Gladding and Blair, I can't say. The other two guys are definitely impressive. This is one scary guy. Whatever and whoever he is, he is both formidable and very battle-scarred.

We keep him cuffed and under close guard, Benjamin. I've got to follow up on that call I made earlier. You go and make sure our team gets the message loud and clear when it comes to Mr. X here."

Ben Marlowe stood for a moment watching his mentor walk away. Masters was the most astute person that Marlowe had ever met in his entire life. His appraisal of this unknown man definitely gave Benjie some serious reason for pause. He had never heard Masters talk that way about anyone before—never.

❖

Masters determined that he would give this one more shot before having to go outside of their location here in upstate New York to get the answers he needed.

"I'm going to try one last tactic, Benjie, before going upstairs with a request," Masters said. "Get me Gladding and Blair together. Bring them here to me... "

"Whoa! Hold on, sir. Together? You want these two men to sit here with you alone... I mean... is that a safe and smart move, sir?"

Masters smiled. He appreciated the depth of loyalty and concern that he received from Benjamin Marlowe. As a result, Masters was not upset that Marlowe's words could be construed as questioning the decision of his superior. Marlowe was young and inexperienced, but he was in no way insubordinate.

"Thanks, Benjie. Appreciate your concern. These two men are former sworn federal agents. Whatever their motive was to come snooping in Bergam's factory, I assure you it was not based upon some criminal or selfish reason.

Yes, I will be perfectly fine. Besides, you will be right next door to me with eyes and ears on all that is going on."

❖

Together for the first time since they drove to the Bergam plant the night before, Jonas smiled broadly when he spotted Gladding. Bill reached over and squeezed Blair's arm. Within minutes, the two men were seated at the table with Phillip Masters.

"So, gentlemen, I assume that you are being treated well by our staff here?"

Gladding smiled and spoke first.

"All the comforts of home."

"Yeah," Jonas said. "Like a pleasant stay in a bed and breakfast. Except that I have not received any breakfast. Have you, Bill?"

"Matter of fact, no, I have not either. Do I order my eggs and choice of sausage, ham, or bacon with you, Masters, or is there someone else who handles that?"

Masters smiled.

"After our time here now, I will be sure that we get you men something to eat. First, it seems that the list of mysteries continues to grow.

You have not yet told us just what prompted you to break into Bergam. What is it you were looking for?"

Gladding and Blair remained silent.

"Now another mystery surfaced. Who is this man that you are working with? How does this guy merit the highest level of clearance with the FBI and the same status with the CIA? That's some serious stuff there, gentlemen. Would either of you care to explain?"

Gladding smiled. Somewhere over the years, he had come across Phillip Masters' name. Although he had never met nor worked with the man, the word Gladding had received was that Masters was a top-notch agent—clean, honest, and well qualified.

"I am sorry, Masters. We can't help you there."

"Can't or won't, Gladding?

Listen, man, you've got an outstanding reputation. You have enough medals and accreditations to fill a damn library. You've served your country extremely well.

And you, Blair. A hero. Wounded in the line of fire while helping to save the life of another agent.

Now married to a former FBI agent with a baby...uh...is that a son?"

"Yes, a boy," Jonas responded. "I'd show you a picture of him, but I, as you might expect, don't have my wallet with me at the moment."

"Listen to me, Gentlemen. You could be facing felony charges and even some time behind bars. And, who knows what our investigation will come up with. Could also mean some jail time for your wife, Blair.

You upset some top-level government officials by pretty much destroying the covert operation we had going at Bergam. That is not going to help make anyone very sympathetic towards you guys."

Masters paused for a moment. Took a deep breath and spoke again.

Work with me and I'll do whatever I can to make things better for you. It's the least we can do for men of your caliber.

But I need you to work with me."

Blair cringed at the very mention of Sally possibly facing criminal charges, but he remained calm and silent. Gladding was unmoved. He shook his head and spoke.

"I did not tell you this before, Masters, but I have heard of you over the years. Everything I ever heard about you has been positive. I respect that. I am sure that you are smart enough to realize that Jonas and I have been where you are now. I certainly have been many times throughout my career.

So, you've got to know that if we are not talking to you right now, it has nothing to do with a refusal on our part to cooperate with you. We simply *cannot* say anything more to you, Masters. We are under that same cloak of high-level confidentiality. I am sorry for that, but, right now, that's all we can say and do.

Believe me, our hands are tied on this."

❖

"I am not sure that Jonas Blair is under that same level of secret clearance, but I have no problem whatsoever believing that Gladding is, indeed, under a government edict," Masters said when speaking to Marlowe. "We are not going to get what we need from either of these two men…"

"What about putting the squeeze on Blair when it comes to his wife?" Benjamin Marlowe interrupted.

"It may come to that, Benjie, but men of this caliber might prove to be useful to us if we can win them over to our side.

Also, I don't know just what I am sensing, but there is something deep, some kind of uniquely strong bond between these three men. Maybe we could make some progress over time, Benjie, but time is the one thing we no longer have. Already our folks are drawing up the criminal indictments, getting court orders and search warrants in place, and all that we will need. The secrecy of our investigatory work on Bergam is ended. We are into major damage control now."

Masters knew where he had to go and what he had to do if he wanted to proceed any further. He shuddered at the very thought.

❖

Masters could have directly contacted the FBI. He had two of their former agents in custody and a third man whose identity was hidden away in the FBI files.

Instead, Masters made a call to Langley. NCS Deputy Director Thomas J. Westfield. TJ was more than the head of the National Clandestine Service and The Counterterrorism Center. He was Phillip Masters' mentor and friend. The two men traced their relationship back to the days when Masters was a rookie and Westfield was his supervisor. The relationship remained strong and positive over the years. Masters called Westfield to seek his advice.

"I, myself, do not know the details of who your man is and why he is so shielded in a cloak of secrecy, Phil. I am not sure even I can get the file open to you on our end and even if I could, the FBI is the lead on this file. We need both agencies to concur.

What I think you need to do is work the old 'agency vs. agency' tactics here. Get the FBI believing that if they assist you, we will be beholding to them for something they need now or in the near future.

As a mere formality, I will pass this by Bob Patterson, but you will primarily be dealing with me and some key person over at the Bureau."

Bob Patterson was Robert J. Patterson, Deputy Director of the CIA and further proof that Westfield could immediately push buttons and reach people well beyond Masters' sphere of influence.

"Once I give you the formal go-ahead," Westfield said, "use my name. I will back that up. Play the *quid pro quo* on this one. I believe that once you open the door on this with the Bureau folks, I'll be getting a phone call from Director Spellman before you even leave the building."

Within the hour, Masters received the clearance to proceed from T.J. He would move quickly on this.

❖

Masters played his cards well. He showed up at the FBI headquarters on Pennsylvania Avenue in the nation's capital. As anticipated, he was ushered from FBI Chief of Staff Charles Hayes to Deputy Director William Spellman. As Hayes ushered Masters into Spellman's office, the Deputy Director turned to Hayes.

"Okay. Thank you, Charlie. I'll take it from here. Nothing on the books about this meeting, okay?"

Hayes nodded and left the room. Spellman, his hands folded on his desk, listened without saying a word as Masters made his request. Masters cited national security issues, an ongoing CIA investigation, and his case for a strong "needs-to-know" reason for him to be granted a Level 5 FBI Clearance. When he finished, Spellman sat there saying nothing. Masters also sat in what was now an awkward silence. Spellman's pause lasted about forty-five seconds. Masters believed Spellman wanted him to think that he was deciding upon the matter, when in truth he already knew what he intended to do before Masters had even finished speaking.

"You are, I assume, staying overnight here in D.C., Masters?"

"Yes, I'm at the Embassy Suites on 10th Northwest."

"Excellent. What say you come see me tomorrow morning? Say around 10:00? Will that work for you? Not interfere with any appointments or flight plans you may have?"

"That works perfectly for me, Director. I'll be back tomorrow morning at 10:00."

The two men rose from their chairs, shook hands, and Masters turned and headed out from the office.

It was later that evening when the call came in to Phillip Masters' cell phone. The caller was Tom Westfield.

"Hey, Phil. Okay, my man, you're all set. You'll be granted the clearance you need in the morning. Already had my...uh...chat with Bill Spellman. Not sure what you've got here, but Spellman was negotiating pretty high with me on a few things that the FBI wanted from us."

"Man, I'm sorry, Director. Didn't mean to put you in a squeeze."

Westfield chuckled. "Nah, not to worry. No problem, Phil. Truth is we already intended to turn those files over to the Bureau anyway."

Oh...uh...one more thing, Phil. Spellman says the Bureau has an agent working on something not too distant from your location. Guy's name is Marshall Price. He is going to provide Agent Price with a general summary of what has transpired and what you guys are working on. Price will be available to you all, as needed.

When you come up for air, Phillip, make the trek here to DC and come see me. We'll line up a home-cooked dinner with Marlene," Westfield said, referring to his wife.

Chapter Twenty-Five

The Proposal

This time, as they sat alone in that same bare room, Masters removed the cuffs from Kent Taylor. This time, as Masters opened the discussion, he had already turned off the camera and audio. Whatever would be said between these two men would not go beyond these four walls.

"Is there anything that I can get for you, Commander?"

Taylor said nothing.

Masters pressed on, much more gently than in times previous.

"I hardly know where to begin, Commander Taylor. Over the years I have interviewed and interrogated people under some pretty unique circumstances. Must say, you are the first dead person I have ever sat across the table from."

The slight smile on the face of Phillip Masters was neither a sign of nervousness nor contempt. He was still piecing the story together from what limited knowledge he had. The files he had accessed covered the story of a decorated Navy SEAL gone rogue. The most significant discrepancy was that the file ended with the death of Lt. Commander Kent Taylor in a fiery car crash following a high-speed pursuit by the FBI. Masters did a double take when he noted that the federal agent who led that chase and filed the death report was none other than Special Agent Bill Gladding.

"Listen to me, Taylor, I read enough to understand what motivated you to strike back as you did. I am not justifying revenge killings, sir, but I am no fool either. You were betrayed. You were grossly cheated of a future that no one had the right to take from you. I get it, Taylor.

Please listen to me, man. I am now in a quandary myself. I have to present a proposal to you. A proposal handed down to me from my superiors. This is one of those instances when I am truly 'just the messenger.' "

Taylor made eye contact with Masters, but remained silent.

"I need you to hear me out, Commander. Your next decisions will likely determine just where and how you spend the rest of your life."

Taylor's body was tilted a bit more towards Masters. His lips were slightly parted and his gaze had more focus. He was interested in what this man had to say. Threats meant little or nothing to Taylor. He was not easily intimidated by anyone nor anything. Nevertheless, he sensed that Masters had something of genuine interest to say, something that came from other sources.

Masters began by revealing the concern over a major terrorist threat.

"So here's the deal, Commander Taylor. They want you to volunteer to go to Africa, to the Congo. There's a man there that you are to recover and bring back to the United States. He's an insider. One of three men who had infiltrated the gangs there. His two colleagues were discovered by the gang and murdered. He's been in hiding. His only hope is for us to get him out of there.

We have every reason to believe he knows the identity of the kingpin here in America who is playing a major role on this terrorist threat.

If you agree to do this, we will provide all your supplies and transportation needs. You can take a small team with you. You do this, Taylor, and the slate is wiped clean—for you and anyone who goes with you or assists in any manner. Right now, at the very least, you can negotiate on behalf of Gladding, Jonas Blair, and, of course, Jonas' wife, Sally.

One condition will be that absolutely no one, other than your limited team and a handful of others needed on this end, is to ever know about this. And if you or any of your men are captured, you are completely on your own. We deny any knowledge whatsoever."

Taylor stared ahead and initially said nothing. Then he leaned forward, smiled, and placed his hand on his chin.

"In other words, you want to use the 'dead man' and a makeshift crew—people who are dispensable. No big deal if they never make it back."

❖

The room that Gladding was now housed in on the second floor was a somewhat normal bedroom, complete with a full bathroom. It was furnished as one would expect such a room to be. The only difference was that the windows were reinforced with bars bolted on the inside and not otherwise noticeable from the outside of the building. A reinforced bedroom door would withstand any effort to be forced open from within.

Phillip Masters sat in a chair strategically placed near the door. Gladding was seated at the small desk that centered the outside wall. Gladding's initial reluctance to share anything relating to Kent Taylor began to thaw the more he realized that Phillip Masters had obviously gotten top level clearance and read the files relating to Taylor and the"Ghost Assassin" Case. He also outlined the proposal that Taylor was being requested to accept.

"Aren't you the one who stated that we were not going to engage in game playing? Wasn't that your idea, Masters?"

Masters remained calm and made a concerted effort not to appear defensive.

"Please, call me, Phil. I'm not your enemy, Gladding. The more I have discovered who you are, who Taylor is, and Jonas Blair's profile, the more impressed I am with each of you.

You and I, we've lived in a world fraught with lies and deceit. I realize that it is difficult for you to believe a word I say. Truth is, despite your legendary career as a federal agent, I am in the same position when it comes to trusting you.

I've given you all I have at the moment. Problem is a miscalculation on your part or mine can be very costly in this instance. Simply stated, let me summarize everything again.

The powers that be, few in number, but superior to me, want to utilize the skills and talents of Taylor to help get a certain someone out of Africa. This would be an unofficially sanctioned CIA mission."

Masters spotted Gladding's body stiffen and the angry look that began to form upon his face. Gladding rose to his feet with his fists clenched.

"Hold on, Gladding. Calm down. Be seated… please. Let me finish with everything I have to say to you."

Gladding twitched, shook his head, then sat back down.

"Hear me out, please, before you react."

Masters gave every appearance of sincerity as he sat before Gladding. The man was correct, however. It *was* difficult for Gladding to let his defenses down and trust someone, especially a federal agent with some strong needs. Sadly, lies and deceit often seemed to be at the very apex of everything that federal agents were dealing with most of the time.

"Listen to me, Bill. I scoured through everything that was available in Kent Taylor's files several times. It makes sense to me that a deal was struck years ago on behalf of Taylor. I believe that people, people with more authority than you had then, or I have now, for that matter, agreed to fake Taylor's death and let the man go. You were ordered to do what you did in officially reporting Taylor's demise. But there's no official record of any of that.

There is mention of cooperation between Taylor and the government consisting of an exchange of information in return for protection of his surviving family members. There is reference to the fact that it was deemed as not expedient at that time to bring Taylor to trial, so as to protect certain government operatives working overseas.

But there's nothing to indicate that Commander Taylor was ever absolved of his crimes—several counts of first degree, pre-meditated murder, I should say. And the only official record we do have is a false report drafted and executed by you, sir, stating that Taylor died in a car crash while being pursued.

The records are such that it could be construed that he tried to escape custody some time afterwards and purportedly died."

Gladding's nostrils were flaring, his elbows were held wide from his body, and his chest was thrust forward. He began flexing his fingers, his eyes, his facial expressions tightened. Under most circumstances, Gladding was skilled at hiding his emotions. At the moment, Gladding did not care what he revealed. He was angry. His pulse rate was more rapid and his heartbeat was pounding.

"You go to hell, Masters, and take your superiors with you.

Now you listen to me. This is a setup and you know it. There's no request here. It's a damn blackmail. I don't give a damn what those records say. Our government set the man free.

You are setting this man up for something that might be nothing more than a suicide mission.

I don't really care what you or your superiors think. Taylor gave his all to serve our country and ended up betrayed and stripped of everything he valued in life. If you think for one minute..."

"No, Gladding. No. You are wrong. I am not the author of this. In fact, off-the-record, I have voiced my complete disapproval to my chief contact at Langley. He's putting some pressure on from his end even now. There is no question that this would be a high-risk mission.

However, like it or not, Gladding, they've got the three of you right where they want you—in positions where you either cooperate with them or they put the noose around your necks. Taylor could face indictment for capital murder, all three of you would be charged with felony burglary. Blair's wife will likely be indicted as a conspirator. If Blair and his wife end up serving time, what happens to their baby?

You could also face felony criminal charges for filing a false report on the death of a notorious killer. Everything you ever accomplished in your illustrious career goes up in smoke."

Gladding sat in silence after Masters left the room. He reflected upon all that he was currently feeling. His own reactions greatly surprised him. He was indifferent. He could not care less about his own fate. Damn them. He had served his country. Served it well. He left his position with the Bureau with both his dignity and his integrity intact. If someone sought to destroy that, let them do so. He knew the truth. Besides, he would never go down without a fight.

What surprised Gladding most was the deep concerns he had for Kent Taylor and Jonas Blair. Jonas had a young marriage, a newborn baby, and had already had his future altered because of the severe injuries he incurred in the line of duty. Taylor had been lied to, cheated, and betrayed, while losing everything he cherished. Now, finally, after so many years, the man had found a measure of joy, peace, and contentment. He was only here because he responded to Gladding's message that Jonas and Sally could be in trouble.

Gladding slammed his fist down on the table.

"Damn," he muttered, "I am sorry that I ever contacted Kent and dragged him into this mess."

Even as he thought about that, Gladding could not help but marvel over the fact that this seemingly started out as a local problem and had escalated into a worldwide conspiracy.

Gladding's anger soared.

Damn these game-playing, hypocritical powers-that-be sitting behind their desks at the Bureau and the CIA. Constantly playing around with other people's lives. Constantly manipulating others. Damn them. They sit safe and secure in their government offices pulling in a paycheck, while others do their dirty work.

Gladding had to calmly think all of this through, consider his options, determine what leverage, if any, he might have. The one thing Masters had accurately stated was that Gladding and his two colleagues were currently in a precarious position. And, for the most part, the people wielding the power would likely not lose any sleep if Gladding, Taylor, and Blair were to go down.

Chapter Twenty-Six

Behind Every Great Man

Another sleepless night. His mind was filled with a multitude of pressing thoughts. Kent Taylor was struggling with a haunting fear that he could not shake.

He did not fear going into Africa to find and recover a man. He was not concerned that he was "out of practice" after so many years. He knew this would be a dangerous mission, but he was not afraid of the enemies he might face nor the challenges he would encounter. What Taylor feared was within himself.

In the past, when Navy SEAL Kent Taylor was deployed for a covert mission, he left home with a mindset that was much different, far darker, than the life he led at home with his wife and children. In order to survive, Taylor placed himself deeply in a world of secrets and shadows. The things he witnessed and the things he engaged in at those times were things that he never spoke about with his wife, Rose. They were locked deeply within the caverns of his own mind.

Kent was no longer a SEAL. He had slowly, over time, freed himself from the painful memories of the past. He was also married to a woman who had reached in and helped free him from the self-imposed prison in which he had been living.

Taylor had purposed to never again bury himself deeply in a penumbra of secrecy and deceitfulness. He feared that if he ever went back into that world, he might never be able to free himself from it again.

Kent Taylor realized that there was a possibility that he would never make it back alive from Africa, but that was not his greatest fear. Rather, he was tortured by the thought that, if he did return safely, just who would Kent Taylor then be?

❖

Before Taylor entered the Bergam factory, he had spoken to Katie and informed her of all that was occurring. Now after several days, Katie was not hearing a word from Kent. She possessed an incredible level of confidence in her husband and his abilities, but she was troubled as the days passed.

Katie met Bill Gladding before he retired from his position with the FBI. She was at the hospital with Jen Roberts, the sister of Jonas Blair, when Jonas had been admitted after suffering severe injuries in the line of duty. Taylor, living under a false identity, disappeared from Katie's life, leaving behind the woman with whom he had a shared love, the very woman who had been the catalyst in resurrecting him from a secluded existence. Soon afterwards, Katie heard a report about an unknown man who had saved the lives of FBI agents Jonas Blair and Sally Forrester.

That day, at the hospital, Katie approached Gladding.

"I want to tell you, Agent Gladding, about a man I came to know. I fell deeply in love with this man and I am certain that he loves me."

As Katie continued to speak, it did not take very long for Gladding to surmise that the man Katie was referring to was, indeed, Kent Taylor. Eventually, Gladding revealed Taylor's identity to Katie and played a major role, along with Jonas Blair, in reuniting Kent and Katie.

Katie knew that her husband would not be pleased if she left the safe haven they shared on the Caribbean island of St. John, but once Miss Katie made up her mind about something, it was very difficult to dissuade her—especially something related to the man she loved with every fiber of her being.

Masters hung up his phone and waved at Benjamin Marlowe to come into his office.

"Just got off the phone with Deputy Director TJ. He has been my "go-to" guy in the CIA for years. I trust that man with my life, Benjie. Believe me, in our line of work that is an amazing thing to be able to say.

I wanted to be sure that any promises we make to Taylor and anyone involved with him are upheld. TJ assured me that he will get behind that and make sure that we keep our word."

Marlowe stood quietly soaking in another object lesson from his mentor—the man he would trust without any hesitation.

"We have got to remain true to our word, Benjie. Take that away and we are not one bit better than the enemy we fight and the people we condemn."

❖

"Phillip Masters is either one of the best liars I have ever encountered in my life," Bill Gladding stated, "or the guy is being straight with us."

"Which means, bottom line, you believe he is telling us the truth," Taylor said with a smile.

Taylor signaled to Gladding and Blair that they should continue talking as he began to quietly move about the room.

"Right," Blair added, "we all knew when we were working under Bill at the Bureau that there was no way we could ever get anything past him."

"You mean like the astute school principal?" Taylor said with a laugh.

"Yeah or the mother with eyes in the back of her head," Blair said.

"Okay, okay, very funny, you guys," Gladding said, while trying to hold back from laughing with them. "If I ever become Mr. Infallible, I'll be sure to let you know."

Gladding, Blair, and Taylor were together for the first time since that fateful night at Bergam six days earlier. Federal agents had already moved against Bergam officials. Factory searches under court-sanctioned warrants had been conducted. The feds were continuing to build their case.

Richard Kelser and Paul Martin were being interrogated in the presence of their respective legal counsel. Others at Bergam would soon also be in the same position as their CEO and CFO. As best the CIA investigators could determine, Kelser and Martin were involved in the Coltan trade for the money it generated. To date, the investigators had not found any link between these two corporate officials and the terrorist threat.

Masters addressed this directly in an earlier conversation he had with Director Tom Westfield.

"Looks to me like Kelser and Martin were making the big bucks thinking they had the full picture when, in truth, they were also patsies being used by others whose goals were more than money. We are still looking deeper into that RedMark company. Got a team in Chicago working with the FBI on that one. They have grown some 385% in the last three years with their small household appliances sales globally. We also think they had a deal, possibly unknown to the Bergam folks selling Coltan to certain terrorist groups for use with smart bombs."

Although Taylor, Gladding, and Blair remained at the CIA compound, the pressure had eased quite a bit. They had more freedom even to saunter within the fenced backyard, ate solid meals, and each had a nice bedroom to sleep in. Blair had been permitted to speak to Sally and arrangements were being made for her to come and visit him. Kent did not dare to contact Katie. He was convinced that the feds were unaware that he was married and living on a tropical island under the identity of Jonathan Nova.

While they were joking around with Gladding, Taylor had been conducting a search of the room. He was now convinced that they were no bugs.

"I'm with you on that, Bill," Taylor began. "I think that Masters is telling us the truth. This idea of a mission to go to Africa and bring back their man is what they want. There's just one very important thing we all have to understand when it comes to Masters and this deal."

"What's that?" Jonas asked.

Taylor chuckled as he spotted Gladding nodding with a look that indicated he knew exactly what the one important thing that Taylor had in mind.

"Care to elaborate Mr. legendary fed guy?" Taylor said, as Gladding laughed aloud and Blair's face bore a broad smile.

"What Kent is alluding to is that since Masters is not the originator of this proposal, he will be limited in upholding the promises made once we undertake it."

Taylor's head spun towards Gladding. He raised both hands in the air, palms forward.

"Whoa! Hold on," Taylor interjected. "Where did this 'we' come from? It's *me* they want to undertake the mission... "

Gladding feigned anger, pointed his index finger, and glared at Taylor.

"You better not be implying that I am too old to engage in a mission."
Blair was next.

"Yeah. It's got to be the three of us.

You've heard of the Three Musketeers, the Three...uh... "

"Stooges? Little Pigs?" Gladding added.

"Amigos? Blind mice?" Blair said.

"Coins in the fountain," Gladding continued.

Taylor could not hold back from laughing with the others. He was touched by the strong support of these men. He could not think of any others he would trust more than Bill Gladding and Jonas Blair.

"Jonas, I appreciate your willingness, but, once again, you do have a young son and a wife... "

"Get a grip, Kent. That argument fell by the wayside some time ago. Besides, you've got a wife, also. And Bill has his family and little granddaughter near him out on the west coast."

"Of course," Kent said. "What am I thinking? Look how well things have worked out. We have free room and board where we are now. And in addition, we are being offered an all-expenses paid trip to an exotic continent filled with adventure."

Gladding had a more relaxed and sober look on his face as he spoke next.

"Listen, Kent. Jonas is right. We all have something to lose and none of us will ever take that lightly.

The key here is that we can trust each other. You know, as well as we do, that is not something you can manufacture. You don't ever want to find out when your life is on the line that you trusted someone who doesn't have your back.

Find a role for each of us, Kent, and let's start making our plans now. The sooner we get this over with, the sooner we can get back to our normal lives."

It had been a long time since Taylor ever engaged in something with men whom he would trust with his life. He made steady eye contact interchangeably with Gladding and Blair. He breathed deeply, wanting to savor the moment and the special feeling that seemed to fill his heart.

"There was a time, Bill, when you once told me that I would have made one hell of a good federal agent. At the moment, I can't help but think that the two of you would have made two great Navy SEALs."

The three men laughed together, but this laugh was riddled with some very real heartfelt gratitude for each other.

❖

She had no problem whatsoever navigating in her rental car to her desired location. No need for a GPS. She knew the area well. After all, she had lived here for years. And she knew this property very well. She had fallen in love with the prior owner and had formed a strong friendship with the neighbors who lived next door.

Sally heard the vehicle approaching even before it turned onto her property. She did not know anyone with an all-wheel drive current year Audi A6.

She peered from the window and spotted the woman who exited the vehicle. Pretty, brunette hair that extended to her shoulders, somewhere around 5'5" in height. Her sunglasses hid the color of her eyes.

Sally studied her as she approached the side kitchen door. Sally's initial impression was that the woman was in no way a threat. Nevertheless, who was she? Sales people never travel down the remote unpaved road leading to the home where Jonas and Sally live. The woman did not have a Bible nor something that would hold a vacuum cleaner, household items, or women's beauty products.

Sally responded to the knock at her door, somewhat curious that the woman chose to come to the kitchen door, rather than the front door that led into the living room. As the woman drew closer, Sally thought that she looked familiar. It was as if Sally had seen her somewhere before, but try as she did, Sally simply could not place her at all.

"Yes, may I help you?" Sally's instincts were in high gear. She was on full alert. She saw nothing threatening at all about this visitor.

"I am sorry to show up here without any advance notice. I-I assume you are Sally—Jonas Blair's wife?'

Sally nodded.

"Sally, my name is Katie. I am the previous owner who sold this house to you and your husband. As I recall, your husband had your power of attorney at the closing, so I did not have opportunity to meet you back then."

"Oh yes, Dunham. Katie Dunham. You were good friends with Jen Roberts next door...uh...Jonas' sister. Please come in. Have a seat."

"Thank you," Katie said. "I hope I am not interrupting you."

"Oh no, not at all, Katie. Taylor is taking his afternoon nap. I was just catching up on the laundry. A baby sure seems to generate a great deal of laundry," Sally said with a smile.

"T-Taylor? Your baby is named Taylor?"

"Yes. Yes, he is. The name is quite special to my husband and me."

Sally immediately perceived the change in Katie. The blood drained from Katie's face. Her lips quivered. Katie was not quite as poised now. She knew about Jonas and Sally. She was aware that it was her husband who saved their lives. But she did not know if they knew Kent's true identity."

"Sally. I-I am here looking for my husband. I-I am concerned. Have not heard from him in quite a few days and..."

Suddenly Sally jumped up. She was laughing, but tears filled her eyes. Her laughter was more throaty than normal. Her eyes were aglow, despite the tears. Katie, unsure of all that was happening, also rose to her feet.

"Oh my God. Oh my God. Of course. You're Kent's wife. You are *that* Katie," Sally exclaimed as if that was the first time Katie's name had been mentioned.

Sally reached over and embraced Katie.

"I recently learned the identity of your husband. Prior to that he was simply the man I saw once before in my life. The man whose face I could never forget. The man who is the reason why Jonas and I are even alive."

Everything changed after that. Sally updated Katie on all that she knew about Kent, Jonas, and Bill. Of course, Sally did not yet know about a proposed overseas mission. She knew that the three men had interrupted a federal investigation of the happenings at Bergam. Most importantly, she knew that they were safe, secure, and in some way purportedly assisting the investigative team.

"I am supposedly going to be brought there soon for a visit with Jonas. I wonder if you would be able to join me."

A startled look covered Katie's face. "Kent has no idea that I am here," Katie said, "and it is very possible that the feds do not know that I even exist in Kent's life."

Sally shrugged.

"Okay, too much to try to figure out so soon," Sally said. "Let's take a breath and take some time to get to know each other."

"I'll need to head to town reasonably soon and line up a place to stay. I might want to meander a bit away from Halston. There are a good many people around here who would remember me…"

"Oh no, please," Sally interrupted. "Please stay here with me, Katie. Please do. We need to be together. This way we can keep track of things happening with our husbands. I would love to have you stay here…uh…that is if you don't mind that you will hear a little baby cry from time-to-time."

Katie laughed. "I'd be honored to stay with you, Sally. And the sound of little Taylor will be like music to my ears. I am already looking forward to meeting him."

"Great. Awesome. I am so happy that you are here, Katie. Listen, let's get whatever you need out of your car. Then, just in case, let's put your car on the far side of our shed where it will not be visible unless someone actually goes back there. With the possibility of any of these federal agents showing up here, the less they know the better."

As the two women headed towards the kitchen door, Sally took Katie's hand, then leaned in and hugged her again.

"I am so happy that you are here, Katie."

Chapter Twenty-Seven

The Camp

The strategy behind the mission into the Congo was coming together very quickly.

"We've got two specialists coming in from Langley tomorrow," Masters said in a meeting attended by Benjamin Marlowe, Kent Taylor, Bill Gladding, and Jonas Blair. They will be bringing in two individuals, both extensively trained, who will be added to your team… "

"Just a minute. Hold on, Masters." Gladding was red-faced, shaking his head, with his arms crossed against his chest. "I thought that Taylor gets to choose whomever he wants for this little foreign sojourn. You never said anything about having a couple of strangers put on a team."

Masters held his hand up, palm facing outward. Once again, he maintained his poise. "Okay, let me rephrase that, gentlemen. These two guys are coming with high recommendations and strong reasons to want to take on this mission, which will be fully revealed to you. If you have any objections after meeting them, just let me know, and I promise you, I will push back."

"Fair enough," Gladding said. "Kent, Jonas?"

Both Taylor and Blair nodded in agreement.

The three men, along with the two Langley coordinating agents and the two recommended team additions, were all to be trained at a camp that was set up on a farm about twelve miles north of Chester. It was officially named the "Tactical Preparedness Training Center," but most everyone referred to this place as "The Camp." The training, preparations, and strategy would be set forth and refined there.

Benjamin Marlowe, along with two other CIA agents, transported Taylor, Gladding, and Blair to their new location. It was already 3:00 p.m.

when they arrived. Marlowe was the only one of the three CIA agents who would stay there with the others. A small staff of agents who manned that location greeted the men as they arrived and showed them the rooms where they would sleep. The Camp also included classrooms, a cafeteria, an exercise room, a firing range, an indoor lap pool, and a recreation room.

The three men and Marlowe headed towards a room where the training sessions would be held. The room was pretty much set up as a classroom. Upon their arrival, Marlowe and the three men discovered that the two agents from Langley and the two recruits to be added to the team were already seated.

"Save the intros for later, gents. We got us Willie and X-box here, he said pointing to an African American man and a Latino. We've got us a lot o' work ta do in a short amount o' time. We gonna hit the ground runnin' here."

They would learn later that the agent speaking was Bobby Frazier. His partner, who had not spoken yet, was Jaime Velasquez. Marlowe sat further back in the room and simply observed all that was going on.

At a quick glance, Taylor noted that X-box was a tall, perhaps 6'3" tan-skinned Latino with a whole bunch of tattoos on the parts of his body that could be seen. Willie was an African American, somewhere in the range of 6' tall and 210 lbs. on what appeared to be a chiseled body at first glance.

"What say we first go over some initial introductory facts here. Make sure we all got our acts together, ya know? Jaime."

"Okay," Velazquez began, "the subject here, he is one Jean-Pierre Muamba."

"Yeah. Lock in on that, boys," Frazier interjected. "Muamba is the dude we gotta get ahold of and bring to the US."

"What's the profile on this Muamba?" Blair asked.

Frazier clicked on a hand-held device and a photo popped up on a big screen at the front of the room.

"So, this *hombré,* he is the star of our show, none other than Jean-Pierre Muamba," Velasquez said. "The man, he is a native of the Congo. Yes? He was born in Katanga Province which is the area where you will land and pick up your package."

Frazier spoke again.

"In addition, we had us Fabrice Zakuana and Muteba Kyenge. These three dudes was workin' with us. They infiltrated one of the armed groups we most interested in. They was workin' undercover for us until somehow, some way that we just ain't figured out yet, they was discovered. Last we heard Fabrice and Muteba had their tongues cut out. They was tortured, then beat, then hacked to death with hatchets before being hanged out in public for everyone to see."

"These thugs, they are like gangs, you know?" Jaime added. "They demand absolute loyalty. They operate based upon fear. The tongues, they cut out, so everyone, they see what happen when you talk—you know? Give information to others like these two men do with us, they find out and you gonna pay big time for that."

"So our boy, Muamba," Frazier said "took to hidin' from the group. They find him, he's dead meat. No questions asked. He knows that. So you dealin' with a guy who is, how you say it, Jaime—mucho scared?"

Jaime laughed."Haha. *Si. Muamba está muy asustado.* He very much afraid. He runnnin' and hidin'. We finally hear from him after many days."

"So, we can assume that you have coordinated a time and place when we will come and get him," Gladding said.

"Indeed, we have," Frazier said. "And we got us some work to do ta make sure we get there as promised. We miss this dude on the first go-round we may never see him again. He either gonna go so underground it would take a damn dragline excavator to unearth the guy or..."

Jaime interrupted this time. "Or he gonna be six feet under after them bad guys, they catch him. You know?"

Kent caught the African American recruit staring at him from time to time. Every time Kent looked back at him, the man turned his head away.

The trainers introduced the fact that within three days, this team would be flown into the Republic of Zambia.

"Long damn flight,' Frazier said. "Onliest good thing is you gonna be flyin' in one of them doctored up C-37As, so at least they make for comfortable flyin'.'"

Blair with a quizzical look on his face, turned towards Taylor.

"The military has taken the Gulfstream V, a business jet," Taylor said, "and adapted a souped-up version for their use. They refer to it as a C-37A. The plane can hold up to sixteen people and has a range of some 6,500 miles or 12,000 kilometers."

"They got any of them hot stewardesses on board?" Brown blurted out.

Even the two trainers laughed at that comment.

"Afraid not, boys," Frazier said. "Just be happy you ain't in no cargo plane sitting on the floor or on a wooden crate."

From Zambia they would fly by helicopter to an area just outside the Grand Karavia Hotel and near the Lubumbashi Golf Club.

"That spot we talkin 'bout," Frazier continued, "is about two miles from the center of Lubumbashi, which is actually the second biggest city in the whole country. You'll be in the Katanga Province."

"Anticipated opposition?" Taylor asked.

"If we play our cards right, you guys gonna be in and outta there before anybody of negative attitude ever knows a thing about it," Frazier said.

"You will, of course," Velasquez said, "be fully armed and in position to defend yourselves, yes? But as long as no one from the armed groups knows, we do not anticipate any problem."

"Yeah," Frazier added, "and jus' ta kind of sure things up a bit, we paid off the manager at that there Grand Karavia Hotel. He gonna do some things to make sure nobody gets too excited if they happen ta spot a helicopter landing. He gonna tell folks they got a photographer takin' some aerial pics. That'd be a reason why people are bein' asked to stay outta that area."

"Speakin' of that helicopter," the African American recruit was speaking now, "watcha got, man?"

Jaime Velasquez answered quickly. "Good question, Willie. You not gonna fly into no African country in a military helicopter. No. We got us one of them Eurocopter EC-225's. Plenty of space for people and any equipment you got. They built to handle offshore and onshore crew change missions. Got long-range capabilities, too. They a Category D copter, which means... "

"Means it's got a cruise speed in the category of 141-165 knots or 162 to 190 miles per hour," the African American interjected.

"Sound like you know your copters, son," Frazier said. "That's good. I ain't allowed to say more on this subject 'cause it's classified, but we juiced up this particular bird some. So you can take that speed and projected range and amp them up. You got wings that will get you there and back with no problem."

"An' we gonna provide you with a pilot whose got the experience," Velasquez said.

❖

They broke for dinner, which would be in the mess hall or cafeteria in thirty minutes. The men were not under close guard, since the property itself was enclosed and guarded. The area they were in was surrounded by a high voltage electrical fence.

Benjamin Marlowe called into Phillip Masters to provide him with an update. Gladding and Jonas headed to their rooms. As Taylor was walking towards his room, the African American recruit caught up with him and walked alongside him.

"Willie," he said, as he extended his hand.

"Nice to meet you, Willie, I'm... "

"I know who you are, Commander Taylor. I been knowin' for a while now. I volunteered for this mission when I learnt that you was gonna be in the lead."

"I'm not sure that I am following you, Willie. How about filling me in."

"Any chance we could take a few minutes and sit somewhere, sir?"

Taylor was caught off guard by the sudden change in politeness and protocol. He pointed to a picnic table, set off by itself in the nearby field.

"Some time ago, sir, I was in the Phillipines with a bunch of mercenaries. There was this one guy, he was older'n the rest of us. Had a Navy background. Never learnt a whole lot more 'bout him because he never told us a whole lot more. He were a very private dude, ya might say.

Most mercenaries are guys with some tactical training, some big-time stuff, I might add, who messed up somewhere along the line."

"Does that description fit you, Willie?"

"Yes sir, I ain't proud of that, but it do. Got me admitted to RASP, Commander" Willie said, referring to the Ranger Assessment and Selection Program—a grueling 8-week course of training.

"Went on to Ranger School. Made it through all three phases of the crawl, walk, and run. Damn near killed me, but I made it. Earned me my Ranger tab. Saw some immediate action, but I was too big for my own britches, Commander. Had me a chip on my shoulder the size of Texas. And I ain't even from Texas.

Long story short, one fight too many, then charged with punching out a commissioned officer and I was dishonorably discharged."

"So you became a mercenary?"

"Wasn't finished being a soldier, even though the Army was finished with me. Then some of the guys in the Philippines was charged with war crimes. Say our platoon kill some innocent villagers after rapin' some women and stealing some stuff."

"Were you guilty?"

"Ain't never happened, sir. Leastwise, if it did, ain't none of us that done it.

Tell you what I was guilty of. I was guilty of accusing the military of being liars and responsible for the death of my own daddy."

Taylor said nothing. He liked the spunk in this young man. Saw the rebellion, but also believed there was something deeper that had tipped his scales to the negative.

"My daddy died in the line of duty, Commander. He was a Navy SEAL. His name was Brown, Wilson Brown. I'm Wilson Brown, Jr."

Chapter Twenty-Eight

Good Payback

Taylor was speechless, frozen where he sat. This could not possibly be happening. He could not be sitting with the son of a fellow SEAL, a friend he watched die in a dank cave years ago.

"This man and me, we was in a city, sittin' in a pub, having a few brews. Guess the beer loosened him up a bit. He started talkin' 'bout a time when he was servin' as part of an underground unit in the Middle East. He starts to tellin' a story 'bout some Navy SEAL who against some incredible odds, somehow saves two other SEALs from becoming charcoal after a bomb done killed everyone else in their camp."

The young insurgent clearly had Taylor's attention now. His head was down, staring at the ground as he continued to speak to Taylor.

"I been putting some pieces together for years, tryin' to get me a better picture of how my daddy died. Y'know my momma, she never did marry nobody. Said she could never replace my daddy no matter what. She died a young woman from breast cancer, they say. I personally think she died from a broken heart.

My daddy died overseas in Yemen where he was on a mission to bring back a major terrorist. I was told that they caught the guy, had him in custody, and was preparin' to bring him back the next day. They never made it. Their camp was bombed. Cooked, Commander. They say that there fire ate up everythin' and everbody in sight, exceptin' for three men. They was three Navy SEALs and my daddy was supposedly one of 'em.

The story I got was that this SEAL, he was messed up pretty big-time, but he carried and dragged the only two other men who was still alive. Took 'em to a cave or somethin'.

Help never came. Guy tellin' me the story said them SEALs woulda gone there ta rescue them three in a heartbeat, but they was prevented from doin' so by a bunch o' politicians and military bigwigs."

Brown lifted his head for a moment and made eye contact with Taylor. Kent could see Brown's eyes glistening from the potential tears that this man refused to release.

"I know you that man, Commander. You the one that tried ta save my daddy's life. You the last person on earth ta see him before he passed.

At first, as I begun ta check things out years ago, I heard tell that you was dead."

Taylor was moved by the words being spoken by Wilson Brown, Jr., but Brown had made a statement that set off some inner alarms in Kent.

"Willie, before I talk more about your father, I have a few questions I need to ask you."

"Ask away, sir."

"Willie, did you first volunteer for this assignment or did someone approach you?"

"Yeah, they come ta me. I been servin' time in Jesup...that's the federal prison in Georgia. These two men that come ta me, they bigwig feds. Said they was CIA. They come ta me, got me outta my cell and tell me about this special mission. They tell me that if I choose to do this thing, they gonna wipe the slate clean with me. Set me free. No more prison time."

Kent was all ears.

"At first, ya know, I'm thinkin' I don't trust these dogs as far as I can throw 'em. Then one of 'em tells me that this mission gonna be headed up by a former Navy SEAL they jus' come in touch with after years of thinkin' he were dead. Man by the name of Taylor. Was thought ta be dead from more'n a dozen or so years ago, but he ain't.

Bingo! I'm thinkin' that's my guy right there. So I up and volunteered."

"Did it strike you as a bit strange that they came to you thinking you would put two and two together and conclude that they were talking about me, the man who was with your father in Yemen?"

"Hell yeah, Commander. I figgered I was being suckered inta signing up for a mission that has a real good chance ta fail. They need it done, so they settin' up a team they can afford ta lose."

Taylor simply waited for Willie to say more.

"I didn't pay me no mind ta that, Commander. Firstly, I was rottin' away in some prison over some trumped up charges I ain't never gonna get around. And second... "

Wilson stopped talking for a moment.

"Well, hell, sir, second, if I 'bout ta die, dyin' with the man that tried ta save the life of my daddy, sounds like an okay deal ta me."

Taylor placed a hand on Brown's shoulder.

"And what about this other guy with you?"

"Name's Xavier, Xavier Domingo. He go by 'X-Box.' I ain't never met him before. Says he's been in a lockup in Lewisburg, Pennsylvania. Says he was a Marine, Green Beret. When he come out, he get all o' them tattoos on his body. Starts hangin' round with a bunch of druggies. Ended up with sellin' and possession charges. That's all I know 'bout him.

One mo' thing I want ta tell ya, Commander, 'bout what this guy said ta me when he was talkin' 'bout what happened to y'all in Yemen. The man says that he an' a bunch o' his buddies, they all believe that your camp was hit by friendly fire. Says somebody set y'all up ta capture this guy, then intended ta kill y'all. Claims the guy y'all nabbed knew too much damagin' stuff against the CIA ta stay alive.

Ya know, I could be wrong, Commander, but I can't help but think that we could be in a same situation as that now."

"How so, Willie?"

"Well, ya know, I wonder if this Muamba dude knows too much that some peoples on our end would jus' as soon like the guy ta never make it back. Ya know?"

Taylor smiled. "You have good instincts, son. Truth is, we are going to have to keep our eyes open at all times."

Taylor talked with Wilson Brown, Jr. about his father. The conversation went along the same lines as the discussion he once had with Katie. He spoke about Wilson being an excellent soldier, a great guy to be around, and someone you could trust with your life. He mentioned having met Willie's mother, Gloria, and confirmed the fact that Wilson planned on marrying her. He told him that Willie's dad had asked Kent to be his best man.

Two men with open hearts sat together talking about a dead man who had a place in each of their lives. Taylor confirmed what Willie's mother had told him.

"Your daddy adored you. Talked about you all the time. He called you 'Hashbrown.' "

This time Willie shed those tears. Kent did also.

❖

Kent, Bill, and Jonas spent some time after dinner walking along the perimeter of the property. The guards were eyes-on, but, despite that, these three men had opportunity to speak privately.

"So based upon what I heard from Willie, I believe that there is a very real possibility that we are all being set up."

"How so?" Jonas asked.

Gladding smiled. "I believe that Kent is saying that the presence of Brown and Xavier Domingo could very well mean that our overall safety is not a priority."

"Right," Kent responded. "They are putting together a team that they can afford to lose, if necessary. Or maybe even dispose of once the job is done.

Somebody went looking for Wilson Brown, Jr. and dropped my name knowing he'd take the bait. I'm not sure what all of this means, but we are going to have to keep our eyes wide open and come up with a Plan B to anything we may encounter."

The three men agreed that Jonas would attempt to dig in a little deeper with Xavier Domingo. Bill would stay in close touch with Ben Marlowe and use him as a conduit for anything they want to get to Masters.

❖

Benjamin Marlowe caught up with Kent Taylor during a break in the classroom strategy sessions on the second day they were at The Camp.

"Gonna need to get with Jonas Blair," Marlowe said. "Agent Masters is asking me to go and bring Jonas' wife in for a visit, as he promised."

"You're pretty close with Masters, aren't you, Ben?"

"Yessir. He's a good man. Can be a tough taskmaster. Can be petty about a few things," Marlowe started to laugh. "Shoes. Hahaha! The man has a bit of a fetish that everyone under his command has their shoes cleaned and polished every day without fail. But you know, he's got a lot of responsibility both at our Chester location and here at The Camp. The paramilitary troops here are currently working under his command.

So, I guess if having polished shoes is the worst thing we have to deal with, well, that's not really all that bad."

Taylor laughed along with Ben as Marlowe headed out to find Jonas. Taylor liked Ben, just as he had developed a growing trust in Masters. He admired Ben's loyalty.

❖

It was, indeed, Phillip Masters who made sure that the promise to Jonas was kept. He sent Ben Marlowe to pick up Sally and bring her to The Camp where her husband and the others were located. D-day was tomorrow. They would begin their trek to Africa. On the following day, the copter would arrive at the designated spot to pick up Jean-Pierre Muamba.

Jonas made the call to Sally in Marlowe's presence and introduced him to Sally. Katie would remain hidden and she would be the one to stay and take care of little Taylor in Sally's absence. Under this plan, there would be no need to communicate with Jen Roberts and alarm her to all that was going on.

Jonas was super excited about seeing Sally again. At the same time, he had a list of items that he, Gladding, and Taylor had compiled to give to Sally. It would not be until Sally arrived that they would learn about Katie's presence with Sally at the Blair home.

Sally's initial reaction to the news that the three men would be engaged in a mission to the Congo was not positive at all.

"Listen to me, Sal. We're going to be just fine. No big deal. We fly in, fly out, end of story. We've got a really solid team. You and Katie need to not fret. We will not take any chances. Safety comes first above all else."

Sally did not have any direct contact with Gladding or Taylor. She did see them from a distance, standing with Wilson Brown, Jr. They waved to her and Gladding gave her a thumbs-up signal.

Ben Marlowe, who made a positive impression on Sally, drove her back home.

"I was not able to actually talk with Kent or Bill, but Jonas assured me and I got a strong impression that they are okay," Sally told Katie. She had already informed Katie of the mission to Africa, and the Coltan that was found in Bergam's building. She also went over the list that Jonas had given to her.

Katie, as expected, shed some tears, but expressed confidence in her husband, as well as Gladding and Jonas. She was very relieved that the three men would be together.

"I did not know Kent when he was an active SEAL and was deployed on covert missions. I can only imagine what Rose must have gone through every time her husband left home—wondering if he would ever come back."

Sally reached out for Katie's hand. "Let's agree right now, Katie, that we will remain positive and confident as we wait for our husbands and Bill to come back home."

"Agreed," Katie said.

And the two women looked into each other's eyes with a growing bond of trust and friendship.

Chapter Twenty-Nine

Within the Ranks

The fresh, crisp morning air rode on the back of a light breeze. The morning sun was ascending to its rightful position for the day.

They ate a hearty breakfast, gathered up the few things they would take with them, and prepared to enter the van. The automatic weapons and all the needed supplies would be waiting for them further down the road.

As Taylor, Gladding, Blair, Wilson Brown, Jr, and Xavier Domingo stood outside near the van, they were approached by two men they had never met before.

"Good morning, Gentlemen. I am Agent Trevor Hunt and my partner here is Agent Peyton Norris." Norris nodded in greeting. "We will be the ones taking you to the location where your plane is located," Hunt said with a smile.

"Glad to be able to report," Norris added, "that it looks like clear weather for flying all the way to your next destination."

"Isn't Ben Marlowe going to travel with us to the plane?" Blair asked.

"Ah! Sorry. Thanks for reminding me. Ben got called back to the Chester area headquarters during the night. Not exactly sure what that was all about. He did ask that we send his regrets for not being here on this final leg. Wishes you all good luck and a safe and successful return."

Everyone was in the van and driving away from the property within minutes. Taylor eyed the agents at the front gate, as they pulled away from the property. Confirmed. He remained on full alert.

❖

Vincent J. Sachar

Phillip Masters hung up his cell. He sat motionless at his desk and stared outwards with his eyes seemingly focused on nothing. He felt a hardening or clenching in his stomach. He fought to calm down and control his thoughts, but they were racing beyond his control.

They did this to Tom. I know they did. He was trying to stop them. He knew what they were up to. My fault. Should have never gone to him.

He forgot his nitroglycerin? No way! And of all days, forgot it on the day that the episode was far more than angina pectoris? They did this to him. I know they did. After his heart attack five years ago, after being further diagnosed with debilitating coronary microvascular disease, Tom would never dream of ever walking out the door without his nitro. No way! They did this. I know they did.

The news that Thomas Westfield was in an ICU Unit at Langley Air Force Base Hospital left Masters stunned. The report he received was that Westfield was found unconscious in his office. Masters' call into Westfield's cell phone was actually answered by Tom's wife, Marlene. She was at the hospital. She was weepy, but communicative.

"Only answered because I could see it was you calling, Phillip. We are perplexed by this whole thing. They say Tom apparently forgot to fill the little pouch he kept his nitro medicine in. They found it empty on the floor in his office—like he was trying to take it and found out the pouch was empty. So hard to believe," Marlene said. She broke up and cried when she informed Masters that her husband was in critical condition.

"We just don't know for sure if he'll make it. I already contacted the children."

Masters sat at his desk simply staring at nothing in particular. He was overwhelmed with concern for his mentor. Suddenly, he broke free from his negative thoughts and considered that whoever had done this to Westfield might also strike out in other ways. He thought of Benjie and the men at The Camp and immediately began to call. His calls went unanswered.

Masters was getting frantic now as his calls to Marlowe remained unanswered. He summoned agents Micah Jensen and Albert Sweitzer to his office.

"I need you to listen closely to me. Albert, get a team up now. SWAT. We head out in ten minutes. I will follow up with the details."

"You got it, sir," Sweitzer said before leaving to carry out his orders.

"What goes, sir" Jensen asked.

"I'm not exactly sure, Micah. Something is out-of-kilter, both at Langley and at The Camp. Hang tight on this, Jensen. If my suspicions are right, this could get real sticky for all of us."

❖

A small convoy headed to The Camp. Masters was seated in the front seat of the vehicle he was in. He continued to check his phone for messages every twenty seconds or so, even though he did not ever expect to receive a return call.

He felt a tightening in his chest. He needed to concentrate on what was now occurring and remain in charge of his men. Yet, he could not escape the thoughts that were constantly barraging his mind.

My fault. Damn it! Should have known. Should have seen it coming. Can only hope I am not too late.

All efforts to reach the van transporting Taylor and the others failed. Masters sent an additional team of his agents to where the plane was located. He knew, however, that would prove to be futile. By the time they would arrive, the plane would be gone.

When the convoy arrived at The Camp, no one was at the front gate entrance. He had his agents take caution and spread out searching the premises. They began to find evidence of what had occurred throughout the property. They found dead bodies lying on the mess hall floor. Two men were killed while taking showers.

Bobby Frazier and Jaime Velasquez were each found in their respective bunk rooms. Frazier's neck had been snapped from behind. Velasquez had been stabbed. As he lay on the floor dying, he apparently dipped his finger in his own blood and started to write something on the wooden floor."T-A-Y..."

As Masters was called to the scene, he was certain that the name being written was "Taylor."

They found a number of bodies in one of the storage barns towards the back of the property. The dead bodies were stacked. The pattern was clear.

Everyone not linked to the men in charge of the van and with the plane was dead. Masters stared in disbelief. His pulse was racing. Good men. Patriots. All of them too young to die.

There was no sign of Benjamin Marlowe in his room nor among the stacked bodies in the barn. Masters' hopes soared that Benjie was taken away with the others in the van. He would certainly be a good hostage, if needed.

Behind one of the buildings, they eventually found the body of Agent Benjamin "Benjie" Marlowe. When Masters looked at the body, Marlowe looked like a man asleep. A single bullet to the back of the head had completed his execution. His cell phone was on the ground near his body. When Masters picked it up, he quickly spotted that Benjie was accessing his speed dial. He was attempting to call his mentor, Phillip Masters.

❖

In the presence of his men, Phillip Masters appeared to be calm, strong, and decisive. None of them could see inside the man where everything was in turmoil. He was grieving over the loss of his men and the personal loss of Benjie. He blamed himself, since this occurred on his watch.

Masters had two men and one woman who were trained extensively in crime scene investigative work. He placed them in charge and assigned several others to assist following the leadership from those three experienced agents.

Before sending the others back to the headquarters near Chester, he huddled together with Micah Jensen and Albert Sweitzer. Micah would remain at The Camp in leadership over everyone. Albert was to communicate what constitutes an all-points bulletin with regard to Taylor, Gladding, Blair, Brown, and Domingo. Taylor's name was still not universally known, so he was only identified by a photo and referred to as an unknown male. Sweitzer would return to the Chester area headquarters.

"Remember, we've got a team that will be reporting back in from the location where the plane is housed. I need you two to communicate with each other and communicate to me. I will make a full report into Langley. You will be able to reach me by phone at all times. I will let you know anything else we need to do. For now, this is totally hush-hush. No one talks to anyone but you two or me. Is that clear?

We'll also follow up with death notices to families and all else later."

"Can't believe that three guys we caught over in the Bergam factory are somehow responsible for this slaughtering of human lives," Sweitzer stated.

Sir," Jensen said as Masters began to walk again. "These men and woman were friends of ours, like family, sir. I'm assuming the three men who spearheaded this will be on the run somewhere here in the States. I just want you to know that if I'm ever in position to take one or all three of 'em out, sir, I'd consider it an honor to do so."

Masters said nothing. He was certain that Jensen would never have any such opportunity at all. He was sure that if the people who had Taylor, Gladding, and Blair now were successful those three men would never make it back alive from Africa.

Masters drove away quickly and raced towards his destination. He knew that it was likely impossible for him to reach Taylor, Gladding, and Blair. He would go for the next best thing.

Chapter Thirty

Trust is Elusive

They heard the knock on the kitchen door. Katie quickly disappeared into the living room with little Taylor. Sally was frightened. She quickly pushed the thought out of her mind that this man was here to provide notice to a next of kin.

The man showed Sally his credentials. He was anxious. Beads of perspiration crowned his forehead on a day when they had no reason to be there. For a man of his stature, he was surprisingly nervous or agitated, even to the point that he occasionally closed his eyes in what appeared to be an attempt to remain calm.

"I realize that you do not know me, Mrs. Blair, but I am the man who sent Agent Benjamin… uh… Marlowe to you to bring you to your husband Jonas."

Sally said nothing. She had gone to the door thinking she would quickly dismiss the man. Now, he had her attention. Something was amiss. Yet, at the same time, the man did not appear to be threatening in any manner. She remembered that Marlowe had specifically mentioned that his supervisor, an Agent Masters, was the one who upheld a promise that Sally would get to see her husband. Masters was not the kind of name a person easily forgets.

Suddenly, everything changed."Mrs. Blair, what I have to talk to you about is urgent. It is of the utmost importance. I am asking you to trust me." Then Masters did something that was most perplexing. He lifted his hands in the air and pulled his lightweight jacket open revealing his holstered gun.

"Mrs. Blair, I am asking you to take my weapon from me. Feel free to keep it pointed at me, if you so prefer. Please do this. I must get to a point where you believe you can trust me. What I have to tell you may be the difference between life and death for your husband and the men he is with right now."

Sally was riveted on the man now. She hesitated for a moment, then took his weapon and did point it at him.

"Please, Mrs. Blair. We need to talk. Now."

❖

Peyton Norris drove the van. The van was equipped with the driver seat and passenger seat up front, and two bench seats behind them. Trevor Hunt rode in the front passenger seat. He sat at an angle where he could both see and chat with the men seated behind him.

Taylor, Gladding, and Willie Brown sat in the first full seat. Xavier Domingo sat at the window behind Taylor. Jonas Blair sat next to him.

"Give or take another twenty minutes or so," Hunt said, "and we'll be there. Everything you need, including all weaponry, has already been loaded onto the plane."

Taylor nodded. Gladding spoke next. "Do you have confirmation that all the audio equipment I will need is also there?"

"Roger, that," Norris said from the driver's seat. "Got a confirmation on that earlier this morning."

"Yeah," Hunt added. "Even though you're in a grounded copter with all its noise communicating to the guys outside the craft, you'll be able to hear each other loud and clear."

"Great. Thanks."

"Impressive," Taylor said with a smile.

"Thanks," Hunt responded. "Just trying to do the best job we can to keep everyone safe and achieve our goals.

Taylor retained his smile. Hunt was completely unaware that Taylor's positive comment related to the excellent acting job he was witnessing.

❖

Sally had a stranger bearing CIA credentials sitting at her kitchen table. She had no problem keeping the handgun pointed directly at Phillip Masters. Baby Taylor was asleep permitting Katie to eavesdrop on the conversation.

Masters confirmed that he and his agents apprehended Blair, Gladding, and Taylor from the Bergam factory. Sally quickly noted that they had now identified Kent Taylor. Masters then added the fact that in apprehending Taylor and Blair, the CIA had actually saved them from the Bergam security team that likely would have killed them. He jumped quickly to the point that Jonas, Gladding, and Taylor were now engaged in a mission to recover and return a man who has been working with the CIA.

"There are details, Mrs. Blair, that I am not at liberty to disclose to you. Just coming to you now is already a protocol and security breach that could result in my loss of a position as a federal agent and criminal charges filed against me."

"So why are you here, Agent Masters? What is it that you want from me?"

"I suspect that this mission has gone rogue. The agents running the show now have their own agenda. I don't exactly know what it is, but I have my suspicions. Your husband and the men with him are in grave danger.

I need you to contact me in the event that you hear from your husband, Mrs. Blair. I want you to relay a message to him and the others with him."

"You're asking a great deal from a man whom I have never before met and have no real reason to trust, Masters."

"Trust..." Masters stared off. A cynical look was on his face. The woman was right. In his profession, one that she once labored in, trust was extremely elusive. Masters had often considered the irony that lying *to* a federal agent could net a person time in prison. Lying *by* a federal agent was not necessarily a chargeable offense at all. In fact, it pretty much occurred every day.

"I am asking a great deal. I realize that. Damn it, I told you that from the moment you laid eyes on me. I am sitting here with you pointing my own weapon at me—a weapon that I voluntarily surrendered to you.

Look, I don't know what more I can do to get you to believe me. You were a trained federal agent yourself. When is it your responsibility to rely upon your own instincts, training, and experience? When does the burden shift to you to decide?

I've done my best to give you what I have, Mrs. Blair. Do what you want with it."

Sally sat motionless, staring off at a point somewhere beyond Phillip Masters. A pensive expression dominated her face, as she pondered the pros and cons of trusting this man. A slew of "What ifs?" raced through her mind. She shook her head, then pushed her shoulders back, stiffened her posture, and made direct eye contact with Masters.

"Call me, Sally," she said, "and tell me just what you want me to do."

Sally placed Masters' weapon down on the table in front of her.

Phillip Masters took a few calming breaths and turned his face upwards. A slightly more relaxed appearance now dominated his face. He made a serious attempt not to smile too broadly. The man had taken a chance. He had come here in the hope that he could somehow get Jonas Blair's wife to trust him. Every fiber of his being was active since he first was unable to reach Benjie and throughout the time that he witnessed the horrific scene there.

"Thank you. Thank you, Sally." Masters paused again and breathed deeply. "The phone number I am giving you is a 'throw-away.' Until now, only two people had this number. One of them is in critical condition in a DC hospital. The other died this morning."

Masters eyes dropped downward for a moment. Then he looked back at Sally. "Please, if you hear from your husband or any of the men with him, pass it on to them. Tell them I will be available to assist in any way that I can. Fill them in on what you know.

And Sally, I will be reachable to you. If I can help please do not hesitate to contact me. I...I hope, deeply so...that we can get out of this with no harm to your husband and the men with him. It-it was never supposed to be like this."

Masters stood up to leave.

"Thank you, Agent Masters..."

"Phillip," he said. "Please, call me Phillip."

Then he turned and walked out the door.

Chapter Thirty-One

An Agency within the Agency

As Masters drove back towards the Chester area headquarters, what he would term"crazy thoughts" bombarded his mind. He wished that his father were still alive. A successful anesthesiologist with a sharp mind, much wisdom, and a great listening ear. Screw confidentiality, to hell with protocol, he would tell his dad everything and seek his counsel.

He wished he had never joined the CIA, wished he was still playing ball with some team, in some league, somewhere. He could not escape the heaviness that dominated his mind and heart. He wished that his marriage to Helene had not ended in divorce. He wished that he was with his two children right about now.

Hah! They expect us to be like robots, like machines, devoid of any feelings at all.

He had dedicated his life to an agency he believed was fighting to make the world a better place and find the bad guys who stood in the way of those goals. And now, the bad guys were not all that difficult to find at all. They were on the hallowed roster of his own agency. They were right under his nose.

His mind flashed back to images of dead bodies strewn throughout The Camp—to Benjie Marlowe lying still behind a building, killed while desperately trying to reach Masters on his cell phone. His thoughts turned towards Kent Taylor, Bill Gladding, Jonas Blair, and the others, over whose lives he had now lost any semblance of control. Until that moment, he had images of people who were dead. These men were still alive. That was where he needed to focus. He needed to do whatever he possibly could to keep these men alive—if he had not already lost the ability to do so.

Phillip Masters disclosed all that Sally Blair needed in order to win over her confidence and put her in position to pass a message on to Blair, Gladding, and Taylor. In his heart, he seriously doubted that Sally would ever hear from

Jonas. The men that he and the others were with had their own agenda and neither Masters nor Taylor, Gladding, and Blair were privy to it.

Masters suspected that these rogue agents planned to use the team to lure Muamba out of hiding and then kill everyone. The helicopter would likely be met by the same thugs that had already killed Fabrice Zakuani and Muteba Kyenge.

They don't want Jean-Pierre to be able to help them get to whoever the key players are in the States. They want to start a war. They want to have a terrorist attack occur on American soil to force our country to go to war in the Middle East. These are radicals, some within the CIA, likely others in the military and Congress who believe that our country has been too soft on the extremist groups that are terrorizing the Middle East.

Phillip Masters never mentioned to Sally that there was evidence found at The Camp crime scene that pointed towards Taylor being behind the mass slaughter of CIA agents. He never mentioned it because he did not believe it was valid.

❖

Taylor recalled the words of Bobby Frazier, as they continued their trek in the van.

"Boys, you gotta remember that our guy Muamba is real jittery right about now. He's been livin' like a rat in a New York sewer ever since his two buddies was turned into chopped liver. You gonna have to be real careful when you first encounter him after y'all get offa that there whirlybird. One wrong move and Muamba will be gone. And after that, we may never have a chance ta rescue the dude again."

"What has he been told to expect on that end," Jonas asked.

"After he lose his two compadres, communication with him been real sketchy for a while, you know?" Jaime responded. "But we finally got the chance to talk. We tell him when and where the rescue, it would happen, yes? But that hombre, he want to know jus' who is comin' to get him."

"Yeah, so we agreed ta send the dude pics of you guys. He got him some pics of Taylor, Blair, Gladding, Brown, and Domingo. We ain't had much of a choice. Had some higher-ups that was dead against us sendin' him pics, but we done it. It were either that or we was afraid that Muamba would be a no-show," Frazier said.

As Taylor reflected back on this, it explained a great deal. In fact, it was likely the difference between life and death—the only reason why he, Gladding, and Blair, as well as Brown and Domingo were not killed with the others.

❖

Katie's face was pale as she entered the kitchen after Masters drove away. She heard everything he had to say and did not have any answer as to what she and Sally should do next.

"I still have contacts at the Bureau," Sally said, "but I am not sure who I would reach out to and what difference anyone could make. What would they do? And is there enough time?"

Katie breathed deeply before speaking.

"Sally, we are talking about three incredibly talented men. Kent mentioned in times past that Bill Gladding might very well be the best field agent that the FBI has ever had. He also told me how deeply impressed he was with Jonas.

And as for Kent, if I had not seen him with his shirt off, I'd swear the man had a blue uniform with a big red "S" on his chest."

Sally chuckled despite the fact that she and Katie were both on the verge of sobbing.

"Listen to me, Sal. I think what we have to do right now is the toughest thing of all. We have to wait. We wait and we trust that our guys are smart and talented enough to handle this. Hopefully, Phillip Masters and others will do what they can to help our guys. But, we just have to believe that our three men will find a way to get through this."

As she spoke, Katie's eyes filled with tears. Sally's eyes did the same.

Katie summed it up perfectly. They wait and they trust—the toughest thing of all.

❖

The flights into Zambia took an entire day. Two American soldiers, Jake Helton and Dalton Kepler, joined the team. Helton was an intimidating man at 6'6" and weighing somewhere in the range of 240 lbs. His shaved head and dark piercing eyes added to the image. Kepler was shorter, standing at about 5'11" with a broad build, red hair in a crew cut, and deeply set green eyes. Kepler was the spokesperson. Helton pretty much never spoke at all.

"We'll be joining with you gentlemen," Kepler stated, "all the way in to provide added backup. So get used to our faces now."

Norris and Hunt would not be on the helicopter. Taylor considered that these two new additions must be expendable.

The Eurocopter EC225 that Jaime Velasquez spoke of back at The Camp was actually an H 225 Super Puma. Normally equipped with two powerful Turbomeca Makila 2A turbine engines, a five-blade main rotor and Spheriflex rotor head, the H225 provided long range, fast cruise speeds, and flight endurance. The eight men who boarded were well below its capacity to carry 19 passengers. Bobby Frazier's statement that the copter to be utilized had been 'juiced up" to provide even greater speed and range was true. This bird would get the team there and back with no problem at all.

As promised, the weapons and audio equipment were on board. Interestingly, only Kepler and Helton bore pistols. Taylor silently wondered what Trevor Hunt would think when he noticed that his weapon was no longer in its holster. Instead, it was snugly tucked in the belt of Taylor's pants.

The pilot, Pankaja Conteh, was a tall, dark man with a heavy African accent. As a native of the Congo, he purportedly knew the area they would be flying into very well.

Gladding was seated towards the front of the craft, closest to the pilot. Taylor was seated alongside Blair. Xavier Domingo was seated behind Taylor with Wilson seated to Xavier Domingo's side. Jake Helton and Dalton Kepler were seated together behind the others.

Lift off was surprisingly smooth with low vibration and sound levels further enhancing the aloft.

Ten minutes into the flight, they made their move. Gladding placed a knife against the pilot's throat. Taylor pulled his handgun and pointed it directly at Helton and Kepler. Blair moved quickly and took their weapons from them. He then gave one of the handguns to Gladding.

Just as Gladding turned his head back towards the pilot, Xavier Domingo pulled a knife he had hidden away. He lunged directly towards the back of Taylor's neck. Just as the knife was about to plunge into Taylor's neck, Domingo's head was snapped to the side. Two thick hands had a vice grip on the man's neck. Wilson Brown, Jr. continued to squeeze until all signs of life were gone and Domingo's limp body slumped to the floor.

Taylor turned his head as his eyes locked in with Brown.

"Well, you know what they say, sir. Ya gotta 'pay it forward', " Willie said with a big grin. Taylor nodded and softly thanked him.

Gladding pointed his weapon at Pankaja Conteh. "You keep steady in our flight pattern, No sudden moves. No radio contact," he commanded the pilot.

Meanwhile, Blair pulled out some rope he had tucked away prior to takeoff and, with the help of Brown, tied and gagged Helton and Kepler.

Gladding then turned towards Wilson.

"Now's the time we need to know, son. Can you fly it?"

That now familiar large grin once again covered the face of Wilson Brown, Jr. "What? You kidding me? That's a Roger, sir. You bet I can. One hundred percent."

Taylor spoke next. "Bill Gladding has the coordinates and will assist in guiding you in, Willie. We will need to drop down before we reach the meeting spot and I will jump out."

"Huh? You gonna do what? How low you need me ta get, man?"

"We do not have another choice, Willie. The way I see it, There's going to be a team of thugs in the area waiting for the bird to land and Muamba to show his face. Once that happens the fireworks go off with the intent that everyone dies. I need a chance to quickly search the area, hopefully find Muamba and…"

"Well, hell, Commander. If anyone else can fly this machine, I'd love to make that drop with ya. I mean ya gonna need some help. I'm sure I ain't gotta be the one to tell ya that you gonna be jumpin' into a hornets' nest."

"Wait, please, wait," the pilot screamed, his voice heavily accented and tight with fear."I do it. Let me do this. No one fly this aircraft better than me. No one, he know, this area better than I know. I do this."

"Why would we trust you?" Gladding asked.

"I favor not these men," Pankaja Conteh said. "They threaten my family, if I do not fly for them. But now, I think, they kill me too. I must live to protect and support my family."

Over the next few seconds, Gladding, Taylor, Blair, and Wilson took turns looking at each other. No one spoke.

Conteh broke the silence. "My name, 'Pankaja'—it mean 'one who is born in dirt.' My family, they very poor. We lived in small village, but my father, he was an honorable man. I, Pankaja, I am like my father. I do this. I do as you say. Only you promise that I live to return to my family."

So, they agreed. Conteh would fly the copter, while Taylor and Brown would make an early exit.

Chapter Thirty-Two

Like Riding a Bicycle

It did not matter that Sally Blair was a former field agent with the FBI. It did not matter that Katie Nova was married to a former Navy SEAL and hidden away with him on a Caribbean island.

At this moment in time, they were two women deeply concerned about the welfare of their husbands. So, they did what any two women would do. They spent a great deal of time talking about anything other than what Jonas and Kent were currently going through.

Sally was fascinated to hear the story about how Katie and Kent first met and how many things they shared together on this very property.

Katie enjoyed learning about how Sally and Jonas fell in love and carefully kept their relationship a secret from others within the Bureau. Although Katie was aware that her husband saved the lives of Sally and Jonas, she was enraptured by Sally's account of all that occurred on that day.

Between the exchange of stories, details about how and where they each grew up, and spending time with the baby, the two women were doing a great job pretending. They pretended that they were not absolutely terrified over all that their husbands and Bill Gladding were currently involved in.

❖

Pankaja Conteh did just what he promised. He dropped the craft to a height where Kent Taylor and Wilson Brown, Jr. could leap out with the least risk of injury. He also dropped them off far enough away from the planned landing spot.

Taylor and Brown began running quickly, remaining parallel to each other where, at least for now, they could communicate with hand signals.

Despite the fact that they could communicate with each other, as well as with Gladding, and Blair via the audio system, the two men on the ground avoided speaking as much as possible.

They ran swiftly, yet amazingly quietly. Meanwhile, the craft drew near, then lifted up again and circled away. Conteh called in to someone on the ground. He spoke in an African dialect, further requiring Gladding and Blair to trust that the man was not betraying them.

"I tell them," Conteh said to Gladding and Blair, "that the winds change and I must circle back and reenter. A helicopter, it must always take off and land never downwind—only into the wind. This buy us a few extra minutes. We fly near enough to make noise. Help drown out movements of our men, yes?"

Gladding nodded affirming Conteh's statement that the noise from the copter would benefit Taylor and Brown. Blair knew, however, that Gladding's actions did not carry a great deal of confidence with them. They had not heard from Taylor or Brown since the initial communication that they were safely on the ground.

As the two men ran together, they stayed within sight of each other and continued to rely upon hand signals. Suddenly, Taylor spotted two men in front of him at a distance of about thirty yards. He also spotted a lone figure within range of Brown.

Taylor's signal to Brown about the man that Wilson would soon encounter was met with a thumbs up and a wide grin. Taylor reached his men first. He grabbed one of the men from behind and positioned his victim between himself and the second man. His chokehold had his man gasping for air. Taylor held tight while shifting his body into position to land a powerful kick on the second man. As the man began to fall forward, his weapon already fallen to the ground, Taylor let his first man slump unconsciously to the ground. He then put both hands together and swung his arms upwards as if he were teeing off with a golf club. The blow made immediate contact like a boxer throwing a devastating uppercut, snapping his target's head back violently. Victim number two was unconscious before he ever hit the ground.

Within seconds, Taylor emptied the clips from the automatic weapons of the two men he had encountered and then turned towards Wilson Brown, Jr.

Willie had his man in a chokehold and was fully in control until two more men came through the brush and spotted Brown. One of the men, the shorter of the two, quickly turned his weapon on Brown and fired. Wilson Brown was hit, but managed to grab the assault weapon and was grappling with the man who had just shot him. The second man stood at 6'8" with a physique that would have served him well as a professional in the National Football League. Brown was twisting and turning in such a way that the giant was not yet able to fire without possibly hitting his partner.

The behemoth moved with surprising agility and positioned himself to where he would be able to come behind Willie. The tall man pulled a knife that hung from his belt and moved forward in position to slit Brown's throat. The knife was out and moving forward when Taylor hurtled his body through the air and struck the man. The force of Taylor's body was enough to knock the knife from the man's gargantuan hands and stagger him, but this giant did not fall to the ground. Instead, he was in position over Taylor who was on the ground. He quickly moved closer to Taylor and swung his leg in a powerful kick. Taylor knew that he now had some cracked ribs. The second kick was aimed directly at Taylor's head. Kent caught only the side of the man's boot as he deftly moved aside. He then quickly grabbed the man's calf, twisted his leg, and brought him down.

Taylor's punches were fast and solid. A smaller man would likely already be unconscious, but this man, though severely rocked, was still trying to fight back. He grabbed the knife that had fallen to the ground and struck at Taylor drawing blood to the side of Taylor's neck. Kent grabbed the man's wrist as the knife was drawing ever closer. The huge man made a final thrust. Taylor quickly spun to the side causing the knife to strike the ground. Three successive punches to the giant's throat fractured the man's hyoid bone resulting in forced strangulation. Brown dispatched of his man and watched as Taylor's victim succumbed to his fatal injuries.

Taylor quickly turned towards Willie.

"How bad are you hit, man?"

"Ah! Got one in the left shoulder. Another grazed the upper thigh in my right leg. Ain't got time to check it out too much, but I'm thinkin' I'll live.

Got some bleedin', but we gotta get a move on here. These goons heard the shots. They gonna be all over us any minute now."

Wilson was right. The gang members were now aware that something was wrong here on the ground. Muamba was probably already on the run. Odds are he'd be heading out of this area so fast, they would never have any opportunity to take him away.

The helicopter was drawing close again. The sounds of its engine and the air displaced by its rotors was louder now. Taylor was ready to abort this failed mission and do whatever he could to get himself and Brown back on the Super Puma and out of this area as quickly as possible.

That was when the first miracle occurred.

Taylor grabbed onto Brown. Willie hobbled, but moved with Taylor to a spot west of where they had been located. Taylor's plan was to leave the immediate area where the shots were fired and circle around to where they could relocate. He wanted to find another area for the copter to land while he and Brown positioned themselves to take out anyone who attacked.

As the two men quickly rushed through the bushes, Brown still running despite his injuries, they suddenly came upon a man crouched down, hidden in the brush. Taylor and Brown both pointed their weapons at him. The man began to cry out in fear. His body was shaking. He began to shake his head and plead for his life. Taylor and Brown had found Jean-Pierre Muamba.

Taylor quickly bent down, covered Muamba's mouth, and whispered directly into his ear.

"We have come here to save your life Jean-Pierre. So, if you want to stay alive, do not make any more sounds and decide now if you are willing to trust us—totally. Understand?"

Muamba nodded his head and whispered his assent.

"Yes. I trust you with my life. Please. Save me. I do not wish to die."

Chapter Thirty-Three

Freebird

Taylor provided the coordinates of where he, Brown, and Muamba would be for pickup by the helicopter. "Once these guys figure out that the copter is not going to land where they expected, you can be sure that all hell will break loose," Taylor informed Gladding and Blair. "I will cover for Brown and Muamba as they head towards the bird. Then y'all can cover me."

"I'm coming out once we land, Kent," Blair said. "You can head for the copter right behind Willie and Muamba."

"You'll be able to cover for me from the fuselage, Jonas. Don't take any unnecessary risks."

Taylor looked over at Brown and Jean Pierre. A large patch of blood was seeping through Brown's pants and growing in size. Muamba was shaking uncontrollably.

"Willie," Taylor said, "you are bleeding pretty bad from the leg wound. Plus we know you were also hit in the shoulder. Can you make it to the copter with Jean-Pierre?"

Brown stopped and stared directly at Taylor. "Watcha think, Man? Ya think a little discomfort in my leg and shoulder gonna keep me from finishin' the job we set out ta do? That jus' ain't gonna happen, Commander. I ain't gonna let it happen."

Taylor said nothing. He simply kept his gaze upon Brown and waited. Brown's eyes seemed to soften, as he reached out and placed his hand on Taylor's forearm. His eye contact remained steady, as he moved his hand to Taylor's shoulder. His desire to repay the man who had attempted to save his father's life was evident.

"Lissen, man, I can't deny that I'm hurtin' right now. Ain't no doubt somebody gonna have ta tend to my wounds. But first, we gotta get our butts outta here or ain't none of us gonna have anything alive ta tend to. I can make it, sir. I can do it. Hell, what I gotta do ain't nothin' compared ta what you done years ago for two of your fellow SEALs."

Taylor reached out, placed his hand atop Brown's. He nodded.

"Let's go," he said to both Brown and Muamba."It's time to go home."

❖

Masters was finally making strides. Micah Jensen and Albert Sweitzer were working with him in establishing a team that Masters could rely upon. "I'm counting on you guys to find men and women that we can trust. We've got some dirty business to tend to and there is no room for mistakes here." His confidence soared following the call he received from Langley.

"Phillip Masters, this is Marisa Reynolds. Please hold the line for a moment." Another person joined the call. At first, her presence on the line sent a jarring fear throughout Masters' body. It was Marlene Westfield. The wife of TJ quickly assured Masters that her husband was still alive.

"Tom is actually doing much better, Phillip. They removed him from ICU, placed him in a standard hospital room and, despite the fact that he is listed in serious condition, he is definitely headed to having that downgraded to stable." Marlene Westfield then informed Phillip that her husband was not permitted to make phone calls, but he had a message for Masters that Marlene was carrying. "Tom says he wants you to rely upon Marisa Reynolds. You can trust her. She will work with you. I do not know details as to what is going on and I am not permitted to know. So I am now going to get off this line and let you speak confidentially with Marisa."

Masters quickly expressed his thankfulness that TJ was improving. "He'll be out of that place before we know it, Phillip. And don't forget. Tom promised you a home-cooked meal."

Marlene stopped speaking and Marisa took charge of the conversation. "By now you are undoubtedly aware that we have a faction within our own agency that have gone rogue. I am not going to lie to you, Masters, and pretend that we know everyone who is involved. What we do know is that they are attempting to thwart the recovery of Jean-Pierre Muamba from the

Congo. Their goal is to make sure that a terrorist attack on American soil does occur. They believe that Muamba can identify key players within the U.S. We have to do everything we possibly can to stop them from succeeding."

Masters sighed deeply. "We've lost control of the small team sent over to recover Muamba. They could all be dead by now. Muamba could be dead along with them."

"Last word we received," Reynolds said, "your guys are still alive and were headed by copter to the rendezvous spot where they are to pick up Muamba."

Marisa's statement startled Masters. "Last word you... "

"Yes," Reynolds said, "we've got someone over there, in Africa, at the location where they met up with the copter. Goes by the name 'Fargo.' It is difficult at times to hear from our contact, but this is someone who can be trusted, Masters. Of course, right now, we are all powerless to do anything. We just have to hope and pray that somehow the team and Muamba make it back in the helicopter."

Hope and pray, Masters thought. *That's not a hell of a lot for the world's greatest intelligence agency to rely upon.*

❖

The clearing that Taylor chose was on the Lubumbashi Golf Club that bordered the Grand Karavia Hotel area where the copter was supposed to land. The plan was for the copter to begin landing at the planned location, then abruptly fly back up, speed over to a nearby new location, make a quick drop, and take off. It did just that.

Unfortunately, the African gang members were spread out enough so that some of them were able to quickly move towards the area where the copter was now landing. The Puma was down. Taylor was poised and hidden away, while Brown and Muamba raced towards the craft that would take them out of this area. Just then, several Africans arrived on the scene with automatic weapons aimed at Willie and Jean-Pierre. Taylor began firing his weapon catching the Africans by surprise. Four Africans lay dead on the ground, as Muamba and Brown climbed into the craft.

Taylor made his run, quickly crossing an open area and reaching the copter when additional Africans arrived on the scene. He evaded their fire. Blair, Gladding, and Willie Brown began launching a barrage of shots from the helicopter, but it was clear that time was of the essence. They would have to leave now. Blair dropped a ladder, as the copter began to slowly rise and leave the area. Taylor grabbed on and was hoisted in from the air—hanging on, still a target for the men on the ground.

Conteh swerved the helicopter to increase the difficulty of a shooter being able to hit Kent, while Gladding, Blair, and Willie Brown continued to fire away.

Faster now—the roar of the engines confirming that the special equipped H225Super Puma was lifting higher and moving faster, as Kent Taylor hung tightly to the only thing separating him from certain death. Once they were out of range, Blair and Wilson Brown, Jr. reached down and pulled Taylor up to the craft. The straining and pulling tore at Brown's shoulder wounds, increasing the bleeding. Willie screamed out in pain as he continued to work with Jonas in assuring that Kent Taylor was safely on board. Once Taylor was inside the helicopter, Willie Brown sat back and passed out.

Chapter Thirty-Four

Where Do You Go?

At first, Jean-Pierre Muamba was silent. It was apparent that the man was still frightened. Blair turned to him and spoke. "Jean-Pierre, give me a hand here. Let's see if we can help Willie a bit."

Muamba nodded his head. "He save my life, along with all of you. Yes, I help."

Blair reached over to tend to Willie Brown. Willie opened his eyes, his head still swooning, as Jonas gave him some water to drink to appease the voracious thirst resulting from the loss of blood. Jonas examined Wilson's wounds.

"Okay, Willie, looks like the bullet did not graze your left thigh. It passed right through, my friend. There's an entrance and exit wound there. As to the shoulder, I'd say you still have a slug in there that will have to come out. Need you to stay still for now. You've lost more than enough blood for today."

Willie whispered a quiet thank you, drank some more water fed to him by Muamba, then closed his eyes and laid back quietly.

Taylor's ribs felt like they were on fire, but he did not even mention his injuries to anyone. There was also an ugly abrasion on the right side of his face from the giant's second kick. Kent was unsure whether his right eye would swell and close up. Taylor still figured he got the better deal. He was alive. The giant was dead. Besides, assessing his injuries was by no means the most important consideration or concern that Taylor had along with the others. The Super Puma was cruising along, widening the gap between its occupants and the murderous Africans on the ground in Lubumbashi. The major issue they now faced was where they could safely land and how they would be able to get out of Africa once they did land.

Gladding spoke first. "Way I see it, if we return to Zambia, we'll have a whole lot of people there who were expecting us not to make it out of the Congo."

"Right," Taylor said, "but going back to where we first boarded the copter, we end up where there are planes and that's the only ticket we really have to get out of Africa."

Panjaba Conteh spoke next. "Originally, they tell me I bring helicopter back to where we first find it. We know now, they expect me to die in Congo. Maybe as we draw near, I call in, say I am returning. Act as if that is what I expected. I tell them that no one else make it back with me. Enemy strikes. They all die. I have no choice, but to fly away."

"I think that is our only hope," Gladding stated. "They might buy it. It could give us just a momentary element of surprise."

"I'll take a moment," Taylor said.

"There exists no location where anyone can jump out early, as in Congo," Conteh continued. "Much too open. No place to hide."

"And we have a couple of wounded guys here," Blair added. He and Gladding had both noticed Taylor wincing in pain and surmised that he had broken ribs.

"We have to land as close to an available plane as possible. Our greatest exposure will be getting from this craft to one of the planes. Possibly, the very one that brought us to Zambia," Taylor said. "Plus we're going to have to help Willie get... "

"I help," Conteh quickly responded. "It is something I am able to do."

"I also help. Anyway I can," Muamba said.

"We'll need me, you, Bill, and you, Jonas, handling the automatic weapons and holding off any intruders," Taylor said.

"Roger that," Gladding responded.

Blair spoke next. "What about the plane? Who's going to fly us out of ..."

"I can fly it," Taylor said. "Might not be able to serve everyone with snacks and a drink, but I can get us out of there."

The strategy was set. The plan was in motion. Realistically, its success was highly in doubt, but at least they did have a plan.

❖

Phillip Masters was on edge and jumped when his cell phone rang. It was his government-issued phone and not the throwaway.

"Phillip, this is Marisa Reynolds. Listen, we were able to make contact with Fargo over in Zambia."

Masters was all ears.

"No word on the plight of our guys and Jean-Pierre Muamba, but at least Fargo is ready to help should the team return to where the plane landed. It's not much, but at least it is something. Wish I had more Masters. I really do."

❖

As the copter approached the airstrip where it initially took off for the Congo, Conteh made his call. He spoke in English. Gladding had instructed him on what to say and how to say it.

"H 225 Super Puma, Punjaba Conteh to home base."

"Come in Puma."

"Ready to land. Heliport three."

"Permission granted."

"Conteh. This is Emerson. What is your status?"

This rebel group in Zambia had a key contact in the Congo. Dikembe Botende, whom they referred to as"Bo," secretly updated the team in Zambia on all that was occurring on his end. At the same time, he was the one who tipped off the African gang about the time and location when a team was to arrive to rescue Muamba. He lied claiming to have gotten this info from the manager of the Grand Karavia Hotel, rather than his sources in Zambia. The African thugs interrogated and tortured the hotel manager, even cutting out his tongue before killing him.

When Botende was killed in the fracas with the men on the helicopter, the rogue troops in Zambia were left in the dark. They had no idea what had occurred in Lubumbashi.

"I am alone," Conteh responded. "All others, they are dead. I have no choice but must fly away alone or I must die also. Bullets even strike the Puma."

"And Muamba?"

"He is dead. I see him shot many times."

George Emerson, a former Congressman from Ohio, cut off his communication with Conteh and turned towards Rascoe Infante, a former US Marine Raider Regiment special operations force member. Infante lost his right leg to a land mine explosion while overseas in Afghanistan. Rascoe spent over two years undergoing surgeries, skin grafting for the burns on his left leg, stomach, and chest. His anger festered as he witnessed what he felt was weak and indecisive US reaction to the insurgent terrorist groups in the Middle East.

Emerson had just recently flown into Zambia to keep a first-hand look at this recent incident. Infante had been there for several months and was generally regarded as the leader when men such as Emerson were not present.

"Let's question Conteh, hear just what he witnessed before he was forced to leave. Have to think those left there on the ground are all dead, but no harm getting more insight before we kill Conteh," Emerson said.

The grin on Infante's face actually troubled Emerson. George was more than willing to take action and even kill when necessary. Infante seemed to regard killing someone as others would view partaking in a delicious meal.

"Consider it done," Rascoe responded. "Matter of fact, I just might slit Conteh's throat myself," Infante said with a chuckle. "Kind of a shame, though."

"Shame?"

"Yeah," Infante continued. "A shame that Taylor guy didn't make it through. I was hoping for an opportunity to kill him. He's a former Navy SEAL, they say. Supposed to be a tough dude. That's just the perfect kind of guy that I would love to kill, you know?"

As Infante walked away, Emerson reflected upon the fact that he was working side-by-side with a full-fledged, no-holds-barred psychopath.

❖

"I did not see any hangars when we landed here," Taylor said. "That plane, or any plane, will be out in the open somewhere."

As they drew nearer, the C-37A was sitting out in the open.

"It's been moved from where we landed," Blair said. "Hopefully that means they serviced it and it is ready to fly again."

"Right," Taylor said with a wry smile, "except they certainly did not prepare it for us."

"Okay, Punjaba," Gladding said, "we pretty much use the same tactic as back in the Congo. Approach the heliport. Give the appearance that we are landing. Then take off, fast as we can over to the plane."

Blair spoke next. "We provide cover as we get on the plane. Kent, you first to get the plane ready?"

Taylor nodded. He did not like the idea of boarding first, but knew that Blair was right. A team sitting on a plane that was not ready to fly away would be like sitting in a death trap.

Conteh feigned an approach and a landing before heading straight for the plane. This was the very plane on which the team had flown in.

When the copter landed next to the plane. They quickly spotted men headed towards them, along with several jeeps and trucks now racing to their location. Gladding and Blair were firing away at those who were approaching, forcing some to position themselves behind vehicles that had stopped. They were now firing their automatic weapons at the men boarding the plane.

Taylor was on board and already had the plane revved up. Conteh was big and strong enough to quickly get Willie Brown on board. Muamba was right next to Conteh, assisting him. Jonas motioned for Gladding to board next. Gladding continued to fire from the copter. His mouth was wide open. His eyes widened in shock. Jonas was racing towards the plane with his back exposed. Two men in one of the jeeps were now racing towards the plane with their weapons aimed directly at Jonas. Gladding was firing, but could not stop their approach. There was no way that Blair could reach the plane before enemy bullets would bring him down. Gladding screamed. Conteh and Taylor turned to see what was going on. Kent even considered leaving the cockpit to assist Blair, despite the fact that his efforts would be in vain.

Blair was closer now. Running as fast as he could, as the jeep was racing forward at a speed greater than the man on foot. The jeep passenger leaned out from the side of the vehicle and took aim directly at Jonas. His finger moved forward and a multitude of shots rang out.

The shots all traveled at a projection above the plane itself as the passenger's bullet-riddled body fell out from the jeep. The next shot traveled through the back of the jeep and struck the driver. Taylor already had the plane moving, the moment Blair was on board. They heard additional gunfire and watched as Rascoe Infante shot and killed the woman who had saved Jonas Blair's life.

It would not be until much later that they would all learn who was responsible for saving Blair. They had encountered Fargo. Capt. Wendy Adkins had served her country as a member of a special women's' unit in Afghanistan. Upon retirement from the military, she learned that a group of rogue soldiers were conspiring to help bring on a major terrorist attack on US soil. She volunteered to work undercover in that group and eventually ended up with the team in Zambia.

Now, she had paid the ultimate price for her service to her country.

Chapter Thirty-Five

Going Home

Taylor had the plane cruising. Conteh sat next to him. The African man had some flight experience with small single-engine planes. Taylor was now familiarizing him with the operation of a jet.

Gladding came forward to speak with Taylor. "We are going to have to come up with a plan, Kent. No way we make it all the way back to the States. We need to get some medical attention for Willie. For you also."

Taylor ignored the comment about himself. Not much anyone could do for a couple of broken ribs and his facial swelling had already subsided.

"This is Phillip Masters. Can you hear me? Masters here. Are you receiving this?"

The call into the jet shocked Taylor, Blair, and Gladding. They would soon learn that Captain Wendy Adkins did one last thing before saving Jonas Blair's life. She signaled Marisa Reynolds and left a twelve-second message. "Team from Congo made it back alive. Headed towards the plane that brought them here. Trying to escape." Reynolds immediately called Phillip Masters. They agreed that Masters would attempt to reach those on board.

Taylor looked over at Gladding and Blair. Bill Gladding nodded his head indicating his thoughts that Kent should respond to the contact.

"This is Taylor. Yes, we hear you, Masters."

Phillip Masters paused before responding. "Taylor, thank God you're alive. The others?"

"We are all alive, Masters. We've got a medical need for Willie Brown. We also have Jean-Pierre Muamba and the helicopter pilot, Panjaba Conteh, on board."

"Thank God. Great to hear. Listen, I have a key contact out of Langley who can assist us. We are aware that we are dealing with a rogue group... "

"Rogue is kind of a soft description, Masters," Gladding interjected. "A damn agency within your agency is what you've got, Masters. Good luck finding anyone you can trust."

Masters said nothing. He knew the caliber of trained professionals he was dealing with in Gladding, Taylor, and Blair.

"We do need help," Taylor said. "Thankfully this bird was refueled, but we will need a stopover before we can make it back to the States."

Masters was prepared. "You are about six hours from the United Arab Emirates. Al Dhafra Air Base is about twenty miles south of Abu Dhabi. It's a military installation operated by the United Arab Emirates, but we have a presence there. We've got American personnel and planes. It is definitely a safe haven for you. You will all be safe. Plus, we've got people there who can help get you back... "

"We've had enough of your help, Masters," Taylor snapped. "So, here's what we need and want. We land at Al Dhafra. You get us refueled, food, supplies, and medical assistance for Willie. Medic is the only person we let on board. Any other attempt to board or stop us on our way will be met with lethal resistance. Is that clear?"

Masters paused before responding. He was intent on doing whatever he could to communicate without further igniting the anger of Taylor, Gladding, and Blair.

"Listen, I know you guys are upset. Don't blame you," Masters said, "but if you want to get back here, you're going to have to trust me."

"Trust you? Damn you, Masters," Gladding shouted, "which of the CIA teams are you on? The one that sent us out on a potential suicide mission realizing that we might not make it back or the one that did everything to assure that we would not make it back.

How the hell can you talk about trust when you and your cronies... "

"My people are dead," Masters interrupted. "They slaughtered everyone that was stationed at The Camp. That's why none of the people you were familiar with were around when you boarded the van headed towards the plane. We arrived too late. Found...found them all dead."

"The trainers ... Frazier, Velasquez?" Blair asked.

"Dead," Masters responded.

Gladding hesitated before asking the question that was pressing on all of their minds. "Benjie? Ben Marlowe?"

There was a hesitation before Masters spoke again. "Found him behind one of the barns. Shot in the back of the head. His cell phone was on the ground. He was trying to call me when they gunned him down."

At first, no one said anything.

"Man, very sorry, Phillip," Gladding said. "Damn shame—all of it."

"You pegged it right, Gladding. Two sides, a schism, within our agency and beyond. I...uh...I never lied to all of you. I just...I just never saw it coming."

The silence, ultimately broken by Taylor, seemed to have been much longer than it actually was.

"Okay Masters, okay, we need and want your help. For now, we stand by our decision. You get everything we need brought to us. We stay on the plane. No one other than someone trained to help Willie comes on board."

"Roger that," Masters said.

"Hey, Masters," Blair was speaking now. "Any chance you would be willing to contact Sally and let her know that Kent, Bill, and I are okay?'

"Hell! You kidding me, Jonas? I'd consider that an honor." Masters responded. "It will also be the first bit of good news I have shared with anyone in days."

❖

Willie slept most of the way to the Al Dhafra Air Base. He was in a weakened state, but they had definitely stemmed the blood loss. Conteh was like a schoolchild as he eagerly listened to everything that Taylor had to share about flying an aircraft such as this. Blair marveled at yet another skill that Taylor demonstrated.

"Hey, Kent," Jonas said. "Is there anything you can't do?"

Gladding chuckled a bit as he witnessed Taylor blushing for the first time since he met the man.

"Aw, Jonas, there's a whole lot of things I can't do. A whole lot."

"Name one." Blair was having fun now.

"Okay, well...uh... I can't dance. It's like my upper and lower body parts simply do not agree when it comes to dancing." Taylor was laughing now and everyone was laughing with him. Willie Brown opened his eyes for a moment and commented.

"Ya probably don't have no rhythm is the problem there, Commander. Ya know, some people's born with it and some jus' ain't. I'd get up an' show ya, but I ain't in the best condition to do that right now."

Muamba was still quiet, but the camaraderie that he sensed among the others was comforting to him.

As they continued flying, Gladding spoke quietly to Conteh."Give me the name of your village and family members, Punjaba. We'll send word to our contact in the States and see what they can do to protect them—even if they have to pull them out of there."

The tears in Conteh's eyes spoke louder than his quiet thank you.

Muamba spoke quietly with Taylor. As he did, he opened the small backpack he had taken with him from the Congo and removed a small object. It appeared to be an animal bone that had been hollowed out, then sealed, and carved until its exterior was smooth and polished.

In my country, we call things such as this *fetishes*. Please do not confuse what I am saying with your meaning of such a word. To us, a fetish is something that we believe possesses great power. This one I give you, it has within it the power to reveal much wisdom. I wish to give this to you, sir. I entrust it to your care. If I die, it speaks when I can no longer do so."

Taylor held the small object in his hand. It was in the range of six inches in length.

"Is this a good luck charm?"

"Oh no, sir. You must not say that. To refer to a fetish as charm that brings good luck would be to undermine its great power and purpose. Please, you must keep it with you at all times. Remember to recall its power in the event that something should happen to me.

Please, sir, can you promise me you will keep this with you at all time?"

Taylor nodded his assent and placed the object in his pocket.

A few more hours into the flight, a broadcast from Masters came through once again.

"Option is yours, gentlemen, but I can get you a military plane, pilot and co-pilot, and medical care you need on board. You'll have a stopover in the UK. It's a quiet air base, Royal Air Force Fairford. It's in Gloucestershire, England. They will fly you to the very upstate New York location that you originally flew out of. We have regained and secured control of that secret area where your plane was waiting. Choice is yours, but I just wanted to present this to you."

"Thanks, Phillip," Gladding responded. "We will discuss on our end and get back to you."

Gladding turned towards Taylor. "Kent, what say you?"

Taylor waited a bit before he spoke. "I am okay with a military jet, pilot, and co-pilot. Anything funny on their part and Punjaba and I will know it. We keep our weapons. They have none."

Blair was next. "Yes, okay by me. Too much for Kent and Punjaba to keep flying. A military jet will get us there faster and the pilot and co-pilot can share flight time."

Gladding turned towards Conteh. The African smiled as he responded.

"I thank you that you honor me with the opportunity to decide with you. I want you to know that I accept whatever choice you gentlemen choose to make. I pledge to remain alert and help in any manner that I can."

Brown was asleep again. Taylor spoke a bit quieter. "I trust Masters, but hell if I'm going to trust any others within that hornet nest of an agency. If it is okay with you, Jonas, I suggest that Masters have Sally waiting for us when we arrive. Katie might also be with her. We just do not mention who she is to Masters. Let them think she is a neighbor or friend."

"Fine with me," Jonas said. "What are you thinking, Kent. You want Sally to take us all somewhere?"

"No. I want her to get Willie out of there, away from these CIA folks, as quickly as possible. He's got a prison cell waiting for him or worse if these people renege on their word. Seems to me that's something they're pretty good at doing. Especially now, when they do not need Wilson Brown anymore."

Taylor then revealed his plan for Wilson Brown, Jr.

❖

Brown woke up another time or two before they reached UAE. Each time, Blair and Muamba checked his wounds. Blair also helped him sip some water. Of course, Willie had not eaten anything for hours, but that was also true for all of the others.

As always, even despite his injuries, Brown was in good spirits.

"Ya know, I could get use ta having ya feed me liquids like you done so far, Blair. Only my preference runs more ta things like tequila, vodka, or a good beer."

Blair laughed. "You get yourself healed up, my friend, and I'll get you all the tequila, vodka, or beer you would like."

"Careful, Jonas," Gladding said upon hearing the conversation. "The man's a U.S. Army Ranger. They have a saying, *Sua sponte,* which translates to "of their own accord."

"Yeah, that's right. It's one of our favorite Ranger quotes," Willie said.

"And?" Blair responded with a smile. "What's that got to do with promising a supply of liquor to our Ranger Brown."

"Well," Gladding responded, "Among other things, I think it may mean you can fill a Ranger with alcohol forever and they will still walk away from the bar *on their own accord.*"

Everyone laughed, including Wilson Brown—despite his pain.

Before long, Taylor began the plane's descent. Everyone breathed a collective sigh of relief as they began their approach to the Al Dhafra Air Base.

Chapter Thirty-Six

Where To?

Americans and nationals from the United Arab Emirates were both present to greet the plane when it arrived. Taylor radioed Masters before they even opened a door of the plane.

"Okay, Masters. We've decided we will leave this plane, but our weapons go with us. Need you to assure everyone that we mean no harm. Nobody gets hurt, provided we do not feel threatened."

Masters agreed and he actually connected them in to his communications with officials at Al Dhafra. The doctor, Abdul El-Assaad, who would tend to Willie Brown, was a UAE national who earned his degree from Weill Cornell Medical College in Qatar and did his residency in Chicago. The nurse practitioner, Lucy Niles, was an American from Des Moines.

As Taylor stated, they agreed to leave the plane bearing their weapons and remaining together. Masters had done a good job communicating with everyone at the Air Base, as they all remained calm during their encounter with the team that had just arrived.

Dr. El-Assaad examined and treated Brown. He personally came to speak with the team.

"The news I share with you, it is quite positive and, under present circumstances, rather surprising. The patient, he received four wounds associated with gunfire. I believe that is double the number that you originally believed.

Wounds on the upper right thigh and left shoulder pierced the skin and entered Mr. Brown's body. These two wounds resulted in the most significant amount of blood loss.

Speaking positively, both missiles also exited the body and did so without damaging any major organs or vessels. This man was, indeed, most fortunate.

If one is ever to be a victim of gunshot wounds, four gunshot wounds I might add, this would be the least damaging way to experience that."

The doctor smiled at his last remark indicating both his attempt at levity and his desire to put everyone at ease.

"Two additional gunshot wounds resulted from bullets grazing the skin, but not penetrating the body. One such wound is at the left side of his torso at a beltline level. The other at his left forearm. The two non-penetrating wounds merely required us to dress the wounds to protect against infection.

We have dressed and heavily bandaged the other two wounds and the patient is currently receiving IVs to restore nutrition, as well as to administer antibiotics."

Before anyone could ask the inevitable question, Dr. El-Assaad spoke again.

"It is my best medical advice that the patient remain in bed in a clinic, under medical care, receiving IVs, and resting as he is now. However, I am quite sure that is something that neither he nor you will choose to do."

Dr. El-Assaad waited for a moment. When no one responded, he spoke again.

"This patient can travel, if need be. I would suggest as little movement as possible and a regular changing of bandages. We will send along antibiotics and pain medicine for him. We would like to teach at least one person among you the best method of changing those bandages and dressing those wounds. I would specifically ask that you refrain from taking him away until after the current IVs being administered are completed."

They alternated keeping two men with Brown and two who took turns showering and changing clothes. Punjaba Conteh was also given an automatic weapon. John-Pierre volunteered to learn how to tend to Brown's wounds.

When it was time to eat, they all ate together in the same location as Willie Brown. Willie was given a lighter diet, but he did have his meal supplemented by each of the other men.

While they ate, they discussed their plans.

"I know we are all tired," Taylor said. "I suggest we rest in shifts on the flight back to the States.

"Sounds good," Gladding stated. "I'll be more than glad to take a first shift.

"I would remain awake with this man," Conteh said. "I can assist him in assuring that the flight remains on course."

"I like that idea," Blair said. "Kent and I can take the next shift. Means we will have one of our two most experienced pilots awake at all times.

"Hey, y'all forgettin' 'bout me?" Willie Brown said. "I got a few holes leakin', but I sure as hell ain't dead or nothin'."

"Hey!" Blair said, while working hard not to laugh. "Chill, man. You been laying around doing nothing for a while now, except stealing some of our food against the doctor's orders."

"The way I see it, Mr. Brown," Gladding said, "the last thing we need is you bleeding all over everybody because you refuse to remain still. You know if you give us a hard time, we could always leave you here."

"Whoa! Hold on now," Brown said in mock fear. "You seen that head nurse they got. Man, she's bigger'n me and could probably whup my butt without blinkin' an eye."

They all laughed together.

"We do need you to rest and get as much of your strength back as possible, Willie," Taylor said. "As we discussed, landing back on American soil will not be the end of the road for you."

Brown nodded. He knew that what Taylor was saying was right.

The United States had a KC-10A craft at Al Dhafra that could be used to transport the men back to the United States. Ultimately, a decision was made to continue using the C-37A, with a stopover at the RFA Fairford base mentioned by Masters. One American Air Force pilot would fly the plane. Taylor provided a backup, if needed. Conteh could also assist in an emergency.

Steve Grayson was the Air Force pilot who would fly them into the United Kingdom.

"Okay, gentlemen, next stop RFA Fairford in Gloucester, UK. We're talking about 3,030 nautical miles. We've got us a bird that can fly at about 600 miles per hour. So give me somewhere in the range of 5 hours and I'll have us touching down. My orders say that another US Air Force pilot will be waiting at Fairford. Some time for refueling, food and drinks, and a doctor will come on board to check out Mr. Brown. Then you'll be back in the air headed for the USA."

❖

Throughout the flights to the United Kingdom and on to the secret government location in New York, Wilson Brown, Jr. continued to improve quite rapidly. Muamba regularly changed Willie's bandages.

Jean-Pierre openly talked more about his experiences within the African gang. He did not discuss anything related to who the chief contacts were in the United States. Muamba was aware that the knowledge he had was his key bargaining point for himself and his family members to receive political asylum.

Phillip Masters called in several times. As promised, when the plane landed in upstate New York, Sally was waiting, along with Katie. The two women rushed into the arms of their husbands, greeted Bill, and were introduced to Jean-Pierre, Willie Brown, and Punjaba Conteh.

Conteh and Muamba assisted Brown in getting to his feet as Taylor turned his weapon towards Masters. "Sorry, Phillip, but we do not have any room for error here. Wilson is on a tight schedule, so we will need to say our goodbyes and get him quickly on the road."

The hugs with Brown were heartfelt and meaningful. . .

"I never forget how you help me," Muamba said.

"You good man. It is my honor to know you," Conteh stated.

"You take care of yourself, young man. Make sure you take the time to heal fully," Gladding said.

"Pleasure, Willie. Yes, take care of yourself, man," Blair said.

When Willie reached Taylor, he was, in turn, careful not to hug Taylor tightly and press against his ribs. "You never gonna be able ta know how much meetin' you has meant to me, Commander. Ain't possible no more for me to ever be with my daddy again, but bein' with you was like the next closest thing, ya know?"

"This man," Conteh interjected referring to Kent Taylor, "he is a father to you?" the African said naively.

The soft laughter that followed was shared by Taylor, Gladding, Blair, and Brown. "More'n a father. To me, he is a hero."

Brown turned to Taylor one last time, saluted, thanked him, and quickly turned away in the hope that no one would see the tears forming in his eyes.

Willie then entered the backseat of Sally's vehicle. Sally and Katie would bring him to a man, waiting in a van, with false documents that would get Wilson Brown, Jr. over the border into Canada and on to Nova Scotia. Taylor had spoken with Gladding earlier to set all of this up for Willie. Katie and Sally would then return to the Blair home and await the return of their husbands and Bill Gladding. They all watched as Sally drove away.

Another vehicle arrived on the scene. Two men stepped out of a black limo and presented their credentials as being associated with the Congolese (Dem) Representative Office in New York, The United States. These two men from the Permanent Mission at the United Nations Plaza, the Congolese embassy, would take custody of Punjaba Conteh and assist him in obtaining asylum in the U.S. There he would also await the arrival of certain family members from the Congo who were already under the protection of CIA operatives.

Jean-Pierre Muamba was taken into protective custody by the team Masters brought with him to greet the plane. He stood with Masters outside the vehicle that would transport them to the CIA Chester location. Phillip had notified Marissa Reynolds that Muamba was safely in the U.S. She was already aboard a plane on her way to the Chester headquarters with two others from the Counterterrorism Center of the CIA. They would begin questioning Muamba at that location.

The limo driver opened the door for Conteh to climb into the back seat. When he did, the driver, using the remote, locked the door. The two Congolese embassy reps were standing with Masters and Jean-Pierre.

The driver stood in place while anxiously looking around for someone or something that was not there. He waited, looked again. Then saw the two men from the embassy preparing to come to the limo.

"If you please, Jean-Pierre, do know that we are also ready at the embassy to assist you in any way at any time," one of the Congolese reps said to Muamba.

"We will maintain contact with these men," Masters said."When we have completed our sessions with you, they will be notified and can assist you as... "

The shots rang out and the two embassy men fell face forward turning the brown dirt beneath them red with blood. The next shot struck Jean-Pierre, he also fell to the ground. Masters attempted to grab Muamba and bring him to cover and was shot during his attempt to do so. He fell along with Jean-Pierre and found himself staring upwards into the gun of the chauffer-assassin. The killer began to pull the trigger when three shots struck him in the head, killing him instantly. Taylor, after firing the shots, ran over to Masters. Gladding and Blair joined him.

Chapter Thirty-Seven

Kill Order Fulfilled

Deep in the inner sanctums of the Pentagon, Sergeant Omar Santana jumped to his feet at the sound of his desk buzzer. U.S. General Victor"Bugler" Monroe used this as a signal when calling for his administrative aide.

Monroe was a West Point grad who worked his way up the ranks. He earned the nickname"Bugler" because he was a skilled trumpet player who performed in times past at some local clubs. He accepted the nickname often saying that"trumpeter" sounded much more awkward.

Bugler had recently reached the age of sixty. There were powers-that-be that made it clear to Monroe that he was not yet ready to retire. He had a full head of hair which he kept very short and gray. At 5'9". The man was not particularly tall, but his strong, solid frame help him give the appearance of being a larger man than he actually was.

"Yes, sir, you signaled for me?" Santana said while stepping in from the outer office. As he did, he saluted the general and remained at attention, his body stiff and unmoving.

The general pushed back in his chair, reached for his cigarettes and lighter, and violated the building no smoking rules before even looking at Santana. Monroe opened a side drawer of his desk, pulled out an ashtray, flicked his cigarette ashes, and then finally looked up at his administrative aide.

"At ease, Sergeant. What I want to know is where the hell is my report on today's activities?"

"We have not yet heard anything, sir. Not a word."

The general's face began to redden, his eyes protruded, and he dug his fingernails into the palms of his hands.

"What do you mean by that, Santana? Have you attempted to reach our man directly? When I sanction someone to do a job, I expect to hear back from him. And if we do not hear, I expect you to do your damn job and find out what in the hell is going on? Do you understand that soldier?"

"Y-yes, sir, I... "

The general's eyes narrowed. He leaned forward and glared. "I am not interested in any excuses, Sergeant, I want answers. And I want them now. Am I making myself clear? Do you understand me?"

"Yes, sir, I fully understand, sir."

"Great. Then get the hell out of my office and go get those answers."

Santana stood up, saluted the general, and waited for his final word.

Without even looking at his aide, General Monroe spoke.

"Dismissed."

On that Command, Sergeant Santana, whirled and exited the office.

❖

Taylor was the first to reach Masters and Muamba. Blair immediately went to the limo driver. Gladding went to the two embassy representatives.

"Got two dead ones over here," Gladding called out.

"Ditto on the limo driver," Blair said. He then went over to the limo to release Conteh from the back seat.

"Need a wagon right away for Masters," Taylor said, indicating that Phillip was alive and in need of medical assistance. Blair called for an ambulance as Gladding walked over to Taylor.

"We're going to need you to remain still Masters," Taylor said. "I have done what I could to help stem the bleeding, but you have lost quite a bit of blood. Don't want you to bleed out or go into shock."

"Thank you," Masters replied. His voice was weak, but he was fully conscious.

"Muamba?" Masters asked.

Taylor shook his head. "No, he didn't make it. Looks like whoever hired this guy got the results they wanted without having to fork over any additional funds to their hit man."

Gladding shook his head. "How in the hell did this happen?"

"Our only communication was directly to the embassy," Masters said, as he grimaced in pain.

"Okay, Masters. You just need to hold still now," Taylor said, as he tightened the tourniquet he had wrapped around Masters' right thigh.

"Ambulance should be here any minute, sir," Albert Sweitzer said, as he walked over towards Phillip Masters. Sweitzer made eye contact with Taylor, nodded his head in thanks, and looked out towards the entrance where the ambulance would arrive.

Blair spoke next. "Now isn't that something? We go all the way over to freakin' Africa to bring this guy back safely to the U.S. and he gets gunned down in our own backyard."

As Gladding, Taylor, and Blair stood by, Masters was placed into an ambulance and taken away to the nearest hospital.

When Muamba's body arrived at the morgue, the medical examiner quickly ran an electronic fingerprint exam. Muamba's prints were on file from the time of his involvement with the CIA. The ME also had Muamba's dental records.

The doctor stepped out of the examining room and took the call on his throwaway cell.

"Thanks, doc. Nicely done. Appreciate your quick work. Nice to know we have our guy."

"Dead people don't talk," the medical examiner replied.

"You checked the body? No implants? Nothing else that might contain hidden info?"

"Nothing," the doctor said. "Whatever this man learned in the final stages of his time over there in that God-forsaken country goes with him to the grave."

❖

Sergeant Omar Santana knocked on the door and waited for a response.

"Yeah, enter," the voice bellowed granting Santana the access he both needed and dreaded.

"I have the report, sir, that you requested."

"Okay, then sit down and tell me what I need to know, Sergeant. And do it now."

"Yes, sir. Well, sir, first and foremost, Jean-Pierre Muamba is dead. The report I received is that he died on the spot before he ever got into one of the cars that was to take him over to the CIA Chester location."

"And that is a definite?"

"Yes, sir. His death was confirmed by the ME who examined the body. Muamba was shot to death by the driver, our man, Peter Gent. I also have confirmation that both men from the Congo embassy were shot and killed. CIA agent Phillip Masters was wounded in the fracas."

"Where the hell were our other two men, Felix St. Claire and Carmine Alatamine? They were supposed to be on sight with Gent in order to take out Taylor, Gladding, Blair, and Brown. Where were they, Sergeant? I am not hearing anything about them?"

"They...uh...apparently they made a wrong turn somewhere and...th-they...they got lost, sir. They never showed up at the site."

The general said nothing as he sat, stared, and pondered all that he was now hearing.

"No others were wounded, sir.. The word I received is that Gent placed Conteh in the limo and, in doing so, had positioned himself to shoot Muamba. He executed the two men from the embassy and followed that with the execution of Jean-Pierre.

That is all that I know at this time, General Monroe."

Monroe was shaking inside. Yes, Muamba was dead, but several others were supposed to be killed also.

"Huh, oh yeah, good, Santana. Keep your ears open and let me know whenever you learn more."

After Santana left the room, General Monroe sat quietly at his desk reviewing all that he heard. Muamba was dead. Santana was right when he labeled that first and foremost. He did not care one bit about the driver having been killed. He would have preferred that Gent's body not be lying there to enable the CIA to make an identification, but there was always a chance the hit man could go down. He would also have preferred that Taylor,

215

Gladding, Blair, and Brown were also dead, but that could be accomplished in time. At least for now, the problem of Jean-Pierre Muamba and his ability to name key individuals involved in this plan was no longer an issue.

General Victor Monroe hoped that the others would be satisfied with this result. In truth, he knew that they would not be.

Chapter Thirty-Eight

Much Needed Closure

Phillip Masters was beaming from his wheelchair as he entered the large conference room along with Marisa Reynolds. "Please, I would like everyone here to know that I offered to wheel Director Masters into the room, but he absolutely would not hear of it. It is only as a gesture of peace that I yielded to his manly pride and chose to walk alongside his carriage."

Everyone, including Masters, laughed at Marisa's remarks. Within the past two weeks, Phillip had successfully undergone one minor surgical procedure and had two more on the agenda. He looked around the room and chuckled.

"I must say that I have never had this many distinguished guests at one meeting in Chester as we have here today." His eyes scanned the room again, acknowledging each person seated at the conference table. Bill Gladding, Kent and Katie Taylor, Jonas Blair and Sally Blair were seated along with Albert Sweitzer, Micah Jensen. An elderly man, unknown to all the others except Masters and Reynolds, was on a secured phone line connected to a speaker on the conference room table.

"I want to thank each of you for joining with us today. We asked you here to join with Marisa, me, and our two colleagues, Micah and Albert, because there is something we all are desperately need. It is a thing called closure."

"And before we take one step more, Phillip and I want to introduce to you the Deputy Director of The National Clandestine Service of the CIA, under which our unit the Counterterrorism Center operates. The director, whose name will remain anonymous, is joining us by way of a dedicated phone line.

"Sir, are you there?"

Thomas Westfield would remain an unnamed voice, with occasional reference to him as "T.J." Only Phillip Masters and Marisa Reynolds knew the man's identity. Nevertheless, the mere mention that the Deputy Director was on the phone generated quite a stir among all the others.

Westfield spoke next. "I am, indeed, honored to be here with you all today. I have endured a few recent physical maladies myself in recent times, making it impossible for me to travel to be with you in person today. Let the record show, however, that my current use of a cane is a far less dramatic means of transportation than that of Phillip Masters."

Westfield generated a laugh from all present, but the smiles were quickly erased as Westfield began to speak on a much more serious subject.

"I deeply regret that all of you, in various ways, were drawn into something at a time when our own federal agency is forced to hang its head in shame for so much that occurred under our own eyes."

Masters spoke next. "I am sure that you—Kent, Bill, and Jonas—quickly became aware that a faction within the CIA had gone rogue and were working on their own agenda."

"Yes," Kent responded. "Did not take us long to realize that they did not want Muamba to make it back to the States and reveal who was behind this plan to lure a terrorist attack in our country and generate a war in the Middle East."

"There's something I haven't figured out," Masters said. "At some point, you guys determined that the men traveling with you to the plane after your training at the Camp were rogue. How and when did you spot that?'

"It was Kent who first spotted it," Gladding said, "and keyed Jonas and me in on it."

Masters turned to Taylor. "But...how, Kent? What tipped you off? I mean when... "

"Shoes," Taylor said. "Benjie and shoes were all I needed."

Taylor's reference to Benjamin Marlowe startled Phillip.

"Benjie told me one day what a great guy you were to serve under. He laughed when he referred to one idiosyncrasy he associated with his beloved mentor."

"My insistence that all men under my command have clean and polished shoes or boots every day?"

"That's the one," Taylor said with a smile. "I noticed that the men who joined us on the way to the plane and the men at the front gate when we pulled out of the Camp had dirty shoes."

Masters smiled broadly. Thomas Westfield whistled quietly under his breath before speaking.

"I believe this man would be a good one to have in our agency," Westfield said with a big smile.

"Forget it, sir," Gladding said. "I did all but recruit the guy years ago and never got to first base."

Everyone laughed again.

Thomas Westfield's demeanor changed before he spoke again. His brow was furrowed, his eyes were initially down, and he fidgeted with a pen he pulled from his pocket. Despite the fact that no one else could actually see the man, he conveyed his feelings by way of his voice intonations and pauses when speaking.

"Before we go any further, I must call your attention to something of the utmost importance. In doing so, I will be completely honest with you all.

I am afraid that each of you are not yet out of the woods. You must be very careful and alert. Your lives are still in danger."

"And you are going to elaborate on that, I assume." Gladding interjected.

"Special Agent Gladding," Marisa Reynolds said to inform T.J. as to who was speaking on her end.

"Yes, indeed, I am, Agent Gladding. You all need to know that Muamba's death, though a terrible tragedy for all of us and his family, was not the end of the road in our ability to learn who is behind this conspiratorial threat to our national security.

Marisa, please."

Reynolds responded immediately to Westfield's cue that she elaborate.

"When our agents recovered Muamba's family members from Africa, we brought them safely into the United Kingdom. It was after Jean-Pierre was killed that we learned that he left a sealed envelope with his family members. He told them that if anything ever happened to him, they were to let us know that they had information from him. In return, they wanted further assurances of asylum and protection."

"Which we intended to provide in any event," Masters said.

"So, as a result, we have significant insight on who some of the players are here in the States. We are moving deliberately on this as we continue to shake the apples from the trees," Westfield added.

If you all had not gotten Muamba to leave Africa safely with you, his family would never have cooperated with our agents in also leaving their homeland. We owe you all a great deal for the significant inroads we are making. You have provided us with a much greater assurance that we will be able to prevent a major terrorist attack on our country designed to provoke us into a declaration of war.

We are making great strides, but we do not yet have a complete handle on everyone involved in this somewhat epical conspiracy. We also do not know when and where the attack will occur. Until we do, none of us are completely safe."

Katie smiled and took Kent's hand in hers. He looked at her and returned the smile. Without saying a word, her message was conveyed. As long as Katie had Kent in her life, she would always feel safe and secure—nothing else really mattered.

Jonas Blair spoke next.

"Muamba and his cohorts infiltrated an African gang that was involved in securing significant deposits of Coltan. How does that link him to knowledge of who is involved in the plan to stage a major terrorist threat here in the States? How would he learn names of Americans involved in this sordid affair?"

"Excellent question, Agent Blair," T.J. responded. "The African gang that Muamba, Zakuani, and Kyenge infiltrated was paramount not only because of their strength. They were working directly with both Middle Eastern and American contacts behind this master plan. Muamba was able to glean who was communicating with the African gang leaders."

"Remember," Marisa Reynolds interjected, "There is no honor among thieves. Time and again, the gang members received assurance that they were dealing with people who would guarantee that they get paid and assure that they would not suddenly find themselves under attack by U.S. Special Forces during the night, once the gang was no longer needed."

"Right," Masters said."Muamba and his two partners were familiar with many people of prominence here in America. This enabled them to catch on quickly whenever a name was mentioned on their end or a direct contact was made."

"Muamba told us on several occasions," Reynolds added, "that there was much distrust of Americans among the gang members. Their leaders had to constantly convince them that they were not being played by our country."

"We were told," Westfield added, "that there were actually a few visits by Americans to help stabilize the African gang members."

Gladding shook his head.

"And there is a significant piece to this puzzle that you all have not yet disclosed to us. Closure rises from the truth, not from leaving out key information."

Initially, no one said a word. Masters was flushed. Reynolds' lips were tight. An uncomfortable pall of silence hung over everyone.

Finally, T.J. spoke.

"You are also a very astute man, Special Agent Gladding. And you are very correct in what you have said. My response is both disturbing and deeply embarrassing.

Yes, someone of significant authority and influence within our own CIA has been secretly working with the conspirators. This person undoubtedly revealed that Muamba, Zakuani, and Kyenge were working with our agency. It goes without saying that this person greatly undermined our own efforts."

"And," Kent Taylor interrupted, "this person, this traitor, is still unkown to you."

Another hesitation, followed by another response from T.J.

"Yes, I am very sorry to admit. At the moment, we do not know who it is within our ranks who has betrayed their oath of loyalty to our nation."

Things remained somewhat stilted and awkward, until Sally Blair spoke, addressing her question to T.J.

"Sir, so much of what lured us into this whole thing started with that Bergam company and the death of Deputy Andy Maynard. What light, if any, can you all shed on that?"

"Right," Jonas joined in with his wife. "Andy was aware of some suspicious things going on within the Sheriff's Department. At the same time, he was questioning people at Bergam about the disappearance of one of their employees."

Masters spoke up next.

"Those are subjects that I will be able to provide some insight on."

Chapter Thirty-Nine

Where It All Began

All eyes were on Phillip Masters as he spoke next. They had the questions. Now they wanted some answers.

"Much of what I am going to share now has come from agencies such as the FBI and the NY State Bureau of Investigation and some others. Marisa discovered a great deal while I was in the hospital.

Remember, this is still an open case so things can change. As of now, we are confident that, despite Andy's awareness of some suspicious behavior involving the sheriff, a few deputies, and a local burglary ring, the responsibility for Deputy Maynard's death did not emanate from his workplace.

We believe that a man by the name of Carlton"Sonny" Goodall killed Deputy Andy Maynard.

Goodall and his thugs, along with two Bergam employees, gave the appearance that they were working on behalf of Bergam. They were not."

"Right," Marisa said."Goodall was seemingly fully committed to Bergam, along with his team. Two Bergam employees also did a great job concealing the fact that they, like Goodall, were actually on the payroll of the rogue CIA team."

Blair's mind immediately shot to Richard Kelser and Paul Martin when Marisa Reynolds finished her statement.

"The two Bergam employees were Frank Melvin and Howard Dandley."

"Whoa," Jonas blurted out."I had Kelser and Martin in mind."

"Kelser and Martin were dirty," Masters said,"but their only involvement was in the illegal black marketing of Coltan and money laundering. Those two greedy men never anticipated that Melvin and Dandley would actually kill an employee named Fred Wilpin."

223

"Yeah," Reynolds added"and we suspect that once that occurred, Kelser and Martin knew they were in deeper than they anticipated.

We also believe that Melvin and Dandley killed Louis Merkel, though we still have not found that man's body."

"Right," Masters added."We have gleaned quite a bit of insight from a Mary Sterling. She's the head honcho HR lady over at Bergam. She's willing to talk in exchange for some leniency.

That flash drive that Mr. Merkel brought to your office, Jonas, would provide evidence of a second set of books or records regarding Bergam shipments. Additionally, the encrypted files detail money laundering transactions conducted by Bergam. Nothing on that drive is contained in the official corporate financials—the records that the Board of Directors see. Louis Merkel was prepared to reveal that illegal 'off-the-record' shipments were coming in and going out. We also believe that Merkel knew what they were."

"And Sterling believes that Merkel suspected that Wilpin somehow became aware and was murdered," Marisa Reynolds said.

"Okay, listen to me," Masters said."When T.J. warns us of the possibility of danger, he speaks with authority. I mentioned to you that Richard Kelser and Paul Martin were only involved in making money through the illegal importation of Coltan and money laundering. Once they learned that Fred Wilpin died suspiciously in their factory, those two men were on the hook. They realized that there was far more behind the Coltan imports, but, even then, they did not know what it was. They only knew that it apparently was worth killing over."

Marisa Reynolds spoke next."Neither of those two men will ever stand trial nor be able to turn state's evidence on anything they were involved in."

"Uh oh, I have a feeling there's a lot more to this statement," Jonas Blair said.

"Yes," Marisa responded. "They were both indicted and awaiting trial. Richard Kelser died of an apparent heart attack. Paul Martin, also under some suspicious circumstances, committed suicide."

"We said all of that to say this," Masters stated. "We do not know where Sonny Goodall and his cronies or Frank Melvin, and Howard Dandley are right now. We have law enforcement officers searching for them. We believe we will find them, but so far we have not been able to do so."

"These men are dangerous," Marisa stated."We believe they are also responsible for the murders of Rosanna Castro, another Bergam employee, and Melissa Alvarez, a friend of Ms. Castro in Nashville, Tennessee."

"And you can throw in an old man who lived in an apartment next to Alvarez."

"Tennessee?" Jonas Blair stated.

"Right," Masters said."They tracked Castro to an old college roommate in Nashville, killed the roommate, then eventually caught up with Castro in Arkansas, where her body was discovered."

"And that's the point," Marisa Reynolds said."The tentacles of Sonny Goodall and the rogue group reach far and wide. These people are formidable."

"Also, I assume you are saying we will be playing a game of 'who do you trust?' when it comes to a group like this one."

"Commander Taylor," Marisa said aloud, confirming the speaker.

"I should like to respond to that, Commander," T.J. said."You are precisely correct, I am sorry to say. There's a damnable web of conspiracy out there. As I speak, our agents, along with the FBI and others are getting a much greater grasp on things. But until we do, all of us must be aware that we cannot be sure with whom we might be dealing at any given time."

"Well, that's certainly one hell of a comforting thought," Gladding said. "With all due respect, Director, we have every right to expect that you and your people will keep us informed. Your agency falls apart and fails to see the cancer growing under their own nose. As a result, our lives are on the line and we may never know who and what may be moving against us."

An awkward silence draped itself over the room and extended to the Deputy Director of the NCS.

"I wish that I could say that you are wrong, Agent Gladding," Westfield stated, indicating that he now recognized the former agent's voice,"but you are spot on. They hunted down a human resources employee to the foothills of the Ozarks where they killed her and left her body lying in the woods.

Yes, I am afraid that you all have inadvertently stepped into a worst-case scenario. We will do all we can to help protect you."

Taylor kept his thoughts to himself.

You mean like the way you protected Jean-Pierre Muamba?

❖

General Victor "Bugler" Monroe sat with his feet up on his desk and poured himself another shot of Jim Beam. The impromptu meeting this evening would include FBI Associate Deputy Director Parker Nolan, U.S. Congress Homeland Security Chairperson Rep. Margaret Russkind, former Congressman George Emerson, and U.S. Senator Thurman Gibbons.

Two quick knocks and Sergeant Omar Santana, the general's chief aide, stuck his head in the door before entering the office.

"Is there anything else you require, sir, before the others arrive?"

"Uh...no, Santana...uh...thank you."

Santana saluted and prepared to leave when the general called out to him.

"Sergeant ...uh...Omar...I would like for you to join us at the meeting."

The general had a grim twist to his mouth. His breathing was slow and even. His arms and legs were weighed down in a heaviness that seemed to permeate his entire body. The man was in no way looking forward to tonight's meeting.

Santana had never seen the general look so tired and subdued. He was also sure that Monroe had never called him by his first name before now. He quickly nodded and responded.

"Yes, sir, I will attend and remain available to you throughout the time."

"Thank you, Sergeant."

Hmm. Another first. The man just thanked me.

Everyone arrived within three or so minutes of each other. As they took a seat in the conference room attached to the general's office, there was no chatter at all. Senator Thurman Gibbons was the first to speak.

"Why don't we begin by having you provide us with the details surrounding Jean-Pierre Muamba's arrival back in the States, Victor."

"Yes, well as you all know, a team sent over to the Congo was successful in getting Muamba out of Africa... "

"Whoa, stop right there, Victor." Margaret Russkind stared at the general with cold, hard eyes, flexing her fingers before crossing her arms and leaning back in her chair. "You want to tell us how some makeshift team was able to get through every effort we made to assure that Jean-Pierre *never* got out of Africa alive? Would you care to explain that, General?"

General Monroe sat rubbing his hands together, swallowing excessively, and shifting in his seat in an effort to get comfortable. Sergeant Santana had never seen his boss so unsettled. He almost felt a sense of sympathy for the guy.

"Well...ahem...we...uh...knew that we had two men, namely Gladding and Blair who were well-trained by the FBI," Monroe began. His gaze momentarily fell upon Parker Nolan at the mention of the FBI. "But we believe it was Taylor, a former Navy SEAL who masterminded the mission to get Muamba out. Perhaps we underestimated this Taylor... "

"Underestimated?" Russkind's face was reddened, as she stood up from her seat and pointed fingers directly at Monroe. "We've got so much at stake and you talk about underestimating? Seriously?"

Senator Gibbons turned to Margaret Russkind.

"Please, Margaret, let's stay calm. Please sit down. Your anger and frustration is certainly warranted, but, if we intend to resolve some things here, we are going to need to remain calm and focused."

Russkind sat down. She feared no one, but she did respect Gibbons.

"Taylor, Gladding, and Blair were three of the men who were over in Zambia when I was there. How do I know these men cannot identify me? Those men were supposed to be dead already." George Emerson stated.

"We don't know for sure what those three men picked up on. We only know that they are to be taken seriously," Senator Gibbons said.

"And another point, Monroe," the Senator continued, "you used Peter Gent to take out Muamba. Gent ended up getting himself killed. How long before Masters and his people find out that there's a link between Gent and several of us here today?"

General Monroe spoke again.

"Once again, from what we have learned, it was the quick action of this Taylor that resulted in Gent getting killed. We... "

"And where the hell is this Wilson Brown, Jr.? Word I got is that he disappeared and no one knows where the hell that guy is. You have no freakin' idea, do you General?" Margaret Russkind said.

"Brown, Taylor, Gladding, Blair, even the pilot Conteh, they all know far too much to be out there on the loose," Parker Nolan stated.

"Okay, okay, okay, here's the deal from my perspective," Senator Gibbons stated. "We've still got Sonny Goodall and his team, plus Melvin and Dandley. These guys can get the job done.

Parker, thanks to you we already have a key FBI agent keeping us in the loop."

"Yes," Parker responded, "Marshall Price. And, of course, we have others within my agency who are fully aligned with us."

"With that in mind," Gibbons continued, "what say you take the lead, Director Nolan, and we eliminate Taylor and his cohorts now before they cause any more trouble for us?"

Nolan leaned back in his chair, placed his hands behind his head, and nodded.

"You're on. Before we meet again, Taylor, Gladding, Blair and all others will be dead. Consider it done."

Chapter Forty

It's in the Wind

Later that evening, Kent, Katie, Jonas, Sally, and Bill Gladding were all seated together at the Blair house following an evening meal.

"Steaks were great, Bill," Sally stated in reference to the fact that Gladding had grilled them outside.

"I'll say," Katie added. "Have you ever considered working as a short order chef now that you retired from the Bureau?"

Gladding laughed.

"Sal and I appreciate your concern for us, but we feel a bit guilty having you all stay here, away from your own homes," Jonas said.

"Listen, Jonas, we are all in this thing together," Taylor began. "No matter where any of us are, we can be targeted."

"Exactly," Gladding said. "At least for the moment, we are all together and able to watch each other's back. We will give it some time before we decide what our next step should be."

"I honestly hate the fact that we have no idea how and when someone might strike at us," Sally said. "As far as having you all here with us, I actually love it. Please do not ever think otherwise."

"Okay," Gladding said. "Guess I can have my furniture shipped in."

Everyone laughed. "And permanently move away from that little granddaughter of yours?" Jonas said. "Can't see that happening."

"By the way, have I shown you her latest fifty pictures," Gladding said.

These five individuals were doing a great job staying loose at a time when there was a threat hanging over their heads. They planned to confer again with Masters next week. Until then, they would simply remain vigilant.

"Hey, any chance we all might want to venture into Comstock one night this week. Eat at a local restaurant and walk the shops a bit," Taylor asked.

"Sounds good to me," Sally responded. "We'll just need a little advance time to arrange for a babysitter, with Danny and Jen gone."

Taylor froze for a moment. The reference to Danny and Jennifer Roberts, neighbors to the Blairs and Jonas' sister, immediately caught his attention.

"You say the Roberts are gone?"

"On vacation. Packed up the kids and headed out yesterday afternoon. They're headed to some friends who have a beach house on the North Carolina Outer Banks," Jonas added.

"I have heard those beaches are beautiful," Katie said with a smile.

Kent Taylor was not smiling at all. His face was ashen, his brow wrinkled, and his lips pressed flat.

"Okay, listen up," Taylor began. "We only have a few hours before it gets dark. Here's what we need to do."

❖

Their black SUV was parked around the far side of the house where it would not be readily seen should anyone enter the property. No big deal. They had arrived just as darkness had moved in. Since that time, no one had come anywhere near the place. Why should they? The Roberts family drove away yesterday afternoon and the house was tucked at the very end of an isolated country road.

It worked out well that the Roberts family had left to go on vacation. The original plan had been to kill all of them. Not that any of the current occupants would have a problem with that. But the Roberts were not the intended targets, so their absence just made the ultimate job a bit easier.

Tony Giovanni and Michael "Mugsy" Portello were the two individuals currently on guard—Tony at the front of the house, Mugsy at the rear. Giovanni looked more like a handsome entertainer who might be found singing in a small club somewhere. He had been working for Goodall for nearly three years now and had proven his mettle with the boss man.

"Waste of damn time," Mugsy muttered to himself. "Sittin' out here in the damn woods. Ain't nobody gonna show up here, 'cept maybe a few raccoons."

Mugsy was particularly irked because while on duty he could not smoke. Also, he wanted to be in on the poker game inside. Sonny Goodall, Frank Melvin, Howard Dandley, and Edward "Bullmoose" Hendrix were engaged in the game, seated at a table in the kitchen. Between Sonny Goodall's cigarillos and Howard Dandley's cigarettes, the room had a gray cloud cover and bore a strong need for some fresh air.

"Ain't gonna be long now," Sonny said, as he clenched the small cigar between his lips. "Taking these people out at night should be a freakin' piece of cake."

"I don't know, Sonny," Bullmoose said, "word is these guys are pretty tough, ya know?"

Goodall stood up. His face appeared to be as red as his curly hair. He leaned close to Hendix' face. "Tough? You wanna talk tough? You wanna know who is formidable 'round here? Wanna know who ya don't mess with?"

Hendrix shrunk back. Then Goodall roared with laughter.

"Hahaha. Ah'm, jus' havin' me some fun with ya, big guy. But there's a whole lotta truth in those words you jus' heard. Keep that in mind at all times. Ain't never a good idea to mess with Sonny Goodall."

"I'm really lookin' forward to tonight," Dandley said. "A lot of the crap that's happened over time started with that damn attorney Blair stickin' his nose in stuff where it don't belong."

"I warned him," Goodall said with a grin. "Oh yeah. I sure did. Can't say Sonny Goodall didn't give the guy a chance."

Sonny's eyes narrowed sharply. He removed the smoking cigar from his mouth and pointed with it as a tool of emphasis. "You don't want to find yourself ignorin' Sonny Goodall. No, siree. Not a wise choice or good place to ever find yourself.

Frank Melvin peered over the top of his cards and caught Goodall's attention.

"Hey, Sonny, let me ask you a question here, eh?"

Goodall nodded. He hated interruptions when playing cards, but Melvin was a good man to have on the team.

"So, you ain't particularly said nothin' about that baby they got in there. Watcha got in mind when it comes to that kid?" Melvin asked.

"Ah, yes. Thank you, Mr. Francis Melvin for your astute observation. Well there is no question that the subject of what to do with an innocent little one raises, shall we say, some very serious discussion centered upon humanitarian concerns. I mean this type of thing is exacerbated when you consider that we will be killing all the adults. Let's not be so crude that we lose sight of all human kindness here."

Sonny had everyone's attention now.

"It would be cruel, absolutely barbarian, to leave a child alone in this world with no one to care for it and nurture it to adulthood. No child should ever be subjected to a life devoid of love and caring, eh?"

Sonny's eyes narrowed to slits. He shrugged his shoulders and stuck both arms out with the palms on his hands facing upwards.

"As you can see, that leaves us with no alternative other than to make sure that baby is dead before we ever leave that house."

The silence that ensued was quickly followed by a cackling laughter from the red headed leader of the pack. Then Sonny Goodall was the first to speak.

"Okay, I'll raise you fifty," Goodall said, as he tossed a few additional chips into the pot.

❖

It surprised Katie as she glanced at her husband. She remembered when she first met Kent and sensed from time-to-time that there was something dangerous about him. From then, even to now, she never felt personally threatened or uncomfortable with Kent.

As she stared at him now, his face was expressionless. His eyes seemed flat, dull, and uninviting. He did not reject Katie in any way when she stood next to him and took his hand in hers. Yet, she sensed that he was somewhere far away. Katie was unsure where that somewhere might be, but she was sure of one thing. Wherever Kent was, she wanted to be there with him—always and forever.

Chapter Forty-One

The Secret of a Web

The two of them sat alone in a quiet corner at a café on 2nd Street NE in the nation's capital. Their conversation was soft, but somewhat awkward and strained.

"I really like this place," Senator Gibbons remarked. "As I am sure you noticed from the menu earlier, they specialize in Italian cuisine, but have an excellent cross-section of other foods. Quite frankly, no matter what I have ordered, I have never been disappointed.

You have been very quiet this evening, Margaret. I certainly hope that you enjoyed your meal."

The Congresswoman was in a foul mood and not at all interested in discussing food or any other trite matter.

"Yes, the meal was very good, Thurman. Thank you."

"Talk to me, Margaret. I consider you to be a friend, as well as a colleague."

Russkind opened her mouth twice to begin speaking, then thought better of it and said nothing.

"We are in this thing together, Margaret. Your opinion matters to me. It matters a great deal."

The Congresswoman leaned forward, tightened her hands into fists, then spoke.

"I don't know how you can act so calm and reserved after learning what that incompetent buffoon who wears a couple of general stars did. Why in the world would any of us ever entrust anything to that man?"

"Now, now, Margaret. Take a breath and chill out. Muamba is dead for starters. You must not forget that was our primary goal here."

Thurman Gibbons had agreed to take on the responsibility of calming Russkind down after the meeting they attended with General Victor Monroe.

Others, including those who were in attendance and those who were not, expressed a growing concern about the Congresswoman from Pennsylvania.

"The man is a freaking incompetent clown," Russkind continued. "I wouldn't trust that pompous ass with my laundry, let alone handling the elimination of key people who might otherwise help put all of us behind bars."

Gibbons placed his palm up facing Russkind."Stop, Margaret. No one is going to end up behind bars. You need to get a grip on yourself and your emotions before you end up making some costly mistake."

A vein in the Congresswoman's neck began to pulsate, as she slammed her fist down on the table causing glasses and dishes to rattle and a few heads to momentarily turn in the direction of these two diners.

"How dare you sit there and talk about me making costly mistakes, Thurman. We've got an over-inflated idiot who could not work his way out of a paper bag handling things that are way the hell over his head. He uses Peter Gent, Peter-Freakin'-Gent, on a highly-sensitive and extremely important mission. Gent is a known felon. Gent could be linked to several of us on the team and Victor Monroe sends him as a hit man. Dear God!"

Senator Gibbons was not about to try and convince Russkind that her points were not well taken. He felt the same anger and disgust that she did, but he knew that they all had to remain calm and keep their heads clear.

"You will get no argument from me, Margaret, on what you are saying. All I am trying to say is that we must remain calm.

We've got things under control now. Monroe is through. Believe me, he may be stupid about a whole lot of things. But I assure you there is something about which he is not stupid. The man knows that his days are numbered.

Right now, we have FBI Associate Deputy Director Parker Nolan handling things. I've known Parker for many years. He's a good man. Whatever he touches turns to gold. Okay? I do not need to tell you that this is not Nolan's first rodeo. He will take care of things.

Meanwhile, we all need to remain calm, lay low, and let things play out as they will."

The server came to their table with the NV Damilano Barolo Chinato that Gibbons had ordered as a digestif.

The server poured two glasses of the wine, left the bottle, bowed, and walked away.

"Before we drink this wine, I want to take just a moment to share a little something with you, Margaret.

When a spider weaves its web, most every strand is sticky in a way that any insect that touches it becomes permanently affixed to it and a victim of the spider. When constructing the web, the spider leaves just a few strands that are not covered with the sticky substance. But only the spider knows which strands it is safe to walk upon.

We have also built a web, Margaret. It extends far and wide. Our web will entangle anyone who comes near to it. Only we know the strands that will capture someone and the few that will not. Trust the web, Margaret. It is a very powerful tool that we built to capture whomever we desire."

Margaret Russkind smiled for the first time that evening.

"Thank you, Thurman. You have, indeed, helped me."

"Now, back to the wine I have chosen for this evening's dessert wine.

It features some wonderful aromatics like rhubarb, orange peel, and cardamom."

Senator Gibbons extended his glass towards Representative Russkind, inviting her to join in a toast. She did so.

"To success for us and for our common cause both now and in the months and years to come. God bless America," Gibbons said.

❖

"Excuse me, sir," Sergeant Santana said upon entering the general's office. "Will there be anything else that you require, sir, before I depart for the evening?"

Santana was unable to detect the smell of alcohol from where he stood facing General Monroe.

"Huh? What's that? Uh... no... Sergeant...nothing. No."

"Well then, I bid you a pleasant evening, sir."

"Huh? Yeah, okay then."

The general then proceeded to clean out his fingernails with a toothpick, which in turn caused Santana to feel at liberty to turn and leave the room.

When the general finally realized that he was alone, he reached back into his desk drawer, took out the whiskey, and continued to drink straight from the bottle. He then slowly rose from his chair, walked over to the window, and closed all the blinds.

As he returned to his desk chair, his mind reverted back to the meeting that had been conducted in his conference room. In his mind's eye he could see the face of Margaret Russkind spewing out her hatred towards him. He pictured each person in his mind.

Former Congressman George Emerson—the man hates me. Always has. Senator Thurman Gibbons—much too slick to display his animosity, but there is not a chance in hell that man would ever stand up for me. Parker Nolan—that man would drive a stake into my heart and never think twice about it.

Monroe continued to picture one person after another. In each instance, he came up with the same response. He could think of no one, absolutely no one, who would ever defend him.

These people do not believe in carrying excess baggage. If they find someone who knows too much is no longer needed, they eliminate that person—for the sake of country and liberty. Hah! God bless America, eh?

I am a walking dead man. Either I find a way to spill the beans to someone and get myself protected or I wait for the day when unexpectedly, it is my turn to leave this earth. Hahaha! Funny. Leave this earth.

Monroe continued to drink from the bottle until all the liquor was gone. Then he held the bottle by its neck and flung it across the room where it shattered against the wall. His words were slurred. He lifted up the silver name plate that was on his desk and stared at his own image.

"Once a bottle like that is empty, why it is of no use to anyone anymore.

Hey, that sounds like…hahaha…that sounds like me.

You are the empty bottle, General Monroe. You, sir, are of no use to anyone.

Watcha gonna do, Monroe? You gonna wait around until they fling you against the wall and shatter you? Huh? Is that what you gonna do, General? Huh?

Nah. I got me at least some dignity left, and no one is going to take it from me. Hahaha. Especially that wicked witch Margaret Russkind, or Mr. Senator slick Gibbons or that vampire Nolan. No siree. Aint givin' none of you guys the pleasure."

Then just as suddenly, General Victor"Bugler" Monroe's laughter turned to tears, as he dropped the name plate, wailed and cried.

He reached back into another desk drawer and removed the small Chief's Special .38 caliber pistol that had been nestled there.

Monroe placed the barrel of the gun against his right temple and fired.

Senator Gibbons had been right about one thing. Monroe certainly knew that his days were numbered.

Chapter Forty-Two

First Assault

Six black shadows, further darkened by the black clothes they were wearing, moved furtively towards the home of Jonas and Sally Blair. Two entered the property through the woods and passed behind the lone shed that stood further back from the road. Two others walked on the shale road, passed the house and pond, and walked in front of the woods on the side of the house.

The final two came through the woods and crossed over the property in front of the shed. The shadows stood and waited. They could see the image of the tallest shadow who raised his hand to signal a command to move forward.

In accordance with the plan, Howard Dandley and Frank Melvin were the first to enter the house from a side door leading into the kitchen. Sonny laughed when he first revealed his strategy.

"Better watch out for those two," Sonny said with a big grin and chuckle. "They may end up killing everyone themselves and leaving no one for the rest of us."

Sonny and Mugsy would enter through the front door. Tony Giovanni and Bullmoose Hendrix waited for a moment before following Dandley and Melvin at the side door.

All three bedrooms were on the second floor. Sonny and Mugsy would proceed to the master bedroom and, to the disappointment of Howard Dandley, kill Jonas and Sally Blair and their infant son. Dandley's disappointment in not getting to kill Jonas Blair was somewhat offset by the fact that he and Melvin would enter the bedroom that housed Kent Taylor and his wife and execute them.

"I ain't never got to kill a Navy SEAL," Dandley said when the strategy for the night was revealed.

"What's the diff, man," Frank Melvin said at the time. "We got a job to do, we do it."

Dandley shrugged.

"I don't know, it just sounds real nice on a Resumé, man."

Tony Giovanni and Hendrix were assigned to kill Bill Gladding.

In each instance, whenever the kills were made, that team was to move out to the hallway and be poised to assist any other team that might need assistance.

"Tony and Bullmoose will cut the phone wires and knock out the power," Sonny said with a smile.

Howard Dandley hinted at something that was pressing on his mind.

"You know, Sonny, from what little we seen, I wish I had me some time to enjoy Taylor's wife before we kill her, ya know?"

Sonny addressed everyone.

"There will be no, and I mean no, extra-curricular activities this time. Sorry fellas, maybe on our next gig, but the money and importance of this job is way beyond doing anything that increases the odds of something going wrong. *Comprende?* Capisce?"

"Yeah, yeah, yeah, Sonny, we understand. We get it," Mugsy Portello responded.

Sonny smiled. If Michael"Mugsy" Portello understood, then everyone else surely did also.

Giving credit where credit is due, Mugsy moved silently as he and Sonny approached the master bedroom. Not a single word passed between them.

Sonny stood quietly for a moment as he stared at the two figures lying in the bed and the baby in a nearby crib. A sense of elation raced through Sonny's body. This would be even easier than he thought.

Sonny moved over towards one side of the bed. Mugsy was on the other side. Sonny pulled out a knife and Portello did the same. The plan to use knives to slit the throats of their victims assured that no one throughout the house would awake to the sounds of gunfire and create havoc among the teams.

Sonny raised his free hand and used fingers to count along with Mugsy. One finger-two-three, go! They pulled back the covers simultaneously and thrust the knives forward. Both men recoiled in shock at what they saw.

❖

"Who in the hell gave them the word to go ahead?"

His normally calm and controlled disposition was replaced with a reddened face, wide protruding eyes, flaring nostrils, and a fist that repeatedly pounded against his desk.

The two FBI agents, Cayden Verne and Isaiah Harrington, had never seen their boss, Associate Deputy Director Parker Nolan, this angry.

Cayden Verne finally dared to speak.

"We think it was Agent Marshall Price, sir, who convinced Sonny Goodall and the others to move in and kill everyone while they were together in the Blair's home."

"Marshall Price," Nolan uttered the name with disgust. "Who the hell is Price working for? Who authorized him to do anything?"

"If I may say, sir," Isaiah Harrington said,"Price has been running free out there in the country with nothing but his hat size increasing on a daily basis. The guy's been unchecked for too long."

Parker Nolan said nothing in response. Harrington's assessment was probably true and, now he had far more important things on his mind.

Goodall and his thugs were making a move against everyone currently in the Blair home and it was too late now for Nolan to either stop it or add to it to assure success.

Parker spoke at a more normal decibel level. Verne and Harrington were not at issue here. They were simply the messengers who had learned about all of this and immediately contacted Nolan. Despite the lateness of the hour, he asked these two agents to meet him in his office.

"In my opinion, you do not proceed against men like Taylor, Gladding, and Blair by storming the house in which they are residing. These guys are too smart for that. There's no telling what they may already have set up to thwart an attack like that.

Gladding's reputation as an FBI special agent is legendary. Blair proved to be brilliant in the relatively short time he carried a Bureau badge. And Taylor? From what I have gleaned, the guy is off the freaking charts.

You know if Sonny and his people fail, it will only serve to make our job that much more difficult."

❖

"What the…? Mugsy, go check on the others and see what we've got here."

It did not take long at all for the message to become clear. Pillows, extra blankets, a baby doll, all served to make it look like each of the bedrooms was occupied.

Suddenly the cat became the mouse. The predator became the prey. Seven men were trapped in the Blair house with no idea where their targeted individuals were.

Sonny Goodall took a moment to acknowledge FBI Agent Marshall Price who had tagged along at the last minute.

"Couldn't just sit this one out, eh Price?"

"Well you know me, Sonny. I like to be in the midst of the action—or should I say in this case, the non-action?"

Sonny did not waste his time acknowledging Marshall Price's attempt at sarcastic humor.

"All right, guys, search everywhere. Closets, maybe an attic. Whatever. If they ain't in this here house, I'm bettin' they're still somewhere in the neighborhood, eh? Hahaha. In the neighborhood. I like that.

We still got seven to their three, maybe four with Blair's lady toting. Plus, they got to protect an infant. All's we got to protect is ourselves, eh? Yeah, protect our own hides. Hahaha"

Goodall laughed at his own comment. All the others, with the exception of Marshall Price, laughed along with him.

"First, we search this place thoroughly. Then we take turns exiting through the front and side doors. People inside the house cover for those exiting. Those already out find a spot where you can protect yourself and still cover for others. Everybody got it?"

Marshall Price spoke up.

"If these guys are outside, Sonny, we've got to figure that by now, they have already positioned themselves to pick us off when we step out a door.

I, for one, don't like them odds at all. No, not one bit."

"What do you want us to do, Mr. FBI-Man? Maybe we should raise up a white flag and beg these guys not to hurt us if we surrender nicely?

Hey now, there's a great idea, eh? Hahaha. Raise up a white flag... Hahaha."

Price was not amused.

"Well, Sonny, we could do nothing. We got the house. We got the food and shelter. They got nothing. We wait them out. We keep an eye on the outside during the night. Plus, once it is daylight, we will be in position to spot them and pick them off whenever they move or show their faces. Hell, get the power back on and we even got television in here."

Goodall shook his head, causing his red curly hair to fly about.

"Nah, we ain't waitin' for nobody. These people got cell phones. They'll end up calling for help and then we will really be penned in. We gonna get 'em now and make 'em pay. We can't even be sure they ain't already called for reinforcements."

It did not take any time at all to determine that they were not in the house. Sonny got everyone set at the doors.

Marshall Price was right. Taylor and the others had hidden away in the shed, after making it look like they were all asleep in their respective bedrooms. Now Gladding had the side door covered. Jonas was poised to cover the front door. Sally would remain in the shed with a weapon to protect herself, Katie, and the baby. Kent Taylor would roam free, joining in or improvising as needed.

Taylor expected that the occupants would likely attempt to run from the house at the same time, in the hope that Taylor, Gladding, and Blair would not be capable of handling seven men. He was right—at least about the tactic of running at the same time.

Taylor first heard shots coming from the side kitchen door, followed almost immediately by shots at the front door. He ran to the front, saw one individual fall to the ground, while another charged out and a third ran in a different direction. Taylor took the third shadow, while Blair shot the second one. Meanwhile, Taylor ran to the side door. As best he could tell two men were down already, when two more ran out.

As he did with Blair, Taylor shot the second man, while Gladding shot the first.

"I'll check them out, Kent," Gladding shouted. "You go and make sure Jonas is okay?"

"Roger that," Taylor responded as he ran towards the front.

Taylor understood Gladding's concern. It was dark. It was not easy to determine whether someone was dead or merely wounded. A wounded victim could still be extremely dangerous.

When Kent arrived at the front, Blair was carefully checking the second person lying at the front. Taylor approached the third man and immediately learned that he was alive. His gun was on the grass within reach. Taylor immediately kicked it away. Using a small flashlight, he shined the light on the victim's face, but did not know who he was. Jonas Blair walked over.

"Well, if it isn't my old and dear friend, Marshall Price."

Jonas then turned to Kent Taylor.

"Price is an FBI agent, Kent. I knew this piece of garbage was dirty from the first time I met him. He dropped in on me a few times and delivered some subtle threats."

"Well, Agent Price," looks like you won't be making threats against anyone again—unless they do things like that in hell," Taylor said.

"D-don't...uh...be...s-so sm-smug, Taylor. Th-they got s-some n-nice surprises [cough, cough]...lined up for you...and y-your little..."

Taylor reached down, grabbed the man by the back of his neck, and pulled his head upwards.

"My little what, Price. My little..."

Taylor shook the man and asked again. "My little what?"

Jonas moved closer and placed a hand on Taylor's right shoulder.

"Too late, Kent. He's gone."

Taylor let the man's head drop to the ground. Kent then stared out into the night, hoping against all hope that this criminal hiding behind an FBI badge was not saying what Taylor thought.

Jonas Blair ran over and joined Gladding. The two men proceeded in confirming whether the men laying on the ground were dead.

Gladding cautiously approached another victim who was lying face down on the ground. As he did, the tall redhead whirled over from his stomach and pointed his weapon at Gladding. Bill was too quick for a weakened Sonny Goodall. Instead of shooting the man, Gladding actually kicked the weapon out of Sonny's hands and stood over him. As he did, he stood there and stared down at the man as blood poured freely from Goodall's body.

Just then Jonas Blair ran over and stood next to Gladding.

"That how you killed Andy Maynard, Goodall?" Jonas shouted. "Laid there on the road and shot him when he came over to assist who he thought was a man in trouble?"

"W-watched th-that deputy die l-like a ro-...road k-kill...ha...[cough]..."

Gladding put his arm on Blair's shoulder in a gesture to both calm and comfort him.

"Hey, Jonas. Anybody ever notice that this guy looks like that hamburger chain clown?

Nah! Come to think of it, that clown is a whole lot better lookin'."

Blood evidencing internal bleeding dripped from Sonny's mouth as he began to speak.

"Y-you...think it's over, Fed-men? It's not...not over for you... and y-your friends. Not for ...any of...Hah! ...It...it's...just begin...beginning. Ha...ha. Just beginning... "

"Well at least it's over for you, Goodall," Gladding said."And that's a really pleasant thought."

Blood poured out more freely now from Goodall's mouth.

"Y-yup...but...it's been...one...hell of...a ride. Ha... "

Goodall's body convulsed, then stopped moving entirely.

Based upon everything Gladding had heard and Jonas knew about Sonny Goodall, they both simply stood over the man's body and smiled.

Chapter Forty-Three

Clean Up

Bill Gladding had already made the call to Phillip Masters, rather than the sheriff's department, before the attack occurred. Despite the lateness of the hour, Phillip Masters showed up in his wheelchair along with Marisa Reynolds and an entire team. Gladding called again while Masters and the others were already on the way and Masters then called for a team of crime scene investigators to come to the Blair property. As that team went to work on the crime scene, Marisa and Phillip took the reports from each of the five who had prevailed on this night.

Masters kept shaking his head and muttering the same words. "Incredible. Unbelievable."

"And not a scratch on any of you," Marisa exclaimed.

Kent Taylor made every attempt to be polite and attentive to all who were around, but his mind reverted to a moment in time. The words uttered by FBI Agent Marshall Price continued to resound throughout Taylor's thoughts.

Price referred to some nice surprises for Kent Taylor and his little... something. Price died before he could complete his sentence, but the possibilities of what the man was about to utter troubled Taylor deeply.

❖

As they sat in the kitchen drinking coffee and hot tea, they had time to discuss all that had transpired. Sally turned to Kent.

"Katie is the only one among us who has not had any formal training to handle situations such as we experienced tonight. And she was as calm as any trained agent I have ever seen. She was absolutely awesome."

Katie blushed a bit, smiled, and responded.

"Aw thanks, Sally, but I was tucked away in the midst of four of the very best people you would ever want to be with in an emergency situation like this one. It was easy being relaxed."

The smiles across the room were broad.

"Okay, everything happened so fast, but, Kent, what tipped you off to the fact that we were likely to be attacked tonight?"

"Well, Jonas, you and Sally really set things in motion when you mentioned that the Roberts family had left for vacation in the afternoon. Yet, sometime after dark, I heard a vehicle slowly creeping past the house on the road and headed to the Roberts' place. At the time, there was no reason for me to think that it was anyone other than the your neighbors."

"How is it," Sally asked, "that you heard that while none of us did?"

"I think my husband has some kind of super hearing," Katie said with a big smile.

"Yeah, I've noticed that before with Kent," Jonas said.

"Bats have great hearing," Gladding said. "He could be Batman."

Everyone laughed.

"What about Superman?" Jonas asked. "Doesn't he have super hearing/"

"Wait. Dogs have great hearing and, as I recall," Gladding said, "Superman has a dog."

In the midst of all the laughter, Kent gave his explanation.

"You all probably did hear that vehicle or, at the very least, could have heard it. Only difference is I was trained over the years to focus my hearing or sight on even random occurrences. Kind of like hitting a button to tune in when something, even something seemingly unimportant, is occurring."

Jonas made eye contact with everyone in the room before resting his eyes on Kent. "You saved our lives, Kent. Once again, we owe our lives to you. I want to be sure to thank you."

Everyone began to express thanks, until Kent raised his palm.

"Listen, I appreciate what you are saying. I honestly do, but please let's not give too much credit to one man when what we just saw tonight was the concerted effort of everyone here working together as we did. Having you all in my life and Katie's means more than we can express.

❖

"Damn it all. Damn it. All of them. They're all dead? You're talking about Goodall, Melvin, Dandley?"

"Yes, sir, plus Tony Giovanni, Michael "Mugsy" Portello, and Edward "Bullmoose" Hendrix."

The conversation between FBI agents Cayden Verne, Isaiah Harrington, and Associate Deputy Director Parker Nolan was fraught with tension and angry interruptions by Nolan.

Neither Verne nor Harrington wanted to be the one to pass on an additional news item, but they both knew that the man had to be told. God forbid he ever found out later that they were aware and had not said anything.

"There's something additional, sir...that we...uh...that you need to know... " Cayden Verne began.

"Sir," Harrington interrupted, "we were told that Special Agent Marshall Price was there also."

"What? Price too?"

"Yes sir," Verne said, "and Price is listed among the casualties."

Nolan stood up from his desk chair and walked over towards the room windows. He stared out silently, his feet planted in a wide stance, his shoulders pushed back. His posture strong and true. After a few minutes, he turned back towards Verne and Harrington.

"Gentleman, we have much to do and, believe me, we will get things done successfully. You know that we have somewhere in the range of four hundred Bureau agents already working with us. We know we can increase that number into the thousands, but we are not yet ready to do so. We do not want things to get too cumbersome to control at this stage. We have members of the United States Executive Branch, Congress, military personnel, the CIA and others all aligned in this effort to restore dignity to our nation and a shield of liberty to our allies. We cannot fail and we will not.

I am going to need your help in aligning some of our FBI and military team members. We need to clean up the mess left behind by Goodall, Price, and the others. Let's not underestimate Taylor, Gladding, and Blair. When you talk about people like Goodall, Melvin, Dandley, Giovanni, Portello, Hendrix, and Price, you're talking about a pretty formidable group. And they are all now dead.

We need to take care of this quickly and...Yes?"

Wendy James, Nolan's administrative assistant poked her head in the room.

"Please forgive the interruption, sir, but I have a rather urgent call for you that I need to bring to your attention now."

"Thank you, Wendy," Nolan said, as Verne and Harrington scurried out of the room.

Wendy looked over at Parker Nolan. "Vice President Harrison Michaels is on the secured line, sir."

Nolan reached into a drawer at the base of his desk. He pulled out a phone that had been hidden there, punched in a code, provided a verbal password, and waited.

"Parker, how are you, my friend?"

"Mr. Vice President. Good to hear your voice, sir."

"Hey, heard we had a bit of an incident last night in upstate New York. Sounds like it was a rough night, eh?"

"Yes, Mr. Vice President. An unauthorized attack, apparently prompted by an Agent Marshall Price of my Agency, sir. And, yes, it obviously did not go very well."

"All of our guys were killed, I am told?"

"Yes, sir, that would be seven of our men numbered as casualties last night. They were the only casualties, I might add."

"Hmm, impressive. Too bad those guys doing the killing are not on our team, eh?"

Nolan was at a loss for words at this point. He was sure, however, that the Vice President of the United States would not call him simply to regurgitate news that he already knew. He was also sure that if he had been written off by the Veep, he would not be receiving a phone call. He would be taken out by someone, somewhere, when he least expected it.

"Listen, Parker, I did not call to talk about last night's unfortunate malady. I was wondering what your breakfast schedule is like tomorrow. I would like to meet with you, Senator Gibbons, and George Emerson.

To be perfectly frank, Parker, forget about last night. A mere bump in the road. Besides, I know you neither authorized it, were aware of it, nor have had time to establish your own strategy.

Listen, things are proceeding very well for that much-needed incident on our turf. What we have all been fighting for is coming closer to fruition. Time for us to chat a bit more. An attack such as the one coming will have our nation ready and raring to strike back at full force.

I fully concur with the recent consensus that you are the man who should lead the effort to remove these few key individuals whom we have identified as needing to be removed.

As we both know, Parker, Commander Taylor is on that list for a number of reasons. But I am pleased to say that we have acquired what we need to bring that man to his knees."

"You're not telling me that you have finally located them after all these years?"

"Indeed, I am, Director. It will all be over soon."

"Tomorrow at 8:00 a.m. at *The George* over on East Street Northwest?"

"Know the place, Mr. Vice President."

"Great. See you then."

❖

The home on Bayou Black in Houma, Louisiana was situated on twelve acres of land. A long, winding driveway bordered on both sides with Southern Live Oak trees decorated with draping epiphyte Spanish moss plants led to the home of the Bennett family. The house itself boasted five bedrooms, three baths, a large living/den, and a commercial kitchen. A screen and sunroom overlooked a large pond that fronted a wooded area. A Gambrel or Dutch

Style Barn stood off to the side of the pond. A small boathouse was attached to the dock itself.

Despite the beauty and grandeur of the home, Marcia Bennett had never fully embraced it over the past fifteen years. It was the home Lisa Grazier and her husband, Arthur, acquired with the help of a federal agent named Gladding. That was when the Graziers became Bennetts and were forced to live under a form of a Witness Protection Plan. Their niece, Emily Taylor, became a part of their family bearing the fictitious name of Rosemary Chambers.

"It's a beautiful home in a beautiful setting," Lisa once told her husband, "but I keep thinking that we acquired it through the blood of my dad, mom, sis, and nephew."

I would give up the home, the blue heron, the white egrets, and all that we have in return for my mom, dad, sister and her husband, and my nephew.

Those thoughts prevailed in Lisa's mind, despite the fact that they could never be fulfilled.

Chapter Forty-Four

Until It's Over

The mood at the Blair home had radically changed. Bill Gladding was back at the grill working on what he referred to as his "mouth-watering-ribs." Kent and Katie were taking daily walks in the woods. Jonas was seated with a beer in one hand, a cane pole in the other, fishing for catfish in the pond that fronted his property.

Jonas, Bill Gladding, and Kent Taylor remained in daily contact with Phillip Masters. Although everyone remained cautious and alert, the deaths of Sonny Goodall and others eliminated a major threat that would otherwise be looming against these five adults currently together at the home of Jonas and Sally Blair.

Katie also spent a great deal of time with Sally, as they bonded together in a growing friendship. At times when he was alone, Kent Taylor reflected upon the fact that, even though it was a temporary situation, he was suddenly immersed in a great deal of normalcy.

Who would ever believe that several former federal agents, a former widow, and a revenant soldier would forge a friendship. Hardly seems possible.

After a train of thoughts such as this, Kent would find himself basking in a warm inner feeling with a smile covering his face. At the same time, he was saddened by the fact that the time had arrived for this group to disband and return to their everyday lives.

Katie and Sally insisted that they would cook a special meal on the last day that they would all be together. They made a list of food items they would need and the three men drove into Halston to shop for groceries.

When the men returned, everyone sat together in the living room.

"Okay, I am going to be honest with everyone," Bill Gladding said. "It may well be that Kent, Jonas, and I were the strangest trio to ever be shopping for groceries together."

"Well, especially," Jonas began,"when we all learned that former Special Agent Gladding may be a barbecue expert but the man does not know a carrot from a stalk of celery."

"We found him with his head in the freezer moving cartons of ice cream around looking for eggs," Kent Taylor said.

Laughter filled the room.

Despite the fact that they were fifteen days away from Thanksgiving, that was the theme that Sally and Katie chose for their special meal.

Early that next morning, the women prepared and stuffed a turkey and placed it in the oven. Their list of items included mashed potatoes, cauliflower, green beans, and peas in brown gravy. They baked several pies, ice cream was in the freezer, and there was plenty of beer on hand.

"I don't know what to make of the threats we heard from Price and Goodall before they died," Taylor said in a conversation with Gladding and Blair.

"Problem is," Bill Gladding said, "we cannot sit around for the rest of our lives waiting for another attack to occur."

"I agree," Blair added. "Plus if Masters and Reynolds are right that these people are behind some master plot concerning a terrorist strike on American soil that spurs us into a major war, you'd think that's where their attention would be directed."

"But you're both forgetting one thing. We already know too much, as do people like Masters and Reynolds. The people behind all of this have already shown that they are very willing to kill to assure things go their way. We can't afford to ever lose sight of that."

❖

He pushed back in his chair, reached down to his lap for the fine cloth napkin, and folded it before placing it on the table. "I always enjoy the food here," Vice President Harrison Michaels said."Simply superb."

The waiter approached the table adding coffee to the cups. Harrison put his palm up. "No more for me, thank you. And please be sure to pass my compliments on to the chef and kitchen staff." The waiter nodded, assured Michaels that he would relay the message, and left the area.

"So," the Vice President continued, making contact in turn with Parker Nolan and George Emerson, "you concur with the plan?"

"Yes, sir," Parker said."That is my highest recommendation."

"We all know that Muamba left a list of names in an envelope with his family. Not exactly what we were hoping to see happen, but, by no means the end of the road for us. I already learned that the list was incomplete.

What we need to stop is anyone learning the names that were not on Muamba's list."

Parker Nolan responded.

"I admit I am a bit lost here, sir. Muamba is dead. The two men who worked undercover with him in Africa are dead. There is no one left to be talking."

The Vice President smiled, before speaking again.

"We have learned that the envelope and information that Muamba entrusted to his family, was based upon information that Muamba and his partners had some time earlier. Our sources tell us that it was afterwards that Muamba and the two others learned of the additional key names and where and when the terrorist act will occur.

Muamba was no fool. He revealed nothing while still alive and only left messages to be revealed in the case of his death."

"The plane!" Parker exclaimed."Taylor, Blair, Gladding, maybe even Brown..."

"Exactly," Vice President Harris exclaimed."Well done, Parker. You are spot on, my friend. We have to assume that somehow Muamba would convey additional information to one or more of the men on that plane—even if they are unaware that they have it."

"Therefore... " George Emerson began.

"Therefore, all of those men must die," Parker Nolan interjected.

"Ah! You catch on very quickly, my friend," the Vice President said as he turned to Nolan and smiled.

"What I would like you to do, Parker, is forego any plans or focus you may have had with regard to Mr. and Mrs. Blair and William Gladding. We will apprise you of what we have contrived for the elimination of these folks."

Harrison Michaels then revealed the plan that had been formulated to kill Taylor.

"We got us a couple of top-notch experts who will be a welcoming committee for the Commander and his lovely wife.

"I like it," Parker Nolan said.

"Then what we are now asking you to do is formulate a backup plan, a Plan-B in the unlikely event that Taylor and his lovely bride somehow escape our clutches. As such, we will provide you with the new information that we now have le with regard to Taylor's long-lost family members.

As I alluded to a moment ago, I do not honestly believe that there is much of a chance that a back-up plan will be needed. What we are asking you to do may be an exercise in futility. Nevertheless, it never hurts to cover all bases now does it?

To further assist you, Nolan, we will provide you with the new information that we now have regarding the whereabouts of Taylor's long-lost family members."

"I will get on this right away, Mr. Vice President."

"Very good," Michaels said. "We have got to get this done quickly and efficiently. At the same time, we will be eliminating a few others."

Harrison Michaels leaned forward and spoke in a much stronger tone to Parker Nolan.

"I am sure that I do not have to tell you, Director, that if Taylor somehow slips out of our net, whatever you come up with must absolutely work. You should proceed as if your life depends upon that."

The cold chill that raced through Parker Nolan's body generated a lack of composure uncommon to the federal agent.

Nolan fully understood the words uttered by Harrison Michaels.

He breathed in for a moment to further assure that his response would not reveal the torrent of fear that raced through his body.

"Yes, sir. I understand fully."

The Vice President placed his hands up behind his head, leaned back in his chair, and smiled.

"Splendid. Good to see things falling in place so very proficiently."

❖

Bill Gladding was the first to leave. Although he had a great deal of latitude in the security consulting work he provided, his primary West Coast client had a major function coming up.

"I called in already and set up a strategy meeting later this week," Gladding said. "That will give us plenty of time to do what we need to assure that all is secure."

"Seems to me," Jonas said, "you should just hire Kent to set himself up on the building roof and you would be all set."

Everyone laughed.

The men rode together to bring Bill to the airport. Katie stayed back with Sally and the baby. The 'goodbyes' were filled with smiles and some tears shed by Katie and Sally.

As they drove to the airport, the men discussed the need to maintain awareness and stay in contact with each other.

"Okay," Gladding said, "so let's come up with a plan to remain in contact with each other."

"Right," Taylor said. "Let's schedule a call, say every three days."

"I'll schedule that," Jonas said, "and send invites to everyone's phone."

"I think we should include Katie and Sally. Let them see that we are being proactive," Kent added.

"Yes, I agree," Gladding said.

Kent and Katie had already scheduled a flight out on the following day. Katie's rental car was still on the property, so she and Kent would drive themselves to the airport.

Gladding rested all the way to California and felt a peace as he reflected upon the friendship he shared with the Jonas and Sally and Kent and Katie. He slept well that night in his own bed.

It was not until the following morning that his peace was replaced by fear and a sense of urgency.

Chapter Forty-Five

Too Close to Home

He never paid much attention to his landline phone. His cable company threw it in at a nominal cost to him when he bundled his wireless internet and television coverage. Occasionally, he would have a voicemail from a telemarketer, despite the fact that he registered the line on the"Do Not Call" list. This time the message left on his phone was very different. It shocked him.

Gladding felt a surge of fear racing through his body. He carefully examined his phone. He always took preventive steps to safeguard himself, but he had been unexpectedly away for a considerable amount of time. His blood ran cold. His heartbeat started racing. He stared off into nothingness as he contemplated his next moves. He decided to leave the bugging device in place. No sense tipping anyone off that he was aware.

There was no time to do a search for any other bugs. He was certain there were more. He dressed quickly, grabbed his cell phone, walked over towards the window before leaving his fourth floor condo to call Kent from a safer location. A button from his shirt broke loose and tumbled to the floor.

The shot came without warning, easily penetrating and shattering the glass as the bullet sure and true struck his head, its intended target.

❖

Phillip Masters was in his Chester office when he saw two dark figures outside the window of the house that served as a temporary main office for his CIA team. In recent times, he had posted two men to stand guard outside the building. He immediately tried to reach them by radio. No answer. From his office, Phillip could not see their cold lifeless bodies lying on the ground.

He quickly called Marisa Reynolds who was stationed in the office next to his, but she did not answer her phone.

Masters grabbed his handgun, rose from his desk, and moved slowly towards the door. There were times when he left the door open. This time, he had left the door closed. He moved closer and froze in place. He could hear footsteps approaching. He knew they had come for him.

Masters waited, standing quietly to the side of the door. It would open towards him, which meant he would not immediately be able to see his attackers. At the same time, they would be incapable of seeing him. His heart thumped as he saw the door knob turning ever so slowly. He worked very hard to control his breathing and offer no advantage whatsoever to his deadly visitors. The door was beginning to open, the crack widening in tiny, quiet increments. Just then, Masters heard someone coming from a short distance down the hall. He heard two sounds, much like a staple gun, in quick succession. Shots with a silencer. He was sure of it.

Masters had seen two figures, so he anticipated that more than one person would be coming for him. The door continued to open—more rapidly now. Perhaps the stalkers did not want to chance another inadvertent visitor coming down the hall.

Suddenly, the door opened with a burst, the men entered the office and were quickly surprised to find that Phillip was not at his desk. They felt the bulk of his body behind the open door. Masters spun quickly and shot the front man. He charged the second man and as he did, Masters' weapon fell to the floor. Phillip quickly grabbed the man's outstretched hand that held his weapon and the two men were now grappling in a life and death struggle. They twisted, turned, kicked, and attempted head butts until they both fell to the floor. In that moment, Masters lost control of the man's hand. The man was now kneeling on top of Masters when he raised his weapon to Phillip's face. The shot resounded, blood splattered everywhere, and death was immediate.

Masters lifted his head and saw Albert Sweitzer with his weapon in hand standing over the dead assailant. Their eyes met, as Phillip Masters mouthed a thank you.

"Marisa... " he whispered, as Albert pulled Masters to his feet and they raced to the office next door.

Vincent J. Sachar

Reynolds was lying on the carpeted floor next to her desk chair. The carpet was soaked in rich red blood. The bullet had entered her forehead. Marisa likely never knew what occurred.

Masters knelt down, felt for a pulse that he knew would never be there, and looked back up at Sweitzer.

"She's gone. I heard shots. Someone else..."

Sweitzer started to speak, then turned his head away from Masters to avoid having him see the tears that were forming.

"It's...uh...M-Micah, sir. They killed him."

Micah Jensen had entered the hallway leading to Master's office when he was shot and killed.

Sweitzer took charge alerting everyone in the building who immediately went into emergency mode. The building and grounds were searched. No other assailants, no other dead bodies, other than the two guards, were found.

Masters grabbed his cell phone and continued to call, but his calls went unanswered.

"Get me a small team," Masters said to Sweitzer. "We need to head out immediately."

Within minutes Masters, along with another vehicle and a total of six men raced ahead towards the home of Jonas and Sally Blair.

❖

Kent and Katie arrived at the airport, prepared to return the rental car.

"Everything okay with your vehicle, Mrs. Nova?"

Kent wondered whether the man at the agency was beaming as part of his customer service image or the joy he felt when he tallied up the totals for renting a vehicle over such an extended length of time.

As they headed towards the gate, Katie wrapped her arm within her husband's and smiled. She was happy to be headed back home, happy to be with Kent, happy that they had survived this latest ordeal.

Kent gave some thought to making a quick call to Gladding and inquiring about his trip back home, but decided against it. He was aware

258

that Bill had a full agenda in preparing security on behalf of a major client. Taylor mentioned that to Katie.

"Bill's probably sitting in some sleek office with his feet up on a desk spewing out his strategy to a top-paying client. By now, these folks likely believe he hung the moon. And you know they may not be too far off on that."

Both Kent and Katie smiled.

As they sat together at the gate, Katie, once again observed the opposing characteristics at play in her husband. Kent was relaxed, cheerful, and friendly. He was also extremely vigilant, aware of everything around them, always on full alert. It was as if not one little thing occurred without passing through some type of inner filter that Kent possessed.

After a while, Katie got up to use the women's restroom. Very shortly afterwards, Kent also got up. He walked towards the men's room. It was located down a hallway off the main floor. He walked towards it, then kept going. He turned into a small alcove where supplies were kept and waited there. He did not have to wait long before the man who had followed him arrived. Kent grabbed his shirt and threw him against the wall. The man was tough. He bounced right back and spun with a high kick. Kent's spin enabled him to take it on his left shoulder, rather than on his face. The man immediately charged Kent and had both hands around Taylor's neck. He was strong and his squeeze was powerful enough to block Kent's breathing. Taylor kicked the man in the groin, then head butted him, and watched him fall. He bent down, grabbed the man with his left hand and pummeled his face with four hard punches with his right hand. Then he let go of the man and let his head strike the floor.

When Katie entered the restroom, it was empty. She stepped inside a booth. When she opened the door to come back out and walk up to the lavatory, there was a woman standing there applying lipstick at the mirror. Katie smiled and reached for the soap. Suddenly, the woman's scarf was tightly around Katie's neck. Katie was struggling to breathe.

Tighter, tighter still, all of Katie's attempts to twist, turn, and somehow free herself from this death trap were unsuccessful. She could feel the lightheadedness moving in. She knew that she would be unconscious very soon. Death would certainly follow. Her eyes began to close. It was as if her body was telling her that it was time to let go and accept death.

Then just as suddenly, she was in someone's arms. The scarf was gone. The woman who attacked her was lifeless on the floor. Her eyes were open and she could see the face of the person who saved her. At first, Kent's eyes were cold, lifeless, and frightening. As he gazed upon Katie, his eyes softened and he smiled.

Chapter Forty-Six

Something's Happening

It had been a while since Sally visited her husband at his law office. With all that had happened lately, Jonas and Sally decided to take steps to bring some normalcy back into their lives.

Sally made arrangements with a photographer to have some pics taken of baby Taylor. Afterwards, she and the baby would visit with Jonas and take time to have lunch together.

The drive to Comstock would normally take about thirty minutes. Sally strapped the baby into a car seat and headed out. She was traveling on the two-lane stretch between Halston and Comstock when a black Ford F-450 XLT came racing up from behind her.

"What's your hurry?" Sally mumbled to herself.

Fortunately, there was no traffic coming from the other direction, so this lumbering four-wheeled monster would be able to pass Sally quite easily. Sally slowed down a bit to assure that the truck would pass and leave her behind even more readily.

The Ford truck moved over to the opposite lane, began to pass Sally, then stayed even with her, side-by-side. Sally slowed down even more, but the truck did the same in order to keep its place at her side. Sally hit the horn and screamed aloud for the truck to pass her, but it did not. She knew that if a vehicle approached from the opposite direction both she and the truck would be in big trouble.

It was on a stretch where there was no shoulder to her right. A deep ditch that served as a water runoff ran parallel with the road. The trucker made his move. He began to veer closer and closer to Sally until he was scraping the side of her vehicle. She hit her brakes in an effort to get away from the other vehicle. The slower speed at which she was now traveling enabled the truck to veer at an angle in front of her. Sally skidded, swerved, and lost control of the vehicle.

The truck sped off and drove away with the driver staring in his rear view mirror to watch Sally's vehicle rolling over again and again into, out of, and back into the ditch. At last glance, the truck driver could see Sally's vehicle lying in a mangled heap upside down.

❖

Kent carried Katie to the door of the restroom. "If I hold you real tight, Katie, can you walk?"

Katie's blue eyes were locked into Kent's. She could hardly speak. Her breathing was quickly restoring itself, as her body cried out for the oxygen it so badly needed. She smiled, nodded her head, and mouthed a silent "yes."

Kent held Katie tightly and headed for a car rental stand. He threw money down quickly, gave them his license, proof of insurance, and expressed his urgency. The young man at the rental car station had his name "Simon" displayed on his nametag.

"Hey, Simon. I need to know if you can help me in a special way." Kent placed a $100 bill on the counter. "My wife and I need a vehicle quickly. We just learned that her father suffered a major stroke. He has been rushed by ambulance to an upstate hospital about an hour from here. As you can see, she is not feeling well. Appreciate anything you can do to expedite things for us."

The clerk flew into fast mode, aided by the large tip Kent gave him. He started listing the available vehicles when Kent interrupted him.

"Uh, thanks buddy, but find something with four wheels, a running motor, a steering wheel, brakes, and we are set to go."

Simon proudly upgraded them to a better vehicle. Kent thanked the young man.

"All the cars are out there on the lot," Simon said as he handed keys to Kent and a decal indicating their assigned vehicle was in space A-16. During this time, Katie had been seated in a chair near the counter. She had a very light scarf in her purse that she used to cover the abrasions on her neck.

Kent reached out to Katie. She was increasingly better, but Kent held her tightly anyway. As they began walking towards the rental car lot, Kent spotted a tall man with sallow skin and jet black hair that was in serious need of a brush or comb. He was the man who had been seated at the gate with the woman that attacked Katie. Now, there was another man with him. He was shorter, stocky, with a shaved head.

Kent spoke quietly in Katie's ear. "We've got two men interested in us, Katie. I expect we will encounter them out in the lot. We will head for the car. I want you to take the keys. When you get to the car, get in the driver's seat. Do you feel well enough to do that?"

"I do, Kent. What about you?"

"I will be fine, darling. I just need to know you are in the car, safe, doors locked. If either man comes near a car window, you take off. Drive away. You can come back and pick me up afterwards."

Kent leaned over, kissed Katie on the cheek, and smiled.

An attendant was standing at the entrance to the lot. Kent showed him the A-16 decal.

"That'd be Aisle A, sir, which is that one right over there. Number 16 is down a ways. Numbers are very easy to see..."

Kent handed the man a $50 bill. "Listen, friend, can you help us, please. My wife is not feeling very well and we just realized we left a small bag back at the gate. Could you take her to the car while I run in real quick?"

"Glad ta help, sir, but you don't have to tip me like this. I'm more'n glad ta help, sir..."

Kent smiled.

"The tip is not only a thanks to you, but evidence of how important this woman is to me."

The young man escorted Katie to the car. Kent turned and spotted the two men walking towards him. He looked over at them. Then his eyes narrowed, tightened, and appeared cold and hard. He neither waited nor turned away. He walked directly to them.

The tall man pulled out a knife. Kent stared back at him, smiled, and moved closer.

"This will be your only warning, gentlemen. Move on and you will not get hurt," Kent said.

The man lunged, Kent moved aside, reached forward, grabbed his arm in a locked position and snapped the bones. The man screeched and cried out in pain. Kent threw a punch striking the man in his throat. The big guy replaced his screeching with choking and gasping.

"Everything in me wants to kill you for that attack on my wife, but I'll just take it out on your friend here."

The stocky man wanted no part of Taylor now, but he quickly learned that the choice was no longer his. The man was frightened, but took a chance and charged Kent hoping to use his burly body to slam and pin Kent against a nearby vehicle. Taylor stood, widened his stance, welcoming the man to come at him. When the man was close enough to actually grab Kent's body, Taylor spun until he was standing beside the man. Taylor grabbed him, and threw him into that same vehicle. Before the man even had a moment to adjust, Taylor was on him with a series of punches so fast, and so many that they seemed endless. By the time Kent stepped back to let the man's unconscious body hit the ground, Taylor's opponent was not recognizable as the same man. His nose was broken, his eyes were already swelling to a close, his lips protruded like the beak of a mallard, and several ribs were broken.

Kent quickly jogged over to the car that Katie was in and ran into the young man who escorted her.

"You got a couple of guys back there who obviously got into a fight," Kent said. "From the looks of them, neither one looks like a winner. Anyway, just wanted to be sure you know."

Taylor hopped into the passenger seat letting Katie drive since she had everything all set. Besides, he had seen Katie drive many times. The woman was not afraid to let things fly.

Chapter Forty-Seven

Game On

Katie drove, while Kent continually tried to reach Jonas, Sally, and Bill Gladding. All the calls went unanswered. +

"I'm getting nowhere, Katie. Can't reach anyone. I'm going to call Phillip Masters."

Before Kent could do so, his phone rang. It was Masters.

"Taylor? Phillip Masters here."

"I was just getting set to call you."

"You and your wife okay? Where are you?'

"We left the airport after both Katie and I were attacked. They're on the loose, Masters. I have been trying to reach Jonas and Bill, but no one answers. We're in a rental headed back to the Blair's place.

Masters was silent for a moment as he made an effort to collect his thoughts. Taylor was right. They were coming after everyone. They obviously intended to clean house on this day. It also was an indication that major events on their agenda could not be very far behind.

"They...uh...they hit us here too, Commander. Marisa Reynolds is dead, along with one of my key men. They would have been successful in killing me were it not for another one of my men."

It was Taylor's turn to be quiet for a moment.

"I am sure that explains why we are not hearing from Gladding, Jonas, and Sally," Kent said.

"Listen, Taylor, I'm on my way to the Blair's now with a team. I'll meet you there."

"Roger that, Masters...Hey, Phillip? ...watch your back going in there. Watch for a vehicle tucked away somewhere before you turn into the road fronting that property. They'll follow you in and you'll be trapped front and back. They could also come at you from the property at the very end of that road."

"Thanks, Kent. Will do."

❖

Jonas was on his way back to the office from the courthouse. The men waiting for him were angry when they arrived only to learn he was not there. They had gone to great pains to verify his schedule and he was supposed to be in the office this morning, especially with his wife and baby coming into town. But Judge Lambert called Jonas and asked if he could come by to the judge's chambers for a quick discussion along with opposing counsel on a case that was pending trial in a few days. Jonas was now on his way back.

He noted that both Kent and Phillip Masters called him while he was in the judge's chambers. He would call them back after he checked in with Sally.

His call to Sally when straight to voicemail. He considered that she was on the phone herself and might be attempting to call him. He smiled at the thought of having Sally and baby Taylor with him in Comstock for a portion of the day.

At first, when the two men arrived at the office, Claire Reeves thought they might be federal agents, unwilling to reveal much to her. It did not take long for Claire's keen instincts to kick in and her discomfort with these men to soar. Under the pretense that she was headed to the copy room, she went into Jonas' office with her cell phone and attempted to call Blair to warn him. Suddenly, one of the two men was standing behind her. He reached around her from behind, slit her throat, and left her to bleed out on the carpeted floor.

Jonas had a designated parking spot on the side of his building. He once tried to convince Claire to park there but she refused. "The attorney who heads up this office needs to be parked there," she told him. "If I ever get a law degree and become a partner here, we can have this discussion again," she said, as they both laughed.

On this day, Jonas had pre-arranged for Sally to use that spot when she arrived with the baby. When he could not find a spot across the street where

Claire parked, he drove around towards the back, found a spot on a side street, and approached his building from the rear. That door was pretty much only used by the young man who cleaned the office to dump the trash bags in a dumpster that was back there.

As he walked along the alley behind his office building, he saw a man standing in his private office. He carefully grabbed hold of a ledge, pulled his body up, and peered as best he could into the room. He only had a few moments before his arms would tire and he would need to drop back to the ground. A few moments was all he needed. He spotted Claire lying on the carpet in a pool of blood. He knew immediately that she was dead.

Jonas started calling Sally on her cell.

❖

"Still no answer?" Katie asked after Kent attempted to reach Bill Gladding for the umpteenth time. "You know he could be tied up in a meeting and not able to answer his phone."

"I thought of that, Katie, but knowing Bill, once he would see that I have called this many times, he would know there is some type of emergency on our end. He'd excuse himself and call back."

Katie knew that her husband was right. They had every reason to believe that something was wrong, seriously wrong on Gladding's end. She found herself wishing that no one had ever left and they were all still huddled together in the Blair home.

"I am sorry, Katie, sorry that once again I have managed to drag you into this mess. I am sorry you ever had to get mixed up with a guy who... "

"Kent Taylor, don't you ever talk to me like that again. I don't ever want to hear that kind of talk from you."

Katie's face reddened. Her hands tightened on the steering wheel and were moving in a jerking motion, causing the car to swerve.

"No one, Kent, not you, not anyone ever dragged me into anything.

Besides, I was not dragged at all. I chose to be with you. I wanted then and want now to always be with you.

I love you, Kent, with all my heart. And I appreciate your protectiveness.

But I am *not* some super fragile piece of china that will shatter at the slightest jarring. And I do *not* want to be treated that way.

You remember... you remember what I said to you, Kent, when you found me...uh... waiting on the porch in St. John?

Do you remember that I told you it was *my* right, *my* choice to determine whether *my* life would be better off with or without you? Do you remember that? And do you remember that I said I wanted to be with you?

It was *my* choice, Kent. I came looking for you. I knew then that I wanted to spend the rest of my life with you.

That has not changed at all, Kent, and I am convinced it never will. Not now. Not tomorrow. Never."

Taylor sat quietly for a moment, then smiled and responded.

"Are you finished, Katie?"

"Well, I suppose I am," she said, as she fought to suppress a smile.

"Because I want you to know that I hear you loud and clear. Thank you. And by the way, I love you so incredibly much, you know?"

Katie did know and soon they were both laughing aloud.

❖

Masters reached Jonas even before Taylor did. Jonas had already received a call from emergency personnel and was on his way to the hospital where Sally and the baby had been transported by ambulance. At this point, no one could shed any light on their condition. Blair told Masters what he had seen at his office.

"Jonas, let's leave that alone for now. From what you saw, nothing can be done to save your employee and I am very sorry to hear that. I am going to send a few of my people over to the hospital to provide some back-up for you and your family. You concentrate on your wife and child. I am very sorry, Jonas. Above all else, it is my deepest hope that your family members will be all right."

Masters informed Jonas that he, Kent, and Katie were headed to the Blair's home, along with a few of Masters' team members. Jonas told Phillip where he could find a hidden key to the house.

In an attempt to bring some levity to Jonas at a time when he was so justifiably distraught, Masters said, "No need for a key once Taylor arrives." It worked as Jonas, despite his pain and anguish, smiled.

Masters then called Taylor and told him all that was happening. Kent was shocked and immediately informed Katie, who cried while continuing to drive.

"Listen, Taylor? I suggest we all meet at the Blair's house as planned. I am sure that you and Katie would want to be there with Jonas and his family, but until we have a better sense of where our attackers might be, you both would only increase the target size for the enemy. I have a few of my people headed to the hospital to further protect Jonas and his family."

Masters was correct. Kent and Katie both desperately wanted to go to the hospital to be with Jonas and check on the conditions of Sally and the baby, but it was best that they stay away at the moment.

Despite her tears, Katie continued to drive and Kent continued in his efforts to reach Bill Gladding.

❖

The two men drove out of the parking lot beneath the building that enabled them to fire the shot to kill Bill Gladding. The hats they wore pretty much covered their faces, although the lens on the camera at the entrance/exit was still covered with black spray paint.

Normally, Raymond and Edison worked alone in their capacity as hit men. In this instance, those hiring them agreed to pay double to be sure all went smoothly. It was also because each man, without the other knowing, would receive a bonus if it was necessary to kill the other. This was based upon someone getting caught. If both were caught, a Plan B team would have to be sent in.

"I would have liked an opportunity to go over there and gather up all them"ears" we planted in that condo," Raymond said,"but you know once they find a former federal agent with a bullet embedded in his brain, ain't nobody like us gonna get within fifty miles of that place."

"Yeah, you got that right," Edison said. He entered the ticket and paid for the parking in cash."Especially when the victim is some legendary dude like the late Bill Gladding, eh?"

"Ah! No big deal, anyway," Raymond said."Nothing there is traceable back to us. Even that slug hidden there in his cerebellum is common ammo."

They turned onto the street and drove away. Soon they would be long gone with a good chunk of cash deposited in their foreign accounts.

Chapter Forty-Eight

What Now?

It was like waking up in a cold dark cave located somewhere deep in the bowels of the earth. Or maybe this was hell itself in the aftermath of death.

Soon the whooshing sounds surfaced in his ears making the presence of hell more likely than a subterranean chamber. He was not sure if his eyes were open or blindness replaced the vision he once had. The throbbing pain in his head seemed to defy the existence of death.

He reached towards his head and felt a gooey liquid all over his hand. He did not need to see it to know what it was. He felt blood many times before. What he did not know was how bad the source where it came from might be.

His senses slowly began to come alive once again. His mind was striving to determine where he was and how he had gotten here. He began to recover the use of his hands. He moved his fingers along the floor and felt shards of glass.

Things around him began to slowly come into focus. He could see that he was lying on the floor, glass and blood around him, noise from traffic and activity on the streets below became increasingly apparent. Noise. Glass. The window had to be broken. Something struck him through the window.

He wanted to lift his head, even get to his feet. He needed to look around and get a better sense as to what happened, but he was too weak to do so. Even now, he was battling to remain conscious. He felt as if he had narrowly escaped death. He had. Much closer than he knew. But for a button, he would now be dead.

❖

The conversation was fraught with more emotions than should be contained in any single conversation.

"Thank God, Jonas. Oh, Kent and I are beyond relieved. I-I c-can hardly..."

Katie was too choked up to continue talking, so Kent took over again.

"Katie summed it up perfectly, Jonas. We are so relieved and thankful. So what does this mean in terms of hospital stays and all."

"The concussion that Sally has likely means she stays in tonight. They appraise things again tomorrow. It's possible she will stay another night, but maybe not. She's got stitches in above her right eye, but they are confident she will not have a permanent scar. She's bruised and sore and you know how it goes with those kinds of injuries."

"Sure do," Kent said."You hurt more in the following days than you did initially."

"We were so lucky, Kent. Taylor was unscratched. The little guy was crying when the emergency crew pulled him from the car. The doctor said they searched him once, twice, then a third time and you'd never know he was in that kind of accident."

"Jonas, you stay focused on Sally and the baby. Afterwards, I promise you we are not going to rely upon luck to assure everyone is safe. Between Masters' team, whomever we may be able to trust from your old employer, and us, we will find out who's behind this and put a stop to it."

"Thanks, Kent. Yes, we all need some closure here. Uh...Kent...Bill? Anything yet?"

"No, not yet. We've got Masters using his contacts to get some people over to his condo. I'll let you know when we hear something."

❖

Phillip Masters was now with Kent and Katie at the home of Jonas and Sally.

"I've got a team stationed at the hospital. There will be personnel there as long as Sally and the baby are there. We pulled some strings and arranged for your little namesake to be in the same room as his mother and a private nurse to be on duty with them at all times. Jonas can sleep there, also. Not sure if he will, but either way he is coming home to gather up some things for Sally."

Just then Masters was interrupted with a call. He took it in front of Kent and Katie. His facial expressions and responses revealed the nature of the call.

"They just found Bill Gladding. He has been shot. Narrowly escaped being killed. He is currently admitted to a hospital in critical, but stable condition. The FBI has assigned 24-hour guards outside his hospital room."

❖

When Rascoe Infante lost his right leg in a land mine explosion in Afghanistan, some who knew him said it justified the release of the remaining demons that, until then had been dormant. Rascoe was a Special Forces officer in a US Marine Raider Regiment at the time.

He retained enough of the leg to warrant below knee prosthesis. Over time, following advanced therapy sessions and strenuous exercise, Infante had better mobility than many who had two sound legs. This was a rather unfortunate development, because George Emerson was certain that Rascoe Infante was a dyed-in-the-wool psychopath.

"I never have studied it enough to distinguish between a sociopath and a psychopath," FBI Associate Director Nolan Parker once told Emerson,"but whatever Rascoe is, the boy definitely comes in handy when we need someone to do the dirty work that has to be done."

As a result, Infante would be on the team assigned to the dirty work next on the agenda.

Nolan Parker was sitting with Senator Thurman Gibbons and George Emerson outlining that next"dirty work" mission.

"Heading up the team will be Hank Madsen," Parker said."Hank's a former decorated Green Beret. He's a good man. He'll get the job done. May sound a bit like overkill, no intended pun," Parker said with a chuckle,"but we have six other operatives that will be working with Madsen and Infante."

"When will all of this take place?" Gibbons asked.

"They're all set to go. We had us a little hiccup in that the hit on Gladding was supposed to occur after he contacted Taylor and told him about the voicemail message, not before. We are thinking that Gladding spotted the bugging device in his phone, left it in place, and suspected there would be other bugs in his condo. We think he was preparing to leave and call Taylor from a more secure location. Our guys were poised and when they saw the former special agent standing at his fourth floor window, they took action. We are working now to get the word to Taylor. Believe me, once we do, he will head straight for bayou country." Parker was smiling now.

Gibbons was fidgeting a bit and did not smile at Parker's comment."I do not like hearing about hiccups. Hiccups can be the death of all of us, the reason..."

Parker interrupted."I always find it interesting, Thurman, that people like you sit back in their plush D.C. offices, shuffling papers or hobnobbing with some corporate sponsor, while the rest of us get the real work done—the work that will get us to where we all need to be. My advice to you is tread lightly, my friend, before you agitate the wrong people."

Gibbons said nothing. It was now George Emerson's turn to smile.

Chapter Forty-Nine

Me Gotta Go

K ent and Katie remained at the home of Jonas and Sally Blair. They took turns checking on the status of Bill Gladding and also had assistance from Phillip Masters. Kent had considered flying out to the West Coast, but the doctors assured him that Gladding would not even be aware they were there. All anyone could do at the moment was wait things out.

Two days had passed since the accident. Sally was doing much better now and baby Taylor was perfectly fine.

Masters had moved from Chesters to a hidden location with an even greater level of security. His contact with Kent, Katie, and the Blairs was limited to secure phone conversations. Masters was working closely with NCS Deputy Director Thomas Westfield and a team seeking to identify those behind the rogue operations of several agencies and independent sources eager to spur U.S. warfare in the Middle East.

An afternoon phone call from Masters to Kent Taylor generated some group activity. Kent informed Masters that he was placing the call on speaker so that Katie, Jonas, and Sally could also listen.

"Good news is that Bill Gladding's doing much better. He'll be laid up for a while and we do not yet know about his level of functionality afterwards, but it looks like he's going to be around for a good number of years.

This was a very close call. Seems the last second, Gladding quickly bent his head downward. The sniper's bullet slammed against the side of his head. It was a powerful slug that did its damage. If it would have penetrated, Gladding would have been dead on contact."

Everyone breathed a collective sigh of relief. Their joy quickly vanished as they listened to the additional news that Masters had to relay.

"From the moment Bill Gladding regained consciousness, he kept talking about some kind of message, urgent message for you, Kent. We were having difficulty understanding all that Bill was saying, but when he mentioned something about a voicemail message on his condo landline, I sent an operative over there to check things out.

We recorded that message, Kent. I am going to play it for you now.

The four of them sat rigidly listening to the voice of a young girl. Sally's mouth fell wide open. Katie gasped. Jonas' eyes were squeezed shut. Kent, despite the inner turmoil that already was at play, was on full alert.

Agent William Gladding? Sir...my name is Rosemary Chambers, but I believe that you would otherwise know me as Emily Taylor. Mr. Gladding, I understand that you knew my daddy. I know the history of everything that occurred, but was wondering if we could talk. I am willing to do whatever it takes to arrange that with you.

I want to know more about my daddy. I am also hopeful that you might be in position to help me learn more about my mom...

The message ended with Emily saying that she was a student at Louisiana State University in Baton Rouge. She left her phone number and stated that she would call back.

By the time the message ended, Katie and Sally were both in tears. Jonas was shaking his head and making a concerted effort to refrain from speaking until they all first heard from Kent.

Katie had never seen her husband's face so devoid of color as it was now. In fact, his face was tight and his breathing was heavy.

Phillip Masters spoke first.

"We will stay on top of this. Whatever we need to do, Kent. We are here for you..."

Taylor's response was curt.

"Thank you. I will let you know."

No one said a word until Jonas finally broke the silence.

"What are you thinking, Kent?"

Kent was pensive. He appeared to be deep in thought, processing all that he had heard and considering what his next moves would be.

"Obviously, the fact that Emily knows her true identity and has reached out to Bill means she and my family could be in great danger. I know where they are. I'll have to go."

This was the first time that Jonas was concerned about Kent Taylor's judgment and clarity of mind. He was deeply concerned that Taylor might react based upon emotions that he kept locked up and under control for many years.

"Kent," Katie said, "all we know at the moment is that Emily left a voicemail message on Bill's phone. We don't know anything more."

Taylor was deep in thought and reacted as if he never heard Katie's statement. A few moments later, he shook his head as one awakening from sleep and turned towards Katie. His demeanor was soft and gracious, but his words carried a sense of urgency.

"No, Katie, I'm afraid we know a whole lot more than that."

Kent sighed and made eye contact, in turn, with Katie, Jonas, and Sally.

"We don't know exactly when Bill accessed that voicemail message. I believe we have to assume it was the morning following his arrival back at the condo. It honestly does not matter exactly when he first heard it. What matters is that he had not yet called me when he was shot.

If Gladding's only concern was that Emily was exposing herself to potential danger, he would have called me immediately upon hearing her message. But he did not. Why?"

Jonas responded. "Because he had reason to believe that it was not safe for him to do so from his condo."

Kent nodded evidencing his agreement.

"You mean his phone was bugged," Katie asked.

"His phone and his condo," Kent answered. "So he was likely headed out to call me from outside of his place, but was shot before he could do so."

Katie gasped. Her face turned pale. For a moment she looked as if she was going to faint. Instead, she walked over to Kent. He took her into his arms."

"Th-that…means…" Katie stuttered.

"That means they know," Kent said. "The wrong people know how to find Emily and my family."

"You know if you go there," Jonas said, "it could very well be a trap."

"Yes. Yes, I expect that it will be. But maybe I can use that trap against them."

❖

Taylor's first argument was with Jonas in front of Sally and Katie.

"No, Jonas. I am grateful to you, but this is something I am going to have to do by myself. It is too dangerous for you to get involved. This time you have to think about Sally and the baby.

Look, I appreciate it, man. But my strategy will be to work by stealth and be ready for any moves they make."

"But Emily is in Baton Rouge in a dorm..." Katie interjected.

"No, they will be sure that Emily is back home in Houma when they make their move. They will not want to alarm an entire campus and generate that kind of attention. They will make it look like a home burglary gone bad or maybe even a murder suicide by a family member.

I am going to have to handle this one on my own."

Kent headed straight to the bedroom where he quickly began to gather up a few things. Katie followed him and that was when his next argument ensued.

"Not this time, Katie. This is way too dangerous. There is absolutely no way you can get involved in this—no way. This is a world you do not belong in, darling. It's a dark, evil, dirty world. I lived in it once. I know it's rules. I know how it works.

Trust me, the people we are dealing with will slit your throat without thinking twice. I am sorry, Katie."

"Maybe if we get Phillip Masters to help us..."

"No, Katie. That's just it. Any false move on anyone's part could result in them killing everyone. If I can get there before any of them arrive, maybe I can strengthen our odds a bit. That's what this is all about.

I have to do this, Katie. I have no choice. If I never show up, they may kill everyone and leave a trail knowing I will come after them.

You see, it's me they want, Katie, so it's me I have to give them."

I need to use the rental to get to the airport. I am going to charter a private jet and lease something on the other end.

Time is of the essence."

Kent started to walk past Katie and leave the room, when he turned back, reached out for her, and held her in his arms.

"I love you, Katie. No matter what happens, I hope that you will never forget those words.

Hey, I'll take care of this and be back here before you know it."

Katie felt as if those last words constituted the most empty expression she had ever heard her husband express.

He pulled away.

"Kent..." Katie cried out.

He turned. Smiled at her and walked out.

On the way out of the house, Kent passed Sally, hugged her quickly and walked outside. The moment he exited the door, he spotted Jonas waiting at the rental car.

"I'm coming along, Kent," Jonas said.

"You sure this is something you want to do, Jonas."

"I'm sure."

Taylor paused, sighed deeply, then handed the car keys to Jonas.

"Then you drive. I have a lot of planning to do."

Jonas moved around the car towards the driver's seat, passing Taylor on the way. As he did, Kent reached around, grabbed Jonas from behind, and locked his arms around Blair's neck until Jonas passed out. Kent gently laid Jonas on the ground.

"Much too risky, Jonas. This is something I am going to have to do alone."

Taylor started to enter the car, then turned towards Blair's prone body one more time.

"I may never get to tell you, my friend, how much it means to me that you were willing to come along. But, I didn't save your life so that you could die with me.

Stay home. Raise that son of yours and live out your life with Sally."

Chapter Fifty

Greatest Mission

"Hello, this is Rosemary."

"Yes, hello. This is Bill Gladding. You left a message for me?"

Emily froze. She felt paralyzed at first to hear the voice of the former FBI special agent. She had doubted whether a man, such as Gladding, would ever return a phone call from someone he did not really know."

"Y-yes, sir. I..uh.. I did. I-I appreciate you calling me back."

The caller went on to remind Emily that her identity and that of her family must remain uncompromised. He then was able to learn that Emily would be driving to Houma for a long weekend.

"Perfect. I will be in New Orleans during that time. Here's what we do."

Emily was told that she would receive a text from Gladding on the Sunday that she intended to return to Baton Rouge. He would provide her with a place in the Crescent City where they could meet for a few hours before she headed back to school.

"I am assuming that your uncle and aunt talked with you."

"Yes, they told me all about my parents and my real birth name."

"But they do not know that you have contacted me?"

"No, sir. No one knows. I have not said a word to anyone."

"Okay then, young lady, if you want me to talk with you, I must be assured that absolutely no one else knows that we will be meeting. Is that clear?

I am under a government order of confidentiality and I can get myself in some very hot water for even meeting with you."

The caller hesitated for a moment, then spoke with a greater intonation of empathy.

"Listen, I have a daughter, Ms. Taylor. I understand your desire to know more about your folks."

Emily's body shook with excitement. She assured Bill Gladding that she would not say a word to anyone.The caller hung up and smiled.

"Well, that was easy enough," Senator Thurman Gibbons remarked.

"Splendid," Vice President Harrison Michaels said."Well done, my friend. You were most convincing, indeed."

❖

As he drove towards the airport, Taylor called his chartered jet service company to arrange for a flight. He used his phone GPS to locate the offbeat store he would stop at to pick up the things he needed.

When he arrived at the airport with his backpack and the duffle bag he was now carrying, Taylor felt a rush of emotions stronger than any he had felt in years. He remembered the times when he was deployed on a new covert mission, heading for unknown challenges, relying on skills upon which his very survivial would depend. However, this was most assuredly the greatest mission he had ever undertaken.

He smiled, nodded his head to no one but himself, and took a deep breath. He would be ready.

Dear God, he *had* to be ready.

❖

Lisa pulled out of the long twisting driveway and headed towards the grocery store. She would have time to pick up the things she needed before Emily arrived from Baton Rouge and Arthur returned home from a day in New Orleans.

Arthur, Jr. was away at college in Tennessee. Stacey was spending this semester as an exchange student in London.

As she drove away, Lisa smiled as she reflected upon her list of grocery items for things Emily would eat before returning to school in a few days.

"My, my." she muttered aloud, her eyes moistening a bit with tears."So many of your favorite foods were the very things that your mom loved to eat. Must be in your genes."

❖

As he sat aboard his chartered flight, Kent's mind was inundated with the awful truth. He was the reason why his loved ones were tucked away and hidden here some fifteen years ago. He was the reason why their lives were now in danger. Hell, he was always the reason why someone was in peril. He was the reason why Katie had almost been killed.

In all truth, there were those who feared that Rose might have said things to Arthur and Lisa before she died. And that was the chief reason why they had to be hidden away. Yet, no matter what, Kent was always prone to blame himself.

Fifteen years ago, he was powerless to stop the murders that shattered his life and future. He would not let that be the case now.

But why? Why were these people so intent on killing him? Why were they also so focused on killing Bill Gladding and Jonas and Sally Blair?

He thought back on all that had transpired. Jean-Pierre Muamba was dead. He was the one who knew who the key conspirators here in America. But Masters said Muamba left a sealed envelope with his family members in the event he should die. Could it be that the sealed envelope did not include everything that Muamba had learned? Was that what this was all about? Yet, even if that were true, Muamba never disclosed anything more during the flights from Africa to New York. Or did he?

Taylor's mind was racing.

What am I missing here? Muamba never said anything more to any of us. He had to know that if he were to die, his secrets would die with him.

Wait a minute. In the event he should die.

Suddenly Taylor was brought back to a moment he had with Muamba while they were flying back to the United States. The words of Jean-Pierre began to resound in Kent Taylor's mind.

"In my country we call things such as this fetishes... bear great power. This one has within it a power to reveal much wisdom... If I die, it speaks when I can no longer do so... recall its power in the event that something should happen to me."

Within it great wisdom? If Muamba dies, it speaks? How can a hand-carved bone speak when Jean-Pierre is dead? Why recall the fetish in the event something should happen to Muamba?

He gave me a bone. A smooth, hollowed out...

That's it! Suddenly, Taylor had the answer. He reached into his pocket and pulled out the small object that Muamba had given to him. He spotted the point where it appeared that the bone had been sealed back together by some type of adhesive. He began to move the blade of his knife back and forth, like a saw. Then he held the fetish with both hands and applied pressure in an attempt to snap it open. When he had it open, he found a small rolled up piece of paper inside.

The writing on that paper contained a few names, including the primary person of influence in America who was leading the effort to generate a major terrorist attack. It also had reference to a date and three primary targets.

Taylor pulled out his phone and immediately drafted an email to send to Jonas Blair. He wished that he had Bill Gladding healthy enough to also assist.

Before he sent it, he hesitated as his mind raced considering whether there was another man he could also trust. The wrong decision now would prove to be catastrophic for Taylor, his family, and many others. Time was of the essence. He had to make his decision now.

Taylor added Phillip Masters as a recipient to his email. Then he pressed "send."

❖

Phillip Masters stared at the communication from Taylor. There had to be some mistake. This could not possibly be true. He personally knew Vice President Harrison Michaels. He had known the man since he was a congressman years ago. He also knew U.S. Senator Thurman Gibbons and a few others listed in Taylor's email. These were people whom he trusted. In some cases, they were individuals that he admired and respected. He believed them to be men and women who loved their country and have served it well. He sat frozen in place, unable to even move. He felt sick to his stomach.

For a moment, the thought crossed his mind that his mentor, Thomas Westfield, might also be aligned with these people. His body shook as he considered that frightening possibility.

Now, for the first time, he began to question his own judgment. Had he been wrong all along? What made him think he was any more of a patriot than those who were listed in Taylor's communication and those he had learned of earlier from the notes left by Muamba with his family members. . These people were not thugs, terrorists, or criminals. Harrison Michaels was the proverbial heartbeat away from the presidency. Thurman Gibbons was generally recognized as presidential timber.

Were they right in believing that something extreme would have to occur before America would deign to declare open war in the Middle East—war on a scale far beyond anything this country had previously been engaged in?

His mind reverted to that infamous day in history.

More than 2,500 died and 1,000 were wounded during the two-hour attack on Pearl Harbor. December 7, 1941. Even so, it was only then that the"sleeping giant" was awakened. And what if the United States had never gotten involved in World War II? Where would the world be today?

Are we on yet another precipice where the future of humanity depends upon the action or inaction that we take? Is that where we are?

Perspiration poured from Masters' face. His hands shook and his heart raced. He made a concerted effort to slow everything down—deep breaths, relax, stop, and think clearly. He had to remain calm. There was so little time and his decision now was crucial.

Should he ignore the communication from Taylor and simply do nothing? Perhaps America did need to be seriously jolted into taking action.

No. Our nation cannot prevail if the only time we can make a decision is after some cataclysmic event where thousands or maybe millions of innocent people are killed.

No. he knows Tom Westfield. Tom would never support anything where people are sacrificed like this. Besides, Tom was almost killed himself.

I trust him. Dear God, I have to trust him.

Kent Taylor is on his way to save his family members. Soon, very soon, people sworn to defend the lives of Americans will be closing in on Kent Taylor. They will kill him and his family members.

The battle raging within Phillip Masters' mind continued.

Taylor could have, maybe should have died years ago. Well, hell, what is that to me? I am just one man. I cannot possibly save everyone. Sometimes people die. Sometimes people have to die.

No. Not Kent Taylor. Not his family.

No. The others did not deserve to die. Not all the men at The Camp. Not Marisa. Not Micah Jensen. Not Benjie…

Masters took action. He had to act quickly. He sent his communication in response what he had received from Kent. As he did, he could only hope and pray that he had made the right decision. If not, the result would be catastrophic for far too many innocent people.

❖

Once the jet landed and Taylor had his rental vehicle, he was in the Houma area in slightly less than an hour. The sun was beginning its descent for the day. Darkness was moving in quickly.

He first passed by the house and made a preliminary judgment that no one was home. He continued to make a couple of quick passes by the house. He measured the distance between the house, nearby homes, and a local quick-stop. He took a number of pictures with the black ops HD camera he picked up at the offbeat gun and supplies store. Even so, he would have to go in blind and improvise as he did.

They once referred to him as the *Ghost Assassin*. He considered that at some point on this day he would have to possess some degree of invisibility once again.

Taylor parked his vehicle on the side of the quick-stop that was located some 2.5 miles from his destination, fastened his backpack, grabbed his duffel bag, and began his jog. He reached the property quickly.

His first challenge would be how he would approach them after so many years of their belief that he was dead. There was a significant part of him that wished that he would never have to reveal himself to them at all, but he knew that he must do so. They had to know and be prepared for what lies ahead. Their lives would depend upon it.

Even after he awoke, it took some time before Jonas could fully shake the grogginess and clear his head. He did not like what Taylor had done, but he fully understood why he had done it. Taylor knew how heavily the odds were stacked against him. He was willing to face those odds. He most assuredly believed that he had no choice but to do so. At the same time, Jonas was sure that Kent did not believe that it was right to expect anyone, other than himself, to take on such a one-sided challenge.

Jonas went inside the house and gathered Sally and Katie. It was time for the three of them to make their own plans.

Kent was hidden within a stand of trees to the west of the house itself when Lisa arrived back at the house. His heart was racing at the very sight of her. She pulled her car into the garage and disappeared from view.

Within minutes, Arthur arrived home. He also opened the garage door remotely from his vehicle and pulled in. Kent's palms were clammy and, as before, his heart was beating faster. His thoughts started to stray to remembrances of Rose and Drew.

"Not now," he whispered to himself. "Can't go there now. I need to concentrate upon the living—upon those whose lives I still have a chance to save."

He waited as the minutes passed. He was certain that Emily was headed home from Baton Rouge. Even so, his confidence began to waiver. What if she had changed her mind? What if he was wrong and they would go after Emily at her college dorm? What if she arrived after they were here? What if..."

Just then he spotted a car pulling into the driveway. Emily was home.

Two current year Hummer H4s, each containing four passengers, drove out from a remote location in New Orleans and headed southwest towards the outskirts of Houma.

Hank Madsen, a former decorated Green Beret, drove the lead vehicle. Nolan Parker, FBI Associate Director, sat in the front passenger seat.

Former special forces US Marine Raider Regiment, Rascoe Infante drove the second vehicle, despite the prothetic device he wore below his right knee. George Emerson, a former Conressman from Ohio was in that vehicle's front passenger seat. Emerson was also a former decorated US Marine and someone who considered Infante to be a maniac.

Emerson was on the phone with Parker.

"Give it about an hour and we'll be there," Emerson stated.

"Sounds good," Parker responded."He behaving?"

Nolan Parker knew how greatly Emerson detested Infante.

"Yeah, okay for now."

"Well, just hold tight, George. It'll all be over soon."

❖

His hands shook. He fought desperately to calm himself. In the past Kent Taylor had stared death in the face and was nowhere near as unsettled as he was now. How do you tell your loved ones that after fifteen years you are not dead, as had been reported? How will they react? What will your daughter say or do? She was only three-years-old when you disappeared from her life. Will she reject you? Maybe hate you? Maybe they will all hate you—hate you for the lie they had been forced to believe, hate you for staying away for all those years.

Emily was seeking to know more about her dad and mom—about her *dead* parents. What will Emily feel when she learns that her father has been alive all this time? Will Kent's appearance tear open the deep wounds that Lisa suffered so many years ago? Arthur, too?

At the moment, Kent Taylor did not feel like an experienced Navy SEAL. If anything, he felt more vulnerable, even fragile, than ever before.

Stay the course, Taylor. The issue is not whether they accept or reject you. Your primary concern has to be that you find a way to save their lives. Once these people show up on this property, your family members are as good as dead. You're dealing with people who are willing to sacrifice more American lives than you can count in order to support their cause. Surely you do not believe that they will heistate for one moment to kill a few people here in southern Louisiana?

Kent Taylor paused long enough to take a deep breath in a concerted effort to calm his body down and flush out all distractions. He did not know whether this was the last mission he would ever undertake, but it was certainly the greatest one. It was also the most difficult one.

Chapter Fifty-One

Full Cycle

He utilized a window at the back of the house to gain his entrance. He did not know the interior layout of this home, so, once again, he would have to improvise.

He could hear voices now. As best he could determine they were coming from the kitchen.

"It's extremely unfair that a professor would give us so short a time to do all the research we needed to do to write an essay. I mean, it's not like his course is the only one we are taking. Everyone was super upset."

His heart leapt. The speaker had to be his Emily.

"There should be someone that students can complain to, you know? Like a dean of some kind."

Taylor was confident that the response came from Lisa.

The male voice that followed was clearly that of Arthur.

"Sure," Arthur said with a chuckle, "the dean of complaints, eh?"

"Well, I'm just saying," Lisa responded. "You've got responsible students who are striving to do well. They should have a voice when someone is treating them unfairly."

"The important thing," Arthur said, "is that fair or not, you got the work done. Nice going, Rosemary."

This was Taylor's opportunity. They were all together in one room. He trembled as he walked closer to what was, indeed, the kitchen. His legs felt like jelly. His mouth was dry. He sucked in a gulp of oxygen and prepared to make his appearance.

When he stood before them, they were all startled, shocked, and frightened. Arthur reached for a kitchen knife. Lisa jumped from the stool she had been sitting on and placed her body in front of Emily.

Taylor stood perfectly still and raised his hands in the air.

As he did, Lisa began to openly sob, shaking her head, her body quivering. The blood instantly drained from her face and a look of disbelief dominated her facial expressions.

❖

Jonas, Sally, and Katie were in full gear now. Katie had already made several phone calls and was pleased at how easy it was to arrange things. Jonas had already gathered up whatever they would need. Made his contacts and went over the strategy several times. Sally was on the road on her way to pick up the babysitter.

It was Jonas' words that had spurred each of them into a controlled flurry of activity.

"We need to focus and think as Kent would."

❖

Any thoughts of burglary, rape, even murder were quickly dispelled when Lisa screamed aloud.

"Kent! Oh my God! Kent. B-but... w-what?"

Lisa ran towards him, then stopped. She abruptly turned towards Arthur.

Taylor calmly looked at each of them in turn. His eyes were misty, but he fought hard against his emotions. Emily appeared to be in a state of shock. She sat motionless and stared. Her face took on a quizzical look, an expression of sheer confusion and wonderment. In that same moment, her body shook and she began to sob without making a sound.

Arthur made the first attempts to regain control of the situation as he dropped the kitchen knife and walked closer to Taylor.

"Kent? You're alive? But, how?"

"They faked my death for their benefit. I could never be in touch with any of you or I would be placing your lives in jeopardy. Bill Gladding helped tuck you all away so deeply, that even the government lost track of you. I did everything I could to avoid ever making contact.

Things have changed. They are headed here now. I had to come to warn you and protect you. We have very little time."

"Whoa! Who are we talking about, Kent? Why not just call 911 and get the sheriff's people out here?" Arthur said.

"No. You cannot call anyone. The people coming will have credentials. I expect some will be military. Others, federal agents."

"Military? Feds? What the hell is going on, Kent?" Arthur continued. "You...show up suddenly after fifteen years...like a man returning from the dead. Now you're talking about federal agents, soldiers all headed here to our home...What?..."

Taylor moved closer to Arthur and placed his hand on Arthur's shoulder. Arthur turned his head, stared at Taylor's hand, and sighed.

Now, for the first time, tears flooded Arthur's eyes. Taylor moved closer and hugged his former brother-in-law.

"I understand, Arthur. You all have every reason to doubt me...to question everything I am saying. I don't have enough time to convince you that I love you all...I never stopped loving you..."

Lisa reacted first.

She reached over to her husband and to Kent. Her body was still trembling and tears continued to fall from her eyes. Yet, in that moment, Kent saw that same fortitude that Lisa displayed fifteen years earlier when he brought her the news that her sister, parents and nephew had all been murdered.

"I-I believe you, Kent. I-I have t-to believe you.

The last time I ever saw you...you asked...you asked m-me to trust you. And I-I did...I d-did trust you, Kent. And everything you told me that day...everything...and...and all that you had us do...it all...it all proved to be true.

We...dear God...we are all alive today because I-I tr-trusted you back then."

Lisa turned to Arthur and he took his wife into his arms.

"Arthur, please....Please, Arthur...I believe, Kent. We need...we all need to trust him."

Arthur's body slackened. He nodded. For just a moment, he placed his hand, in return, upon Taylor's shoulder.

"I need you all to listen to me," Taylor continued. "Regardless of badges, these people have gone rogue. They have splintered off from legitimate government agencies and channels. The sheriff's people would not know that. They would believe these folks are legit.

The people coming here correctly believe that by doing so, they will lure me in. At the same time, they intend to kill all of us."

Lisa gasped.

"Wh-what should we do, Kent? Leave? Run now? Get away?"

"No. We will never be able to get away from these monsters. They're just too well connected.

What kind of guns do you have in the house, Arthur?"

Arthur quickly listed off a few rifles used for hunting, a 22-caliber pistol he had gotten for Lisa, and a .357 Magnum.

Taylor then outlined his plan. He had a few automatic handguns and clips that he would leave with the women. Arthur would handle the .357 Magnum. Taylor would retain his own weaponry.

"Do your best to keep your weapons handy, but hidden. Do not let on that you know that anything is suspicious. Cooperate with them. Do not panic. And under no circumstances mention that I am here."

Then Kent smiled for the first time and made eye contact with each of them.

"But do not forget that I am here. I will not abandon you. Just stay calm."

"What about you, Kent?" Lisa asked.

"I am going outside. I will cover the perimeter of the house. I am going to leave one window unlocked. I can use it if I need to reenter. As I stated, they cannot know that I am here."

Throughout this time, Emily stood as one paralyzed. Her mouth was open. Her face bore the appearance of someone who was in disbelief at what she was seeing.

Then she finally spoke.

"D-daddy... "

Tears were pouring from her eyes. She attempted to speak again, but could not.

Kent walked to her and took his daughter in his arms. It was the first time he had touched her in some fifteen years. The embrace was electrifying.

For a moment, he was overwhelmed with the desire to hold tight and never let her go. Her body trembled and she continued to sob deeply. He reached down, cupped her chin, and lifted her face towards his. A gentle smile was on his face. He kissed her cheek, her forehead, the tip of her nose.

"Listen to me, Darling. We *will* get through this. I promise you.

And afterwards, I have so much to talk with you about. So much time to make up for... if you will let me. I love you, Emily.

Please. Just do as I say for now. Let's all get our lives back, once and for all."

❖

Taylor positioned himself at the very back of the stand of trees that he had come through earlier. Now came the difficult part. He would wait for their arrival. It would not be long now.

When they arrived, they made no effort to hide from the occupants, except that four men quickly jumped out of the two Hummers, while the others remained inside.

Taylor watched as two of the men positioned themselves in an area in front of him in the very same stand of trees. One other man took a position up against the very front of the house. The remaining man went behind the house.

These four men would be waiting outside for him to arrive. The others would likely approach the occupants of the house, present their credentials, and begin questioning Arthur, Lisa, and Emily under some pretense.

It bothered Taylor that he did not know anything about these men. He did not even know their names. As he watched from a distance, it became clear to him that two of the men carried more authority than the others. Those two were Parker and Emerson. The two others who were with them, Rascoe Infante and Hank Madsen, were prepared to enter the home with Parker and Emerson.

Infante and Madsen would likely search the house relying upon some false pretense to do so. He had instructed Arthur, Lisa, and Emily to act as if they believed they were dealing with men properly acting under the dictates

293

of the law. Most importantly, Taylor was banking on the fact that his family members would act as if they were completely unaware that he was alive and here this night.

While he was waiting, he received a text message purportedly from Bill Gladding informing him about the voicemail message left by Emily. The message stated that Bill was using a throwaway phone for added security.

Kent knew, of course, that the message had not been sent by Gladding. It was part of the plan to lure Taylor to the home of his family members.

Kent Taylor smiled.

Nice job, guys. If I did not know better, I would swear this text came from Bill Gladding.

But, the text sent a more important message to Taylor.

Perfect. They do not know that I am here.

Well now, you have the numbers. I still have the element of surprise.

His movements were as silent and precise as a great cat stalking its prey. He had night vision glasses that enabled him to see in the darkness. Even without this artificial aid, he would have spotted the men who were stationed outside of the house throughout the property.

Waiting for my arrival? Kind of makes me feel like the guest of honor here tonight.

Taylor's vantage point was from the west side of the house at the back end of the stand of trees. He fastened his eyes upon the two men also hidden away behind those trees. They were staggered about twenty feet from each other. He would need to take these men out now.

He began to move in closer to them. His every step was silent.

The first man was hidden behind a tree looking towards the house.

Taylor smiled.

My, my. You expecting I'll be coming in through the front door? How unoriginal.

Taylor had his arms around the man's neck and snapped it so swiftly and silently that there was never a concern that the second man would hear anything. He then crawled in position behind his second target. He found a twig on the ground and snapped it. The man spun around just in time for Taylor to fling his knife and watch it sink into the man's heart. Two down.

Tall shrubbery hugged the front of the house. As Taylor peered out from the end of the cover of the trees, he spotted the man who was situated up against the house. At the moment, Taylor was more concerned about the man behind the house, since that was the location where the window was that he had left unlocked. He moved back into the stand of trees and exited at a point facing towards a pond at the rear of the house. He also spotted one of the Hummers parked in the back, but he could not find the man who was hidden back there. He focused upon the small boathouse at the edge of the pond. Through a side window, he caught a momentary movement. He had found his man.

Kent had to cover some ground in order to position himself within striking distance of the boathouse. This was the greatest risk he encountered thus far. He slowly began to crawl forward when he spotted someone opening a back door. Taylor was lying on the ground when the man walked to within two or three feet of him. Kent very slowly reached for his knife, but remained motionless on the ground. For a moment, he feared the man would actually step on his prone body.

He did not. The man walked over to the Hummer, opened the door to retrieve something, then turned around and went back into the house.

Kent Taylor prepared to make his move by crawling to the boathouse, taking out the man hidden there, and then entering the house from the back window, when it happened. A military Jeep entered the property. The man hidden at the front of the house, jumped out in front of the vehicle with his automatic rifle pointed directly at the two men sitting in the Jeep.

"Put your weapon down, soldier," one of the occupants called out. He quickly identified himself and the man with him. They were directed to the area behind the house.

As Taylor lay prone on the ground, the two men were joined by Hank Madsen and Rascoe Infante, who stepped outside.

"De man, he sent us, yeah." one of them stated, with an accent revealing that he was a local."Dey sayin' dat Taylor, he is one tough dude."

"You just a got dat right," the other man interjected."Dat mean we stay and be reinforcements to ya."

Infante spit on the ground before responding.

295

"You tell *the man…*" Infante sarcastically responded, "we can handle Taylor and anybody else and don't need no help from the likes of you guys."

"Ain't gonna be me carryin' no message like dat, I guarantee," the first man said.

"Yeah," his partner joined in, "dat mean we gonna stay right 'chere, podna."

Rascoe Infante and Hank Madsen went back inside the house while the two new men stayed outside leaning against the Hummer, within a few feet of a prone Kent Taylor.

Chapter Fifty-Two

Getting Restless

Arthur, Lisa, and Emily were seated on the living room couch. Rascoe Infante was back inside the house with Hank Madsen, George Emerson, and Parker Nolan.

At first, Emerson and Nolan politely interviewed the family members under the pretense that their family might be in possession of funds that the federal government believed might be laundered money. It was a bogus story intended to engage the family members while waiting for Taylor to appear. Soon, aided by the impulsive personality of Infante, that cover was blown.

Parker Nolan had already taken two calls from Vice President Harrison Michaels informing him of the latest updates on Taylor's actions.

"We got word that he used his credit card about an hour ago to charter a flight. We're just going to have to be patient now. He should be arriving in Louisiana within the next few hours," Michaels reported. "We are awaiting further insight on how many people are with Taylor. If need be, we will send some additional support your way."

It bothered Parker Nolan that the Vice President had purportedly entrusted him with this "Plan B" operation and now seemed to be pushing buttons himself. Nolan could not help but wonder whether Harrison Michaels had less than full confidence in him. Nevertheless, he was not about to question or challenge the Vice President in any manner.

"Yes, thank you, sir. We will be ready on our end."

"Splendid, Parker. We are all counting on you, my boy. Indeed, we are."

Nolan's negative thoughts were suddenly interrupted by Arthur.

"Gentlemen, we have cooperated with you fully. I am not sure what you are up to, but I believe it is now time for us to ask you to please leave our home," Arthur said.

Infante rushed towards Arthur. He grabbed his neck and screamed in his face.

"Leave your home? Did I hear you correctly? You think *you* gonna tell *us* to leave? Is that what you think?"

"Calm down, Rascoe," Emerson said.

"You want me to calm down? I'll calm down.

Let's stop playin' games with these people. I ain't in no mood to play pretend. Okay? I don't care if they know we waitin' for Commander Taylor to show up here."

"What? Kent?" Lisa screamed. "You're waiting for Kent to show up here? Are you all crazy?

Kent Taylor is dead. He died fifteen years ago. Your own Bureau," she said turning towards Parker Nolan, "reported his death."

Infante turned towards Lisa and grinned. Rascoe had become unstable and reckless after becoming a US Marine Raider Regiment Special Operations Force member. Some blamed his uncontrolled, somewhat psychopathic behavior on that a land mine explosion in Afghanistan that resulted in the loss of his right leg and hospitalized him for months.

Others cited the seething anger he bore towards Middle East terrorist groups and his own government's failure to declare open war in the region. George Emerson believed that Rascoe was a lunatic—probably always had been.

In any event, Emerson believed that Infante should never have been entrusted with carrying out a mission such as this one.

"Hah! You can't always believe what any govermment agency tells you," Infante said with a smirk covering his face."Hell, you can't believe a damn thing this here government says."

George Emerson was livid. Now he was torn between his desire to somehow shut Infante up and the need to keep this family calm while everything else unfolded.

"It is true that we are here because we believe that former Commander Taylor is alive and headed this way. It is only recently that we learned that you are his relatives.

Taylor is a a a person of interest to the United States government," Emerson lied."He is believed to be spearheading a conspiracy that is considered to be a major threat to our national security."

Emerson's attempts to calm things down were unsucessful.

"Please let us go," Lisa continued."You're waiting for someone to show up who never will. He's dead. Why won't you accept that? He died years ago."

Infante moved closer to Lisa and placed his face within inches of her neck.

"Whoowee! You one sexy lookin' woman when you get all worked up like this, sugar.

Lissen' here, woman. My folks named me Rascoe. That'd be R-a-s-c-o-e. You got that? Kind o' like a cross between Roscoe and rascal. Hahaha. Either that or my parents was too dumb ta know how to spell. Hahaha. Funny stuff right there, eh?

See? I got me a sense o' humor, sweetie. And I think you one good lookin' lady."

Infante kept his face real close to Lisa's neck as he peered over at Emerson. "She's a fine woman. Ain't she George?

Mmm, an' you smell real good too, honey."

"Back away from my wife, mister," Arthur screamed, as he began to rise from the couch.

Infante whirled, pushed Arthur back down to the couch, pulled his gun from its holster, and pressed it against Arthur's temple. Lisa screamed. Emily sobbed.

"My God, what are you doing to him?" Lisa cried out through her tears.

Infante withdrew his weapon and put it back in the holster..

"I'm not about to tell you again, mister. You keep your mouth shut and remember who's in charge around here. Next time, your pretty wife gonna be pickin' up pieces of your brain scattered around this here room."

"Please let us go," Lisa continued."We've already told you. Kent is dead. Why won't you accept that? Let us go."

Infante turned towards Emerson and Nolan.

"He's dead? Haha! The man we're waitin' for is dead?

Well, hell, then I guess we're waitin' on a ghost to show up," Infante said with a loud cackle that Emerson compared to the laugh associated with an insane person.

"You hear that, Georgie boy? We're waitin' for a ghost to show up."

"Let's just calm down," Parker Nolan said.

"Calm? I'm calm," Infante responded."I'm real calm.

Only I'm havin' me a hard time figurin' out which of these fine ladies I would like to take on first, while we're waitin' for the man to show up."

Emerson glared at Infante.

"We're not here for personal pleasure, Rascoe. We've got a job to do. Focus on that, damn it, and not your animal urges."

As Arthur watched all of this unfold, his thoughts went beyond the moment. Kent was right. These men, if they actually were federal agents, were not interested in conducting themselves in a manner that would hold up in court. Arthur was not an attorney, but he never heard of federal agents coming into a home, searching it without a legally justifiable reason to do so, and threatening innocent people as this Infante was doing.

They don't care how they conduct themselves, because they are not anticipating that anything would ever come before a court of law. They will leave behind no witnesses. They intend to kill Kent and all of us.

Arthur would not share his thoughts in front of his wife and niece, as he did not want to frighten them any more than they already were. He was trying desperately to do something, to do anything, that might help to save the lives of Lisa and Emily, but he could think of nothing. He could only hope and pray that somehow Kent could save them, but, in truth, even that seemed to be impossible.

Rascoe, angered by Emerson's comments, moved towards him with a threatening gesture, but stopped when Arthur spoke next.

"Listen, keep me here. Do whatever the hell you want with me. But leave the women alone. Let them go."

"Well, la-dee-dah, we got ourselves another hero here," Infante said."Heard tell your brother-in-law were some kind of hero—before he turned killer, that is."

Once again, Infante turned towards Emerson.

"Guess bein' a hero must run in the family, eh George?"

Parker Nolan spoke again.

"George is right, Rascoe. We've got an important job to do here. Let's just calm down and remain focused, okay? We take care of Taylor, then you can do whatever you want. Let's just keep our priorities were they should be."

Infante moved away from the couch, turned, and left the room.

❖

Taylor was lying motionless in the grass when he heard a vehicle approaching on the driveway. Once again, the vehicle cleared the front of the property and pulled up alongside the growing number parked in the back of the house. Rascoe Infante was out in that area when it arrived.

"What the hell is this all about?" Infante asked as six men stepped out of an SUV.

A tall, spindley man wearing fatigues, stepped forward. He put his hand out to shake hands with Infante. Rascoe ignored it.

"Frank Summers, Army Reserve, reporting here. Got me five other reservists soldiers.

We got word that little short of an hour ago Taylor booked a chartered flight into Houma," Summers said."He used an alias name, but our sources picked up on it."

Infante continued to scowl. He stared at Summers as if the man had nothing of value to offer.

"So what does that prove, we already heard about it."

Summers remained calm. This was the most exciting thing that he and the other reservists had ever been involved with and he was not about to let some ill-tempered jerk distract him.

"Word we got is he booked two flights for a total of six people, excluding the pilots. So we were sent in by command as a back-up, if needed."

Infante's eyes bore a wild look. Waiting, waiting to kill, waiting to satisfy his consuming lusts and passions warred against his mind. The added people on the property made him increasingly uncomfortable, even though he did not know why. He did not really care to understand why he felt as he did.

He had paid his debt to society and to his country. A portion of his leg left somewhere on an overseas mine field, the pains and scars he bore, the surgical procedures he had alreeady endured, all evidenced the extent and the cost of his patriotism. If anyone was owed anything, it was he who should be on the receiving end.

❖

This was not what Taylor had anticipated. He was trapped by men located within just a few feet of him. And now, he was far outnumbered.

What did those men mean when they said that he had chartered two flights under a known alias. He had done no such thing. He never used a credit card at all when he chartered his flight. Based upon the arrangement he had, he kept an escrow account with the charter jet company from which they withdrew funds after he submitted a confidential code. He specifically had arranged that so that he could travel anonymously.

Taylor had to find a way out of here. The odds were increasingly stacked against him. The options available for what he could do were dwindling. He could not continue to lie here motionless on the grass like a trapped animal.

He was sure there was someone in the boathouse at the dock. He now had eight men at the back of the house and at least two others at the front. Four other men were inside the house.

Of course, two others were dead within the stand of trees, although he presently was the only person to know that.

He had to do something. And he had to do it soon.

Then it struck him. The men currently at the back of the house had all arrived after the original team had come in. He heard their discussions. There was every reason to believe that the new arrivals and the original team members did not know each other. If so, that was pretty sloppy work. In any event, it was a risk he was willing to take.

He would not move forward. He would move backwards, towards the pond, towards the boathouse, towards the man whose identity he would steal.

❖

Two chartered jets landed within ten minutes of each other. By the time the wheels of the second jet touched down, the land travel had already been arranged.

Lester Boudreaux had worked at the airport for years.

"Caw! Been woikin' here right at fawteen year now," Lester said to Beau Guidry, as they prepared for the two jets to land, park, and disembark. "Let me tell ya, podna, in all dem year, I ain't had no two classy jets come in here on de same day like dat."

Beau simply nodded and smiled.

"You know what dat mean, don'tcha Beau?"

Guidry again simply smiled and waited for Lester's next comment.

"It mean dis here might just be de good night for me ta get myself behind some o' dem slots, ya know? When de unusual happen, it normally a sign dat good luck gonna follow. I guarantee."

Chapter Fifty-Three

A Father's Duty

Taylor did not crawl, he slithered. He kept his body as flat as possible against the ground and very slowly pivoted in a half-circle until he was facing the pond. Then he used his arms and the tip of his toes to silently move forward.

He did not like the fact that he could no longer see the men located behind him now, but he had no choice. Silently, he projected his body ahead. When he reached the pond, he spun his body around and slid down feet-first slowly into the water. He managed to do so without generating hardly a ripple.

The distance to the boathouse from his point of entry was about thirty yards. Even without a diving start, Taylor could easily cover that distance underwater without surfacing. When he reached the dock, he took his knife, cut the metal cleat hitch from the end of an unattached dock line, and tossed it at a distance parallel with the boathouse. The man inside immediately stepped out of the building to inspect. When he did, Taylor reached up, grabbed his legs, and quickly pulled him into the water. He kept him under until he was no longer breathing.

Back up on the dock and into the boathouse, Taylor took a moment to wring out his clothes, as best he could. He found a shirt hanging on a hook that would fit him. He also found a ball cap, which he placed on his head and pulled down in the front. On a nearby bench, he spotted a pair of reading glasses, likely belonging to Arthur. He added those to his face.

Taylor headed out in the direction of the back door to the house. Several of the men standing outside in the dark spotted him as he headed their way.

"At ease, gentlemen, don't go pointing something at me that might discharge," Taylor said. "Now that we have so many additional men out here, no sense me staying holed up in that boathouse.

I'll be around if our boy shows up and you guys need some help," Taylor said with a tone of sarcasm.

He continued walking towards the back door of the house.

"Don't you do no worry 'bout us, podna. We know how ta handle ourselves jus' fine," one man said as Taylor reached the back door. As he did, he hoped that no one from inside was anywhere near that location.

❖

Taylor could hear the voices emanating from the living room. He stood outside the room, like a shadow in the night. He removed the glasses he had taken from the boathouse.

From what he could surmise, Lisa was seated on the couch along with Emily and Arthur. The two other men, who he determined earlier to have more authority, were also seated somewhere in the room. Another man was closer to the front door, likely positioned in the foyer that opened up into the living room. The fourth man was restless and moved around much more than any of the others.

"Please, I'm begging you let us go. We have done nothing to deserve this. Please, don't do this. You're wasting your time. You're here for nothing. We've already told you, Kent is dead."

That was clearly the voice of Lisa.

"Man, I'm tellin' ya Georgie-Peorgie," Infante said while turning to Emerson,"I like this here woman when she gets all worked up like this. I could enjoy me a woman like this..."

"Don't talk about my wife like that you animal..."

Arthur did not even finish speaking before Infante had him by the throat once again.

"I done told you already to watch your mouth, boy, before I have ta kill ya right here and now. Besides," Infante continued as he let go of Arthur's throat,"as fine a woman as you got there, I ain't gonna touch her at all."

Arthur was struggling to regain his composure after being choked by Infante, but he was relieved to hear this madman's proclamation that he would not defile Lisa.

"You see, I made my decision," Rascoe Infante pronounced, as if it were something of the utmost importance."I want the girl."

Rascoe walked closer to the couch and stood before Emily Taylor.

"I'm gonna enjoy this fine young filly even before her papa shows up."

Emily began to silently cry. Lisa wrapped her arms around her niece.

"Leave her alone. Don't you dare touch her."

Infante reached over and slapped Lisa across the face.

"You think you gonna tell me what I can and can't do, woman? Is that what ya think? Huh? Is that really what you think?"

Arthur started to get up from the couch, but Lisa grabbed him and pulled him back.

"No, Arthur, please. No."

George Emerson was aghast. Infante's eyes bore a crazed look. Emerson rose from his chair and moved closer towards Rascoe. Hank Madsen came in from the foyer and stood beside Emerson.

"Forget it, Rascoe," Emerson shouted."We've already been through this. Back off. We have a job to do here."

Hank Madsen stepped forward.

"You heard the man..."

Madsen's words were cut short, his eyes widened in disbelief, as Infante's razor sharp knife blade slit his throat. Gurgling sounds broke the shocked silence in the room, as Madsen fell to the floor in a growing puddle of his own blood.

George Emerson stood motionless.

"Tired of you or anybody else tellin' me what ta do, Georgie-Boy," Infante said.

He then pulled up his pants leg revealing his prosthetic leg.

"They tried to stop me when they planted a land mine and, as you can see, that ain't stopped me at all. I am still a hunnerd percent man."

Infante stared at Emily.

"And this here young lady 'bout to learn that."

Infante then pulled out his handgun and turned towards the others in the room.

"Anyone else here want to tell me what I can and can't do?"

No one did.

Infante moved towards the couch to grab Emily by the arm and pull her up.

"You and me, we gonna get ta know each other a whole lot better," he said, as he grabbed her arm.

This was it. Kent knew that he had no choice but to react then. Once Rascoe Infante had Emily isolated in another room in the house, it would not matter what happened outside that room. Taylor could conceivably kill Emerson and Parker Nolan and Infante would still have control of Emily. He could and likely would kill her immediately and then take his chances with Taylor.

Taylor moved out openly into the room, but Infante had Emily between himself and Taylor. No way Kent could shoot the man without hitting his own daughter.

Taylor fired at Emerson, striking him in the shoulder, while tossing the gun to Arthur. The silencer on Taylor's weapon kept anyone on the outside from hearing the shot. Parker Nolan began to reach for his weapon.

Arthur spoke quickly.

"I would not advise that, sir."

Arthur kept the gun pointed at the wounded Emerson and Nolan. At the same time, a blur constituting the body of Taylor struck Infante and knocked him away from Emily. In the collision, Taylor's weapon fell to the floor.

Infante pulled his weapon, but Taylor kicked it loose from his hand.

A huge grin now covered Infante's face, as he drew out his razor-sharp knife and prepared to fight Taylor.

Arthur's voice cried out in terror.

"I-I'm n-not sure I can get him, Kent...w-without hitting you."

Taylor spoke to Arthur without ever turning around to look at him.

"No problem, Arthur, just keep the gun pointed at these other two men. If either one so much as moves an inch, shoot him. Don't hesitate. You got that, Arthur?"

"Oh yeah, Kent. Oh yeah, I got it. Let one of them give me even the slightest excuse and I swear, I will kill him—kill them both."

Infante was still grinning, as he held out his knife against the weaponless Taylor.

"Guess it's jus' you and me, Navy boy," Infante said as he took a swipe of the knife to keep Taylor from rushing him. "We 'bout ta tango, my friend. And I think this is one dance I'm gonna really enjoy."

Infante charged, Taylor pivoted at the last moment, but it was a bit too late. The knife sliced at Taylor's right arm drawing blood.

Emily screamed out.

"Daddy..."

"Oh my, you daddy is bleedin', sweetness. That's his blood leakin' outta there. Hey, you right-handed, Taylor?"

"Appreciate your concern," Taylor said, "but you're going to have to do a whole lot more than that if you expect to stop me."

Taylor then made a quick move, feinted, changed direction, and struck Infante in the face with his left fist, drawing blood from Rascoe's nose.

"That's my left hand, soldier boy. Just in case you really are interested."

Then Taylor began to laugh and taunt.

"Haha. Hey, crazy boy. You missing part of your leg? Haha. What did you step on? My, my, very careless of you. Did you ever find the rest of that leg? Maybe up in a tree branch? Oh, hell, it was probably just an enjoyable snack for some wild animal. Or maybe some native picked it up and is using it as some kind of good luck charm. Wouldn't that be funny? Your leg hanging on the wall of someone's hut?"

Infante's face began to twitch. His eyes were blinking. His face was flushed and red. The man was beyond himself in a fury.

"Calm down, Rascoe," Nolan screamed out. "He's just trying to get you riled up. Get you to do something foolish and... "

Nolan never got to complete his words. Infante was making a strange guttural noise as he charged recklessly towards Taylor. Kent stood still and did not move at all...until...

The moment that Infante was within reach, Taylor stepped to his side, spun, pivoted, grabbed Infante's knife-wielding arm, and raised the man off the floor. The snap of broken bones was unmistakable. Infante fell to the floor where Taylor stomped forcefully on the man's neck. Rascoe Infante was dead.

Taylor never hesitated. He quickly recovered his weapon and walked over towards Parker Nolan. He placed the gun up against Nolan's forehead.

"Now would be a really good time for you to call off your dogs outside and clear the area," Taylor said.

Nolan looked at Taylor and spoke surprisingly calmly for a man with the barrel of a handgun pressed against his skull. A wry smile covered his face.

"No can do, Taylor. I don't think you understand. I am not calling the shots here. None of us are. We all have our orders from on high. Those men outside will let me and George here die before they ever leave these premises with you and your family members still alive.

Sorry, my friend, but you're just as doomed as ever. Once these guys find out that you are in here—we all die."

Chapter Fifty-Four

It's Over

One at a time, Kent Taylor yanked Emerson and Nolan from their seats and stripped them of any weapons. Then he pushed them back into a sitting position.

He walked over to Lisa and Emily and spoke softly to them. While he and Arthur kept their weapons pointed at Emerson and Nolan, Taylor reached over to Emily and placed his arm around her.

"Daddy, you're bleeding."

"I'm okay, Darling, I am just fine. Listen, Emily, I need you and Aunt Lisa to both go into another room together. Lock yourselves in. If anyone comes near a window or tries to come in the door without clearly identifying themselves as me or Arthur, you pull the trigger. Do not hesita... "

"Daddy, no. Please, Daddy. I don't want to leave this room. I want to stay here with you."

Lisa spoke out next.

"I feel the same, Kent. I want us to stay together. Please?"

Kent stood silently for a moment, looking upon the faces of these two females whose lives he was absolutely committed to save.

"Okay, okay, we stay together. But, you have to promise to do what I say. And remember, Arthur and I will take the lead on everything."

Just then, a voice sounded on the handheld radios that both Emerson and Nolan had.

"Seymour here. Headed your way, gents. We got us two dead back in the trees. It's Jansen and Caldwell," he said identifying two of the men to initially come onto the property. "Taylor's got to be here. Also, I'm not getting any response from Engle over at the boathouse.

Our men are searching the premises now."

310

Just then, the front door was pushed open. Taylor whirled, fired, and the man named Seymour fell dead to the ground. The men behind him scattered away from the door. Taylor slammed the door shut.

"Lisa, Emily, both of you quickly get behind the couch. Arthur, help me push our two friends over in front of the door. Then take cover. You position yourself to cover the back door. I'll take the front. We can't possibly cover all windows throughout the house, but at least we will hear them break if someone is coming in from all but the one facing the back near that door entrance.

Stay calm everyone. They will be coming in very soon."

Taylor knew how badly the odds were stacked against them. Too many on the outside. Kent had Arthur, a brave, but untrained accountant, Lisa and Emily on the inside. Damn! It was not supposed to go down like this. He did not even have his backpack with additional weapons.

Suddenly, an eerie silence enveloped the house and property. Kent was poised waiting for the front and rear doors to be kicked in and men to come in charging while firing their weapons.

All these years of fighting so hard to protect his family members were about to be fused together in a futile and losing effort. Too many against too few. Kent Taylor was formidable, but this was not a personal quest to survive. He had three family members to keep alive. He was willing to die if it would spare the lives of Arthur, Lisa, and Emily, but, of course, it would not.

For just a fleeting second, Katie crossed his mind. He wished he could tell her how much he loved her one more time. Oh well, he would simply have to believe that she would always know that until her own dying breath one day.

Then it happened. The loud boom sounded like a cannon shot, as it reverberated and shook the house. It was followed by the sounds of vehicles moving onto the property and the chopping, whirling rotator blades of helicopters hovering above. Through the house windows, Taylor could see bright flashes of light. It appeared as if they were in the midst of lightning and a thunderous storm.

A loud voice resounded.

"FBI. Drop your weapons. This is your only warning," the voice over a speaker screamed out. "Drop your weapons and stand with your hands above your heads. Do it now."

Lights, so many lights, continued to flash. The sound of automatic weapons being fired revealed the fact that someone outside decided to defy the command of the voice they all heard.

No one inside said anything.

The sounds of weapons being fired continued at a feverish pace.

"Kent. Kent Taylor…"

That next voice over the loudspeaker was unmistakably the voice of Jonas Blair.

"Kent. Can you access a handheld? Are you all okay in there?"

Kent grabbed Emerson's radio.

"Jonas, this is Kent. We are all okay.

We've got two of them dead in here and two others incapacitated.

We are all safe."

"Hold your place, Kent," Jonas said, as the sounds of automatic weapons being fired continued. We are rounding up everyone outside here. We'll have everything all ready for you guys in just a minute or two.

That is if it is okay with you that I am actually here."

"Jonas, I…Yes, I am very, very thankful that you are here."

Another voice came through on the handheld.

"Watcha do, Commander? Git youself stuck in another one of them hornet nests or something?"

"Haha," Taylor laughed aloud. "They conscripted you into service again, Wilson?"

"Hey, with all due respect there, Commander, you gotta watch you choice of words, sir. Ain't nobody never gonna make Willie Brown do nothin' he don't wanna do. This here was a party I wasn't 'bout ta miss out on."

Arthur, Lisa, and Emily were all standing with Taylor now. Within minutes, Blair signaled that he and others would be entering the house.

The front door was kicked open. Albert Sweitzer was the first to clear the door, followed by Wilson Brown, Jr. and Jonas Blair. Others followed behind them, some associated with the CIA, some with the FBI.

A team began a complete search of the house.

Taylor immediately signaled Arthur to hand his weapon over to any of the men that were with Sweitzer, Brown, and Blair.

Sweitzer kicked over the chair that Parker Nolan was seated in.

"Oops, my bad, director," he said, as he tightly cuffed Nolan's arms behind his back.

He turned Nolan around so that he was lying on his back. Sweitzer moved his face so that his nose was actually touching Nolan's. Then he began to squeeze Nolan's neck.

"Some good people—a whole lot better than scum like you, sir, are dead because of you. Be thankful there are others in this room or I swear to you, I would already have killed you."

Wilson Brown was cuffing George Emerson. He spotted the bullet wound in

Emerson's shoulder.

"Looks like you got youself some leakin' goin' on there," Brown said.

"Hey there Commander," Brown said, as he saluted Taylor and grinned broadly.

"Nice to see you again, sir."

Jonas Blair walked up to Taylor, smiled, and the two men embraced. Willie Brown followed and did the same.

Kent Taylor stood between Emily and Lisa, as Arthur moved over beside his wife.

"We are safe now," Taylor said.

Then he placed his arms around Emily and Lisa, while also looking over to Arthur.

"And I promise you, no one will ever hurt any of you again."

❖

Jonas Blair worked with Albert Sweitzer and the leaders from the FBI and CIA contingents in coordinating the placement of all the prisoners in vans. They would be delivered to a secure private location for interrogation.

Kent, Arthur, Lisa, and Emily were moved to a hotel in New Orleans, where they would also be heavily guarded. Katie was also with them.

As he paced the large hotel suite where they were housed, Taylor was on the phone with Phillip Masters.

"Can't tell you how thankful I am that you and your family members are all safe, Kent. I assume that Sweitzer briefed you that we have special interrogators from the CIA and the FBI headed to New Orleans to conduct the investigatory work with the people on your end. At the same time, federal agents are poised to move in against Vice President Harrison Michaels, Senator Thurman Gibbons, and a few other high-profile conspirators. Of course, guys like Michaels and Gibbons will lawyer-up before we get a word in."

"No doubt," Taylor said. "And you'll have others from the President on down weighing truth and justice in one hand and political ramifications in the other."

Masters grimaced.

"Man, how I wish I could say that is not the truth.

Well, at least we got something good going. It seems that Congresswoman Margaret Russkind has a lawyer who is working a fire sale with us—leniency for her client in exchange for insider info."

Taylor laughed.

"Sometimes you corner a rat and it suddenly becomes the most cooperative thing ever.

Before we go any further, Phillip, what's the latest word on Bill Gladding?"

"Definitely improving day by day. He told me that his doctor said if he's a good boy and cooperates in working with his physical therapist, the doc might let him have another visit with his daughter, son-in-law, and granddaughter. And...the doc might permit me to coordinate a conference call between Bill and a certain former Navy SEAL, his wife and a husband and wife who were former colleagues of his at the bureau."

Masters could not see the beaming smile on Taylor's face, but he was sure that it was there.

"By the way, Kent, we just arrested Raymond Townes and Hiram Edsen, two professional hit-men, and charged them with the attempted murder of federal agent Bill Gladding. And we linked those two to a couple of FBI agents named Cayden Verne and Isaiah Harrington. No big surprise that those two agents are strongly linked to Parker Nolan."

"Small world, isn't it?" Taylor said.

But, most importantly, Kent, we've stopped the terrorist threat."

Taylor paused, took a deep breath, then continued the conversation.

"Phillip, I want you to know how much I appreciate you sending a team in here so quickly. Things were definitely getting tight. I don't know how you got such a cooperative effort between your agency and the Bureau. Most impressive, I must say."

"Yeah, well you also had some impressive activity generated by Blair, your wife, and Sally. I mean, hell, two chartered jets, one from New York, another from Canada. Man, maybe I should try to hire on your folks."

Taylor laughed.

"Funny thing, too. Katie used credit cards I had under a known alias.

Parker Nolan and his folks caught that activity. They assumed it was me, and that I was still on my way into Louisiana. Actually, ended up buying me more time on this end."

"Yeah, well Albert Sweitzer and another of my agents actually got on the chartered jet along with Jonas, Katie, and Sally. I am concerned now that they will insist on chartered jet service going forward."

Taylor laughed before changing the subject.

"Phillip, we also have the issue that Katie, Sally, and Jonas brought Willie Brown in from Canada..."

"Say no more, Kent. I already have started things in motion. Between Tom Westfield and others with some formidable 'Capital clout,' we will make sure everyone is cleared and given a clean slate. You have my word on that.

Kent, I will also do the best I can to not overly broadcast your identity. Believe me, there are still people who do not want to blow that lid off and create the media sensationalism that will undoubtedly occur if the world learns that the notorious *Ghost Assassin* is still alive.

What are you thinking you will do?"

More people than ever were now aware that Kent Taylor was not dead as had been reported. The government would claim that the name Taylor was simply used to add to the bait of luring in those who were involved in the intended terrorist plot. Kent Taylor knew that he would never be completely free from the need to live with false identities.

"I think it is clear that I will always have to be guarded and careful and I will encourage my family members to do the same.

Vincent J. Sachar

Simply put, Phillip, there is really nowhere on earth where I will ever be free to live as Kent Taylor."

At first Masters did not respond, as he knew that he had nothing to say that would contradict Taylor's own assessment of his future. When he did speak, Masters chose to respond with something that he could express with full confidence.

"If ever, in any way, I can be of assistance to you or anyone in your family, Kent, I promise you that I will be."

"Thank you, Phillip. That means more to me than I can even adequately express."

Taylor could not see the mist forming in Masters' eyes, but he sensed what was happening when Phillip cleared his throat and continued to report on the latest developments.

"I followed up on the message you sent before you went to save your family members. Seems Muamba had picked up on the fact that Vice President Harrison Michaels was a key player in the plot to usher in a terrorist attack on U.S. soil. As I mentioned, we have federal agents moving in now on the Veep. We have also pegged FBI Deputy Director William Spellman, as a conspirator. And there was some strong joint cooperation between the CIA and FBI even before what you witnessed here today."

Taylor immediately picked up on the sarcasm in Masters' voice.

"Spellman and CIA Deputy Director Robert Patterson were working together. I had contact with Spellman when we were first trying to gain access to your Top Secret files. At that same time, Bob Patterson was also made aware. Guess we know how word concerning your identity was spreading to a few places where we would definitely not have wanted it to go. Bob Patterson, freakin' number two guy in the CIA, was also instrumental in the attempt to murder T.J. Who in hell would have ever thought... "

Masters stopped talking for a moment.

"Listen, Phillip, I have traveled down the road you are on right now. It's riddled with betrayals—leaves you wondering whether anyone is clean."

"For a moment, Taylor, I... I questioned whether I had the courage to press on when I realized the powerful people involved and what I was putting at risk."

316

Taylor waited before responding.

"But you did step up, Phillip, and make the choice to move in against some very formidable people. You helped save the lives of others on this end and countless Americans.

I guess I don't have to tell you that you affirmed the fact that some people will rise above the scum and do the right thing."

"I-I lost some very special people along the way," Masters said. His voice was quieter, softer now.

And Taylor knew the list consisted of Benjie Marlowe, Marissa Reynolds, Micah Jensen, and so many others at the Camp whose names Taylor did not even know.

"I am sure I don't have to tell you this, Phillip, but those kinds of hurts never go away. You try to overcome them, but you never do.

All you can do is whatever it takes to assure that they did not die in vain."

Chapter Fifty-Five

Now and Forever More

Long after the team that Masters had sent was gone, Kent, Katie, Arthur, Lisa, and Emily all remained in New Orleans.

Taylor struggled greatly with the question of how a person can possibly make up for so much lost time with his family members and fill in the gaps of all that occurred over the years. He finally reached an answer. You cannot.

Now it was time to walk along new paths. It was time to create fresh memories and treasure whatever was newly available. Yesterdays were gone.

Kent did explain why a plan was forged to fake his death and why he was constrained from ever making contact with them, but he simply invested most of his time renewing his relationship with his daughter and with Arthur and Lisa.

Arthur, Jr, flew into New Orleans for a long weekend visit. Stacey was not yet told anything. They would wait until she was back from Europe.

Emily cried when she learned that her daddy had actually been at her high school graduation. She also cried tears of joy when she spoke with Taylor one day about Katie.

"I absolutely adore her, Daddy. She is so awesome. I know she is not Mom. I realize that I have a mother that was stolen away from me. I know she can never be replaced.

But, I already feel such a closeness with Katie. And I see how special she is to you, Daddy. I love what I see.

Just let me in. Find some space there in your life with Katie and let me squeeze in a bit—that would be most special of all."

Kent continually marveled at the poise and maturity of his daughter and considered Emily's words to be among the most sublime he ever personally heard.

One night, while Katie and Emily were chatting together in another room, Kent spent time with Arthur and Lisa.

"Never—I can never say enough about the love you have shared with Emily."

"Listen, Kent," Arthur responded. "I am absolutely convinced that there are no limits to what you would do to protect Lisa, me, and the kids. We can see that. We can feel it. We know. The more we have learned, the more I realize that there was a huge target on our backs simply because of the scandal Rose uncovered and our link to her. You saved our lives, Kent, even when in a very real sense you lost your own."

Lisa spoke next.

"I knew how devastated you were when you lost Rose, Drew, and my dad and mom. I am so incredibly hap…"

As her tears poured forth, Lisa held up her hand as if to signal to her husband and Kent that she intended to finish her statement.

After a delay and a concerted effort to regroup, Lisa did just that.

"Y-you…have made me s-so happy, Kent. I am be-beyond w-words thankful, that w-we are together once again."

The days continued to pass. While they all remained together in the Crescent City, teams were at the home of Arthur and Lisa. Following the work done at what constituted a major crime scene, Masters had cleanup crews working now to restore the home and property.

Arthur and Lisa did not yet know whether they would remain at that location. At the moment, they simply wanted to breathe in the freshness of some new beginnings that they were all sharing together.

They all walked the streets of the French Quarter. They ate *beignets* and drank coffee at the *Café du Monde.* They stopped to listen to street musicians and sat awestruck listening to the legendary musicians in Preservation Hall. They laughed together as they ate at local restaurants, and rode a paddleboat down the Mississippi. They rode the streetcars down St. Charles Avenue past the hallowed halls of Tulane and Loyola universities. They walked throughout Audubon Park.

They shopped along Canal Street. Kent and Arthur laughed as they watched Katie, Lisa, and Emily try on a number of new outfits.

As Kent and Arthur observed the beaming smiles and constant chatter between the three females, Arthur commented.

"Amazing! Those three look like they have been together for years, rather than days,"

Kent stood silently for a moment and simply stared at Katie, Emily, and Lisa.

"Maybe they have been together," Kent replied, "somewhere in the world of their deepest hopes and dreams."

They agreed that Emily would drop out of school for the next year and spend additional time with Kent and Katie. Along with time spent in the U.S. Virgin Islands, there was a trip to upstate New York they intended to take. By now, Kent and Katie had told Emily all about Jonas, Sally, and baby, Taylor.

A west coast jaunt to visit a man named Gladding was also on the agenda. And, of course, there would be increased times together with Lisa, Arthur, and their children.

Kent always took the time to tell Emily more about her mother and older brother. He was willing to answer any questions she had about the past and about his own life, but Emily soon found that she did not have all that many questions she cared to talk about.

She was enraptured with the now. Her daddy had come back and he was already fulfilling the last words he spoke to her some fifteen years earlier.

"Always, with my every last breath and beyond, I will love you,"—and he did.

Nothing else really mattered.

The End

About the Author

Vincent J. Sachar is an attorney with a passion for writing fiction. He earned his Juris Doctor from St. John's Law School in New York.

Vince is an experienced public speaker. In addition to speaking at book events, high schools, colleges and universities, book clubs, author meet & greet events, author panels, and more, he has addressed crowds large and small (sometimes with foreign language interpreters) and has done so in very unique situations (including at a prison in Siberia).

Sachar also conducts radio and internet interviews across the nation and has provided interviews for prominent author websites. Contact Vince at: vsach777@comcast.net

Vince and his wife, Gwen, a native of southern Louisiana, met while attending Loyola University in New Orleans. Vince and Gwen currently reside in south Florida. They have three children: David, Victoria, and Jonathan.

For more: Please visit Vince's author site: www.vincentsachar.com.

ADDITIONAL PUBLISHED WORKS:

The Nowhere Man

Nowhere Out

A Twisted Road {Novella}

Cajun Culture Shock {Short Story}

Vincent J. Sachar

COMING SOON: An Exciting Mystery Thriller

Murders at Pearl Springs

At 24-years-old, Heather Lance is the youngest and the first female detective on the Corona Police Force. She has also just become a divorcée.

In an effort to escape from the hurt she has just endured, Heather drives to a remote campground to spend a few days alone. On the first morning of her stay, a young woman is found dead along the shores of a lake. The murder will be the first of a series throughout the area and Heather will soon find herself immersed in an investigation that places her own life in danger.

With a series of twists and turns that keep the reader guessing who is behind these killings, this classic "who-done-it" will have you glued to the pages as the mystery unfolds.

Heather Lance had come to the Wandering Nymph Campground seeking healing from a shattered heart. Now she is striving just to keep that heart beating.

Chapter One

A Time Away

Heather Lance was driving much too fast for the winding, twisting mountain roads on which she was traveling. As she drew nearer to her destination and farther from her point of origin, she would have a difficult time determining which brought her greater joy—the "to" or the "from."

Heather had immediately driven away from Corona County Courthouse and the divorce proceedings that ended her marriage. There was nothing in Corona City that she cared to think about—certainly not Dominick, her now ex-husband after nearly four years. She had her job as a Corona Municipal Police Department detective, the first female to be in that position, but right now, she did not want to even think about that.

At twenty-four-years-old, 5'5" 125 lbs, blue eyes, blonde hair that extended to her shoulders, and pretty "girl-next-door" looks, Heather did not look like a police detective. She also did not immediately conjure up thoughts of someone who was an excellent sharpshooter and trained in martial arts and kickboxing.

Heather's keen mind, incredible instincts, and strong work ethic earned her the reputation as a top-notch detective. She also credited her "good stock'" with a grandfather who had been a county sheriff, a father who had been a detective with the state police, an uncle who was a chief deputy in a nearby county, and another uncle who had been a state trooper when he died from a sudden heart attack. If that was not impressive enough, Heather also had two cousins who were in police academies in two neighboring states.

Many, even most, police departments have a minimum age requirement of twenty-one. Corona accepted cadets at age eighteen. Heather entered the Department straight out of high school at eighteen years old. She had to

Vincent J. Sachar

overcome male resentments and chauvinism to reach the point that she now had.

Nevertheless, at the moment, she did not care to reflect upon the accolades associated with her job. Who knows? Surely, her dedication to work, the countless hours she committed to her career, added to the breakdown of her marriage. Of course, it did not justify Dom bedding down a girl with the IQ of a mud turtle and ten years younger than him.

Damn! Seemed as if no matter what track her thoughts began on, they somehow ended up back at her divorce. Twenty-four years old, both parents dead, and already divorced. This was not how she had pictured her life.

She reached over on the passenger seat, found the windproof cigarette lighter she purchased just before the trip and lit up another coffin nail. Damn! She quit smoking a good year before she even graduated from high school and in recent weeks started again. She had to stop. She intended to stop—just not today.

It was Heather's hairdresser, Lillian Belton, who first told her about the Wandering Nymph campground located some seven miles east of Pearl Springs. The campground, built around Lake Folly, was primarily a fishing camp. Twelve cabins were neatly situated in the surrounding woods.

"Now you lissen at me, girl," Lily said during Heather's last hair appointment. "You gotta get yourself away for a spell. Slow down. Catch your breath. Otherwise you ain't gonna be much good to yourself or nobody else."

Lily told Heather about the Wandering Nymph, owned and run by Lily's uncle and aunt, Oscar and Helen Wainright.

"They more'n my aunt an' uncle. They helped raise me after my daddy left an' my momma spent most of her time in one bar or another an' with too many new men for me to count or care."

So now, Heather was booked for five days in a campground cabin. No interruptions, no crimes to solve, no haggling with lawyers, no Dominick.

"Kind of interesting isn't it?" Heather was talking with Millie the night before her divorce proceedings. Sergeant Mildred Jameson served on the Corona Police Force with Heather—the only other woman. She was also one of the only genuine friends that Heather had. Jameson was 5'9" 170 lbs. with light brown curly hair. At 35-years-old, Millie was eleven years older than

Heather, but she often said that her young friend infused life and caused Millie to feel at least ten years younger.

"Since I've been with Corona PD, I have been hit on by fellow police officers, lawyers, an assistant district attorney, and a senior citizen judge. In each instance, I avoided ever getting involved with any of them. But Dominick somehow could not resist some bleach-blonde bimbo who has been around the block countless times.

Oh well. I honestly cannot remember the last time I simply settled in somewhere and did nothing."

"Getting away will be good for you, Heather. Believe me, once you get there and turn off to all you've been going through, you'll see just how therapeutic a little time away will be."

As she drove closer to her destination, Heather reflected back to what likely was the last time she was alone. It had to be three years ago, on the day following her father's funeral. She stood alone in the house where her parents had lived for so many years. Two years earlier an aneurism shockingly and unexpectedly took the life of her mom. Now once again without warning, a heart attack ended her father's life. Her older sister, Angela, never even showed up for the funeral. Twenty-one-years-old and orphaned. Where's the fairness in that? Well, at least at the time, she had Dominick...

Heather slowed down as she entered the town of Pearl Springs. She crept along driving well within the small town speed limit. Her thoughts were rampant dominated by a feeling that she had just stepped back in time.

Quaint. Kind of attractive in its own way, but talk about small. Hah! This is definitely one of those "don't sneeze or you might miss the whole place" towns.

The primary building in Pearl Springs was a tall, wide, old country-style building with a large front porch. Two men were seated there playing a game of checkers. This stately building was clearly identified as the "Pearl Springs General Store." From all appearances, this was the place to come to for groceries and most everything else. She also spotted a privately-owned drug store, connected to a small clinic. A restaurant named "Mama's Kitchen," was located across from the little clinic. "Brother's Auto Repair" was the next establishment, followed by "Creamy Delight," an apparent small town version of a *Dairy Queen*. At the very edge of town, a large garage identified itself as the "Pearl River Volunteer Fire Department."

Heather stopped the car, turned it around, and headed back towards the general store, where she had spotted what she now realized were the only gas pumps in town.

Maybe it was the attraction of her current year Ford Mustang GT Convertible. Or maybe it was the attraction of Heather herself. Perhaps it was the rarity of any non-resident human showing up in this tiny mountain town. Or maybe the general store owner, Nester Whitlock, and his friend, Wesley Summers, always interrupted their checkers game to greet anyone pulling up at the gas pumps.

Anyway, for whatever reason, Heather found them standing nearby as she began pumping gas. The two men looked to be somewhere in the range of their early seventies.

"Howdy, Ma'am," Nester said in greeting as he introduced himself and Wesley to the attractive blonde who had just showed up in town. "Jus' passing through, are ya?"

Nester and Wesley might be in the seventh decade of life, but they both certainly knew pretty when they see it.

"Well, hello to you. I'm Heather. Actually I'm headed to the Wandering Nymph Campground."

Nester smiled. Wesley nodded his head.

"Right nice place," Nester said. "Well, as you likely know, it's a straight shot through town and about seven miles up yonder. Got good signs. Can't miss it. Oscar and Helen Wainright are the proprietors there. They're good folk."

"You don't much look like someone who fishes," Wesley said, finally breaking his silence.

"Guess that depends upon what someone who fishes would look like," Heather said while instantly realizing that her attempt at humor sailed completely over Wesley's head.

"Well, I'm just looking for a quiet place to rest and catch my breath a bit," Heather responded with a smile, as she hooked the pump back up and closed the cover to her gas tank.

"Hey, I don't see a police department here in Pearl Springs."

"Nope. Ain't got one," Nester responded. "This here town and surrounding areas is under the jurisdiction and direct supervision of the Lyming County Sheriff's Department."

Wesley, increasingly bolder joined in. "They situated some twenty-two miles from here in the city of Monmouth. That's also our county seat."

"An' my biggest competitors when it comes to shoppin'," Nester said with a chuckle.

Just then an older model Chevy pickup pulled in. A man bounded out from the driver's side and called out.

"Hey, Unc, you got them traps I been lookin' for?"

"They layin' out in the back, Randy, where I done told ya they would be."

The man looked to be somewhere close to Heather's age. His 5'9" body was lean, his face narrow and tight-lipped, his brown hair tucked underneath a ball cap bearing the logo of some insurance company Heather never heard of.

"Well, well, well. What have we here?" the younger man said, as he fixed his glare on Heather.

"This here's Heather. She's fixing to get some rest and relaxation over at the Wanderin' Nymph.

Heather, this varmint is my nephew, Randall Cobb. He does most of the huntin' and trappin' in these parts. Probably knows these mountains better'n anybody 'round here."

Cobb glared at Heather as he spoke.

"Well now, Missy, you need somebody to show you some of the hidden mountain paths or help you a bit with your restin' and relaxin', you just give me a holler."

Heather said nothing as Randall added to her discomfort appearing to undress her with his eyes. She was relieved when he pulled his truck around to the back of the store, picked up whatever he needed, and drove away beeping his horn at Heather.

"Don't mind him," Nester said. "Somewhere along the line, he got ta thinkin' he's God's gift ta women.

Hey, you get a hankerin' fer some really good home-cooked food, come back in ta Mama's Kitchen. Mama is Wesley's sister, Maude. Believe you me, that woman can flat-out cook."

Wesley was beaming now as if his sister's culinary skills somehow increased his own stature.

"Well, I might just do that," Heather said with a smile as she climbed back in her car, waved goodbye, and drove away.

As she did, she never noticed Randall Cobb, who had hidden his truck behind some tall shrubbery and was standing behind a tree with his eyes glued on Heather Lance.